Also by Ron Swan

Through the Kindness of Ravens
The Evolution of Hoke's Focus

For information about the author
and his art and writing,
visit RonSwan.com.

THE
KITE
and the
COIN TOSS

RON SWAN

THE KITE AND THE COIN TOSS

iUniverse books may be ordered through booksellers or by contacting:

iUniverse
1663 Liberty Drive
Bloomington, IN 47403
www.iuniverse.com
844-349-9409

ISBN: 978-1-6632-1773-8 (sc)
ISBN: 978-1-6632-1775-2 (hc)
ISBN: 978-1-6632-1774-5 (e)

Library of Congress Control Number: 2021902844

Print information available on the last page.

iUniverse rev. date: 02/25/2021

For every man and woman
who has fought for
or fought to maintain
freedom.

Instead of cursing the darkness, light a candle.

—Benjamin Franklin

Catching Lightning with My Hands

I now know
What I must do.
It won't be easy—
That's nothing new—

Like counting tyrannized
Grains of sands
Or catching lightning
With my hands.

He owns the cards,
Recognizes the faces,
Deals heavy hands,
Keeps us in our places.

But now it is he
Who has forced my hand.
So count him out
As you count the sand.

For his sands of time,
They are quicksand.

And as each grain counts
For each grain you see,
As oppression's pressure mounts,
Pushes back to be free.

How much are you willing
To pay to be free?
This cost I am willing
This cost, it is me.

PROLOGUE

Present day, October 24, 2021
Joshua Nolin Franks
Anderson Raines Lightning Lab in the royal city
of George's Cross, Province of Burgoyne

T HE KING WANTS ME DEAD. I SHOULD FEEL HOPELESS AND SCARED OUT of my mind right now. And I suppose I do. Still, in this flash of a moment, I find I ponder histories.

Funny thing about histories, we all have them—personal histories; family histories; and even local, cultural, and global histories. We all have them, and to varying degrees, we all share them. The broader a history's scope, the greater the chance it is shared.

I can think of no history with a broader shared reach than the king's. As of recent, the king has consumed not only my history but also my future. He has pushed me to the point where I must try to make some global history of my own.

My options are to either die by the king's hands, the very hands that already have a stranglehold on most of the world or die by my own in my fight for freedom from them. In an attempt to make my decision as a free man, I choose the latter.

Others in history have faced these choices as well.

A moment in history over 240 years ago shared the same opportunity for transformation. It was a time when some very brave revolutionaries, my newfound heroes, faced the same decision.

I've always known how their story ended but have only recently learned some truths surrounding it by reading a firsthand account written by Benjamin Franklin's son William. In it, William, having just witnessed his father's hanging, provided revelations on how his father and the fellow rebels were resolved to their fates. Their lives were a price they were more than willing to pay in their fight for freedom.

As it was, these so-called "rebels" paid that price, as they were publicly hanged, drawn and quartered in a single event now known as the Signer's Day of Reckoning.

Coincidentally, the spectacle occurred in nearly the same location where I am. Back then, however, the city was not known as the royal city of George's Cross in the Province of Burgoyne, but as Philadelphia. And a map of its time would place it within the colony of Pennsylvania.

I am amazed and equally saddened at how a path taken in a fork in the road at that time could lead to such a history as ours.

I am also amazed at how I managed to get my life so tightly knotted within the results of such a history, and all in just the past couple weeks. Two weeks ago, I was a no one, just another cog in the machine doing my royally mandated part to keep the machine running. In that short time since, I've turned from a no one into a someone, with the most powerful person in the world wanting him dead.

Two weeks ago, I would have thought my story had begun at my birth. However, I now understand it is merely and hopefully the long overdue end story of a fight for freedom and the end of a revolution that began over two centuries ago.

I apologize for my rambling. But like a clock at the end of its wind, I am exhausted and out of time.

I know I have been vague. I know my story sounds as if I have told it all without having yet told you anything. In my current state, I have merely provided a fifty thousand-meter view, though in doing so, I have laid the groundwork on which my story might run.

My story is one of histories. More significantly, however, it represents the classic battle between the history that makes you and the history you make.

"Men make history."

PART I

History and How It Happened
Heads Will Roll ... Or
Tales of Freedom

— CHAPTER 1 —

Friday, February 23, 1781
Philadelphia, Pennsylvania

BENJAMIN BACHE WIPED HIS EYES DRY. HE DID NOT WANT HIS MOTHER to notice he had been crying. But he had just discovered the last of his siblings had been sent away and he had just been told to gather his own belongings and change his name.

"But, Mother, I don't understand. My name's Benjamin Franklin Bache."

"No, as I have told you, your name is now Francis Nolin Franks. I know this is hard for such a young man of eleven to understand, but understand you must. Your life and safety depend upon it. I never want you to forget being a Franklin or a Bache, but you must hide your pride within; it is no longer safe to be known as either. Now, finish gathering your necessities as I have asked."

She had spoken in haste. She had spoken firm. She had spoken with tears in her eyes. He had never seen his mother cry.

All his life he had witnessed the accomplishments and benefited from the results of the genius he shared—or at least used to share in last name—with his grandfather, Benjamin Franklin.

At least I am still in his bloodline. They cannot take that away, he thought.

He had watched as his mother supported his grandfather and the revolutionary effort as a political hostess, as well as led in relief work throughout its course.

He had always been amazed how he could find evidence of his grandfather's inventions, from the church steeple top to the cast-iron woodstove to the streetlamp and peering through his bifocals, no less, when he would let him.

All his life, he had been told how proud he should be to carry the name *Franklin*, and he had always genuinely been proud of it.

But now, after the recent turn of events, his mother told him to bury his pride inside and gather his necessities. She said he was to go with his "Uncle" Silas, but he had never known he had an Uncle Silas; nor did he believe the man was actually his uncle. But his mother said he would live with Silas and his wife on a farm in a town southwest of their home in Philadelphia. He had been put into too much of a hurry and had not even caught the name of the town. *Or was it that she does not want me to know it yet?*

His mother also told him the British Army had captured his grandfather, along with all his other heroes, and their fight for freedom was over.

She grabbed him by his shoulders, turned him square, and then looked into his eyes. And for the last time, she reminded him of his new name. "It is no longer safe for you to carry the name Benjamin Franklin Bache. Your new name is Francis Nolin Franks. Francis Nolin Franks. Repeat it back to me."

"Francis … N-Nolin Franks."

"Again."

"Francis Nolin Franks."

He had overheard her tell his "uncle" that Francis was the name of her brother who died of smallpox when he was four.

He did not know where his other siblings had gone. He had seen three of them—the youngest, Sarah, Eliza, and Louis—go with a lady their mother called Mrs. Cook, an "aunt" he never knew he had.

His brother William had left with a younger couple. He had heard no name and had not recognized them, and William had left as he collected his things and with no goodbye.

He had thought to himself, *Apparently "Uncle" Silas can only support one of us. I suppose I should be thankful.* But that thought had done nothing to stop his head from spinning, nor to keep him from feeling frightened.

His mother kissed him on the forehead one final time and then promised the separation would only be temporary. She would come get him, round up all the kids, as soon as she could ensure their safety.

Those were the words she had told him, but her crying eyes told him otherwise. Though he firmly believed she wished the words true, he equally believed he had just witnessed the first time his mother had lied to him.

The last thing she had said before rushing him out to the horse-drawn cart on which he was to leave was, "I love you ... Francis Nolin Franks."

She had turned away quickly in an effort to hide her emotional breakdown. Though he had not seen her face, the body language he had witnessed through his own tears had revealed the cracks in the force of strength he had always known her to bear.

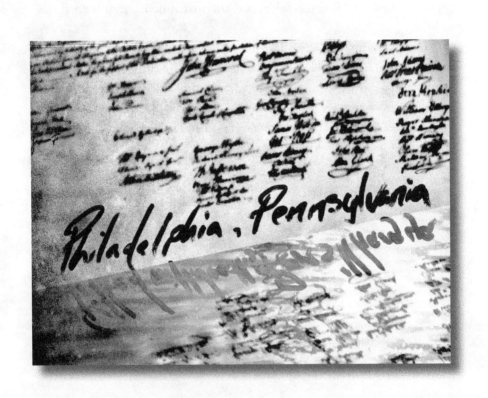

— CHAPTER 2 —

Sunday, February 25, 1781

Prison guard Jonathan Elders made his way up from the captain's quarters, where he had just learned he had received a promotion.

It was another cold February morning aboard the HMS *Romney*, anchored just off the coast of Philadelphia, and the newly promoted King's Guard subconsciously braced himself for the cold wind that would hit him the instant his head appeared deck level. Consciously, his mind swam between the ebb and flow—the high tide of happiness about the promotion and finally getting a chance to leave the miserable prison ship, mixed with the low tide of relief that this call to the captain had not been for another disciplinary inquiry. In his long career as a soldier in the King's Navy, he had become used to the disciplinary floggings, but the scars on his back were still too fresh this time to not issue a sigh of relief. Though he had long been a ship prison guard, the flaring of fresh scars always reminded him how he equally felt a prisoner in life.

He watched on as, in the exhale of his sigh, he could see his breath.

"Elders!"

As he had reached the deck, Jonathan had not needed to look up to know who had just beckoned him. Miles Westbrook and he had been jailers on the HMS *Romney* since it left the banks of Mother England for the godforsaken land known as America.

Miles had already gotten back from a day at Pennsylvania's south shore, from where Jonathan had just learned he too would be going.

"So how do you hail now, Jonathan Elders?"

"I think you know, you bastard. You heard the same bark from the captain this morning, didn't you?"

"Ah, so you're hailed as King's Guard now too eh, Jonathan Elders? No longer just a lowly prison guard, are ya?"

"King's Guard may have a regal ring to it, but I prefer the ring of extra coin in my pocket." To support his statement, he shook his now hopeful, but still empty pockets.

"Did he tell ya you'd earned the honor, lifelong service to the crown and all?"

"Honor, my arse! We'll just be guarding more prisoners as we've done throughout this bloody revolt."

"Ah, Elders, but these prisoners aren't just any prisoners; they're the Signers. Among the lot, we'll be guarding the likes that penned and signed the treasonous declaration—Jefferson, Adams, Franklin, and even General Washington.

"Of course, they'll be hanged by their hands and legs, drawn and quartered, treason against the crown and all, but not before we hang them by their necks first. The king wants to make a statement by silencing the voice of the dissenters."

Pain from the statement his captain had wanted to make during his own recent flogging had just sent another jolt, reminding Jonathan of his lot in life. "Miles, don't you ever get the feeling we are not so different from the prisoners?"

"Elders, let's not get on about that again. I know what you mean, but it'll do you no good and you better not let anyone else hear ya either. Take your mind off of it all and take in this opportunity to witness history from the right side of the rope."

Miles continued, "The captain said after we quarter them, they'll be piled and burned in the town square, ashes upon which'll stand a statue of the king. A royal spectacle is to be made of the whole event. They've already a name for it, the Signer's Day of Reckoning. An' did you hear, we've already got our marching orders into Philly, to the statehouse?"

"The statehouse?" As if he could see the building on this cloudy day from where they were anchored south of Windmill Island, he glanced toward Pennsylvania.

"Aye, that's where we'll be guarding them. The Pennsylvania Statehouse, where they signed their bloody declaration, has been turned into their very jail cells, and they're calling it Hell's Gate. And get this, they're building the Signers' hang stations and gallows from every window, even adding on to fit the lot. Come Signer's Day, they'll hang at once from the windows of Hell's Gate, and in front of the king."

"In front of the king?" Jonathan scratched his head. He wondered where Miles had picked up all this information, as he had only learned general details surrounding his new duties.

"Aye, the whole royal family will be here. They're sailing from the motherland unto this new world. Going to establish the monarchy here once they've a worthy place for them."

"Balderdash!"

"No, 'tis true. It's what I've learned on the day's venture to shore. Fact be told, our marching orders are to fall in with the Fusilier's 23rd Regiment. That's why I'm back, to round up your arse, and the ferry's waiting."

"Ah, it is good to be on the right side of the prison bars and the right end of the noose," Jonathan quipped.

"Aye, that it is."

While on the ferry, Miles carried on about the thises and thats, but Jonathan's mind drifted as the ferry drifted from the prison ship. He looked back at the ship for hopefully the last time, though he doubted it. He had, many a time, felt like a prisoner himself on that damned ship.

He pushed his thoughts away from his own woes and onto the Signers' lots—*all for penning for their freedom; and look where that got them.*

Having reached the ferry landing, Jonathan and Miles disembarked and fell in with the awaiting 23rd Regiment. Jonathan had expected to hear Major Mecan's call to duty, but Miles explained that duty now fell to Major Frederick Mackenzie. Mecan had recently fallen to violent fever. So it was under Mackenzie they marched north up Front Street and then west up Chestnut and into the heart of Philadelphia.

As they marched by drum cadence, a phrase popped into Jonathan's head. He had been thinking on what he'd like to say to the damned

Signers. He thought it was the cadence that set the words right in his mind. They rolled in cadence in his mind, as if they marched in step alongside him.

Philadelphia, Pennsylvania, fill'd with death, ya pens'll hang ya.

The words repeated in his head as they marched.

Philadelphia, Pennsylvania, fill'd with death, ya pens'll hang ya.
Philadelphia, Pennsylvania, fill'd with death, ya pens'll hang ya.

In no time, they reached the corner of Chestnut and Fiefth. Having reached their destination, Jonathan and Miles fell out from the regiment's line, who still had miles to march before reaching their day's destination.

Standing before and facing the Pennsylvania Statehouse, Jonathan glanced up to the tops of the scaffolds at its entrance. They looked like bones, only on the outside of its body.

Taking in all the windows, he turned to Miles, who had instantly picked back up his rambling mouth from where he'd left it at the ferry.

When Jonathan finally spoke, it startled him. "I can't count like a merchant, but you need not be a merchant to see not a window, come gallows, for each of the soon-ta-dangles. They'll be sharing ropes."

"Aye, but that's why they're building up. And look here," he replied, pointing to what looked like a castle moat. "They're digging down to make room for the dangling feet from the lower windows as well."

Eager to see the lot worthy of such attentions to have become the exclamation point in the king's statement, Jonathan made his way into the makeshift prison, with Miles still jabbering in tail.

Entering what must now be the guards' main office, he spied several other guards gathering at a table on the far left. He knew the guards had seen them enter, but they made no effort to acknowledge the newcomers.

Miles instinctively drifted toward the lot, but Jonathan's eyes scanned the surroundings and landed on the only closed door. He glanced back to the other guards, noting how they appeared to gather at the farthest point from the closed door.

Miles must have shared with the guards what he understood to be Jonathan's intentions, as three of them appeared to then direct Jonathan to said door, as if to affirm it was where he should go.

He opened the door to a hall and then continued down, with intent to do his first official rounds. As he walked, he thought, *Signed for their independence—hell, they signed their own death warrants, and my promotion papers. They'll be hanged, drawn and quartered in the very city and from the very building where they signed—the fools.*

As he reached the end of the hallway, it curved and opened up into a grand room filled with makeshift cells. The rough-and-ready structures still had the awkward appearance of offices, remnants of their former lives, but now made adequate cells. Jonathan scanned through the bars of the three large cells and spied the lot of the crammed prisoners. Even as prisoners, however, they carried a surreal and stately air about them. He'd seen thousands of prisoners in countless prisons in all his years, but something about these felt different.

The chant of the prisoners' fates he had repeated in his head throughout the day had reared its way back into his mind like the never-ending drone of marching feet, only this time he was thankful. *Philadelphia, Pennsylvania, fill'd with death, ya pens'll hang ya. Philadelphia, Pennsylvania, fill'd with death, ya pens'll hang ya!*

Compelled to mock these stately fools, fools who had so carelessly written deadly words with poisonous ink, he walked toward the man who he had believed had held the pen that drafted the deadly declaration. Thomas Jefferson was the name he recalled.

Though the man may have looked the part, strong in conviction and bold enough to dare drafting their treasonous declaration, the man, Jonathan would later learn from Miles, had not been Thomas Jefferson, but the general himself, George Washington.

The prisoners had been stripped of visible rank, and the general stood dressed as if to work the fields. The clothes were fit for that but failed to make their wearer fit the role. The general stood tall, and though a prisoner, his presence still managed to inherently demand respect. He had seemingly not even taken notice of the guard's entrance.

In fact, none of the prisoners had even seemed to take notice of his existence.

Not even at my new post for a quarter hour, and I've been completely ignored twice.

Now standing before the prisoner he had singled out, he stared directly into the man's eyes. He had to look up to do so, and a chill ran down his spine as he realized he was peering into eyes far more fearless than his own.

9

He looked back toward a rustling in the hall, comforted to find his fellow King's Guard comrades had gathered at the entrance looking on. He would later learn, they only wanted to see if he had felt the same chill they had, and they had just been comforted in recognizing that he had.

On a roll for mistaking things, at the time he mistook their comfort as strength to build up his own courage. So, within earshot of his fellow comrades, he rounded up enough nerve to face the prisoner and finally spew the mantra that had bounced in his head all morning. It was the first time he had spoken it aloud beyond his own earshot. "Philadelphia, Pennsylvania, fill'd with death, ya pens'll hang ya!"

He had directed the verbal jab at the one prisoner but believed his words had pierced all ears present.

As it was, the prisoner had remained unaffected and lost in his own thoughts.

In irony, as his fellow guards had heard the message, they had already started talking about how the world would come to hear his words. They would listen. And this lowly King's Guard would find celebrity as the man who had bellowed what would become the catchphrase of the bloody war.

Jonathan, however, had come to realize that the men in this prison were driven by powers beyond his comprehension. Their strength bled unhindered through the bars and sent the second chill down his spine for the day.

Riding the wave of hearty responses from the other guards, he repeated his phrase, ending it this time with his own declaration, "Declaration of Independence? Tis more the Declaration of In-th'end-dance—the dance you'll be doing at the end of a rope, you damned soon-ta-dangles. To be a fool not uncommon. But ahhhh, give a fool a pen," he snarled, "and he'll give uncommon reason to earn a date with the noose. I, fool with a pen, I, King's Guard Jonathan Elders, will introduce you to your noose. In fact, I'll even entertain you with one of my favorite tricks. I'll throw the rope 'round the sun." On a roll, he gestured a noose being pulled around his neck and the subsequent act of being hanged.

He tried to cap his statements with a hearty laugh, but his voice only cracked. His words were strong, but his voice turned weak, and the man to whom he had directed the gibes remained unaffected.

Courage spent, he made his exit and joined Miles and the other guards, who were already placing bets whether they would ever hear their king repeat the words of one of his servants, a lowly prison guard.

— CHAPTER 3 —

As the guards left, the chatter of distraction resumed between cell mates.

However, the man of mistaken identity, George Washington, whose eyes had held no fear and whose ears had ignored the guard's shining moment, stood stolid.

His mind had drifted to an excerpt from one of his captain's journals, noting how his soldiery had marched through snow for days, to the point their shoes had worn out and their bare feet had left blood in the snow.

Then General George Washington recalled the name of a soldier he considered a hero, Captain Nathan Hale.

This young captain had been a Yale graduate, but it was in his capacity as a spy George found himself reflecting. Nathan had been betrayed by a traitor to the revolution and called out by Tories who identified him. Rumor had it one of the Tories may have been a cousin of his.

Captain Hale had been awarded an execution without trial, and it was at his introduction to the noose where he was said to have quoted Addison's *Cato*. His final words, "How beautiful is death when earn'd by virtue! Who would not be that youth? What pity is it that we can die but once to serve our country?"

The general's reflections flowed to others' actions and quotes inspired by the scent of freedom. Freedom, he thought, had been so close they could smell it, and they had risked everything to reach it, but fate would never allow them a taste. Then Washington remembered Patrick Henry's fiery declaration, "Give me liberty, or give me death!"

He knew that Patrick Henry was in the same cell and turned to find him in the back carrying a distractive conversation with John Adams, distractive, George assumed, only in its ability to dull his mind of his impending fate.

The general stared deeply into the eyes of Patrick's fiery words. He could feel an answer in them, but it had been elusive. Then it hit him, "Give me liberty, or *give* me death?" The key was in asking to be given death, seemingly by the very hands that prevented giving liberty. Acting on the epiphany, he approached Mr. Henry, hoping to both clarify his thoughts and, if they rang true, inspire this downtrodden lot of fellow soldiery.

"Mr. Henry."

He noticed Patrick Henry's head had popped up immediately. He had also seen John Adams had turned typically, head angled down, eyes pierced by the interruption of a good distraction. The piercing eyes had relented some, perhaps George thought, as he had realized who had instigated the interruption.

General Washington continued, "Mr. Henry, did you mean all you so fervently spoke when you declared to be given liberty or given death?" Still wrapped up in sorting his thoughts, he had asked it half-rhetorically and half in question.

Regardless, Patrick Henry responded, "In certainty, sir. And each time I say it I mean it more!"

Snapping out of his thought cloud, George detected a touch of defensiveness in Patrick's tone. He replied accordingly, "I have no doubts of your, nor any of these men's'"—he gestured to encompass all in the prison around him—"shared conviction that liberty is a cause worthy of death. Where I myself have long echoed your sentiments, I find myself in conflict."

George witnessed the impact of his statement as he noticed Patrick, and all within earshot, appeared to stand in shock and disbelief. In his mind, he predicted, asked, and then prepared to answer the question he believed going through their minds. *Does our leader now doubt the value of our cause?*

Benjamin Franklin had been over in the corner of the cell writing with a pencil stub in a journal he previously had stashed in his shirt. He was afraid the guards would take it all away, his homemade journals and pencils, if they had the chance. He had been writing all he witnessed, to capture and provide a true historic reference, a true depiction of the events and mood he sensed in this company of freedom's would-be heroes. A voice in the back of his mind told him his journal would never reach reading eyes. However, he knew if he did not write it, there would be nothing written that would contain the truth.

It was for this reason that, before his capture, he had hidden what he'd started as an autobiography. He had started the autobiographical account back in 1771, while in England, originally written in the form of a letter to his son William. Along with the autobiography, he'd hidden sorted and condensed versions of his science journals, political writings, and other documentation he had kept that would provide proof of his thoughts, actions, and accomplishments—his story.

Now in the jail cell, Ben's perceptiveness captured all the underlying fear that spewed from the guards, who would only come near the cells when they needed to. He knew that fact would be left out of all historic accounts. He could already picture the prison guard who had just left embellishing the story of his shining moment to the guards he had seen cowering at the doorway. So, Ben's pencil had been flying to put down on paper how events had actually occurred.

Judging by the look he saw on the general's face, and the confusion on everyone else's, he knew he had better get over and capture all he could about the thoughts the leader was about to convey.

When he looked into Washington's eyes, Ben suspected the general had intended to plant the confusion. He had seen that look before, believing George had predicted the men's misinterpretation and saw it as an opportunity. Now the general would seize the opportunity, capitalizing on what he liked to call the slingshot effect. He had effectively pulled their thoughts back one direction and was about to release and catapult them further into the opposite and appropriate direction.

Ben smiled at the revelation, causing his spectacles to slide down his nose.

Before the dust of misperception could settle, the general continued as if he had not even noticed the dust he had stirred. "Come closer, my fellow soldiery, for I offer my final stratagem. My conflict lies not in the rights of liberty or death but in how we ask to be given them. This man, who claims a blessed and blood-linear crown, plans to cross the sea to our home country and make ceremony of giving us death. Where we may have lost our fight for freedom in the common fabric of life, I for one am not going to allow him the pleasure of giving me anything, much less death. Though I know our histories will not be publicly taught but skewed or forgotten, I am committed to my very end to make history. I do not feel mistaken in my belief that this very honorable blood flows through your veins."

Honoring an adage the general recalled and firmly believed, he added and repeated, "Men make history ... Men make history."

John Adams, whom like all others had gathered to see the path they were now being led, stepped up with a question. "You have our attentions, General Washington, but not our understanding. What else, pray tell, do you think that small man hiding behind such a large title would be willing to give us?"

George knew all too well how John Adams's tone typically rode the blade of a knife, albeit for butter. He smiled at the opportunity and then attempted to clarify his statements, though they were just coming into focus for him as well. The general continued, "This man who fools call sovereign has us rotting in these jails, waiting for him to have his moment, make his statement. Jailers speak of a ceremony of sorts, a spectacle to be made of our deaths. I have heard of masses of gallows and how he intends to first hang us by our necks, to silence our voices of freedom, all such suspicions validated by the sounds of their construction."

He referred to their impending demise as if he were merely speaking in somber reference to the hardships of a cold winter.

George continued, "This little man intends to make our deaths his moment. I do not intend to give him any moment. As we face certain death, I have reaffirmed my belief in how the forced and final act of a free man would be better served by his own hands. We can let him give us death or escape his hand by recognizing and seizing our final opportunities to make the choices of free men. In freedom, I choose to take death before ever allowing him to give it to me. Make no mistake, death is the answer to all our equations, but as free men, the trick is in how we choose to calculate."

Now, with the audience's ears and understanding, the general continued. "I think on all we have accomplished and all we have not. I know in all my efforts, I have done everything an ordinary man could do. I know this, as it is woven throughout the very fabric of my soul. There is no mirror I could stand before, mine eyes unto my reflection's, without honor in facing that ordinary truth."

Staring into the eyes of the men he spoke; he could see there was not a man among them in doubt. "In my efforts I have attained the heights of all that could be ordinarily expected. All the same, where I have failed myself— most importantly, where I have failed all I have served—is in the lack of extraordinary. I now realize that I have failed in finding and capitalizing on opportunities that had not knocked. These opportunities were there just the same. When against extraordinary odds, one needs to take extraordinary actions. It took the light of our darkest hour to shine on this revelation, but I now know what I must do in redemption for all I have not.

An ordinary man, such as I, would normally and naturally relent to this so-called monarch, allowing him, albeit by servants' hands, to push me from the gallows. An extraordinary man would jump, for in this equation, that would be the extraordinary final act of a free man."

In that moment, George hoped he had managed to at least suppress their fears and replace them with purpose. He believed they needed an extraordinary man, for an extraordinary man, even in this darkest hour, would find some light to shine. He only hoped he had filled those shoes.

At terms with their fates and again fueled with purpose, the men cheered.

The commotion gained the attention of the guards, including their newest celebrity, Jonathan Elders. They dutifully, though hesitantly, stormed the cell block, muskets in hand, fear in eyes, and wavers in voices, as they attempted to demand order.

Having witnessed their meager charge, George thought to himself, *If their demand were the wind, and I a sailor in need, I need not bother to raise my sails.*

Thomas Jefferson had been sitting in the back of the cell when the then nameless guard had planted his seedling legendary statements. The man who had penned the Declaration of Independence may have been in the back of the cell, but he had heard what was said, and all in the cells had surmised the guard had not known whom he had previously addressed.

Now, standing with only bars between him and the grandiloquent codger, he turned, looked him square in the eyes, and said, "I held the pen. I held the pen, and the signature on the document I had penned holds firm."

Guard Elders and his cohorts wanted to silence these prisoners, this prisoner. It was they who had been silenced, left awestruck by the energy that flooded through the bars toward them, leaving them drowning in silence and gasping for breath.

Thomas Jefferson continued, "And though, in the end, it is death that greets us, remember this, death's arms are opened for all. Do not let the bars fool you, for you are the true prisoners. We were freed by the pens and will not hang by them, but yet, will walk the lines drawn by them and cross life's inevitable threshold as free men."

Jefferson had not needed to look around to know all ears had absorbed his words. The deafening silence in response told him.

— CHAPTER 4 —

TIME PASSED, AND BY SPRING 1782, BENJAMIN FRANKLIN WITNESSED how, though skin paled, weight diminished, and physical strength withered, the minds of he and his fellow Signers had remained astute and their destiny with freedom resolute.

Each day the past year, he and his mates, by fate, had heard the construction that occurred seemingly all about them—the planning, the hammering, the sawing, and all the other sounds now familiar to them.

They too had experienced the action in the camaraderie of shared purpose. Some in their prewar times had helped their communities build a new church, reinforce a bridge shared by neighboring townships divided by the river it crossed, or helped a friend repair their house damaged by storm—all to aid their family, their friends, their communities.

He knew full well that such was not the reason for all the construction he heard now.

Ben had himself overheard the stories from the guards echoing from down the hall or through the walls of adjoining offices to the cells.

As spring had progressed, he noticed the shadowed images from the resulting structures hit by the rays of a tired day's sun.

Ben imagined the shadows were mere extensions of the gallows, reaching down as if to try to grab them early. Still, the Signers remained just out of reach; it was not time yet.

But Ben knew that time was nearing.

— CHAPTER 5 —

MONDAY, JULY 1, 1782, A DAY BEFORE THE EVENT OFFICIALLY COINED "The Signers' Day of Reckoning," William Franklin made a royally approved visit to Hell's Gate to see his father.

Prior, no outsider had been allowed to see the prisoners. The king granted William exception for reasons of his proven status as a staunch British Loyalist and position as the royal governor of New Jersey. There had been no question where his loyalty lay throughout the rebellion, given his polar opposite position on the political spectrum from his father's.

William had requested the visit, but he himself had questioned why. Divided by their loyalties, he and his father had not spoken in years. Though he publicly denied it, a part of him understood his father's actions and loyalties. But to William the royal governor, his father's actions were neither practical nor logical. The end his father would be meeting was both inevitable and unworthy of the sacrifice, no matter how lofty and noble the cause.

It was another sweltering summer day, and stepping into the jail, William felt the temperature and humidity jump even higher. He rounded the corner from the guards' station and then made his way down the hall to which he had been directed, to enter the cell row.

His first thought as he caught sight of his father was how he appeared to be melting. Benjamin Franklin, once portly, was now emaciated after almost a year and a half of rotting in the cell.

William spied his father writing diligently in the back of the cell. Their differences melted as he looked upon the frail presence that remained of his father. He watched on as he witnessed his father, hunched on the cell floor, lost in his writing. William made his way along the outside of the cell toward where his father sat.

Standing alongside his father, only the cell bars between them, he spoke the only words he could muster, "Mr. Franklin."

As his father looked up in response, William saw no personal bitterness, only happiness and endless hope in his father's expression. He knew his father had never given up on the hope that someday he would come to understand the "true value" in the freedom he had sought. William recalled their last argument from several years prior, in which his father had conveyed that he knew his son would not join the fight for freedom but hoped he would someday come to recognize it as something worth fighting for.

As William peered into his father's eyes, he saw the fire burning in them was as bright as ever. Ironically, while his father's body had withered, it appeared his conviction had only strengthened. It was as if his physical strength and essence were merely transferred to his article of faith. William asked himself, *How can these eyes belong to the frail old man I see before me? What stokes these flames?*

William cleared his throat, and this time, less formally spoke, "Father, … I do not know what to say … I guess I …" He truly had not known what to say and found he was still asking himself why he'd even wanted to come.

"William, son, I am both incredibly surprised and glad to see you. I want to apologize. I am so sorry for how our differences have driven us apart."

William believed the apology had been genuine, without blame, and noticed how it had made no right or wrong declarations. He sensed and shared the relief from his father, and he realized he would have regretted not having the chance to bury the hatchet. Along with the relief, he felt a sense of reconciliation.

William finally spit out the desire that had been eating away inside him, however conflicted, "Father … I find, despite our differences, a longing to save you, though I know I cannot." He said it so fast, as if he could not control what he had said. He had been denying and burying this feeling over the past year and felt a sense of instant relief. Once spoken, he realized what a poisonous and bitter pill it would have been to have kept it inside him.

"Son, there will be no saving me. My physical fate is cast in stone. But you can save my story, my legacy. I have written an autobiography of sorts, with no hope but to keep at least one accurate account of things I have done and why I did them. I do not ask that you even read it; I have no intent of leaving you to dwell on our differences. In my reflections over the time that has passed, I have come to recognize I will leave you with nothing but the love of a father. Prior to your coming here today, I had no means. But as you are here, I ask that you keep this account and pass it on through generations for no other reason than to let me die believing someday someone may see me and my actions through my eyes. Lastly, I have also hidden several of my other journals, as I know they would be destroyed, otherwise."

William watched as his father pulled a journal from underneath his now baggy shirt and discreetly handed it to him through the cell bars.

His father continued, "Can you collect the others as well, keep them with this account? Son, I accept my fate but will face it in peace if you can do this for me."

William saw no harm in the request and selfishly felt his own desire would be fulfilled in honoring his father's wish. "I will do this for you. I promise."

To this, his father revealed the location of the other journals. A smile appeared on William, as hearing the location hit him with a flood of good memories from his youth.

There was more each wanted to say, but neither could find the words. William tucked the journal in an inner jacket pocket. His eyes locked on the intensity burning in his father's. In them, he could see his father's love, and so much more. He thought to himself, *If I had not seen that life in his eyes, I might have felt sorry for the frail old man before me. Instead, I see my father at peace with his foolish and fateful design, and I can only hope I am so in my own day of reckoning.* He finally managed to muster a simple, "Goodbye, Father."

"Goodbye, son."

William turned to leave, only then realizing there had been no guard in there with him. He thought of the journal in his jacket pocket and held it closer, as if doing so would hide it more. He saw no guard until he was out of the cell block, and down the hall. When he finally came upon a group of King's Guards, he overheard them discussing how the horses to be used for the drawing and quartering had been corralled into the building's rear courtyard. Their comments drew his attention to the sounds he recognized as from horses, restless and neighing.

He remembered how the courtyard had been where the Second Continental Congress had made so many behind the scenes decisions.

As he stepped out of the building, one he had known his whole life to be the Pennsylvania Statehouse, and onto Chestnut Street in the newly renamed city of George's Cross, he witnessed the myriad of gallows and crowds of spectators already gathering for tomorrow's events. Having had almost two years to prepare, he saw how these gallows were not for mere function but intended historical and monumental form.

The Pennsylvania Statehouse had always been a historical and visual form itself, but now William found it wrapped by the skin, or more the skeleton, of the very enemy it had grown to abhor. He looked at that memory with political indifference, thus allowing his thoughts to turn to a personal memory of his father telling him how he had reported the building's first function in his paper, *The Pennsylvania Gazette*.

In a sudden onslaught of memories, he thought, *Less than an hour ago, I was a Loyalist, wanting nothing more than to witness the much-celebrated Signer's Day of Reckoning. But now I see I am so much more. I am a son who knows his father greets his end, and I cannot find it in myself to witness such end. I will leave my final image of him the eyes that reflected the man I have always known.*

He decided, while the events of the morrow were carried out, he would instead make a trip to a giant and old oak tree he remembered picnicking under so frequently as a child. Behind it, he would find, buried in a wooden chest, the remaining portion of a promise he intended to keep.

The tree, he had just remembered, was memorable because the family had always storied that it resembled the famous tree at the end of Abbey Road in London. The very tree, the Tyburn Tree in Hyde Park was originally used as natural gallows for so many hangings in earlier history, until its manmade counterpart gallows replaced it. The natural progression of thoughts on this led directly and immediately back to Hell's Gate. The sweltering heat of the day did nothing to prevent the goose bumps from running up his arms.

He reminded himself how, on their picnic tree, however, they chose to hang pictures they had drawn. With that image, he imagined it would be just a picture of his father being hanged, a memory, not his father the next day.

A sadness for the coming loss overwhelmed William. The feelings that bubbled up confused him as they conflicted with the feelings he had developed for his father over more recent years.

As he continued down Chestnut, sweating in the sun, he wiped his eyes and then forehead with a handkerchief, pulled the book in his jacket pocket closer to him, and firmed his own resolution. He would honor his father's wish.

Maybe someday, he imagined, he might even allow himself to read the journals.

— CHAPTER 6 —

BENJAMIN FRANKLIN KNEW THE NEXT SUNRISE WOULD BE HIS LAST, so he had stayed up all night to witness it.

He had not been alone in this realization, nor at having stayed up all night. He knew all his fellow inmates had stayed up as well. He noted that it had not been a night of nerves. It had not been a night of arguments, desperation, or sorrow. There had been no other visitors, and there had been no crying. It had been a night of individual reflection. Each man had long accepted his fate.

From the cell, Ben could not directly see the sun, but the sun had found a way to see itself in, and Ben basked in the rays that had somehow made it past the gallows. It had not escaped his thoughts how one had his name on it. But for now, he ignored all gallows' shadows, knowing he would greet them soon enough.

Having been up all night, his thoughts had ventured down every avenue of his life. He had thought about his family, recognizing all he had done for them and all he had not.

He had thought about the idea of a united country, an idea for which he had fought and was giving his life, though it had never come to fruition. His memories on this struggle began so many years ago. He remembered how, for so long, he had firmly believed the colonies both could and should reconcile with Britain, recognizing only recently how he had been so much slower than the people he represented at realizing they could not. Though he could not remember the specific day his attempts at reconciliation had started, he could not forget the days he'd finally came to believe he had

25

been blind and misguided. Two dates burned in his memory, opened his eyes, and told him both how he had been wrong and how he could do right.

The first had occurred back on January 29, 1774. On that day, shortly after Ben had admitted to his part in redistributing incendiary letters in what had come to be known as the Hutchinson Letters Affair, he had found himself as Britain's scapegoat for the rebellious actions they had endured as a result. Though Ben had been in Britain at the time, the British held their newfound scapegoat partially responsible for the "Tea Party" held in Boston Harbor the previous year.

Ben had received the Hutchinson letters after the death of Thomas Whately, the British undersecretary in 1772. Mr. Whately had received them from Thomas Hutchinson, who at the time of Mr. Whately's passing had held the position of royal governor of the Colony of Massachusetts.

The letters contained early evidence of the powder keg that had been stirring in the colonies, and Ben's intentions had been to pass them on, using them to assign blame for the colonies' unrest to a handful of people like Hutchinson, so perhaps the colonies would become more willing to reconcile with Britain. He hoped they would see it was not their mother country but a handful of authoritarians the colonies had to blame.

He could not have been more wrong about how the colonists would react. Against his intentions, he had inadvertently added fuel to the revolutionary fire.

So, for his part in sending the letters, Ben stood before the Privy Council, led by Alexander Wedderburn. Ben was standing in the "cockpit" of the amphitheater in Whitehall, and in front of the entire king's council. He stood silent and stone-faced as the council orally tore into him. The crowd laughed and jeered as he stoically withstood the verbal assault.

Thinking back on it now, he remembered how, as he'd finally exited the amphitheater, he had whispered to the council leader, Wedderburn, how he would "make his master a little king for this." Thoughts of his coming execution aside, a smile spread across his face.

A while after that day in Whitehall and shortly after the Ides of March in 1775, while reading American newspapers with his friend, Joseph Priestly, he remembered that he'd cried as he read the colonist's responses to the king's closing of Boston's port. This closing of one of America's busiest ports had been the king's response to the "Tea Party" that had occurred in it.

In a related article that referenced Ben's failed efforts to represent the colonies in Britain, he'd read how Lord Sandwich had declared that the "deft ingrate American, should stick to flying kites in lightning!"

The next day, Ben had set sail for America. He'd worn a new hat that day, having grown weary of the hat of reconciliation. His new hat was one of a passionate patriot. His every effort since, he hoped, would prove him to have been one of the most passionate.

That had been back in March 1775.

Now, on this the morning of the Signers' Day of Reckoning, or what Ben merely recognized as the day he would die, he sat reflecting. He felt pride in recognizing how those two days, seemingly so long ago, had led him to his first decision as a free man.

On the day's upcoming events, he found he was even prouder of the fact he would be making his last, his final decision, as a free man as well.

In balance with what made him proud, he considered his greatest failure. Shortly after having reached the colonies, in November 1775, he had been asked by Continental Congress to seek foreign support in their fight for freedom from tyranny. Having been added to a Committee of Secret Correspondence, he had the opportunity to meet with Silas Deane and a French agent sent to America to see if the colonies warranted assistance from France. This introduction led to a secret letter, with hopes to engage the French government for support in the form of money and arms. It resulted in Ben being added as a delegate of the Continental Congress to a commission for alliance. This commission included Silas Deane, a representative from Connecticut, and Arthur Lee from Virginia. The three men, duties charged, boarded a ship to France.

The commission of delegates failed their mission. This floundering, Ben considered his greatest.

Looking back on it, Ben realized how he had failed and how he could have greatly improved his chance of succeeding. He realized now that the French were romantics who, upon meeting the American delegates, were greatly disappointed. As delegates, they fell short in filling the grandiose images the French held of Americans. Instead, they had focused on trade and commerce and had failed to pluck the far more pure and idealistic strings in the hearts of the French. Ben saw now, albeit too late, that had they done so, the generous nation might have willingly assisted who they saw as the protectors of the oppressed colonies. Quite simply, they'd failed to resemble the Americans the French idealized and would have wanted to help.

Finally, Ben laughed, as the inventor in him wished he had invented a way to communicate back in time. He wished he could somehow capitalize on the lessons of hindsight. As he thought on these lessons, he recalled how his fellow patriot cell mates had also recognized missed opportunities, on which only hindsight could provide perspective.

Earlier that week, he had overheard General George Washington discussing with John Adams how he wished he had ignored the traditions of war and fought against the British in a way that both recognized the limitations of his lesser experienced militia and capitalized on its unique strengths. The general had elaborated on what he considered a missed opportunity to cross the Delaware on Christmas Eve in winter 1776, during the traditional war holiday—the Rites of Spring.

Following the Rites of Spring, the fighting stopped, frozen as were his soldiery, to camp for the winter. He recognized the boldness of the mission that might have been, his army crossing the near frozen Delaware at night, but also what he now considered the greater risk that he had taken by not crossing it. If he had a second chance, he would have sent his army and tasted the victory of catching the Hessian army off guard and on holiday. It had been at a time when his army so badly needed a victory to swing the fate of favor.

As Ben overheard these reflections, these lessons in hindsight, he had quickly entered them in his journal, along with numerous others he had learned over the course of confinement. There were many, but ultimately only a handful he considered critical opportunities that would have made a cumulative difference in the outcome of their fight for freedom. Even though he saw no value in recording these observations of his companions, other than an accurate collection of revolutionary reflection, he was pleased with their inclusion in the journal he had managed to put in the hands of his son. He would die believing his story, their story, their truths would survive, even if only as a collection of journals collecting dust where they remained hidden through time.

A sudden clanging of keys interrupted the Signer's ruminations as King's Guards dressed in full ceremonial regalia filed into the jail.

— CHAPTER 7 —

WILLIAM FRANKLIN FOLDED A GILDED MAP OF THE GALLOWS HE HAD just been handed and placed it in his pocket. Sitting near the royal circle, he should have considered himself one of the "lucky" few, as the other maps made available to the general populace in attendance were printed with a focus on quantity, not quality. However, appreciation of the ornate quality of the map escaped him in the conflict of the moment.

He had fully intended on not attending the event but under royal insistence had come and now watched on as he witnessed the delivery of prisoners stepping through their doors of fate onto the platforms of their gallows. He suspected the gallows directly before him had his father's name on it. He also suspected that was no coincidence.

Royal colors and banners abounded, and he knew this was intended to be quite the celebration.

The trumpeting of horns sounded the arrival of the king and other royalty. Even the loud trumpets were drowned out by the white noise of the masses as they fought for positions to witness the spectacle.

William noticed, though stepping out of their prison for the first time in a couple of years and into a full royal pomp celebration of their impending demise, the prisoners remained calm and unshaken.

As Benjamin Franklin was directed by his assigned guard toward his own window of fate, he noticed the prisoner's names had been written in calligraphy onto signs posted by each respective window. He laughed, as he knew most of the guards were illiterate so could not read them.

As he passed, he read a sign for Benjamin Harrison and then read three more—Robert Morris, Francis Lightfoot Lee, and Lyman Hall—before being led up a flight of stairs to where he would come to realize that the higher your involvement in the revolution, the higher your assigned gallows.

He smiled as he thought, *Was that so we will fall further? Were our gallows prepared with longer ropes?*

Upon reaching the top of the stairs, he saw John Hancock's sign. This time he laughed aloud as he noted the larger sized script in which it had been written.

He had passed a few other signs before he resumed reading them. Samuel Adams, Elbridge Gerry, and Richard Henry Lee he read before being led up yet another flight of stairs.

Well, this is new, he thought. *There used to only be two floors in the Pennsylvania Statehouse.*

Then turning to the guard, he quipped, "I see you've redecorated the place; it looks good. Adding the new level should allow quite the show, and from up here you should have a great view of the fireworks. There will be fireworks?"

He cocked his head back and laughed again as he had noticed the guard he had recognized as the one who'd spoken the catchphrase so long ago now stood shaking and looked white as a ghost.

At the top of this second set of stairs, he realized he must have reached the pinnacle, as to the left at the top of the stairs, he read a sign for John Adams and then passed one that read simply, George Washington. He witnessed yet again how the king had made sure not to recognize any degree of stature by even so much as recognizing him as a general. Ben laughed at the irony. George Washington deserved the title and crown of king more than the king did but was a good enough man he would have rejected it if offered.

As Ben finally approached his window, he reached for the remaining stub of a pencil he had tucked hidden behind his ear and, before his hangman could react, scribbled his signature loops underneath his name on the sign.

He turned back to find his guard standing frozen and stunned by such a simple act.

Ben then handed him the pencil. "Here. I have done my writing in this life. You fancy yourself a man of words. Perhaps you will actually write something worthy someday."

The King's Guard accepted the pencil as if he had no choice. Looking at his facial expression, one would think he had been stabbed by it. He whispered under his breath and to himself, "Perhaps."

Mr. Franklin laughed as he recalled the stories he had overheard that portrayed this guard as courageous. The guard now before him looked anything but courageous. Instead, to Ben he looked lost, confused, just another man who could not see, blinded in royal darkness to the beauty freedom holds.

"You look as if you'd seen a ghost. You're a little bit early for that, aren't ya? One thing for sure, you stand lost to the values of freedom, but you can't seem to get the allure of it from your mind. Well that's OK. You'll have plenty of time to think on it, won't ya."

Ben then regarded the tradition of giving the hangman the clothes of the man he hanged. As Jonathan Elders was to serve as his hangman, he eyed the man for size.

The guard, for his part, stood shaking.

"Well, Guard Elders, it appears these clothes will favor you. Good, as with the pencil, I will no longer need them where I am going. A word of advice, though, you had better take them before the quartering."

Just then, Ben spied the summer day outside his gateway to heaven. He turned one last time to his hangman and added with genuine resolve, "It looks like a beautiful day to die." He then walked himself out onto the gallows, smiling and waving to the crowd below. He waved harder as he realized they had fallen silent upon witnessing his, and apparently, the other Signers' actions and demeanors. Turning to his left, he looked beyond the lined pikes jutting from the edges of the scaffolds where, if he had bothered to think about it, he would have pictured his head on one when this was all said and done. Instead his eyes looked past the pikes to find John Adams making his way out onto his gallows and General Washington already out on his.

The general was leaning over the edge, holding onto what was likely to be his pike for balance, to make sure the people directly below could see his smile and wave. He then stood back, tall and straight, exchanging waves with Ben as he did so. Lastly, he turned deliberately toward the king, offering his broadest smile and most exaggerated wave.

The king's face turned royal red.

Ben's son William watched on, taking it all in.

He knew this gruesome spectacle was all about showing the king's subjects the price paid for treason, offering a visual deterrent. He also learned how the king intended to celebrate the occasion annually as a reminder. The king had already declared a name for the holiday, and today marked the first Signer's Day of Reckoning. He had also approved a committee to design the traditions he would start and plan celebrations to be held annually on the 2nd of July. William shivered as these thoughts reminded him how had been asked to chair the committee. He recalled how, only two days prior, he would have seen the offer of chairing the committee as an honor.

It had taken almost an hour to get all the Signers in place and noosed.

William watched on as Captain Thomas Horner of the King's Guard finally made his way down the stairs of Hell's Gate, having made sure everyone and everything was in place. The captain then crossed Chestnut Street, made his way through parting crowds, and stepped into ceremonial position before the king to formally commence the day's events.

The crowd stirred in a combination of silence and mixed emotional jeering.

Directly below and in front of William, horns-men dressed in full celebratory liveries marched in from both sides and in front of the lower level of the two-tiered platform balcony built across Chestnut Street to seat, on its top level, the royal family and their invitees, William included. The structure itself was draped in the rich velvet of royal colors, trimmed with gold in an all-out display of regality and pomp.

Just above the horns-men, on a platform to the side of the royal balcony, yet appropriately lower, the royal crier began by drawing out his decorated scroll.

The horns were intended to draw the attention of the crowd, to allow the crier their full attention.

Having covered his ears, William was thankful it only took one try to do so.

Reading from his scroll the crier vociferously proclaimed, "Hear ye! Hear ye! By decree of His Majesty, King George the Third, for the acts of declaration against the Royal Crown and rebellion against His Majesty's Kingdom, ye signers of treason are sentenced to death by hanging … drawing … and then quartering."

He had taken an extended pause, William assumed, to allow the crowd to take it in for amplified measure. He figured the crier would then announce how the hanging, drawing, and quartering were to be preceded by a formal and ceremonial hanging by the necks to recognize the silencing of the rebellion.

It was then, with the hangman's rope around his neck, when General George Washington interjected with a cry of his own design. "Hear ye, great public, hear ye!"

All heads and attentions turned and looked upward immediately. No one had expected nor was prepared for such a disruption in formalities. The entire audience, royalty included, listened more out of disbelief than anything.

Again, William took it all in.

Taking full advantage of the silence and attention and before the king or anyone else could snap out of bewildered stupor, the general continued. And looking directly at the king while holding a sign with his name high above his head for all to see, he declared, "Give me liberty. Or in the final decision and act of a free man, I choose death!"

The royal audience, the public crowd, and the guards stared in awestruck silence, all eyes on the vocal dissenter. They were in perfect positions to take in what would happen next, though were by no means prepared for it.

The completion of General Washington's declaration acted as a cue for all free men, the Signers, to leap from the gallows at their own free accord.

William gasped in total disbelief as he witnessed the ropes go taut and tight around the necks of the Signers, his father's directly above and in front of him.

To his side, he saw the king leap to his feet; instant anger had set in. The king yelled up to the guards to cut the ropes.

Reaching up as if his mere royal gesture could prevent the events that had unexpectedly unfolded before him, he shouted in a fury, "Nooooooooo!" Now jumping in rage, the king screamed repeatedly in demand to the hangmen, his guards, "I order you! Do not let them die! Do not let them die! Cut them down, I command you!"

He was determined to have his moment.

William turned back to look at the Signers.

As they had literally jumped from their gallows, the added strain snapped many of their necks upon the impact of their ropes reaching full extension. Thus, many were granted a quick and painless death.

He turned his focus back to his father. Benjamin Franklin was still, a dead weight swaying at the end of his rope, and thankfully, he found, was one such lucky man.

William's own throat tightened both at what he had witnessed but more at the sudden and incredible loss he felt.

He had attended the event, though he had fully intended not to, fearing the invite was yet another test between bloodline and loyalty. He now realized this was the first test he had passed out of fear more than loyalty.

He stood frozen, watching his father until his feet stopped swaying. Though chaos ensued all around him, he stood hypnotized by the pendulum swing of his father's feet. It was not until they stopped that he looked away. The end of the motion triggered the release of his gaze, and he snapped out of his stupor, comprehending that he had witnessed not his father's execution but his escape. William had taken in the complete conviction of his father's expression as he saw him leap to his freedom. Therefore, he had not missed that his father had smiled all the way until the rope went taut.

What he witnessed solidified his intent to carry out his father's wishes. He promised to append a record in his father's prison journal of all that had occurred and would occur because of this turn of events.

His father had stopped, but he had turned toward the movement of the general, George Washington, who had not been so lucky. William could see it had done nothing to sway his demeanor. The general swung at the end of the rope, maintaining the enduring expression of a man at resolve with his fate. He never fought it but held the expression as long as life held on to him.

William took in the audience as they stared at the debacle before them, stunned by the extraordinary act they had witnessed.

The king, in a blood-red fury, continued to shout orders to cut and retrieve but to no avail, as the guards, like all others in audience, stood frozen.

That is except for Jonathan Elders.

Jonathan Elders turned and ran. He ran down the new stairway. He ran down the old stairway. He ran out the back of Hell's Gate and was not sure when or where he was going to stop.

Many onlookers, there to witness the Signer's Day of Reckoning, witnessed him running. Their eyes followed as if to identify who this King's Guard was pursuing. They had just witnessed how the Signers had escaped their programmed execution, but had a Signer somehow managed to have physically escaped his fate?

Jonathan Elders knew what he was running from. It was the conflict in his mind, which he had been experiencing ever since that first day, his first encounter with the damned Signers. At that moment, a seed had somehow been planted. He was not sure how they had done it or if it had even been intentional, but he firmly believed the seed had been sown by the Signers.

Over the course of their period of detainment, they watered the seed within him with their inner peace and strength of conviction.

The seed had grown in strength inside him. Then, as if it had been released as the Signers had upon making their final choice, this desire to be truly free had shed all constraints and risen from its chrysalis in the shadows of Jonathan's mind. The entity stood tall—and in full conflict with everything Jonathan had been beaten over the years into believing was his fate.

While he ran and as if to throw in its twopence, the fresh wounds from his latest flogging screamed back at the abrasive scrapings of the royal ceremonial uniform he wore.

Jonathan fought to suppress the conflict that had risen inside him, but somehow the word *choice* burrowed its way into his mind, perhaps filling the space the entity had left. Or perhaps it had always been there, and was merely the placenta the entity had left behind in its cocoon. Regardless of its origin, Jonathan began to resolve, to reassess what choices he had. Then, as if on cue, the word *freedom* crept in. And now, as if in waves, it cycled through its ebb and flow to crash on the ever-eroding shores of his mind.

He finally understood what the word meant but did not know what he could do with it yet. Jonathan had a feeling, however, that this wave would crash relentlessly until he figured it out.

Finally taking in his surroundings, he realized he had stumbled upon a tavern on Chestnut he had frequented in the past, on the rare afternoon he had been granted leave. The name on the sign swinging above him read, Fraunces Tavern, not that he could read it; he could not read.

He entered the tavern to find it mostly empty. He knew the crowds still gathered at Hell's Gate where chaos had ensued and a very angry king fought to regain order, his order.

The only person who mattered to Jonathan at this moment was the barkeep.

Having gotten his attention, Jonathan managed, "Pooour me a pint, barkeep."

The barkeep, Phineas Dinter stared quizzically at the King's Guard in full regalia before him. He thought about where he believed the guard should have been but sensed a certain aura emanating from the man telling him he should resist speaking on his thought and just do as he had been instructed.

Cold draft in hand and wearing remnants of the beer moustache its first swig had left, Elders asked more of the barkeep. "Ye wouldn't happen to have a quill and sheet upon ye?"

It took a moment for the question to settle in Phineas's mind. Something about the whole scene seemed off kilter. Not wanting to test his concerns, he replied, "Yeah, I do … I do … Shall I retrieve it for ye?"

Elders simply nodded and drew another swig from his pint.

Upon return, Phineas found the guard had downed the draft and sat silently until he had returned to his position at the bar before him.

"Can ya pen somethin' fer me, barkeep?"

"Yes, yes, sir, I can."

As Phineas inked his quill, Elders halted him and then handed him the pencil stub he remembered he had been given by Benjamin Franklin. "No wait. Use this, will ya, and pen this fer me." Then he froze.

A moment later, Kings Guard Jonathan Elders recited a catchphrase opposite the one that had gained him fame. He said, as if again to an audience of his peers, "Philadelphia, Pennsylvania, freed by death, ya pens'll save ya."

Eyes wide, jaw dropped, Phineas wrote as fast as he could, stumbling on the word *Pennsylvania*, as he had seen it spelled with both one *n* or two at its beginning. Haste won out, and he spelled it with one.

As he finished, Elders repeated, "Philadelphia, Pennsylvania, freed by death, ya pens'll save ya. Did ye get that now, did ye?"

"Yes, yes, I got it," he replied as he slid the sheet to the guard.

King's Guard Jonathan Elders stared at the sheet before him. Though he could not read it, he sensed the barkeep had done as requested.

The pint he had downed had calmed him. He now knew what he must do and felt resolved to do it.

He, unlike the Signers, did not have immediate execution before him. Had the Signers had any other choice, they would not have done as they had.

Jonathan Elders, however, had long grown tired and weak. He'd been long depressed, and the over-the-edge feeling he'd experienced the instant the Signers had jumped at their own will told him how much he longed to have joined them.

Phineas Dinter stared. The line he had written for the guard repeated itself in his mind. He recognized immediately how the phrase had been a variation of the catchphrase that had made one King's Guard, a Jonathan Elders, famous. He thought, *Could this be Jonathan Elders?*

The guard before him picked up the sheet of rough paper and stared at its words one last time and then held it to his chest over his heart.

The barkeep had not seen the knife in the guard's other hand. Elders must have pulled it while he had written the quote for him.

Assuming the knife brandished before him now had been intended for him, Phineas leaped back in instinctive defense and disbelief. He had not even had enough time to shriek in response.

King's Guard Jonathan Elders, standing tall now and looking away from the bewildered and scared barkeep, began to shout as if to an imaginary audience, "Give me liberty." Then placing the knife's tip into position as if to pin the note to his heart, "Or in the final decision of a free man, I choose death!"

Elders then thrust the knife into his own chest, using his weight against the bar to ensure the blade hit home.

Blood quickly soaked the paper the knife held in place against his chest.

As King's Guard Jonathan Elders fell forward in death, his final breath carried his final words, "I am free."

PART II

In the Country of New England
A Time for All to See

— CHAPTER 8 —

Saturday, April 24, 2010
On the grounds of the recently collapsed
Anderson Raines Lightning Lab

RICHARD JACOBSON KNEW THE PROVISION OF INITIAL SUPPORT FOR
Lightning Labs was much due to the efforts of the king's advisors.
He should know; he'd been His Majesty King George VII's most trusted
and chief advisor for over thirty years. He had strongly recommended
providing this support to boost the image of the crown in the eyes of his
vast public—to give the king's people at least one good thing to say about
him. The king's support for an effort to tap into naturally occurring
lightning as a source of sustainable and inexpensive power that could
someday provide electricity to the common villages had at least offered
the potential.

Never mind the fact that electric power had been available in the royal
cities for decades. The king would never spend the money it would take to
implement that traditional and much more expensive infrastructure in the
villages. Richard had learned a long time ago, and the hard way, to never
broach that topic again.

Now, he and the king were at the collapsed location of said first
attempt at a lightning lab. Richard knew he had his hands full with this
one. The king was annoyed by the standard appearances he reluctantly

agreed to make during the lab's construction but was now giving a eulogy, of sorts, for the scientists who'd died in the collapse of his "money pit."

The reality was, his support was no more than a token gesture. As with everything else, the money to pay for the program would come from taxing the people. But that thought remained safely in the recesses of Richard's mind.

At the ruins of the brilliant scientist, Anderson Raines's original lightning lab, Richard listened on with his well-practiced loyal face beaming behind the king as he ended his speech. And he should, because standing behind the king meant all the cameras were on him as well.

"As for Anderson Raines, I have lost far more than just a brilliant scientist. I have lost a friend." The king danced around the potential commitment to continue support for the effort of tapping into lightning as a naturally occurring power source and then concluded, "The date and time of the accident, April 22, 2010 at 12:11 p.m., will forever remain in royal remembrance."

Richard may have been behind the king, but he did not need to see to know there was nothing but coldness bleeding from his steel blue eyes. He knew any thought of the king genuinely promising further financial support for such a noble selfless effort lived in the tidbits of dreams that you remember solely because they occurred immediately before waking.

And as for the remembrance, he knew the king had to read the date from the teleprompters, as he had probably already forgotten it.

Upon completion of the speech, the king pulled Richard aside. He motioned off the guards and media, stating how he merely wanted "to take a closer look at the loss."

"RJ, shall we?"

"Yes, Your Majesty." But in his mind, Richard thought, *RJ? As if we are friends. This man has no friends. You can't forge a friendship out of fear. Besides, I know the real reason you want me to join you.*

The king led him behind a wall jutting out of the wreckage and, more importantly, out of the eyes and earshot of the public. This was not for Richard's sake but for the king's. He did not want his public to hear the rant that conflicted with the show he had just put on.

Richard followed the king as was required of him but kept his distance, choosing to stand in the shadows while the king stood as if studying the backside of the wall. Richard knew there was a royal ass chewing coming. There was always a royal ass-chewing coming.

A ceiling panel leaned awkwardly against the inside of the collapsed wall, presumably where it had landed in the ruin. The king shoved it aside, revealing marks on the wall the panel had been covering. He then dragged his fingers across the backside of the wall. He watched as they crossed burn marks he assumed had been created by the lightning that had killed a handful of his top scientists; destroyed the lab; and, more importantly to him, validated his thoughts that he had wasted his time and money.

In a contained fury, the king then directed his own firestorm at Richard. Most of it just bounced off the wall, as Richard had been chief advisor for so long he was numb to the abuse. Toward the end he would start to listen again, as the jabs usually got more creative then.

"The burn marks on this wall are nothing but incredibly expensive skid marks on my royal boxers! I want to rub your nose in them so you can feel what it is like to be dragged through this shit!"

After the rampage, the king took a moment to collect himself before stepping back out before the cameras he knew were still waiting.

They walked back out into the eyes of his public. The king's expression could easily have been mistaken as one appropriately grieving the losses of which the crumbled site should so handily have reminded him. The arm he threw over Richard's shoulder as if they had just shared a moment of silence only further supported this misconception.

Richard knew that, as always, the cameras had failed to catch reality. The king had merely used the gesture as an opportunity to wipe the char from his fingertips onto Richard's jacket.

Once in earshot, the king solemnly commented, "RJ, that is simply devastating. What can I do to keep this vital program alive yet not endanger the lives of more brilliant scientists?" Shaking his head and feigning genuine concern, the king had played his part, and the cameras had caught it all.

As he always had to, Richard Jacobson had already thrown aside the abuse he had received. Holding onto it would do him no good. Besides, that abuse may well have been the cost of living in the tidbits of dreams.

—✦ CHAPTER 9 ✦—

Tuesday, June 30, 2020
At the Great Clock of the Palace at George's Cross
In the royal city of George's Cross in the Province of Burgoyne

S AMUEL THATCHER HAD ONLY BEEN A RESIDENT CLOCK MAKER FOR the Great Clock of the Palace at George's Cross for nearly three and one quarter years. While that may be true, he had been an amateur horologist for well over twenty.

His dream had always been to own his own clock shop. Over the years, he had changed what he would name the shop. At first, he'd liked Son of Time and then had moved onto Giving the Hands of Time a Hand, but that had been too long. There had been others, but he had landed on Gearhead Clock Man, a name he felt made the art of clock-making sound cool.

Sadly, this latest name had only added another page to a dream book he had been writing most of his life, a book he now figured would not be finished until the day he was finished, only without his preferred ending.

He could not complain, however, as his love for clocks had at least gotten him to where he was now. For a man who loved clocks, he was lucky enough to be responsible for the care, conditioning, and winding of the world's most famous clock, residing in the world's most famous tower, and in arguably the world's most famous palace.

In the Palace at George's Cross, the top of Third's Tower held the aptly nicknamed King of Clocks, more commonly referred to today as Big Ben.

Much of the history of the clock was common knowledge. For example, many people knew how Big Ben originally and still referred specifically to the clock's largest bell, the hour bell. The hour bell, weighing in at fourteen tons, was named Big Ben in honor of Sir Benjamin Hall, the chief commissioner of works at the time the bell had been ordered for creation.

Thanks to every history course ever taught over the past two centuries, it would be difficult to find anyone who would not know the clock's tower stood just across the street from Hell's Gate. Hell's Gate had once held the long-forgotten name of Pennsylvania Statehouse but had ultimately become the constant reminder to all as to what happens when you commit treason against the Crown.

The Pennsylvania Statehouse had had its own clock tower. The only evidence remaining of its existence were the clock's hands, which to this date could be seen on display in the Third's Tower Museum at the base of the tower itself. The display was presented, as it was originally to King George III, with the clock hands knotted in royal ribbon. The public display symbolically represented the tying of the revolutionary dissenters' hands, thus marking the end of their time.

Samuel Thatcher was positive that every student to have ever adorned the halls of a school within a hundred-kilometer radius of George's Cross had attended a field trip to the Third's Tower Museum and seen that display—had heard its story. He vividly remembered when he was a student on his field trip and when he had seen the tied hands of time for his first time. It was not for this that he remembered it. Instead, for him, it had been seeing the copies of the Tower Clock's original blueprints, for they had fascinated him and turned him on to his love for clock making.

Much may be public knowledge, but Samuel doubted that many knew that the most famous bell in the most famous turret clock's tower had two cracks. Nor would most know that the cracks had appeared after the bell had already been recast for cracks once before.

In 1859, when the clock had originally been installed and set only to then have its installers discover the cracks in its main bell, it was the astronomer royal George Biddell Airy who had recommended to simply rotate the bell, so its cracks resided farthest from the strike. The bell had been turned and had rung reliably ever since.

It had held firm as the primary voice of the clock. Over time, the hour bell's name, Big Ben, had become common reference for all the bells, the clock, and the tower itself. Therefore, Big Ben, like its all-encompassing reference, had stood and run accurately and reliably for over the past 160 years.

Samuel Thatcher, at least for the past three years, had helped see to it that Big Ben, the clock, would be able to continue doing so. As one of the base level services he provided to enable this, he climbed the tower's 290 steps several times a week to wind it. It was a task he shared and one that had been done every other day since the clock's first wind over a century and a half ago.

Recalling his last entry into the clock's maintenance and use log as he climbed the steps again, he figured he was on his 118th ascent. Since earning his position at the tower, he imagined he would have performed this ascent thousands of times by the time he either retired or died trying.

Each of those times imagined, however, would all be for the sake of winding or regular maintenance.

So what was it that made this particular ascent so different? Why, after he had just been up these stairs less than a day before, did he find himself on an unscheduled trip up them again?

Lastly, having walked these steps so many times before, Samuel had gotten quite used to the exercise, to the point he no longer got winded. This time, however, he had not even reached the level with the knight's armor, identifying it as the climb's midpoint, but found he was nearly completely out of breath. While he now had the physical stamina to easily walk up the steps, he had never imagined he would ever need to run up them.

Samuel Thatcher had heard the storm last night. Samuel Thatcher had felt the storm last night. Who had not?

Intense lightning had flashed throughout the night. The white noise provided by the torrential downpour had failed to pale the din of the lightning's voice—its thunder.

Though he resided in a resident clock maker flat less than a hundred meters south of the tower, he had failed to hear the void. He had failed to recognize the absence of the sounds, thus creating the void that had been filled his whole life by the bells of Big Ben. Big Ben's quarter-hourly chimes were sounds he had been able to count on his whole life, literally like clockwork.

He reasoned, he could hardly be blamed and was by no means alone in this failing. The very thing that had created the void, the storm, had filled it.

It was not until 5:36 a.m. that morning when he learned of the elusive event that had occurred. Even then and awake, he had not directly noticed the certain absence but had to be told about it over the phone.

When the storm had nearly waned, an anonymous caller had first taken notice and rang the palace's public hotline. The call triggered a series of more calls—made by a number of tower representatives who had all also failed to recognize the void—that had ended with the call to Samuel.

His caller, his boss Malcolm Salas, had been frantic, but the message had been clear. The Great Clock of the Palace at George's Cross had been struck by lightning and had stopped. Samuel had received that message directly, but it was in that instant when he indirectly realized he had not heard the sound of the half-hourly bells just minutes prior. In immediate, successive, and logical reasoning, as he had heard the clock's bells announce nearly every quarter hour of his life, he realized he had not heard the bells announce the passing of the half hour, simply because the clock had not resounded it.

It was the first time in the 161-year history of the clock that external forces had ever stopped it.

As if this fact had not been enough to give its resident clock maker a heart attack, the coming Friday was the annual empire-wide celebration of the Signers' Day of Reckoning. It would mark the 238th anniversary of the comeuppance resulting from the Signers having drafted and signed the declaration that ultimately came to be known as their own death warrants. The so-called celebration of the event was more the monarchy's annual reminder to its subjects as to what happens when "you sign your own death warrant."

As resident clock maker, Samuel, upon reaching his one hundredth ascent of the tower for an official winding, had earned as a gift for his service, a watch with a scaled replica of Big Ben's face and the royal insignia on the back. By this watch, it was now 5:52 a.m. So, within sixteen minutes, Samuel had been awakened by the call, had gotten at least semi-dressed, and had hightailed his arse to and up the tower, having now just reached the 145th step, marking the midpoint of his journey up. He knew this to be the midpoint, as this step was also a landing and home of Mortimer Mundane—at least that is how he referred to the knight's armor that stood sentinel in the corner of the landing.

There will be no idle chatter this morning, ol'Mort! he somehow managed to think as he took no pause, trying to maintain pace up the second half of what seemed a much steeper and much longer stairwell on this mad morning. By now, he had broken out in a sweat and was panting to the rhythm of the steps he continued to scale.

As he lumbered up the staircase, he recalled the time was 5:46 a.m. when he had reached the base of the clock tower. At that time, he had witnessed with his own two eyes that the clock had stopped—and over an hour and a half earlier—at 4:10 a.m.

He had also realized that he had not been alone; he already had company. To his right, he had spied three media vans, cameras out, antennas extending, and dishes positioning—all to be prepared to catch the first light of the morning about to reflect off the stopped clock's eastward face.

The more he thought about it, the faster he ran, as if he actually believed he had a chance to prevent the media from having their moment. It was a moment he would not see himself, as he would still be running up tower stairs, and he feared it had already occurred. Regardless, he knew he had to do whatever he could to get the clock back running, or it would be his name associated with its inability to sound off the hour bell during the Signer's Day of Reckoning's royal kickoff at high noon on Thursday. It would be his fifteen minutes of infamy.

He imagined images of the clock face now, sunlit and plastered on tellies around the world. He was not wrong. By then, nearly a billion eyes were staring at the historic sight. Special news bulletins would interrupt all viewing in all time zones of the international empire.

By six o'clock, Samuel had finally reached the top. The clock's east face glowed with the sun striking it. The sun was the only thing striking in the clock; Samuel had obviously not heard the hour sound.

As disheartening as the realization had been to Samuel, he was sure it would prove a godsend of a story for the media. Though the clock had been struck by lightning, literally stopping in its sesquicentennial tracks, thankfully, he could see its faces had not been damaged.

It would not be until Samuel evaluated the clock's internal workings that he could determine the time, to the second, when the clock had stopped.

That night, from an article in *The Burgoyne Bugle*, Samuel read how its author had infused a religious connection to the time in which the world's most famous clock had frozen. To stoke the fire, the writer had attempted to provide this connection as an exclusive news angle on what had occurred. An anonymous source had provided the referential connection between the time the clock had stopped, 4:10, and the Bible's Matthew 4:10, "For He said, we must worship and serve God alone."

Not happy about yet another theory he would have to answer to, Samuel believed that the journalist had metaphorically used the hands of the clock to stir fervor in the pot of the public eye. And why not? The clock had not been using the hands at the time.

He read from the front-page article:

> The early morning sun illuminated the clock so brilliantly,
> its eastern face looked pristine, and much more so than
> it actually was. The sun's intense rays had washed out
> the effects of the very thing the clock had previously
> so reliably kept track of—time, leaving in contrast its
> seemingly ageless hands, roman numerals, and mosaic-
> patterned background for all to see.
>
> The sun, however, did nothing to erase the visual fact
> that the hands had stopped. Clouds raced past, the tower
> ravens circled, and the sun's rays shifted down the tower
> as the sun made its way up in the horizon.

In case these facts were not enough, to make the clock's stopping visually evident, an image with the article displayed a digital clock representing the real time at the clock tower. Though the digital clock clearly showed time marching past 6:00 a.m., the zoomed-in image of the famous clock face clearly read 4:10.

Samuel was only able to read this article, and without worry, as after a long day and thorough investigation into the failing of the clock, he'd found the root cause was limited to the clock's escapement. While the clock would remain out of commission for the night, he knew it would be repaired well in advance of its royal engagement ringing in the Signer's Day of Reckoning's annual ceremony.

—• PART III •—

FHM (For His Majesty)

── CHAPTER 10 ──

Friday, October 15, 2021
King George VII

T HE KING SAT AT ONE OF HIS MANY DESKS IN ONE OF HIS MANY
studies in one of his many palaces. This particular study was located
on the top floor of the Palace at George's Cross.

This particular desk was made from wood recovered from the ruins
of Shuri Castle in Okinawa, Japan. It had been over three decades since,
in what had become known as the South East Conquest, the Japanese had
surrendered to the British. The conquest had added yet another country,
from the shrinking list of those remaining, to the ever-expanding British
Empire.

Several hundred thousand people died fighting in that war, culminating
in the defeat of the Japanese and the ruin of the historic castle. To the king,
the war had been just another successful expansion, and the desk at which
he was sitting was just another desk.

The king's thoughts were focused on an opportunity he had recently
learned that he believed would give him all the advantages he would
need to finally complete the Crown's two-centuries-old push for World
Britannia.

As he sat in royal rumination, he stared out a window overlooking the
location where events in British history were the turning point catalysts

enabling the grand effort, Hell's Gate. As the sun had just risen, he could see the elongated shadows of the gallows stretch before the building as if looking for dissenting necks.

His thoughts were interrupted as his closest and longtime advisor, Richard Jacobson, knocked on the door asking permission to enter.

"Enter. This had better be worthy."

Richard made his way in, head bowed. "Your highness, I have just learned of a horrible situation that occurred earlier this morning at the Anderson Raines Lightning Lab. An employee," he said, glancing down at his notes for the name, "Geoffrey Talbrook, was struck and killed by lightning. As you have requested to immediately be kept abreast of anything learned surrounding the facility, I thought you should know."

Richard now had the king's full attention, as it was a secretive project at that lab that offered the opportunity he had just been ruminating.

Even in Richard's capacity as his most trusted advisor, the king had unusually not let Richard know the details surrounding this project.

Typical investigations lack resources and take time. Not this one. The king had made sure his many resources were aware and prepared to respond on the turn of a dime to anything regarding this facility.

Richard quickly shared what he had learned, ending with information he had requested and immediately received regarding the beginning investigation into the tragedy. "I was told by the detective in charge that they already have evidence and reason to believe it was not an accident. And another employee"—he looked down to the paper on which he had scratched his notes—"a Joshua Franks, is their primary suspect. As it has been but an hour since the event occurred, I don't know how they already have—"

The king interrupted, "I want to know all I can about the employees involved. And as soon as you learn the whereabouts of Joshua Franks, I want him immediately picked up and brought directly to me. I am about to leave here for now, but contact me as he gets picked up, and I will direct accordingly."

"Yes, your highness."

— CHAPTER 11 —

Friday, October 15, 2021
Joshua Nolin Franks

T HOUGH IT HAD BEEN COLD OUT THAT MORNING, AND COLD AS USUAL in the classroom, I still found I was sweating.

Sitting in speech class, I listened to a girl named Tabitha stammer through her speech on her documented history of being stung by bees. I was to present next.

Maybe, I figured, I was sweating because I was still wearing my coat. I'd been so damn cold in this school lately; it had been my recent habit to keep it on.

Then, more honestly, I reminded myself of my current situation. It was more than enough to make anyone sweat.

In an effort for distraction, I turned my focus back to Tabitha, who stumbled on, "When I was ten, I was barefoot and helping me mum in the fields when I inadvertently stepped on a bee." She stomped her foot and then recoiled for dramatic effect. It did not work but did manage to make my best friend, Emerson Flanders, jolt from his catatonic stupor.

I almost laughed, as I had realized the irony in how this speech had no sting to it, and that thought alone may have calmed me a little. But seeing my best friend wipe drool from his chin and off his desk and sporting a glazed deer-in-the-headlights look after being awakened by the stomp turned out to be all I had needed.

I figured, following Ta-BEE-tha (I could not help myself from pronouncing her name in my head this way) should be to my advantage.

I had also settled on a topic I was very familiar with—the history of lightning labs. Although the professor had quite blatantly hinted, though to no consequences, that we should do otherwise, I had little choice, as I had waited until the last second to start preparing the speech. I couldn't help it. I had been forced to put in too many hours working at the lightning lab. Though in my speech I would be sharing information about the lightning lab, I would not be sharing anything about my present duties. I need not be reminded how that would be considered an act of treason against the Crown.

If I was going to make it through these days, I had to keep myself distracted.

Looking back at Emerson, I realized, though we worked together and shared a flat, that I had never seen him do anything to prepare for his speech. I didn't even know what Emerson intended to share, even though, time permitting, Emerson was to follow me in turn.

I turned my attention back to Ta-BEE-tha to find she had pulled her long shirt sleeve up and was trying to show the class where a scar was in the back of her underarm.

I glanced over toward the professor, and it became visibly evident to me that he would take a thousand screaming babies over what he was listening to now. All nervousness gone, I figured my speech should be a piece of cake.

With no hiding the relief in his voice, Professor Langston ushered Ta-BEE-tha Milner back to her desk and then summoned me in his ever-so eloquent way. "Joshua Franks … Joshuua Fraanks, you are the next victim with the opportunity to enlighten. Take your place at the podium."

Why does he always repeat my name twice, and elongate the pronunciation the second time? He never does that to other students' names. And I swear, I actually heard the professor refer to my predecessor as Ta-BEE-tha. Or was that just how my mind now translated hearing her name spoken? Now her new nickname repeated in my head like a bad song.

Distracted momentarily from my own speech, I dragged myself up to the podium, trying to figure out the moniker mystery and still relishing the thought that even the professor could not help but call her that too. Or *had* he?

After reaching the podium and turning to face my fellow classmates, I snapped back to reality, ready to dive into my own speech. Seeing how Emerson had already returned to his zombie state, I thoroughly enjoyed kicking the speech off with a booming and attention-grabbing imitation of the voice of lightning—thunder. It was all I could do not to laugh at Emerson, arms flailing and nearly falling out of his desk.

"Harnessing the power of lightning has not been without its setbacks. In first attempts, a good ten years ago, scientists found themselves running all over the countryside trying to find it—to be in the right place at the right time and to be prepared to tap into this wild and unpredictable source of power."

I could see I had the class's attention at "lightning," and each student who was still awake would swear I was speaking directly to them. For dramatic effect, I swooped my arms around animatedly, visually supporting my description of the "unpredictable source of power."

"For years, fruitless, chaotic, and deadly attempts to capture lightning continued. It was not until the late great scientist Dr. Anderson Raines had developed the world's first lightning lab when the tables began to turn— the concept of which was to create an environment conducive to inviting the lightning to come to him.

"Dr. Raines's first attempts, however, had him trying to create his own lightning in the lab. He quickly learned this approach required the lab to generate the very immense power it was trying to capture. This equated to spending two pounds to earn one, which went against the objective of economically capturing power from a naturally occurring power source.

"Dr. Raines realized, at the threats of the government pulling his grants, he needed to alter his approach—to make it more cost-effective."

Professor Langston scowled at the portrayal of the royal government in a negative light. I think, though he would never admit it aloud, his reaction was one more of fear than of loyal respect. It did not help having several paintings of the king hanging around the classroom, all eyes painted so that there was nowhere in the classroom you could go to shake the fear they were watching you.

Had Emerson witnessed the professor's expression, he would have mocked it in his typical exaggerated and animated fashion. As it was, I had actually captured Emerson's attention. Emerson watched, knowing that his favorite part was coming, as he had watched me practice it the night before at the flat.

I continued, "It was after much thought, when the idea struck the doctor, like lightning!"

Emerson leaped up and crackled his best impression of lightning, making my own display pale in comparison, making the class literally jump out of their seats, and earning him the professor's scowl and command. "Emerson Flanders, you will sit and keep respectfully quiet while others present!" Then back to me, "You may continue, Joshua Franks," and then again, though more hushed, "Joshuua Fraanks."

Emerson had responded to the professor's instruction accordingly but laughed and mocked the scowl directed at him.

Yet again, I noticed the professor had repeated my name twice. My inner voice called him several names I dared not say aloud. In an awkward pause, I repeated each twice in my head before I continued.

"Instead of creating his own lightning, he would create an environment that, like a strong magnet, attracted natural lightning to strike. He would feed the atmosphere in the lab's core, or 'Mother Nature's playground,' as he would come to refer to it, with agents that coaxed the negative ions from Mother Nature to support his effort.

"A positive ion generator beneath the ground of the core, via controls in the lab, released the positive ions to trigger a strike.

"It was his success at selling this plan that kept the program alive. In irony, his success at attracting lightning killed him, leaving him powerless.

"The noble and key objective of this effort was to capture the power of the lightning and use it as an alternative and naturally occurring power source. After having successfully attracted the lightning, it was time to redirect the power from the naturally grounded lab into a huge battery cell located directly beneath the lab. There it would be stored and made available for controlled distribution.

If he had been given a second chance, he would have taken what he had learned and done away with the single large battery cell directly beneath the lab. He would not get a second chance, as he had not survived the first. Directing the full brunt of lightning's power to one cell was simply overpowering.

"There was nothing simple, however, about the structural damage it had done to the lab. The resulting explosion, and subsequent collapse, proved to be the demise of both the lab and its creator. In all, six scientists perished in its collapse, and if it were not for the miraculous and sole survival of Dr. Raines's apprentice, Dr. Elisabeth Rancor, the scientist's immense successes and knowledge would have died with him as well."

Though I did not add this to the speech, in the back of my mind, I thought how I had not known any of the other scientists. Therefore, I knew them only by the small plaques on the wall by the new lab's entrance. The only personal warmth I had ever witnessed regarding them was in Dr. Rancor's eyes whenever she by chance spoke her former mentor's name. That warmth however, always faded, as her next thought would be of his unfortunate demise. She would speak of the loss to science but never of the visually apparent personal loss.

"Dr. Rancor had been mentoring under Dr. Raines for many years; was equally committed to the program; and was arguably, as time would support, equally qualified to see it through. In a later interview, Dr. Rancor told how, after the accident, she had spent months in a hospital bed recovering, going through therapy, and replaying the tragedy repeatedly in her mind. It was then she determined she did not want Anderson's dream, one she shared, to die with him.

"The lab, its design, and resulting accident played like the government-approved reruns of a series on the telly. Unlike those, her mental reruns provided value and paid off."

I knew my last references to the government earned me my second official scowl from the professor.

Unhindered, I continued, "She finally recognized the mistakes they had made in routing all the lightning's power in a monastic series to a single cell beneath the lab. She realized they needed to safely divide the power, routing it to and storing it in several cells and, more importantly, several cells located around, but not directly beneath, the lab. She landed on a design that would separate the power via three separate branches to their respective cells. This breakthrough kept her going, for without it, she would have been just another victim.

"After years of re-petitioning the government for grants and building the new lab, she would finally get her chance to complete what she and her mentor had started. She named the new lab after Dr. Anderson Raines so history would not forget who had stopped chasing the lightning, having figured out how to make the lightning want to come to him instead.

"Dr. Elisabeth Rancor has since earned her own name in the annals of science. As a now fully functional lab powers this very school, the University of Cornwallis, you can see that she has succeeded."

I concluded, "The lab's current assignment, the royally sanctioned project, FHM720, is to standardize the setup and processes needed to economically replicate the success as a means to provide inexpensive power beyond royal city limits and to the villages of our families."

The class, consisting solely of other students trapped under the same umbrella government-working program as Emerson and myself, roared and applauded at the conclusion. All their families lived outside the royal city limits and would greatly benefit from the program's success.

Though Professor Langston III could not "bee" more satisfied with my presentation skills, he still held his final grimace so long he turned beet red. I knew, yet again, I had failed to provide the appropriate—more importantly, required—preface of announcing "The King's Gift" before stating the name of the institution, University of Cornwallis. As well, I had not offered customary appreciation to the Crown for funding both the failed and successful lightning labs.

In his position, the professor's anger was justified, but again I believe his position was triggered more by fear than by loyalty. One never knew what would make it to royal ears, or at least the ears forced to listen for royalty. Sometimes I swear the ears on the pictures of the king were actually listening.

Now using his digital projector remote and laser pointer as a gavel, the professor proceeded to both regain the class's attention and break his third projector remote this semester. In the back of his mind, I am sure he remembered that it was after my previous speech when he had broken the previous one. Though he could probably not remember specifically in this high blood pressure moment, the professor would likely recall later how the first one had to have been somehow connected to Emerson Flanders.

The professor's wife was deaf, and you could always tell when the professor reached the apex of his temperament, as he would subconsciously break into an animated version of sign language in his rants.

"Joshua Franks, Joshuuua Fraaanks, you have once again failed to refer to this institution as '*The King's Gift*, University of Cornwallis,'" he ranted and frantically signed.

Had he just flipped the birdie when he signed King's?

"Also, once again, you have ignored my instruction to select a topic you are not so familiar with. As one of the young scientists, one of the key young scientists I might add, working at Anderson Raines Lightning Lab, I hardly think the topic qualifies. These repeated infractions have only cost you a grade, if you are lucky!"

With that comment, I thought of how I would have loved to tell the class about the lab's most recent discovery and resulting secret endeavor. But I knew better. I thought that the fewer people who knew anything about our most recent discovery, the better.

Just then the bell rang, distracting the professor just enough to redirect him to his closing thoughts. "Saved by the bell again, Franks and Flanders … Now, class, as we are out of time, we will resume next time with Emerson Flanders, when I am sure he will anoint us with yet another exciting speech about lightning labs."

The professor had grimaced at every syllable of pronouncing Emerson's name and had added an incredibly thick layer of sarcasm while conveying his thoughts on Emerson's assumed speech topic.

— CHAPTER 12 —

Along with the flood of other students rushing out of Professor Langton's Speech class, Emerson and I bolted into the hallway. I turned to Emerson, and it only took one look at his spot-on grimace imitation to put me in hysterics. He capped it off with the customary, "Joshua Franks, Joshuuuuuua Fraaaaanks!"

Emerson and I had been best friends for as long as I can remember. We first met at the age of three at the entry testing for the PURPOSE Program. I would be turning twenty-one tomorrow, and Emerson's birthday followed only a month behind mine and to the day. We'd been best friends our entire memorable lives, so I considered him my twin, though by no means identical.

PURPOSE, or Placement Under Royal Proclaimed Order for Specific Employ, was a royal program put in place to identify a child's high-level aptitudes by starting intense testing at the age of three to determine the child's base strengths. The testing took two years, and its results placed the child in an advanced and focused academic program, prepping him or her for a career serving the Crown in that identified field.

The starting age of three was selected in honor of King George III. As many results would prove, it was far too young of an age to start to make that level of an assessment.

Needless to say, Emerson and I had landed in the field of science, thus our friendship. That friendship was the saving grace to forced lifelong employ for the Crown.

I will add that, if no academic strength was identified under PURPOSE, the child was tested for physical strength to serve the Crown in jobs requiring such. And if the child failed there as well, he or she was sent back home, labeled as a societal burden, and left as a disgrace for his or her family to support. Lastly, a tattoo of an albatross, symbolically synonymous with a burden, was branded just below the neck and on the top of said child's chest.

Here in the royal city of George's Cross, you heard these poor souls referred to as "the N'er-do-wells," though I imagine that, back in their homes, they are welcomed and referred to as sons or daughters.

Though I had asked myself countless times, I honestly couldn't say whether I wished I were a N'er-do-well. I was an only child and did miss my parents, but there was a tax burden tied to being labeled a N'er-do-well. As my parents, like most living in the outskirt villages, had nothing, I'd always feared what else the government would take.

So, I, like all other children not labeled N'er-do-well, was placed as a student in a development program in my identified field immediately upon completion of the PURPOSE program. Torn from our parents and families, we students were not allowed to return home until, having reached the age of ten, we could ride the train back to their home village. And even then, it was only once a year, on our birthdays, we were able to do that. Lastly, as the villages did not have any telephone service or postal service, there was no means by which to communicate to our families, except on our annual visits.

As I had started mentioning before, Emerson and I had both tested positive for science. I saw it as a disease, for which we had suffered since. Ironically, I loved science. But when forced down your throat, even candy can taste sour.

At least some of our efforts to help the Lightning Lab succeed had been noble. For example, the time we'd spent working on project FHM720 had felt as if we were actually doing something good. As far as my time spent in PURPOSE, these times had been my happiest.

I'd had dreamed, and I guess still dreamed, of a day we could bring power to the villages. I would consider it my greatest accomplishment if I helped enable the installation of the first electric light in my parents' home.

In another example of irony, where Emerson and I, as well as our other coworkers, were considered geniuses in our respective fields, we were considered typical college students here at "the illustrious endowment from our king," the University of Cornwallis.

As such, Emerson Flanders and I walked directly from speech class to the only other class we shared, history.

To round off our educations, it was not until after mastering our assigned fields that we were able to continue our educations in other courses of study. Even then, it was less by choice but, rather, under royal schedule and mandate.

So, as continuing students, we trudged our way down the west corridor of Benedict Hall, or "Been-a-Dick-To Hall" as we liked to call it, and toward the warmth of the Hall of Kings. I pulled my jacket tight against the October chill coming through the open-arched side of the hall, with its arches facing the outer commons.

"Pep up your step, Emer. Been-a-Dick-To Hall is always so damned cold this time of year." As much as I hated the Hall of Kings, at least it was warmer.

"Yeah, the portraits and tapestries of royal lineage in the Hall of Kings have always creeped me out, but since your latest discovery, I swear the eyes on the pictures follow us all the way through the hall."

I'd been afraid to say anything, but now know Emerson had shared the same eerie feeling. I'd been feeling it in general but didn't think I'd be able to walk through the Hall of Kings again without experiencing Emerson's creepy take on it. Still, we picked up the pace to get to the semiwarmth of the creepy and connected hall.

Thanks to Emerson, upon entering the hall, my eyes went directly to the eyes in the portraits that lined the hall.

Thankfully, as a strange but pleasant distraction and only ten steps into the hall, a short dandy-dressed and evidently newer student approached us. His blond bangs were long and shot up off his forehead like a wave. They looked like something you could sled down, and my eyes were instantly glued to them.

"Excuse-a me, gentlemen ... Surely you find it understand-a-bubble how a fr-reshman such as myself can get lost in the expanse of this illustrious campus? Can you kindly direct me to Benedict-a Hall?"

I stood dumbstruck, trying to reconcile in my head if I had actually just heard him say *understand-a-bubble*.

A sideways glance at Emerson confirmed he too had heard something of the sort. His stare was burning a dumb hole right through the short fellow.

I tried to grab the student's attention, so he would not catch Emerson's apparent loss of responsive control.

"Uh … why yes. We just came from there … Been a Dick—I mean Benedict Hall is just there behind us, through the arch hall in the commons and to the left."

"Why-ya thhenk you, sirrr. Your assistanance is most honor-a-bubble."

I bit my lip, looking slightly away from the character and up to the nearest painting of a king on the wall. I had to in order to suppress the urge to burst out in laughter.

I had never realized that king's nose before. It was large, protruding, and misshapen, leaving me to imagine how birds would have loved to perch on it. An ensuing image of bird crap buildup on the king's cheek appeared. The king's painting failed me as a distraction, so I turned another glance toward Emerson. He held the same stare, only now his mouth gaped open and adorned a spit bubble—or should I say, spit-a-bubble.

I quickly and stealthily swiped a kick at his ankle, causing his mouth to close, and the spit bubble to pop, leaving drool dripping down his chin.

The student now glanced directly at Emerson and then back to me.

After a curious pause, he leaned in toward me, and though not whispering, continued, "Thhhenk you again, kind sir. Uh … your fr-riend here is a spit-a-ging a-allllll over himself-a."

That said, he let out a snobby, "Humph," and marched past us, his campus compass having been reset.

My lip bled from biting it. "*Spit-a-ging?*"

As the student walked on, my own stare followed him, and my thoughts returned to how he was dressed like a dandy. Most students, Emerson and myself included, were dressed in either homemade clothes made of hand-me-down remnants, or the standard government-issue garb, typically revealing their PURPOSE-ful occupations. As if to confirm the thought, I subconsciously slid my hands up and down the lapel of my lab coat.

I assumed the boy had come from some degree of royal lineage so wondered why he would stoop down to ask a question of me. My last thought on it, before returning my and Emerson's attentions toward getting to our history class, was what a queer little event it seemed to have been.

Emerson, spit now having formed a size-a-bubble—*great, now I am doing it too*—a sizeable drop of drool hanging from his chin, had probably already forgotten the event had occurred.

My thoughts circled back to my speech, as the professor's final comments still burned like embers inside me. "I wish Professor Langston the Turd had mentioned the consequence of grade docking for familiarity when he assigned the damn speech! A lot of good it did me to bring it up after I gave the speech. If he does dock my grade, he will end my A streak. Hindsight's a bitch!"

Emerson snapped, "Whatever man! Blah, blah, blah. Will end my A streak. The old turd's right about my report. It just may break my D streak." Then, pointing down the hall, he added, "I'll give you one thing though; you're right about hindsight! Check out Samantha Edmunds's ass in those jeans. Hindsight is a bitch!"

"You are such an arse, god love you, but that was a good one."

"It was, wasn't it. I should tell Emily that one."

"No, Emer. I don't think it is a good time to remind Em of their fallout. It's been hard enough for her lately. Besides, they are too good of friends to do anything to fuel the fire that, if you ask me, was started by someone else but left them burned."

"Started by someone else? It was Samantha who made the errors in the programming code for Em's project that got her demoted. She's lucky that was all it got her."

"Emer, you know darn well who lit the match under that fire and turned them against each other. His name begins with Geoffrey and ends with Talbrook. He started the rumors about Emily having motive to sabotage the programs. And knowing Geoffrey, I wouldn't be surprised if he was somehow involved in the sabotage itself.

"As for Samantha, sure, she was wrong to take it all out on her best friend, but she has every right to be angry. You know it took Professor Rancor all the pull she could muster to simply have Samantha demoted.

Otherwise she would have been sent home, disgraced, and branded a N'er-do-well."

Subconsciously pointing to his chest, Emerson replied, "Albatross."

"Yes, Emer, albatross. And that tattoo is only one ingredient to the disgrace her poor family would have been put through. They can't afford the additional audits and taxes the government would take to compensate for their so-called productive losses."

It got all serious, until I couldn't help but repeat, "Hindsight is a bitch," and get us both laughing again.

We had just reached the door to the history class, so I quickly composed myself and made a beeline to my desk. The professor was a pompous ass, and I would just as soon make my entry as invisible as possible to avoid the wrath of simply being noticed.

I looked up from my desk to find Emerson still up front, being reminded yet again how he was a subordinate and how Professor Jonathan Elders V was his title and name and, more importantly, that it was how the professor was to be addressed.

Even though we are always reminded of our place in society, most people referred to us as students. But in the mind of this self-illustrious professor "subordinates" was a good two rungs higher on the class ladder than he would prefer. Thus, "subordinates" was his idea of a socially accepted compromise.

Emerson seemed to relish the role as a subordinate, as he knew what button to push and always jumped at the chance to push it.

The temporary but common tirade the professor had just thrown had made his normally disheveled hair lay flat. This sight nearly made the "subordinate" and my hero, Emerson Flanders, laugh his way into deeper trouble. He narrowly escaped, breaking away in time and managing to squeak the correct salutation.

Emerson finally made his way down the second row of desks and plopped into the seat of the fourth desk, next to mine on the row to my left.

"Emer, why do you do that, man? You know you just set the tone to how today's instruction will go. This class sucks enough by itself; it does not need your help."

"What'd I do? I called him Perve-fessor Elders."

I mocked in whisper, "You will refer to me as Professor Jonathan Elders ... the Filth, subordinate!" I made sure to stress all the wrong syllables as the professor tended to do when he got flustered, which was nearly always. Unfortunately, I had not yet mastered the professor's ability to spit through the gap in his front teeth in his stressed enunciation of "Fifth," thus the dribble running down my chin, or maybe it was just because I had referred to him as the Filth.

I probably should not have said anything because Emerson, still on the precipice of laughter, could no longer stop from diving into a sea of it. He, therefore, earned his second scolding, and all before the day's lesson had even begun. What can I say? You have to do what you are good at.

Today was lining up to be truly special.

As what I call the "luck of Emer" would have it, he was saved again. This time it was by an angel, the star who I was slated in life never to reach, Emily Etheridge. Emily had herself just entered the room. Spying that our shared friend was already and again in hot water, she distracted the professor with not just a grade A addressing of the pompous ass, but with what I am sure was a lesson-appropriate question.

The pleasant distraction instantly diffused the professor, as if Emily had merely flipped a hidden switch on his emotional grid.

Emerson and I silently applauded as she walked past, proceeding to her own desk two behind Emerson's. As she passed, she pointed back and forth between her and Emerson multiple times, as she mouthed, "You ... owe ... me." It was safe to assume the repeated gesturing was intended to point out how Emerson owed her for far more than this occurrence.

I knew Emily would just add it to Emerson's never-ending tab, but I wasn't even sure if Emerson got it or cared.

Emily had made it to her desk in just enough time to see and hear the customary class kickoff, "Silence, all!"

After a moment of the professor's customary and evil classroom scanning, he began, "Today, I will bless you with a brief refresher of where we had left off and then proceed, as stated in your detailed syllabi, to ..."

Now came the part and proof that all students had always heard about but needed to see to believe. Professor Jonathan Elders V smiled.

The class sat frozen and in awe of the sight.

I can understand how outsiders may not see this as being anything too monumental. The perspective of a student trapped in this class, however, recognized this event as the only thing you had to look forward to. Before the moment occurred, students naturally doubted it was even possible. Some had reasoned that Professor Elders just did not know how to smile; others, that he was just so miserable he saw no reason. It was even rumored that a birth defect had left him lacking the facial muscles necessary to smile. But all had heard from his previous students that this one day would come when they would have the rare privilege to witness, as if it were a once-in-a-lifetime comet making its earthly pass, the smile of Professor Jonathan Elders V.

One might wonder, What cause could trigger such momentous effect?

The answer was simple and was evident in the name of the event that, some years ago, had been dubbed, "Making history *his* story." It had since been passed on as such, and I was sure our class would keep the tradition, passing it on to future history students graced by the honor of having Professor Jonathan Elders V as their professor.

Though his smile was brief, and though it was crooked, amateur, and revealed a nasty set of teeth, it was there. The stories I myself had heard and wondered about were, in fact, true.

The class abruptly snapped out of its collective daze with the sharp and sudden inflection of the professor's voice as he completed the sentence. "The shining moment and the birth of the famous catchphrase of Third's War."

After a momentary self-relishing of what he had just said, as if he were absorbing it all back in so he could bring it back out nice and fresh for the next history class, the professor resumed. "Remember, subordinates, we left off yesterday with the Signer's rebellion squelched and the treasonous 'declarers of independence' captured. In fact, over the course of the next few months, those who fought under the king's colors were tasked with building jails to hold the treasonous rebels. They had time, as His Majesty King George III had decided he would cross the Atlantic and over to his new world. Capitalizing on the momentous and fortuitous events that had transpired, the king had boldly decided to move the monarchy to its newly acquired, and now uncontested, land of opportunity. It made perfect sense, as this vast new world was ripe for molding into the world he dreamt of ruling.

"Immediately, plans had been put into place to establish royal quarters for the royal family. While the royal architects tackled that effort, the king sent a second wave of mentee architects to manage the conversion of rebel facilities into their own jails. Buildings such as where the 'Second Continental Congress,' as they called themselves, solidified their fates with their written 'Declaration of Independence.'

"You are all familiar with where this took place, only you know it as Hell's Gate, the site of the historic and celebrated Signers' Day of Reckoning. To these traitors and at that time, however, it was still the Pennsylvania Statehouse in Philadelphia, Pennsylvania.

"Today, Philadelphia is the very city you live in, only it has been obviously renamed to George's Cross. George's Cross, as you are all well aware, sits in the heart of the Province of Burgoyne, which in the rebels' time had been known as the colony of Pennsylvania.

"Again, it was in this Philadelphia, Pennsylvania, where members of the Second Continental Congress drafted and signed their treasonous Declaration of Independence, in which they declared their freedom from the king's rule in Mother England. And it was in the very building they met, where gallows were also being constructed, en masse, and plans were being made to hold the largest public execution in English history."

Suddenly Emerson realized he had not disrupted his favorite class in almost ten minutes. With no real question in mind, he could not resist the urge, much to the professor's chagrin, to frantically wave his hand as if he had one.

I was reminded again why Emerson was my hero.

"Perv-fessor Jo-blah-blah Blah-ers the Filth," pardon my use of one of his many undesirable monikers, tried as hard as he could to ignore Emerson. After all, he was just about to introduce his great-great-greatish grandfather Jonathan Elders. It's important to note how even the professor would lose count of his "greatnesses," and the guy was his bloody relative.

The professor decided to get the interruption out of the way before continuing on to his favorite part of history. "Subordinate! What inconsequential issue, what small question could that equally small mind of yours possibly have that is worth disrupting the much-needed increase of your meager intellect?"

Thinking quickly (because I knew Emerson had nothing in mind), Emerson stared at the professor, and then scanned the room. Then he turned back to the professor, where he decided to fall back on his favorite disruption. "Professor Jonathan Elders the Filth—"

I had to ask myself whether he actually had just said "Filth," or whether I just wanted to hear it that way.

Before Emerson could spit out his question, the professor interjected, "And you had better not ask me, yet again, whether the tie I am wearing is new! This tie has stains on it that are older than you, Flounders!"

Instinctively, as this was a regular occurrence, Emerson immediately and correctly stated his last name. "Flanders." Also, as he was successfully contested and there was a challenge at hand, he quickly followed up with, "Did you do something different with your hair today? It makes you look an awful lot like the pictures"—now in a sweeping point to the all too many ornately framed paintings on the walls—"of the Royal Guard Sir Jonathan Elders."

Emerson had tried to capitalize on how the professor's earlier tirade had flattened his hair, a tirade also credited to Emerson. The professor looked nothing like his distant relative. The flattened hair only made his beady eyes look beadier and his pointy nose look pointier. As it was, Emerson's ploy backfired, as he had inadvertently given the professor the best compliment he could have possibly been given. The moment he realized this, he regretted saying it, even though the false compliment had just saved his ass.

As Emily sat behind Emerson, I could see she had the same jaw-dropping stare as I had now. We stared at Emerson in complete amazement, as he had never before blown an opportunity to piss off the professor.

Not one to miss the opportunity to accept the compliment, no matter how false, the professor melted in response, "Why yes, subordinate Flippers."

"Flanders." Emerson interjected through the gritted teeth of his personal disappointment, though the professor again ignored him.

The professor adopted the false compliment and worked it back into the day's lesson, his favorite one to teach at that. "In commemoration of Royal Guard Sir Jonathan Elders's celebrated statement, I am honoring him in imitation.

"Picking up where I left off prior to subordinate Flankers'—"

"Flanders."

"Miraculously appropriate observation, the jails were built. It was also at this time, when the honorable soldier marched into Philadelphia alongside the honorable Fusilier's 23rd regiment after having received his promotion to King's Guard. He had been assigned with the task of guarding the jailed rebels as they awaited their treasonous fates before the king."

The smile had returned and, as it was painfully and obviously an alien expression for the man, caused his voice to whine even more than usual.

Clearing his throat, as if that would help, the professor continued. "It was a cold morning, that February twenty-third of 1781. They say you could see your breath in the jail. It was then that the newly promoted King's Guard, Jonathan Elders"—as he said this, the professor gestured to the overly abundant paintings of the squirrelly, scrawny old fart who disgraced the classroom walls, though the pictures were appropriately smaller in size and number and hung lower than the also overly abundant pictures of the king—"graced all in earshot with the phrase that became the catchphrase of Third's War. You see it was in Philadelphia, Pennsylvania, where Thomas Jefferson had penned the subversive Declaration of Independence. And on that morning, in the very building that would hold Jefferson's gallows, the cold air would carry King's Guard Jonathan Elders's words to him."

The professor paused to recompose himself and add what he alone must have felt was dramatic effect. "Yes, on that cold morning, he bravely faced his adversary, and expressed his fate with these unforgettable words. And I quote."

Then, clearing his throat, and having completely left out the fact that jail bars separated the guard from his "adversary," the professor repeated his ancestor's famous words. "Philadelphia, Pennsylvania. Filled with death, your pens will hang ya!"

── CHAPTER 13 ──

"**A**S IF IN ETERNAL ECHO, NO TEN WORDS HAVE BEEN REPEATED AS frequently as *Philadelphia, Pennsylvania. Filled with death, your pens will hang ya.*"

The professor had just kicked off the first minute, of what was to be well over thirty, in an overly rehearsed and fully memorized self-glorifying speech. The speech would, no less, inflate what had actually occurred, inflate his great-great whatever's involvement, and indirectly inflate the professor's ego as if he'd had anything to do with it.

However, much to the professor's chagrin and students' relief, he was interrupted yet again. This time Emerson could not take the credit, unless he had figured out a way to have the front classroom door suddenly and surprisingly open. In the instant following and as I asked myself whether Emerson could somehow have done just that, Headmaster Paul McAllister burst into the room. This, in and of itself, was intimidating on multiple levels. First, in general, why would a school headmaster come rushing into a classroom in such a manner? I had never personally seen him before but had heard stories and recognized him by his oversized picture hung in the main hall of the administration building. Secondly, at over two meters in height, the headmaster was towering in size. He also had the expression and demeanor of man leading troops into battle. These characteristics fueled most of the stories.

The latter reasons were not only supported but also elevated by the two King's Guards who followed him into the room. Though not in full regalia, they were instantly recognizable by their cookie cutter haircuts, gray suits with the Royal Guard insignia on the breast pocket, and the telltale stone-faced expressions they had been trained to wear on their chiseled faces. It had always been said, they were trained to set an example for statues. Their faces were so void of expression, it would probably be easier to imagine how a statue felt.

In the brief instant of having been interrupted again—and during his self-proclaimed most important lesson—the professor's natural instinct would have him tear into yet another tirade. He quite literally bit his tongue as he threw the brakes on the tantrum he was about to spew. He bit it figuratively, as he saw it was Headmaster McAllister leading the interruption, but literally, as he saw the two men with him were King's Guards.

In the split second of having recognized this, and while still relishing in the heights of his finest moment in teaching, he probably thought the surprise guests were there to support his lesson.

Headmaster McAllister, however, instantaneously squelched that fire. He ignored the presence of the professor, though now towering right next to him. With a cold steel glare, he scanned the students and barked, "Joshua ... Nolin ... Franks!"

The professor cowered like a scared child.

I would think McAllister's presence on a good day would be nothing short of threatening. But here and now with King's Guards in tow, *threatening* was too soft of a word.

I was so thrown by the whole event I had not even realized he had just called my name. I was not alone in the moment of incomprehension. But as it sank in for my classmates, I found all eyes upon me.

Having spoken only my name, and only once at that, the headmaster wasted no more time nor words. He merely pointed and motioned for me to present myself.

Before I could even stand, the King's Guards, having followed everyone's eyes, were already upon me. They "helped" me to my feet, confiscated my cell phone from its holster, and continued to "assist" me out of the classroom. I had not had enough time to let anything register. Nor had I the guts to dream of protesting or resisting.

I had no idea where I was being taken. I had just enough sense about me to know I should not even ask. I really did not think the two royal goons would answer anyway. They had yet to even speak.

Within the next couple of minutes, I had been whisked through the indoor portion of Benedict Hall and through a door I had always seen but heard we were forbidden to use. One of the guards scanned an ID card to open it. As he did so, I saw the unmistakable royal insignia impressed upon the card.

Though I had not seen him leave, the school headmaster was no longer with us.

I was then shoved into the back of a black vehicle parked, engine already or still running, and on a hidden driveway I had not known existed.

Upon entering the car, the first thing I noticed was how the clear windows began tinting black, including the window separating the rear seat compartment from the front. The side windows had been rolled down but were quickly closing. They too turned black but were left cracked just enough for me to see what I imagined they wanted me to see. All I remember grasping at that moment was the glowing blue light that filtered through what little viewing space they allowed.

My mind spun trying to take it in, to comprehend what had just occurred. Kidnapped and now being driven very fast and in near silence, I struggled to calm my nerves just enough for me to recognize the surroundings they were allowing. I was so overwhelmed by what was happening, I could not begin to understand it as a whole but decided to focus on one detail at a time.

Taking the first in a series of baby steps to figure things out, I began to focus on the internal surroundings.

First, I realized I was in the back seat of a black Jaguar. I think my eyes needed the time to adjust to the darkness, but I made out the Jaguar logo embroidered in the leather on the middle of the back of the front seat. The amazing smell of the exquisite leather had just kicked in.

Looking up, I witnessed the enabler of this exquisiteness as I spied a Royal Guard Seal embroidered and positioned above my head. It had probably been placed up there intentionally to remind lucky passengers such as myself where we belonged. The all-too-familiar seal—a lion ornately encircled by snakes. The thought of the same image I had seen on the guard's ID card briefly returned, followed quickly by that of the same insignia on their breast pockets.

81

It was painfully evident this was not, even by Jaguar standards, your typical Jaguar. Even the typical would have been twenty times better than any vehicle I had ever seen up close, much less ridden in.

The Royal Guard's ultimate duty was to protect the body and interests of the king, the queen, and then the remainder of the royal family—and in that order. Just from my visually confined location in the back seat of their vehicle, it was apparent they were spared no expense on things they needed to do so.

I had no idea, as it has never been made public, what this vehicle was capable of doing. Nor did I know about any other equipment and weapons they had at their disposal.

Still, an even bigger mystery was how much it all cost, though there was no mystery as to who paid for it.

As if allowed to take in my environment by incremental perimeters, having just finished the inner perimeter, I was now looking out the crack of the window to my left and at the blue blur of the landscape as we zipped by.

The ride was smooth; it gave no indication we were traveling fast, much less as incredibly fast as it appeared looking out the window. I wished I could see the speedometer up front and imagined we were traveling through the city at over 200 kph. In a city where the speed limit topped out at 48 kph and with lights at every corner, this did not seem possible. Even though everything went by in a royal blue blink, I recognized one building. Most buildings looked the same in downtown George's Cross. Most buildings contained government-approved businesses; they had been approved for development but not to stand out. But this particularly large and ornate building took up its own city block. Its towering spires made it recognized the world over as St. Fauntleroy's Cathedral. Though the cathedral took up a whole city block, we were traveling so fast I had just enough time to recognize it and place us as heading north on Wingate Lane.

My mind raced wondering how we could be, much less why we would be, traveling at such high speeds in the middle of the day through downtown George's Cross.

I pictured myself as an outsider, witnessing this vehicle racing through the metropolis. How many onlookers stared frozen and amazed? How many innocent drivers were hazardously displaced, wrecking their own vehicles just trying to get out of the way as they saw the instigator of the chaos witnessed in their rearview mirrors barreling down on them.

I thought for sure we were going to die in a fiery crash and was on the verge of panic. The only reason it had taken that long was that I had yet to accept what was occurring. The thread that held my panic in, kept it at bay, was curiosity.

I finally figured out the source of the royal blue light the blurring imagery we passed had been filtered through—the recognition of which further distracted my progression toward a breakdown.

My mind jumped back to my driver's ed course. The testing had taken place in a car that could only have dreamed of even reaching 60 kph, vastly slower than we were smoothly sailing now. I remembered, but had never before witnessed, one unique feature that the royal black Jaguar I was now in must have on its list of many.

All royal vehicles were equipped with a signal, a beacon that could be turned on to communicate to the traffic network where they were within scope. If I remembered correctly, the reach was over a three-kilometer radius and activated what was referred to as the Royal Lane. All main thoroughfares and intersections deemed suitable for royal use were required to have the Royal Lane built into them. Once activated, the Royal Lane was illuminated on both sides by royal blue lighting that shot up from the road, and as I was now witnessing, created an intense semitransparent blue wall of light on both sides to make its activation unmistakably evident.

All traffic signals were topped with a royal blue, royally crested light, as well. Though I had always seen them, I had never seen one on and had only imagined what they looked like.

Again, taken mentally back to my time in driver's ed, I remembered the laws associated with an activated Royal Lane. All drivers were to immediately clear the lane for royal use. Being caught in an activated Royal Lane was a costly mistake; punishment was equivalent to what you would receive for being caught dealing drugs or stealing.

Though I knew this was all happening in a blink, my mind wandered from costly mistake to cost for the Royal Lane itself. Paying the penalty would only be salt on the wound of having to have paid all the taxes to support the installation and maintenance of this *royal waste*. Then I thought about those who paid the taxes. I imagined how my family, myself included, had helped pay for this ridiculously expensive ride I now found myself on, and in this ridiculously expensive vehicle.

I had lost track of time. It could have been five minutes, or it could have been thirty. I watched the royal blue blur effect of zipping past all normal life. I thought of all the cars in normal lanes, the sidewalks, and the buildings—all full of slower-moving people, normal people, slowed by the taxing burden of paying for all the royal extravagance.

My mental compass registered, though I was not sure it was correct, that we were now heading west. In reality, for all I knew, my captors had been driving in circles, wasting time, leading me to believe we were traveling far, while trying to add to the already incredible intimidation factors I was being subjected to.

I still tried to figure out where we were heading. A Royal Guard station and training facility located over thirty kilometers west of George's Cross, in the city of Benedict, came to mind. What was the name of that place? Then I remembered, it coincidently shared the name of a drink, champagne. Stepping up my memory ladder, I remembered how this building, however, was named after a famous officer of the Fusilier's in Third's War, Captain Champagne. My memory finally landed on the location being the Champagne Royal Hall of Securities.

Picturing in my mind how the two guards who had kidnapped me had to have attended training there, I cringed at the image of a whole facility of people learning how to outdo the stone-coldness of statues.

Though I resided, worked, and attended college in the royal city itself, George's Cross, I did it all in the northwestern part of the city and away from any royal action. In fact, the primary palace and home of the royal family, Wellington Palace, was located just ten kilometers southeast. It was a wonder I had never witnessed an activated Royal Lane before, but I had always heard most regal activity occurred in the southern part of the city anyway, with the northern section filled with lowly government employees, such as myself.

Benedict, on the other hand, was a small city centered on its Royal Guard training facility. I imagined Benedictines saw quite a bit of Royal Lane activity there. Seeing what I had thus far, I was glad I didn't live where this royal pain occurred frequently. I didn't know how any non-royally purposed person could ever successfully drive around in it.

My mental wandering successfully provided a natural defense mechanism to protect me from panicking. This self-preserving distraction had just been interrupted by the realization that we were slowing down considerably. This could only have meant we had reached the destination. I snapped back into the reality of my situation. This was not a joyride, for me at least. I had been kidnapped, by King's Guards no less, and I still had no idea why.

Now that we had slowed down, I was able to read a street sign as we passed. It appeared we had turned right on Champagne Lane and then left into what appeared to be a run-down car wash.

Is the Champagne Royal Hall of Securities located on Champagne Lane? What is with the old car wash?

The neon sign revealed it as a Crown Jewel Car Wash that we had just pulled into. The car pulled forward to the car wash's automated pay machine.

I thought the goons up front had been driving so long they'd forgotten I should probably not be able to see where we were. They had forgotten to fully roll up my blackened windows. I did not even have controls to do it myself, but I was not about to remind them.

Maybe it was the peculiarity of where they had taken me or the cumulative sum of events kicking in, but it was at this point I began to panic.

I watched as one of the king's goons waved his royally insignia-ed ID card to presumably pay. I could only see his hand with the badge and part of a massive forearm. Then the driver proceeded to pull into the flap-enclosed entrance of the car wash. I guess they were in need to waste time or had forgotten about me entirely and had decided to get the car washed.

I laughed at the thought of them forgetting to roll up my window, as I watched us pull completely into the structure and almost into the now spinning roto brushes. In all appearances, this was a typical self-serve car wash—not that I had ever used one, but I had heard about them.

I did not, however, expect what happened next. Behind me, I could hear the large garage door of the car wash closing, while in front of the car but immediately before the spinning brushes appeared a royal blue laser grid. The grid advanced toward and then over and through the car.

I assumed it was scanning the vehicle and its contents.

Then, moments after I witnessed the grid pass through, the car jolted, and I heard what sounded like gears turning—and, from the sound of them, large ones. It was not a loud sound, but a distinct one. Ahead of the car, out the window, I could still saw the rotating brushes churning full speed and heard the sound of water jets, though to my knowledge the car was still completely dry. The only difference was the spinning brushes appeared to be moving upward. A moment later, the ground level emerged and was almost at my eye level. I then realized it was not that the brushes were going up, but that the car was going down. As the sound of the rotating brushes and water spraying lowered, the sound of the gears increased. It took a moment to register what was happening, but I realized the car was being lowered down some sort of elevator. I watched as the ground level disappeared above, and roughly three meters of concrete passed the window. Finally, the light intensified again to reveal a well-lit tunnel. The light we were bathed in was again royal blue, like the Royal Lane we had just left. Or had we ever left it?

As the car settled, and apparently at the end of a curve in the tunnel, I looked to my back left through the window at a car located immediately behind us. I could only see it because of its position in the curve, or maybe it was an intersection.

The car looked identical to the one I was in, and I could see two royal goons sitting in the front seat. They very well could have been the remaining twins completing the set of quadruplets when added to the two in my car.

The car I was in began to pull forward. Moments later, I again heard the sound of the gears, which I could only assume was the sound of the car behind us now going up. Was their purpose to replace us by appearance? One black Jaguar pulls into a car wash, and one spits out the other end, only cleaner? As we proceeded to drive forward in this tunnel, I pictured the twin vehicle actually driving toward and through the rotating brushes and being washed.

We drove on for several more minutes. All I could see out the crack of the window was the succession of royal blue blurs dizzily zipping by.

My attentions drifted as if again hypnotized by the lights. It had just occurred to me that the Crown Jewel Car Wash sign had, itself, been illuminated by the same shade of royal blue. I also realized the Crown

THE KITE AND THE COIN TOSS

Jewel Car Wash was more than just a marketing gimmick but was, to some degree, actually associated with the Crown.

The car came to a sudden stop.

Not ones to waste time, the apparently mute thugs jumped out and whisked me away. I had only a moment to see a clear image of the tunnel we had been driving through. It was nothing but a long series of vertical blue lights on each side extending for who knew how long or to where.

We entered through a plain door and into a corridor. The corridor itself, however, was an ornately decorated hallway. The royal insignia throughout, I now looked down at tapestry-like carpet bearing the insignia woven through a grand battle scene with royal knights on horseback and clearly defeating the enemy to the Crown. I would bet the carpet I was now walking on cost far more than I would earn in my lifetime. Though I was in some hidden corridor beneath somewhere in some city, it was obvious there was nothing common about my surroundings here. This was well above even a location for the guards. I could sense that I was now in a location somehow intended for royalty.

This was only supported by what I now saw as we completed a right turn in the hall. The walls down this part of the corridor were lined with King's Guards.

My legs turned to jelly, but the two goons who had brought me to the location, effortlessly carried me by my arms.

After passing as many as twenty guards, ten-ish on each side, we reached an ornately hand-carved door. The door was intricately carved with intertwining ivy. While we stood there, while one of the guards once again scanned his ID, the ivy mesmerized me. It was so beautifully and intricately detailed, and my eyes followed the ivy as it twisted its way up the sides of the door to a point where it encircled an instantly recognizable symbol, the royal coat of arms, crowning the doorway. The coat of arms was carved complete with the ornate details of crossed swords over a lion, a lamb, and a raven—all of which were entwined by the royal ivy, diagonally crossed by ribbon, and lastly encompassed within the royal badge.

I had just enough time to notice this when the door opened, and I was carried inside, where the guards planted me on my feet. We stood in a small entryway with yet another door immediately in front of us.

The guard on my left leaned forward into a retinal scanner. I watched as royal blue beams of light crosshaired as they scanned the guard's left eye. A screen on the left of the scanner revealed the profile and identity of the guard. I had no time to see any of the information on the screen before the other guard followed suit, but only after an awkward dance of the two switching sides, with me stuck between them. Afterward, it was evident by the way they thrust me head forward into the scanner that it was my turn.

From my vantage point facing the scanner, I managed to catch a glimpse of the screen. My own government ID photo appeared, as well as what must have represented the profile the government had on me. I was only able to make out a handful of words before the screen went black, and the door before us began to open. The words were "Anderson Raines," "lightning lab," and "core."

The door had barely opened when I was shoved and planted into yet another small and ornately designed entryway.

One of the guards finally spoke, though only four words. "Arms up and out." His voice was low, deep and monotone. His gesture mirrored his request, as if I needed a visual aid. He did not need to repeat himself.

The guards stepped in front of me. The door closed behind me, the deep sound of which gave away its size and weight and the gravity and security of its purpose. Glancing back, arms still raised, I could see there was not an emergency exit bar to push—in fact, there was no getting out unless they wanted me to.

I turned back around to the sound of the door before me closing. It made a sound similar to the closing of the one behind me, yet I had not even heard or realized it had opened. The goons must have gone through, as I now stood alone.

I heard the sound of air being sucked out, leading me to believe I had been placed inside a vacuum. Suddenly, I was bathed in yet another grid of royal blue light. This scan, I imagined, replaced the old-fashioned pat down, and I felt violated as the light surely revealed every square millimeter of my existence. I thought of the few coins I had in my pocket, for surely now that they had seen them, they would tax me for them. Someone had to pay for all this.

The scan took only seconds to complete. I must have been cleared, as the door before me reopened, though again, I had not heard it. Again, the two goons greeted me. At least I think they were the same two; they all looked the same. The names Frick and Frack jumped into my head as endearingly appropriate for any two of them.

Humor kicked in, yet another defense mechanism for me, and was not failing me. This nightmare continued to get stranger and stranger, and I hoped it was all just a bad dream.

I had better keep my thoughts to myself, as I did not think the two oafs would take kindly to being called Frick and Frack. Then fear struck as I wondered whether the scanner was able to read my mind as well.

After Frick and Frack reached back and pulled me into yet another room, only to hear yet another door close, I stood with the two directly in front of me. Sandwiched between the door and the immense frames of the guards, there was little I could see.

I may not have been able to see anything, but my sense of smell kicked in.

The smell I picked up was hard to describe because I had never smelled anything like it. The first words that came to me describing it in that brief moment were *clean* and *intoxicating*.

My inner voice kicked in and asked whether the Frick or Frack before me had royal gas.

Their next action only supported the follies of my inner voice, as they proceeded to kneel in front of me. This was a thought that never got a chance to come to full fruition, for what they revealed, or I should say whom they revealed, put an instant stop to all my internal dialogue.

— CHAPTER 14 —

STANDING OPPOSITE THE IMMENSE FRAMES OF THE GUARDS KNEELING before me was the king.

My own instinctive reaction, upon realizing this, was to kneel; only I was too tightly wedged between the door behind me and the arses of the goons kneeling before me. My effort only came off awkwardly, as if I were trying to play leapfrog but could not decide which yahoo to leap over.

Down, humoristic internal defense mechanism, down, I thought but immediately wondered whether I had spoken my thoughts aloud.

I knew Frick and Frack were not much for words, but they could have at least given me a heads-up. It's not every day you find yourself kidnapped by King's Guards and sped down Royal Lanes to be delivered to His Majesty King George VII's feet.

Naturally, as if by divine rule, it would be the king to speak first. "Rise," he commanded. Then, to the guards—his guards, "Post."

With their heads still bowed and in response to these two words, Frick and Frack immediately stood and stepped aside and then back until they had posted themselves on the sides of the doorway we had just entered. This left nothing but royal air between the king and me.

Aside from rising from my half-knelt position, I did not know what I should do. I stood, head bowed and waiting for my own royal instruction. All the common people of the world were reduced to mere loyal and obedient dogs when in the presence of royalty.

After having added a pinch of silent intimidation to the already spicy recipe I had endured, King George VII spoke again. "You may look at me when spoken to."

He paused long enough for me to submissively respond, though I found it difficult to look into his eyes. They were steel blue, cold, intense, and revealed no emotion but reflected a will that instilled a fear all its own. These eyes emanated with a stare as powerful as the crisp inflections of his voice, the uniqueness of the air about him, and the full globality of his world.

Is globality even a word? As far as I am concerned, it is now. Globality is the only word I can think of to describe his all-encompassing scope.

I could not believe I was standing face to face with the king. He stood tall, distinguished, and with an acute awareness of status.

His facial features were chiseled, as was his beard and moustache. I imagined him trying to imitate the king of spades from a deck of cards and then realized the cards had probably been designed to resemble him. I also realized my damn internal defense mechanism was trying to kick in again, and how I would have preferred to meet the jokers. Then I remembered Frick and Frack behind me, and I figured maybe I already had.

All of this was at the speed of thought, as only a second later, he followed with, "I am a man of few words. You are here because you are key in a royally-funded science project. More specifically, FHM724, or 'Peering through 4D glasses' as it has been casually but officially referred to by Rancor."

As the king spoke the official project's ID, FHM724, I reminded myself what FHM stood for, "For His Majesty." My apparently insuppressible inner dialogue kicked in yet again, having me as the king, and calling the project FM724, as in "For Me, 724."

No sooner had I thought this than the king pointed out that he knew how I referred to the project. "You have coined the project, 'Tax Waste 2021.'"

The room temperature dropped twenty degrees Celsius in that instant.

I could only recall having spoken that once. I remembered I had said it to Emerson but could not exactly recall where or when.

I may have frozen, but the king continued as if it were an annoyance unworthy of further attention. He had only mentioned it to let me know he knew. "Your key focus, as of late, has been to gain control of the ability to tap into the time continuum via the 4th-degree properties of lightning. You are credited with having discovered this ability, though you merely stumbled upon it accidently, while in my service, supporting R&D for project FHM720, tapping into lightning as a naturally occurring alternative power source."

I asked myself, *Why is he telling me all this that I obviously know?* but answered as quickly, *Again, because he wants me to know how much he knows.*

As if he had read my mind, and after a brief pause to let me soak in what he had already conveyed, he continued, "Here is something you do not yet know. Your coworker, Geoffrey Talbrook tried, though quite unsuccessfully, to tap into time this morning. He met his immediate end as thousands of volts fried him to a charred and instant crisp."

My stomach fell, and I thought I was going to be sick. I had no idea. Without thinking, I spoke out, "But I told him … I warned him."

Again, as if reading my mind, the king stepped in to concisely finish my broken defense. He seemed to know everything. And as if reminding me that it was he who would do the talking, he picked up where I had frozen, "You warned him not to try anything stupid. You warned him how your own survival from the accident was a miracle and how there were safety precautions still being developed. You even informed him of what you had learned reviewing a recent study on swarms, particularly bees. Lastly, you said, and I quote, 'Geoffrey, what is the hurry? This project only truly benefits the king.'"

I no longer knew if the shock I was in was due to learning of Geoffrey's death or the fact the king literally knew everything, including my disdain for him and everything he stood for.

"Something else you do not know, and in your complacency much less care to, Geoffrey Talbrook was not working with you but competing against you. He strived for nothing less than to be the one to succeed at all costs. You see, where you have the knowledge and ability, Geoffrey had the fire. He believed in his purpose enough to risk his very life to achieve it. The problem, your problem, is Geoffrey believed, to make himself look better, he had to make you look like a failure. In the process and in his sudden demise, he has inadvertently made it appear it was you who was jealous of him. Did you know he sent emails to himself, from your computer, therefore addressed from you, threatening him? They threatened how he had better back off and how the success of the project would result in your glory, not his."

Making sure I knew he intended the question rhetorically, he immediately continued, "These threats had you as a prime suspect in an accident you just learned occurred and in what the inept police force is considering a potential homicide. I have already taken care of correcting the errs of their incompetence. Your work for me is far too important to have it interrupted by an envious imbecile and a moronic investigation. I have brought you here to convey just how important your work is to you—how, because it means anything to me, it must be of utmost importance to you. Again, I have removed unnecessary roadblocks, and what I expect of you is to do the same. What Geoffrey Talbrook lacked in intelligence, he made up in fire. Your highest priority now is to become the phoenix that rises from his ashes."

Just like that, he was done wasting his all-too-valuable time. A mere gesture had me removed from his presence.

Then, it was as if the whole kidnapping sequence played in reverse, only this time I was in the car behind the car lowered from the car wash. We completed the cycle. This time, however, there was no Royal Lane. The goons had completely rolled up my blackened side windows to actually go through the car wash and left them up the entire way back. Though I could not see, I could tell we were not speeding this time.

During the much slower ride back, I reflected on the incident. I realized how important "Tax Waste 2021," or "FHM724," was to the king. It made perfect sense. Imagine the powerful advantage he would gain using hindsight to tweak the dials of time in his favor. He already held the power of the world in his hands, yet he still wanted more. The thought both frightened me and made me hate his monarchial world all the more.

My fear of the king had heightened to a personal level, as his intimidations were most effective. But this fear had always existed, and in everyone, as if it were some mutant chromosome added to the worker ants of society's DNA strands at birth to keep them in line.

What was new for me was the personal hatred. I think where fear of royalty had been instilled as an almost natural component of my makeup, this hatred did not rear its ugly head until the king made it personal.

The drive seemed to take forever, but the car finally stopped, and the guards shoved me out of the now clean, and all-too-expensive, car.

Until one of the goons had opened the car door, I had no idea where we were. One look at the stone lion statue before me though, and I realized they had dropped me off in front of Benedict Hall back at Cornwallis University. Though class was long over, they never bothered to ask where I needed to go; they never said a word. I was not worth one to them.

It was a good fifteen-minute walk south down Hillsborough Avenue and then down one block on Fusilier Road to reach my flat in the North Commons.

I had ridden to school with Emerson that morning.

After what I had just been through, I did mind the walk so much. It was a beautiful but chilly fall afternoon. And besides, I needed to think. I needed to break down and absorb all that had happened.

I felt a brief pang of guilt about Geoffrey, but he had done it to himself. Sometimes you get what you ask for. The guilt blew past as fast as the leaves had across the sidewalk.

A cold October wind railed at my back as if it were just another car barreling down the avenue and I had been its only obstruction. I had been through so much; I had not even thought how lucky I was to have already been wearing my jacket when I was so rudely apprehended.

I laughed at the thought that such a thoughtful and caring royal kidnapping goon could exist who would think to have gotten me my jacket, any jacket, or even a donkey's blanket for that matter. They both wore fancy jackets, and thanks only to a seasonably cold school, I had already been wearing mine.

As I had continued walking, I reigned in my cold and wandering thoughts and directed them toward not just my one-sided conversation with the king but also the entire royal experience.

I realized the incredible amount of power that literally emanated from the king. In his presence, I had lost all knowledge of my surroundings. I could not recall a thing about what the room, much less anything in it, had looked like. The king had consumed all my senses.

I even remember the distinct smell, his distinct smell. It was the quintessence of otherworldly scents, and it was a smell I would never acquire, or forget.

The world was his, and yet he was his own world. In his presence, I was but a distant lowly subject—and only one in nearly seven billion at that. It was only with his permission that I had been able to witness him through the looking glass from my world. The experience teased me and left me longing for the chance to inhale some more of the fresh air of his world. After all, that fresh air only existed because of the labor of another world—my world.

My cell phone rang and startled me. I had not even realized the guards had returned it to me, having slipped the phone back into its holster. The ringtone was a snippet from "Jester's Folly," the new song by my favorite group, the Bambastards. Naturally, Emerson was the only contact I blessed with this kick-ass song as a ringtone.

As I went to answer, the screen flashed alerts, letting me see that I had eight new messages and four missed calls.

I answered my typical, "It's me."

"Joshua! What the hell, man? 'Bout time you answered the cell-ephone! What happened?"

Emerson must have been genuinely concerned, as he never calls me Joshua. It is always "Joshu-blah," "Joshu-arse," or his latest variation including my last name, "J-Wanks."

"I'm OK, Emer. I'll tell you about it when I get home. I'm walking down Hillsborough now. I'll be there in ten minutes. The royal kidnapping gits dropped me off in front of Been-a-dick-to-h-All!"

Immediately after having said this, I thought how the king probably knew that moniker as well. I had better learn to become more careful with my choice of words. The world, his world, had ears.

"Oh … have you already passed the House of Lords Coffeehouse? I could use a lightnin' jolt of caff."

I had known Emerson throughout my memorable life but was still amazed by his incredibly short attention span. Hearing I was OK, he'd already forgotten I had been kidnapped.

"Yes, I just passed it, damn it. I suppose you want the usual."

"Usual what? Hey, man, I've got a record high game of *Billy Club Bobby* going. I'll see ya when ya get back."

Just like that, he hung up. Hell, he had probably already forgotten he had asked me for the coffee. I hadn't intended on buying him a coffee anyway; money was too tight. It was always too tight. Money, or lack of it, was yet another reason why he and I shared a flat.

My mind had not drifted too far from the king. As for buying a coffee, I did not like the idea of the high taxes I would pay, thus further lining his royal pockets. So that was where our money went—to royal vehicles, Royal Lanes, royal secret underground car washes, royal pains. I wasn't sure I would allow myself to enjoy buying anything anymore. I couldn't hide from it all; we paid taxes to breathe anymore, and it wasn't nearly as clean as the air we paid for him to breathe.

The sun already appeared to hang lower on the horizon by the time I reached home.

As I stepped in, I saw Emerson in his all-too-familiar spot in front of the telly. I expected that but also spied Emily back in the kitchenette. It looked like she was steeping a cup of tea. Emerson must have called her to let her know I was OK.

I saw Emily almost every day at the lab, but I was always struck by how amazing she looked out of the lab coat. I must have been staring in a daze, because the next thing I knew Emerson was punching me in the arm.

"What the hell happened? Did they brainwash you?"

"No ... no ... no, nothing like that," I answered immediately but paused in thought afterward. I guess I needed to ask and then answer that question myself. I did not think they'd brainwashed me.

The royal blue laser grid in the vacuum room crossed my mind.

As I took off my jacket, Emily approached—and with two cups of hot tea in her hands. I dumped my coat over Emerson's arm, as he had never stopped using it to hit mine.

"Well, you look good. I mean it doesn't look like they hurt you, but you look cold," Emily said as she handed me a cup of steaming tea.

I repeated what I had told Emerson, "They dropped me off at Been-a-dick-to-h-All, the king's arses! I had to walk home."

"So, do tell all," Emerson kicked in. "Do tell all!"

Looking back at him as I sat on the couch in the living room, I saw he was still wearing his lab coat, but with only boxers on underneath. The boxers were the *Billy Club* boxers that came with the game he had been playing. His hair was a mess, making him look like a mad scientist, not to mention utterly ridiculous. Lastly, he was still holding my coat. I didn't think he'd noticed I had given it to him.

I told them everything that had happened.

Emily sat there, looking visibly and genuinely shook, but beautiful nonetheless.

Emerson had stolen my tea and spilled most of it on his lab coat as he flailed his arms about, repeating nonstop, "Bluuuuuueeee liiiightsssss … b-b-blllllluuuuuuuueeeee liiiiiiightssssss …" He stretched it out each time until he ran out of breath.

Somehow, I knew he would get a kick out of the Royal Lane.

Emily and Emerson proceeded to tell me of how they had learned of Geoffrey's accident and death at the lab.

It turned out, "Professor Poopypants the V," as Emerson now referred to him, had run out of the classroom immediately after I had been royally kidnapped. I think the professor's soiling was the highlight of Emerson's day. Immediately after telling me of it, Emerson began dancing around the room repeating, "OK, everyone, sound out the bowels—'A' … 'E' … 'I' … 'O' and p-U!"

Emily took it from there. "After you were abducted and the professor disappeared, I looked around and the whole class was on their cell-ephones texting about what had happened. The professor returned. He must've changed in his office, though he told the class he'd stormed into the headmaster's office for an explanation and apology. He didn't elaborate on how well that went over. I think he probably just called the headmaster's assistant. Anyway, it was then he told us he'd learned about Geoffrey's demise. The way he talked about him, Geoffrey must've been an arse-kisser in his class.

"His death was horrible, but I'm not surprised. I heard you warn him several times not to mess with lightning, but he couldn't hear you over the noise of his ambition."

There was not a lot of love lost in her tone about Geoffrey. None of us had gotten along very well with him. He was a far too self-ambitious risk taker—and not calculated risks but blind ones, blinded by his desire to make a name for himself. I remembered how the king had referred to him as believing "in his purpose enough to risk his life to achieve it."

"I can't believe the police pegged you as a prime suspect for murder. Geoffrey was actually trying to set you up to advance himself?"

"In a way, yes. Obviously, however, his intention was only to make him look better by making me look bad. I had no idea he was up to anything like that; much less did I even care. I can't believe he wanted to use me as a step to elevate his credit and career. Hell, it's not a career; it's a life sentence."

"I believe it," Emerson added. "Geoffrey was an arse, and he didn't even like the pickles."

"Emer, it was you he didn't like, not the pickles. He only smashed them because they were yours."

Emily laughed in response.

Emerson looked genuinely surprised at the revelation.

"More than anything," I added, still on the thought that Geoffrey had been trying to frame me, "I can't believe the king knew about it. In fact, he knew about everything."

"Everything?" Emily and Emerson responded in unison.

I was briefly impressed by the appropriateness of Emerson's response—briefly being the key word. After a short pause, he followed it with the question, "He even knows about the likeness of him I drew with permanent marker on the inside back of my boxers?"

How do you respond to that?

Emily and I both stared, not in disbelief, but in what could only be described as wonder and admiration. Although the image was nothing less than disturbing, I found the symbolism of the king kissing Emerson's arse all day, every day, and with Emerson's gaseous nature to boot, nothing short of a triumph of underground rebellion or, in his case, underpants rebellion.

I found it best, however, to continue as if he had not said anything.

"The king even knew about the obscure side project we've been working on lately, studying bees and the logic of swarms."

"Our little plasma ball experiment? How could he know about that? We haven't even taken that basement experiment to the project lab yet. Only you and I worked on it."

"He didn't go into details, Emer, but he didn't need to. I seriously think the only reason he took the pains of wasting any of his time on me was to show me how much he knew. His sole intent was to intimidate me—to scare me into being his new and improved Geoffrey 2.0."

Emily's jaw had dropped. "Bees? Swarm logic? Plasma ball? What's that all about?"

"Em, it's just one of the many side adventures Emer and I work on when blessed by rare bits of spare time. We weren't keeping it a secret; it wasn't even worth sharing yet. But the fact you were not aware of it only adds to the mysterious and disturbing fact the king was. It was just a side experiment focusing on improving the productivity of FHM720. But he only pointed it out because it had advanced to focusing on the success of his pet project, FHM724."

━ CHAPTER 15 ━

CAUGHT UP IN THE EVENTS I HAD SHARED, EMILY SUDDENLY remembered the events on the other side of the day's coin—what I had missed back in the history classroom. She picked up where she'd left off with the professor's return. "After he filled us in with what he'd learned about the headmaster's visit, which, come to think of it, he never even mentioned your kidnapping, anyway, he suddenly went ballistic."

"Ballistic? Ballistic about what?"

"Yeah, he was in a real pisser, Joshu-blah!" Emerson chimed in.

"You know how we've always thought he was such a royal arse-kisser?" Emily asked rhetorically. "We were all wrong about that one. His feelings toward royalty are more fear than anything. I think the only thing he's actually proud of is his ancestral connection to"—switching to her best impression of the professor—"Jonathan Elders, King's Guard and orator of the famous Third's War catchphrase, 'Philadelphia, Pennsylvania. Fill'd with death, yer pens'll hang-ya!'"

I applauded her effort, but she sounded nothing like the twit of a professor we all knew and loved—loved to hate that is. She still had not answered my question, "What the hell was he all pissed about?"

Craning his head to appear taller, or maybe just to make room for the extra layers of arrogance, Emerson replied, "Headmasterrrr McAllisterrrr!"

"Yes, Emer, Headmaster McAllister. When he barged in with the two King's Guards, neither he, nor the guards, even took notice of the professor's existence. Once Professor Jonathan Elders V—"

"Perfessor Poopypants!"

Emily, turned toward Emerson and smiled her beautiful smile, but never skipped a beat. "Got past the fear, he focused on the lack of acknowledgement and base level respect he'd received from the headmaster. The professor threw a fit that showed us a completely different side of him. Unbelievably, he holds nothing but disdain toward the Crown, toward the royal establishment as a whole. He began ranting and raving about it, eventually jumping right back into the history of Third's War."

I was blown away. It was now sounding like I'd missed more than they had.

Emily proceeded to fill me in on the connections between the professor's rant and the events of Third's War or, as Emily stressed, the potential of events.

Elaborating on the word, *potential*, she explained how the professor believed, if these events had occurred, we would be living in a completely different world today. The infamous rebels, those of the Signers' Rebellion, might have actually survived the British forces. By doing so, they might have actually succeeded in their revolution.

Instantly, a strange thought, an image appeared in my mind. It looked like hope, but hope had always been an item I longed for from outside of the store window in which it was displayed. Hope seemed a luxury item I would never be able to afford.

Emily continued, "I don't think the professor intended the rant to be an extension of his day's lecture. He was just ranting. But for the first time I've ever seen, the whole class was taking notes. The next thing we knew, the professor had jumped up to the board and proceeded to list the events and their potentials. I was taking notes as fast as I could, but our very own resident genius, Emer, recorded the whole rant on his phone."

Instantly, Emerson frantically searched for his phone. If he found it before he forgot why he was looking for it, I just may get to see the video of the rant. The odds were stacked against me on that one.

Emily pulled a sheet of paper out of her jeans pocket and then continued, "Josh, we can fill in the gaps later. But the gist of them were," she read from a list, "one, don't fight the formal British fight. Two, fight during the winter and ignore the Rites of Spring. Three, let Benedict Arnold be a hero, but catch him when he turns traitor."

She handed me the list while I was responding to the latter, "Benedict Arnold was once a rebel hero?"

"Yes, before turning traitor, he'd actually been considered one of the rebel force's most tactical battle leaders. It turned out he went turncoat on the rebels because he believed he didn't get the recognition he felt he deserved. He was totally in it for himself, like Geoffrey. But look what happened to him.

"Lastly, the professor went on about how the rebels needed to better utilize resources they had available to them. The one example that stands out was how they could've taken much-needed cannons from forts they'd defeated and brought them as firepower for other battles. For example, there was a fort in Canada … It started with a T."

"Ticonderogaaaaaa!" Emerson came alive.

Then, with his selectively incredible memory, and a spot-on impression of Professor Poopypants, he continued to repeat, word for word, the professor's outburst about it. "Those damned revolutionaries of the Signer's Rebellion managed to take, from the British Army no less, a fort equipped with sixty tons of cannons and other armaments but failed to capitalize on their artillery gains! They so badly needed artillery down south yet left a fully-abandoned fortress full at Fort Ticonderogaaaah!"

Then, for realistic measure, Emerson threw in, "And— Dash it all, subordinate Flounders, pay attention! Everything has a cost, if you are not paying attention, who the hell are you paying?"

Emily and I burst into laughter and applause.

Though I had not noticed at the time, I had inadvertently dropped the list Emily handed me. It had fallen and drifted beneath the chair I had been standing next to.

Further answering what he had asked in character as the professor, Emerson boomed in his own voice, "The king! We're all paying the king!"

Emily managed to spit out, though still in laughter, "Emer, your impression is amazing. I can close my eyes and see the yahoo's flat and flappy hair, disheveled from conniption!"

What stuck in the back of my mind, however, was Emerson's reply, and who I too believed we were all paying—the king. My mind drifted back to the professor's list, not the paper I had dropped but the image in my head of the professor writing it frantically on the board. I do not know why, but this list, and the whole idea that conceptually, history could have been rewritten by timely and extraordinary actions taken at forks in the roads of destiny enthralled me. It would consume me.

The forks in the road were there; it was more the rebels had not seen them. But amazingly, reaping the benefits of hindsight from our perspectives, we saw not only the forks but also which of their paths should be taken. Someone from our perspective in the future just needed to look.

I must have stumbled back into the land of my thoughts, as Emily, standing directly in front of me, snapped her fingers in my face and lured me from them. "Hellooooo! Welcome back Wanderlust the Mind Wanderer. You've been doing this a lot lately."

"Sorry," I began.

"Hey, no apologies, especially after what you've been through today. It's getting late though. And don't forget, you still need to get your stuff together for your trip home tomorrow."

In all that had happened, I had completely forgotten. I was going to catch the train from Pendleton Station in George's Cross to the village of Cloister; I was going home to be with my family for my birthday tomorrow—my twenty-first birthday.

I'd always had mixed feelings about going home. I couldn't help it, though it made me feel guilty. Don't get me wrong. I love my family, my parents that is, as I am an only child. But it was always so hard to be reminded how poor common life was. I had lived sheltered from the full brunt of the plights of reality by the grace of my scientific abilities. The government has allowed me a semidecent government flat in the government city near the government school and, most importantly, by the government lab. Being well off is a matter of perspective. Though, I was by no means living in the lap of luxury, my life was far better than it would have been had I not had been beneficial to the government.

Outside of the protective shell, my family lived day to day, toiling their lives away to pay most everything they earned in taxes, and only to support every royal whim of the royal family. They had nothing to show for their labors but the callouses on their hands. Though my life was better, my pay was not. I was wrapped in the irony of wanting to do so very much for them but having so very little opportunity to do anything.

Emily continued, "You told me, for your birthday, your mother always makes you your favorite meal. What's it called again?"

"It's just a poor-man's shepherd's pie, called meat-wish pie."

"Why do they call it that?"

Again, I was reminded that her father's relationship to royalty, albeit five times removed, had afforded her a slightly better home life. They weren't wealthy by any means, but at least her family could afford to add meat to their meals.

"It's called that because it has no meat, but you wish it did."

"Oh, how sad. I could get some for you to take to them."

"No, they are very proud. And I don't want to take anything away from my mother's efforts."

"If it has no meat in it, how come you like it so much?"

"I don't like it for the flavor. I like it for all my mother puts into it."

"You are a good man, Joshua Franks." Then, with her guard down, she lunged forward and gave me a huge hug and a kiss on the cheek.

I had not noticed at the time, but she must have then slipped a birthday card she had made into my shirt pocket.

I worked with lightning, so one would think I would have seen it coming when it struck me—the longings, the desires, the love Emily and I wanted so badly to share. In that flash of an instant, I was lost in her, her warmth, her kiss, and even her smell. I could not take it in enough. I smiled, as I believed I could feel her scent engulf that of the king's. I would take hers any day over the king's, no matter how rare and expensive his was.

But like lightning's flash, the tender moment of our own ions clashing, though powerful, was gone as quickly as it had come.

Emily jumped backward, sweeping her eyes around the room as if she would find someone watching. Emerson had long drifted back to playing his video game, but it was not Emerson she feared who may have eyes upon her. Still, I could tell by the look on her face, the fear in her eyes, she was afraid that we were being watched—that we would be caught.

It was only a moment later that I recognized I shared in that fear, only I figured it was more we were being listened to. Now, reflecting on what the king took pains to tell me he had heard, I realized we had probably said far more than we should have. It took the emotional jarring of forbidden love unguarded to remind me.

I had mentally drifted again, though this time for only seconds. I snapped myself out of it to find Emily had already snagged her jacket and offered a distressed goodbye in a rushed exit.

Left standing there, now only with my thoughts, I reflected on the source of the spike driven between us. It was hard to believe it had all started less than a week ago after I had stumbled upon tapping into the time continuum through lightning. More specifically, it had all started after the king had found out I had stumbled upon it.

Only a handful of days, and yet our lives have been turned upside down.

It took no time for the king to see the additional power he could attain, as if he were not powerful enough already. He immediately changed the lab's focus from FHM720, the project capitalizing on a cheap, alternative and naturally occurring power source for the people, to FHM724, that sought only an additional source of power for him.

FHM724 immediately became our most secretive and highest priority project. The king did everything in his existing power to squelch any distractions or interruptions to its progress.

My budding relationship with Emily was one such distraction. The moment the king learned of it, he had presented the lab with a royal proclamation prohibiting relationships between co-workers. He would have separated us if he had any choice in the matter, but he needed the both of us for his pet project to succeed, and he knew it. But he went out of his way, via his endless supply of resources, to let us know he knew and was watching.

I had never met the king before today. Nor had any of us previously crossed his radar, but we had personally felt his powerful grip tighten once he realized how much he could benefit from his new pet project.

Reflecting on my special one-on-one meeting with the king, I remembered a specific comment he had made. It had been in reference to the Geoffrey Talbrook investigation. He had pointed out how he had "again removed unnecessary roadblocks." At the time, my thoughts had focused on the one roadblock I had just learned about, being prime suspect in Geoffrey's death. Now, however, focusing on the word *again*, I realize he was referring specifically to what he had done to remove the Joshua and

Emily distraction and put a halt to our budding relationship. He'd wielded his royal hammer and driven a spike between us.

Copies of the royal proclamation were specifically served to us, with our family's names listed, as a reminder of his broad reach to ensure the proclamation was upheld. He had not come out and said it today, but he had not needed to. Emily and I both took this reminder to mean that our families were not out of his reach, and his resources could make them pay if we continued with any further actions against the proclamation.

It was clear he intended our complete focus to be completing *his* project.

While getting ready for bed, as I took off my shirt, I found the card Emily had slipped into my pocket earlier while I was lost in her birthday hug.

I opened it to find it was a homemade birthday card. She had written it on a torn-out calendar page from one of her many government-issued journals. The date on the calendar page matched that of my birthday, Saturday, October 16, 2021.

Before reading what she had written at the top of the sheet, I looked down at the image she had drawn. I recognized it instantly as a visual representation of a line in a poem I had shared with her. An enigmatic reference we had since made our own as a secret profession of our love.

The image was of a trailing sunset that left mostly dark blue skies but for an orange line on the horizon. Emily had signed it on the bottom right.

After having taken in the image, my eyes, with a warm smile following in tow, drifted back up the makeshift calendar sheet turned card, to the top where Emily had written a greeting.

The greeting read simply, "Happy 21st Birthday, Josh Franks!"

As she had written it above the image she had drawn, she inadvertently had written it over the calendar page's daily message. Reading around Emily's writing, I could make out that the day's message read, "The Duke and Duchess of Mayfith's 70th anniversary—a momentous celebration of two lives becoming one."

When I refocused my eyes on Emily's message, the two blended and it briefly read like Emily had wished, "Happy 70th Birthday mom." As my focus adjusted, I could see the word mom, was attached to the word, momentous. The whole episode lasted only a second, but it was worth a laugh, and I sorely needed one.

Exhausted, I set the card up on my milk crate nightstand and then retired to bed.

That night I dreamed. My dreams typically consisted of a bazaar series of abstract scenes clipped together. I usually didn't understand them, if I even remembered them at all.

That night's was different. That night's dream was a virtual reenactment—a nightmare of the key events that had recently occurred.

I woke up in a cold sweat.

Looking up at the clock, I realized it'd be another two hours before the alarm was to go off, but I knew I would not be able to fall back to sleep.

A glutton for punishment, I felt like I had to make some sense of all that had happened, so as I stared at the ceiling in the dark, I began mentally reliving the events. I immersed myself in them, reliving the events that had started less than one week back and at the time this hell had begun.

— CHAPTER 16 —

Saturday, October 9, 2021

I T WAS A CLOUDY AND UNSEASONABLY WARM SATURDAY MORNING AND exactly one week before my twenty-first birthday. At 8:00 a.m., though I could have slept in, I had gotten up to drag my arse back into the lab. We typically worked Saturdays, so my half-mile walk up Hillsborough Avenue around that time and day was normal when I chose to walk. The exception was that the lab was closed this particular Saturday for special maintenance. According to the memo distributed, this maintenance required periodically shutting down the lab's power grid throughout the day.

I figured, as FHM720 was the only project I had ever been involved in that I had personally felt provided any real public value, I would unofficially dedicate some of my own time to it.

I didn't know about Emily, but Emerson had decided he would lie to himself and pretend we had been rewarded the day off. Having passed his room on the way out of the flat, I'd heard him snoring away. From the sound of it, he was a good hour or two from seeing anything but the insides of his eyelids. When that stellar moment finally did occur, I was sure it would only be capped with a transformation from blanketed chrysalis to game chair and a multihour effort to beat his own high score on his latest video game obsession, *Billy Club Bobby*.

I couldn't sit still that long. And as the weatherman had called for thunderstorms all day anyway, I figured I would go into work to try and resolve a longstanding opportunity that had reared its ugly head again during yesterday's control testing.

The storms had yet to begin, so I was racing to beat them, hoping to make it to the lab dry. The walk home was its own roll of the dice I would throw when the time came.

Investigating the opportunity would require me to get down near the area in the lab referred to as the core.

The core was a vertical tube, thirty meters in diameter, and acted as the initial and primary safety net standing between us and the lightning that flashed within. The core extended up from over twenty-five meters underground, to where it reached another ten meters above the roof of the lab, where it served as the gateway for Mother Nature's fury.

There were large vents on the core located just above the outer ramp's catwalk level and just below the lab's roof. With the core shut down, I should be able to look through a vent and down into the darkness of the core.

It was within the original version of this core, an invention of Anderson Raines, where the great scientist had figured out how to create a controlled environment that could consistently invite lightning to occur.

Normally, working down by the core would put me too close to the lightning. It was to my advantage that the electricity would be shut down this morning. I would be safe from any lightning being triggered.

I am a visual person; so being in the lab physically would enable me to view the environment within its active scope, which could, in turn, help me resolve the opportunity I had identified. This self-realization and rationalization was fresh in my mind, as I had just entered the lab's complex and had to explain it to an angry maintenance man who I ran into in the hallway leading toward the lab.

Howard Reskin was the name on the patch on his coveralls, but after the confrontation, I found Howard the Arse more apropos.

I had also explained, in response to his repeated insistence that the power would be out, that I would not need the power on, had all I needed, and would make my visit a quick one. I'd brought my trusty journal and pen, as well as a flashlight, as I was not sure if I would even have emergency backup lighting. Even if I did have backup lighting, I was not sure it would illuminate the area I would be working in.

My run-in with Howard made three things appear quite evident. First, and foremost, Howard did not want me causing him any delays. Second, Howard hated being there on a Saturday morning, apparently even more so than I did. Third, and the reason I spent the entire interaction fighting off breaking into laughter, Howard had apparently just finished eating eggs, powdered doughnuts, and something green that looked like kiwi. He was wearing remnants of it all over his face, and they appeared to move with a life of their own, throughout his animated rant.

At first, I thought he was just pissed he had to be there. Or maybe he was upset that I had caught him eating on the job, or both.

But as Howard the Arse turned to make his exit down the hall, I noticed a couple of things that, at the time and in my own haste to get into the lab, I had only managed to find peculiar. In a gap that revealed what he was wearing under his orange coveralls, I am positive I saw that Howard was wearing a suit and tie. Then, as he walked away, the scrape of the shoes, the click of the heels, and finally their appearance now from farther down the hall, made me think he was wearing dress shoes.

Having finally gotten into the lab, my focus returned from the arse in the hall to the occasion I had come to address.

Friday's testing had gone similar to the previous hundred in that the team had successfully created the environment conducive to attracting lightning. Though for a long time, establishing this environment had been the challenge, it had by now become an ordinary task. The problem we faced now was capturing enough power from the lightning attracted. To date, we had been averaging less than a 12 percent capture rate, leaving a ton of its energy to waste. Less captured meant less stored and available for use and, ultimately, more work on our part to catch and maintain adequate power levels to support the primary goal of FHM720—again, one of providing an affordable, sustainable, and naturally occurring power source to fuel the power needs of the people.

— CHAPTER 17 —

I HAD BEEN TOYING WITH AN IDEA BASED ON AN ARTICLE I HAD READ in a science journal I'd found in the break room earlier in the week. Again, I as a visual person, I thought if I came into the actual environment where the lightning occurred and looked at it through the eyes of this potential solution, it would help me see a way to make it work.

The article highlighted an outside-the-box solution to a logistical problem a trucking company had repeatedly been experiencing. I believe the company's name was Peregrine, or at least it had the word *Peregrine* in it. Anyway, the breakthrough program the company developed greatly improved its distribution productivity and, ultimately, its bottom line, or should I say the king's bottom line.

The program, an experiment in itself and the first of its kind, was developed by a group of logistical engineers who modeled route and load calculations off of the abstract and seemingly illogical movement of swarms.

Swarms of ants, bees, locusts, wildebeests, and various birds were studied, with their movements and activities recorded over time. These movements were translated into digital positioning to enable the engineers to analyze the routes chosen and to determine the route most productive.

At first, these scientists were completely lost to the logic. In fact, the article reported how the whole study had nearly been scrapped numerous times, only to experience an apparent breakthrough just big enough to keep it alive. Swarm logic marched to a different drum, seeming to direct decisions against what the researchers considered logical at face value.

In the end, the answers had been in front of the team the whole time. The key word attributed to their success was, in fact, *time*. By sticking with it long enough, the small successes accumulated, leading to a fundamental breakthrough in their ability to see what had been there in front of them all along.

They had finally come to realize the biggest obstacle they had was the humanly natural and invisible wall they had put up in front of themselves. This wall, an all too common detriment to progress, had prevented them from seeing and understanding things that fell outside the boundaries of their present level of understanding.

After having stared at enough simulation results, their minds subconsciously drifted past these man-made and invisible barriers and into a truly big picture perspective, enabling them to see the abstract yet beneficial logic behind the swarming activities they studied.

For example, they realized that swarms acted without specific leadership.

Ultimately, they discovered a logical and beneficial application of swarm logic to logistics planning.

I had made a mental connection with the science between the logistical engineering team's discoveries and the logistical needs of our own. I was trying to discover a logical approach to locate and connect to the illogical and seemingly random paths lightning charted and forged as it struck. Doing so, I believed would greatly improve our ability to connect to, and therefore tap into, the lightning as a power source.

This connection I had made between my present challenge and the article was thanks to the honeycomb pattern of the external layer of the core, which reminded me of the hive for the swarm of bees I had just read about. I had seen the core countless times before, but this time with the thought of swarms of bees still buzzing in my head, the sight of it only reaffirmed and bridged the connection between what brought success to a trucking company and how it could do the same for us.

This connection provided an opportunity with enough potential to solve our problem, enough so that I found my "like-it-visual"-self up on a Saturday morning and in the last place I wanted to be, given the unexpected chance at a rare day off.

I made my way into our lab and then into the control center.

We called it the control center because, during what we referred to as an active run, it was the area with the controls to initiate altering the core's environment to attract lightning. One might envision a large and elaborate technical setup, but the room itself was barely the size of the living room in my flat. We only needed to be in the control center during actual test or live runs, so the only permanent controls in it were the switches to initiate the runs. We brought our laptops into it to set the environmental dials for each run.

The core in the lab absorbed the heat from the lightning. Doing what it was designed to, it not only took the heat of the lightning but also redirected what energy it could from it, converting and channeling it to the three massive power cells safely outside the perimeter of the lab. There the energy was stored for use, taking power from lightning that occurred in a blink, for the purpose of powering and lighting several districts within the city of George's Cross.

Though the core may take care of the lightning's heat, if you were in the lab during a run, you also needed to be in the control center because it was the only area in the lab with walls designed to protect you from lightning's sound and intense light. Its walls absorbed the pounding thunder immediately following the intense blast of light emanating from the lightning striking in the lab's core. The control center also sat suspended on a specially designed shock-absorbing base so neither we nor the computers in the lab were rattled.

Though the control center was small and not much to look at, the safety factors built into it were an engineering and design marvel. The cost of the materials and the center's design were so high they necessitated its small size. Dr. Rancor had conveyed countless times how hard it was to get the approval to build the labs. Ideally, she said she would have not even had the control center designed within the lab, but she could not get approval for enough land allocation to move it off-site. It as a miracle in itself that she was even able to get approval to move forward, but many concessions were made to keep the costs down. She held firm with insisting on the safest environment possible, some of the results of which were in the design and materials for the control center, the area I spend most of my time cramped inside while playing with Mother Nature.

Except of course for the occasional poor soul who had actually been struck by natural lightning, sitting in the control center, or for that matter anywhere inside the lab, placed you much closer to lightning than anyone in his or her right mind should care to be.

I opened the heavy door of the control center, exited, and moved just beyond it. There was not much else to the rest of the lab. Aside from the core, though it was a large lab, it was, for the most part, bare. Not much could withstand the constant rattling from the thunder. We had tables anchored to the ground that we referred to as our desks, at least in between runs. These "desks" were simple wooden tables with a centimeter lip around the edges to keep things from being shaken off.

I headed past the desks and down to the outside of the core.

Where I was standing outside the core, however, was dangerously close to where 427 recorded strikes of lightning had occurred. I knew this because the count was one of the many things we logged and accounted for in the course of a day's work.

I respected the dangers of my job and the immense power of the lightning that we seemingly played with every day. Even with the power off in the lab, I got the jitters as I stuck my fingers into the honeycomb pattern of the core's outer grid.

I followed the winding ramp up along the outside of the core and up to the catwalk that encircled the core, revealing the vents near the ceiling. The core itself extended up and out an additional ten meters, but from the vent I now peered through, I could see inside the core. Looking down inside its massive and deep expanse, there was just enough light to see the bottom ground on the opposite side.

I imagined being able to see the negatively charged ions zigzagging down until they came close enough to reaching ground to have their positive counterparts leap up from the ground at them. The connection they made, the return stroke, was what our eyes could actually see. The flashing surge of the current and resulting blast of power started from near the ground, though to us it appeared lightning strikes down.

My eyes' focus returned from the ground of the core to the honeycomb grid, while my mind's focus returned to the reason I was there. I turned and began my walk back down the ramp. As I circled back down alongside the core, I reached a vantage point that looked out over the control center.

I stopped, and from where I was standing, I had a clear view of the control center and Emily's desk positioned directly in front of it.

I could see the poor excuse for a desk she used and pictured her there now—god how I loved her. Our relationship had grown so much and so quickly, and I could no longer imagine a life without her in it.

I pictured her there, typically logging into her daily planner all the notes and requirements we discussed and tweaked for programming changes.

Though as the chief project programmer she lived on her laptop, she preferred writing in the planner journal to capture any ideas we dreamed up in our efforts to enhance our capabilities. Everything we did was always a work in progress.

Emerson and I typically teased her about her preference to write it down on paper, as opposed to just typing it into the computer also sitting by her on the desk. She said she found writing on paper an escape from what she described as the coldness of a computer. Paper was such a warm and comfortable medium. Emerson called it her pacifier, and he sucked his thumb as he walked by her when she wrote.

Just thinking about Em left me smiling.

Then something that was both completely unexpected, yet ironically, perfectly natural occurred.

Lightning struck.

Though lightning striking was a regular occurrence in this lab, this particular lightning had not been induced but had struck naturally. Though I had never seen nor heard of this having happened before, in hindsight, I feel ignorant for not having recognized it could. We certainly had not put anything in place to prevent it.

If you had asked me before the lightning strike, I would have told you it should have killed me instantly. I had never been that close before. Aside from those dead because of it, and the rare handful who survived, no one else ever had.

The benefit of having the core grid between me and the lightning, and a lot of luck, were the only things that prevented the lightning from touching me. At least, those were the initial thoughts I would have later— later, having survived the strike virtually unscathed, but most importantly, later when I finally realized lightning had even struck.

As the lightning flashed, however, I stood both uncooked and unaware that it had even occurred. Instead, I still stood there in the lab, and yet it was not the lab. At least it did not look normal. But rather, it glowed and took on an almost dreamlike appearance.

Lost in the dream state, I stared at the scene before me. The light made it look surreal, and in a strange way, beautiful and intense. Trying to shake myself from what I thought was my own imagination gone wild, I proceeded walking full circle down the ramp and out until I reached Emily's desk in front of the control center.

Standing directly over her desk, I noticed something on it I had not noticed earlier, Emily's planning journal. She must have forgotten it, which was odd because she would never intentionally leave it otherwise but would have stuffed it as always, into her GI (government-issue) workbag. She was forgetful sometimes, so I bet this was not the first time she had forgotten it.

Lost in the moment, I decided I would write her a message.

Where it was true our relationship had blossomed, at that point in time, it had done so secretly. To our knowledge, only Emerson had been aware of it, but even he had not known how much it had advanced. We were careful to keep it a secret if for no other reason than to lie to ourselves into believing we had something that was our own. Nothing else in our lives of any value was ours. Sadly, the government owned everything, including us.

Only a week earlier, I had shared with Emily a poem I had read. It was called "Finding the Sense in Nonsense," and it captured our secret relationship perfectly, for imbedded in the poem was a verse in which the first letters of each word strung together formed their own secretive yet appropriate message.

I was sure this type of cypher had a name, but I did not know it.

An obscure line in the verse read, "Indigo lights, on violet evenings, yellow orange undertones."

The verse repeated the line twice, and to Emily and me, it came to represent us saying it to each other. The hidden message formed by the first letters declared simply, "I love you."

It was this verse, or at least my half of it, that I decided to write in her journal. I guess my hope was, upon seeing it, Emily would reply in kind, thus completing the circle of the enigmatic declaration.

I opened it to the bookmark ribbon's pages, and with the pen from my shirt pocket, quickly penned the secret proclamation on the first blank calendar page it presented.

Afterward, with the journal back in its place on the desk and the pen back in my pocket, I remained standing there, taking in the aura of the strange moment. Everything around the lab still had a weird glow about it. I decided with all these distractions I was not going to be able to focus and accomplish anything.

I attributed the illuminated scene to the maintenance work my new friend Howie-the-Arsehole must have been doing in between doughnuts. I wasn't sure what it was he had been doing, and I certainly had not expected a light show.

As I turned to leave, having just walked past the anchored tables, I reached the edge of the control center.

Knowing what I know now and looking back on that moment I realize how, as I had tried to leave the control center perimeter, I had inadvertently broken the first connection I had unknowingly made within scope of the fourth dimensional aspects of lightning.

This also had me unknowingly returning to the third dimensional world, where I found myself dangerously close to where the very real naturally occurring lightning had struck.

The minutes I had seemingly experienced while in lightning's fourth dimensional grasp constituted only a flash of a second back in the reality of this three-dimensional world.

The power and crack of the lightning completing its flash occurred while I was at the edge of the dimensions. I believe that was why I survived. I would have probably been killed had I been standing in the three-dimensional world.

We wore special earplugs and radio headsets, as well as had a sound wave filter that shot continuously in its own layer between the outer core and thermal reception layers of the core. The wave filter, like everything but the emergency lighting, was turned off. Not to mention, I was normally in the environmental safety of the control center.

As I crossed the dimensional thresholds, I caught just enough of the final remnants of the lightning to have both been thrown by it and recognize that it had even struck. At the time, shaking uncontrollably on the ground outside of the control center after having realized I had just survived a lightning strike, I still attributed the glow in my time in the fourth dimension to Howie's activities and simply thought the lightning had just then struck.

The uncontrollable shaking occurred, not so much because of the lightning striking but more the realization I had just survived it. As I inspected myself for injury, I found I was amazingly unscathed, though scared shitless. I repeatedly asked myself how I could have survived it, much less without injury.

The shaking slowly subsided. My guess now was that I had sat there around forty-five minutes or more. But at the time, I had no concept of time passing. Losing my awareness of time was yet another thing I figured out later and attributed as a side effect of crossing into and from time's dimension.

Finally, as if having crossed the threshold of a bad dream and woken to recognize it for what it was, a bad dream, I picked myself up and made my way out of the lab.

I never saw my new friend Howie the maintenance man when I left.

As I walked home, the series of events that had occurred played repeatedly in my mind.

Again, knowing what I know now, had my mind been settled enough after my return to the third dimension, I would have realized that Emily's planning journal would not have been there on her desk. As it was, I had not had the sense of mind to consciously take notice, though her desk had been in plain view.

I would come to realize it soon enough, however, when I reached the flat and found Emily there. Finding Emily there, in and of itself, was by no means strange. But finding Emily at the flat holding the planning journal I had written in not an hour earlier and her staring at me with a very confused and angry look on her face was very strange.

— CHAPTER 18 —

I WALKED IN TO FIND EMILY QUESTIONING EMERSON AND LOOKING FOR me. Apparently, she had been trying to call me. Yet another thing I would soon discover was that my trip into time's dimension seemed to have fried my cell phone. I later learned that simply powering it down and rebooting was all it needed to recover.

In that instant, however, I found an angry girlfriend who, upon seeing me enter the flat, redirected her anger from a thoroughly confused Emerson to laser in on me.

I could not understand Emily and had immediately looked to Emerson, who stood eyes wide open and scared. He was in his robe and boxers I remember but with his right arm out of the robe, leaving it hanging off his right side behind him. He liked to say he was geared for gaming mode and that freeing his right arm allowed him better game control. I had gotten used to seeing him in toga form when he gamed, but in the context of the current situation, he looked even more ridiculous than usual.

I fumbled for my cell phone, as if to validate the part of Emily's rant that I could understand, how I had not answered her calls. While I did so, I returned my attention to Emily and, for the first time, realized in her outburst that she had been waving her journal at me.

As she verbally smacked me upside the head, the realization that she was holding her journal virtually knocked me off my feet.

I had seen her journal on her desk at work. I had even written in it. Besides, she had not even gone into the lab that morning. Nor did I think she'd had time to go in after I had left and then drive right past me walking home for me to find her here yelling at Emerson about my whereabouts. Maybe it was a different journal, but why was she so upset about it? How was this possible?

As soon as the latter question popped into my head, I realized too, it was the very question Emily had been asking all along.

Everything seemed to be hitting me at once. Suddenly, I became aware of a distinct smell. Thinking back, I believe I had faintly noticed it in the back of my mind when I stepped in, but the lightning incident and the thundering scene I had just walked into had clouded my thoughts. Now, however, with Emily waving the planner in my face, the waft jumped to the forefront. I stood with a fixated stare on the journal and then subconsciously reached for it.

At this point, Emily stopped the verbal onslaught, ending with, "Joshua! Are you even listening to me?"

Emerson, taking advantage of the brief silence that followed, threw in his first two words, "Yeah, Josh-u-arse!"

Eyes still locked on the journal, I asked the burning question, "What is that smell?"

"You tell me, Joshua!" Emily replied as she opened the book to the bookmarked page.

She opened it to the page I had written the message on. I recognized my message instantly, but something about it did not look right.

Emily had called me Joshua. She never said my full name unless she was in a real pisser.

The whole scene seemed incredibly surreal—Emily upset and with the journal she should not have in her possession, much less in her hand, but there it was in front of me. And though I recognized the message I had written, I not only realized it did not look like how I had written it but had also finally connected with the fact that the paper in the planning journal was the source of the burning smell.

I snagged the journal, turning it around so it was reading side up for me. Focused on the message itself, I could clearly see what made the message look so strange. It was not just that the smell came from the journal; it came specifically from the page I had written on. In fact, it came from the message itself. The message had not been written in ink but had been burned on.

Blown away by this discovery, I turned to look at Emily. My total look of confusion in response to the slow but progressing awareness surrounding the journal must have triggered the similar look I now saw on her face. I could not only tell she had no idea of what had happened, but she had finally realized that the event, or events, that led to her finding her journal smoking were not just a mystery to her, but to me as well.

With a newly added tone of fear in her voice, she asked, "What's happened, Josh? What's going on here? How could this happen?"

After a moment of silence, while I followed my train of thought to the end of its tracks, I reached into my shirt pocket for my pen. Clicking it a couple times while visually inspecting it, I then tried to write something on the opposite and blank page on the journal. The pen would not write. I pressed harder, scribbling to try to get the pen I had used roughly an hour earlier to write the message, to write again, but it would not.

The next revelation, one might have thought, would have been the fact that the roller ball in the pen had been fused to the end of the pen— literally melted into place. That would have been the case had I not first noticed the date on the planner's page on which I had been trying to scribble was the current date, which meant the page with the previous message burned on it was the previous day's date. As if I was not already baffled enough, this new tidbit of information took me to a completely new level of confusion. The page I had chosen to write the message on was blank, meaning Emily had not written on it yet. That would make it the first time I had ever seen where she had not filled the page with the notes and thoughts of the day, an act you could count on as much as the hourly ring of Big Ben in Third's Tower.

I began frantically flipping back through all the pages of her planning journal. None of this made sense. As I had suspected, every single page of that journal had notes, reminders, tasks, and the like on it. Every one of them had been written on. Emily religiously used that planner, leaving me very confounded how the page I had written on was the previous day's date and how that page could have been blank on this, the current day's morning.

Witnessing my actions and the utter depth of my thoughts, Emily reached the point well past her emotional limits. She now stood crying, and Emerson joined her, even though he had much less investment in understanding why.

"Josh, what the … what the hell's happening here?" was all she could manage to spit out, repeating it several times.

I tried to absorb the evidence. In deep thought, I sat down on the floor in the very spot I had been standing just beyond the front door in the entrance of the flat.

Emily and Emerson joined me. Emily had calmed herself, and Emerson followed suit. Neither had a clue as to what was going on, but both recognized the thought mode I was in and trusted, if someone could make sense of things, I would be able to.

Emily referred to my thought process as a gift. Emerson said I was part alien because of it. My boss, who I think is a brilliant scientist, was quoted as having said, "When Joshua thinks on something, questions find answers and problems find solutions." To me, I knew no other way. It was as normal as breathing; it was just how I think.

I absorbed all the evidence, now looking at the lightning incident at the lab from a completely different perspective. I now realized that Howie from maintenance had nothing to do with the strange lighting that had occurred.

Again, I found myself having to visualize things. Doing so allowed me to step back and see things as if from the outside looking in. It allowed me to recognize things most would not, or apparently could not.

I replayed in my mind all that my eyes could have seen in the lab that morning. I started with my encounter with Howie and then moved on through every step I had taken through the lab—up the winding path around the core and then back down. I pictured myself writing in Emily's planning journal. It all appeared normal enough, except of course for the strange lighting that had crowned by the crash of natural lightning.

Answers—I needed answers. But finding the answers was only ever as good as making sure you asked the right questions.

Sitting there, I turned my attention back to the pen still in my hand. A quick and closer inspection revealed that the roller ball had in fact been fused to the metal of the pen casing.

I stepped back through what I remembered, back down the path to where I had realized the lightning had occurred. I saw myself sitting there on the floor of the control center, stunned. This exercise revealed to me just how long I had sat there on the control center floor.

While I had sat there, I remembered that I had stared at the core—the grid. But now, thinking through the events that had occurred as if I were editing film frame by frame, I could see that I had taken in virtually the whole lab from my vantage point on the floor.

Then it hit me. The power of the visual memory hit me so hard it was as if I had been struck by lightning a second time that day.

The visuals of memories, now framed like storyboards in my mind, were of my still-shaken attempt to stand up from the lab floor—the effort of which had me turn my body and, thus, my line of sight toward Emily's desk. It was then that my eyes saw, and my mind filed as a memory, even though I had not recognized it consciously at the time, Emily's journal was no longer there on her desk. I had finally and consciously recognized that fact. Having done so, it still made no sense.

Again, finding the answers is only ever as good as making sure you ask the right questions. The right question had just popped into my mind. Why would Emily not have written in her planner yesterday?

I thought back to yesterday morning. It had started no differently than any other normal workday morning. In fact, the day had gone, as they all seemed to, with Emerson, Emily, and I prepping the lab for the day's runs.

I could picture Emily sitting at her desk with just her laptop and her journal. She was clicking away on the laptop, checking and tweaking the programming settings for the next run. The last field she entered into the run profile would be the specific time and date of when we would trigger the lightning.

I only knew this because I provided her with that time, as it was based on when I had my prep steps completed and was the final step before triggering a run.

While we completed our settings for the next run, Emerson ran down his safety checklist, testing the core, the environment, and the equipment.

Most of the parameter details Emily keyed in allowed for appropriate record keeping of each run. The trigger time, however, played a key role in the actual program's ability to generate the environment that triggered the lightning. We had long understood the need, but not even the late Dr. Anderson Raines fully understood how or why it was necessary. Its need was, in fact, yet another amazing discovery of Dr. Raines, thus earning it the moniker DART.

I am not one for acronyms but have always liked that one. DART simply translates as Dr. Anderson Raines's Trigger.

Though we may not understand all the whys, we did know there was a direct connection between time and the occurrence of lightning. The entry of the DART was translated in code as an address of sorts—an address in time. The program then directed the results of the entry, along with a myriad of complex arrays and algorithms, all with the intent of initiating the inside layers of the core to polarize ions, directing and collecting positive ions from the ground and, at the top of the core, doing the same for the negative.

The negative ions strike down, as if seeking out the positives in an attempt to fulfill a mating ritual. The positive ions stand ground, until the negative ones get close enough and then leap up at them and the clash of the ions begins. All this is invisible to the naked eye, until the clash and the return stroke.

The whole event leading up to the clash in the lab takes only seconds, if even that long, but the instant the actual time hits the DART, the trigger time loaded by Emily, lightning cracks. Our steps in the process had become so normal I sometimes took for granted how incredibly amazing their results were.

Though I have described what we do in a few simple steps, it is far from simple. For example, at the fifty thousand-meter level I described Dr. Raines DART, one might think of it as merely the function of entering a time stamp. Where that may be the simplistic task carried out, the science behind being able to take that time entry and sync it with actual time in its continuum, is arguably the greatest scientific discovery known to humankind.

The time stamp itself represents humanity's translation of time into a measurable value. The translation, however, is merely an invention by man to satisfy his need to try to control things. Actual time knows no measure but runs on a never-ending continuum. Dr. Raines genius was his understandings of the need to, in essence, sew man's measurement to its corresponding point on the ethereal time's path in the continuum. The science behind this discovery is so complex it gets lost in the flash of the results it enables.

But it does enable the results. And thinking back on yesterday's ordinary chain of events, I recalled our postrun reporting session. It is in our post run sessions where Emily would write her notes in the journal. It was then that she would post her typical entries consisting of the time stamp used, the time span from DART entry to lightning, various other parameter settings, and finally the resulting power captured from the lightning.

Thinking on this and actually recalling a memory of my own, I remembered seeing Emily at her desk after yesterday's run and writing in her journal. At least I thought it was a memory from yesterday. It was such a common sight for me to see, however, that it was difficult to be certain. Regardless, the hair raised on my arms as I realized how impossible this turn of events seemed. The journal I held in my hand had nothing on yesterday's page but the message I had burned.

Knowing what I knew about time's connection with lightning, what I remembered about Emily's entering her notes the previous day, and what I saw in that journal in my hands now, the resulting conclusion on what had happened this morning was both simple and beyond comprehension. It was, however, the only logical explanation I could conceive. The culmination of all the evidence pointed me to an understanding of just what had occurred this morning in the lab. Though a complete accident, I had inadvertently, yet successfully carried out the first tap into the time continuum. I had gone back in time and touched the past—the results of which I now held in my hand, a journal from the past with a message burned on it by my pen from the future.

As the pieces fell into place, my next logical question to myself was, *Why that day? Why that time?*

With this thought, I realized I had a question I had to ask Emily. This realization acted as an alarm clock, signaling to wake me and bring me back to present reality. Snapping out of my thought trance, I found I was still sitting on the floor just inside the door of the flat, and Emily and Emerson were still sitting there beside me.

They too seemed to have fallen into meditative states of their own.

Having looked at the clock on the wall, I estimated a good hour and a half must have passed.

I finally spoke, "Emily, when you key in the DART parameter, what does the program do with that setting?"

Emily sat there frozen. After all the commotional trauma of the morning, she had probably allowed herself to succumb to nature's protective mechanisms, calming her into the meditative state. That is a good thing, and she actually looked calm but was still out of it.

I looked over to Emerson. He looked catatonic. A drop of drool fell from his chin to rejoin the collection that had formed on his knee.

Turning back to Emily, I realized it would take more than me just asking her a question to snap her out of her trance. I gingerly grabbed her arm with one hand and, with the other, gently directed her face, and thus her eyes, toward mine as I calmly repeated the question. "Emily … Emily, when you key in the DART, what does the program actually do with that setting?"

Looking into her eyes, I saw my own reflection and reminded myself how there was where I always wanted to be, in her eyes.

Then, as she acknowledged my having asked her a question, she reverted back to the last question I had remembered her asking earlier, only now in a much calmer tone, "Josh, what happened?"

"I'm beginning to understand but am still following the trail of considerations and questions to lead me to the answer. I'll explain what I have figured out, but I first need your help to complete my theory. When you enter the DART into the system prior to a run, what exactly do you know happens with that information?"

She stared back for a moment, but the connection of my question to her in-depth knowledge of the programming was the key to bringing her back. She gave me her typical fifty thousand-foot explanation that resembled what I already knew, but then the final sentence of her explanation hit home and led me to my next question.

She ended with an analogy to explain how her entry and resulting programming influenced our connection to actual time. "It puts a crease in the time continuum at that synced point, thus triggering what Dr. Raines documented as the time continuum bending to where it rubbed against itself. In the third dimension, we know that, when positive and negative ions clash, it creates lightning, but that is only one perspective. From a fourth dimensional perspective, friction occurs when time rubs against time. In the fourth dimension, it is the friction of the time continuum scraping against itself that generates lightning."

"Does that time setting get erased? Or do we simply override it when you enter the next one and we perform the next run?"

"We have never had reason to reset anything, so I imagine the time setting would be in place until we overrode it. Why?"

Her response was just the answer I had been looking for.

"Em, help me wake Emerson from his coma. I have an amazing story to tell." Shaking the journal still in my hand, I added, "I believe I know what happened, and it is nothing short of amazing."

It would take ten minutes to bring our friend back to reality—throughout which he apparently fought an imaginary adversarial ostrich, claiming it had tried to steal his pomegranate. Then there was the dance sequence he broke into.

While I believed I had made an amazing discovery involving tapping into time, I had no explanation for Emerson other than he is Emerson.

It then took the next several hours for me to formulate and convey an explanation for the event that had occurred when lightning struck earlier that morning. At least we had the time. After all, only a disgruntled maintenance man named Howard had to report to work in the lab that day.

I looked at the clock. It was now after 8:00 p.m., and we were exhausted. The effort of mentally wrapping our arms around the concept of reaching through time had worn us out.

Many things had come out of our brainstorming effort. One question I had asked Emily was why she had not noticed the journal smoking sooner. She indicated that it had not started smoking until she'd opened it up. It was as if oxygen hitting the page had triggered the smoky response.

Emily also revealed that, had she realized it had been a message through time, she would probably have gone immediately to Professor Rancor with it. Not knowing it was a message through time, she had just known it was a message from me, so she'd waited until she could come to see me for answers. Also, as it turned out, Emily *had* forgotten to get her journal yesterday.

She had forgotten the journal because she had not had it with her in the control center during the final run but had left it on her desk. As it was our last run of the day, she was in a hurry to leave and had simply forgotten to retrieve it.

It was not until later that evening when she remembered and returned to the lab to retrieve the journal. It was then that she had first opened it to write down the last run's parameters and notes. Finding my message, and assuming it was just a prank, she'd decided she would wait until this morning to ask me about it. Tired and distracted by the smoking page, she had forgotten why she'd come back to get it in the first place. As if her thoughts on it through the night were a flame festering to become a fire, by the time she got to the flat to ask me, her emotions had escalated to confused anger.

The only other person in the lab Emily could have seen at the time she was leaving would have been Professor Rancor. She had seen the professor when she'd come in but, thankfully, not when she left; therefore, she had not told her of what she'd found.

The greatest revelation we made in our energies was recognizing that we'd had the technical capabilities in place to do this for a while now, only had not known it. We had always keyed in a time to trigger lightning but never realized that the time we entered literally acted as a direct connection to an address of sorts on time's continuum. When lightning occurred in the lab, our time stamp provided conduit to its corresponding actual time in the time continuum. It made sense now why we'd never realized it. We were always working in the now—real time.

I believed what had happened earlier that morning was the lightning struck, but the time stamp imprint we had made was still from the setting Emily had input the previous day. Therefore, instead of the lightning tapping into the time continuum at the actual time synchronized with real time as we previously had it, it tapped into the actual time synced with the time stamp of the previous day.

A side thought, but this also meant that the power had to have been on at the time. The memo distributed regarding the maintenance being done indicated the power would be shut off periodically.

If my theory rang true, I realized that, had I ventured into the control center while in this fourth dimension of time, I would have found the three of us sitting there in it. That was why the lab still looked empty at that time. I had not thought anything of it at the time because I was the only person in the lab this morning, so I was not expecting to see anyone else there anyway.

I think the control center was out of scope of fourth dimensional reach anyway.

The reasoning seemed logical, and with its acceptance setting in with the exhaustion, we decided to call it an early evening. The plan had been to get some sleep and reconvene at the lab the next morning with fresh minds to attempt to validate what had occurred.

Emerson went straight to bed and fell asleep instantly, as in the moment his head hit the pillow. It was as if his head hit the pillow so hard the impact knocked him unconscious.

The next morning, I would learn that, with the exhaustion, sleep came easily enough for Emily as well. I, however, could not stop my mind. It was like a runaway train, and I could not regain control of it until I had solidified our next course of action. Lack of sleep, the price to be paid for perpetual thinkers, but I was finally able to drift into a very light and very brief slumber.

— CHAPTER 19 —

Sunday, October 10, 2021

W HEN I WOKE THE NEXT MORNING, I WAS STILL RIDING THE ENERGY wave of what I believed to be a major discovery. It's amazing how a major event and revelation can inject you with enough power to trump the very exhaustion that existed because of it.

Emily was supposed to come back to the flat at 8:00 a.m. The three of us would pick up where we'd left off the previous night trying to figure out what to do next. Apparently, she could not wait, for it was barely 7:00 a.m., and she was already knocking on the door.

Emerson answered, still in only his boxers and with his robe half on. Even he seemed alert and eager to get this new adventure started.

Emerson plopped back onto his ever-familiar perch in his gaming chair, and Emily joined me over by the coffee table, where I sat on my knees overlooking the thoughts I had thrown on paper.

The TV was not on, and the collection of well-weathered comics and graphic novels that normally littered the sorry excuse for a coffee table, had been cleared as well. On its sticky and rutted surface now sat my quickly drawn timelines, flow charts, parameter lists, and notes. It was the completion of penning these items that allowed me to get the nearly forty minutes of so-called sleep I could muster.

I had spent the whole of the previous evening formulating a plan, and it was now time for me to share it. I must have looked the part, sleepless yet informed, as Emily and Emerson sat silently anticipating the results of my labor.

"First and foremost," I began, "we should *not* tell anyone else about what happened yesterday, what we now think occurred, or what we're planning to do about it. Though we're struggling to grasp the base-level impact the single event that occurred yesterday presented, we have to respect the big-picture impact of the overall discovery. The effect of this discovery is nothing short of astronomical—and equally dangerous. For these reasons, I recommend the following course of action.

"We need to investigate and test what enabled what I can only logically describe as a dip into the past. But in doing so, we must change as little of our routine and behavior as possible. I think there are only two things we need to change to do so.

"First, Emily, we'll just have you forget"—I aired the double quotes gesture—"to change the DART setting. This way, we can continue to test with a plausible error to convey should anyone suspect otherwise. This change alone will allow us to continue to tap back into time and, more importantly, to a specific time when we know no one else was in the lab. Equally important"—now directed toward Emily—"we know that your journal *was* there. We'll use your journal as proof of the theories tested.

"The second change, and an incredibly scary one, is that when we perform a run, I'll need to be where I was when the lightning struck yesterday, instead of with you two in the control center."

I was not kidding about how scary this was. Yesterday's experience was a complete accident, and I'd had no idea it was going to happen and, therefore, no reason to be afraid. The thought of knowingly placing myself directly outside the lab's core when I knew we were going to be inviting lightning sounded insane even now, after having realized I'd survived the accident unscathed.

"I thought a lot last night about how I could've survived the incident and came to the conclusion it was because I was at neither instance of time—neither yesterday's nor the day prior's—but at some ethereal time in between. I was, in essence, in a fourth dimensional lightning sandwich. I was between times, therefore in between the lightning that struck in either of them. Had I been at either instance, I would've felt the full brunt of the respective lightning that struck and wouldn't likely be alive now. It's also for that reason, I feel I will continue to survive if I place myself there again."

I tried to look like I was not afraid and that I firmly believed I would be safe. I not only wanted to convince Emily and Emerson of this but was also still trying to convince myself.

After having stated that I would volunteer to expose myself to the elemental and monumental danger of it all, I paused to see if there were any objections or alternatives. All I got back from each, based on the expressions on their faces, was a silent and visually shaken acceptance of the offer.

After a long enough pause to be considered an awkward moment, it was Emily who spoke. "Do you have any specifics on what we can do to validate the testing?"

Thankful for the redirection, I replied, "Yes, I figured I'd keep a dated document on me with your signatures on it, along with statements indicating you knew what I was going to do. That way, I could show it to you when I returned to current time to prove you knew about the resulting change that occurred in the past."

Emily added, "Why don't you write what you're doing in the journal so when I find it smoking, like I did the day before, I won't freak out as much!"

Emily's statement seemed to make Emerson come to life. He broke into a reenactment of her rant from the previous day. He successfully, even if only briefly, melted the fear surrounding the adventure on which we were about to embark.

I would be taking the biggest risk during the experiments, but I believed we would be successful.

I was actually more afraid about being caught. In fact, the scientific and curious desire to be successful was only but a hair greater than the fear of having the success discovered. The idea of successfully mastering tapping into time presented conflicts between what good could be attained and what bad.

Emily's suggestion seemed logical enough at the time. But as time and our first official unofficial test would prove the very next day, we should have put more thought into the specific message and instructions I would burn into her journal.

The first and accidental time I burned a message in her journal, she recognized it only as a message from me, and the burning of it as some kind of prank. That first time, a personal message was all it was intended to be.

This second and intentional message through time, however, carried with it my message to her and how I was doing it. She did not respond the same way because she realized, as I had told her in the message, it had been written through time.

This may not have been a problem in and of itself. But as it was more than just a personal message from me, she felt compelled to share it with Professor Rancor.

I should have told her in the message not to let the professor know. As it turned out, I should also have put more thought into what I should not have written in the journal. Hindsight can be not only twenty-twenty, but as we would find out, it can also be downright painful.

Not even a week had passed since my second run through time.

The mistakes I made in not writing what I should have (do not tell the anyone else, not even the professor) and writing what I should not have (indigo lights, on violet evenings, yellow orange undertones) had so quickly altered the courses of our futures.

When Emily got the message this second time, much had transpired as before. She had still forgotten her journal in her haste that afternoon. She had still returned later that evening to retrieve it, finding only Professor Rancor at the lab. She had still only discovered the message upon opening it.

But because this message was more than just personal, and especially because the message shed light upon the fact it had been written through time, Emily could not keep to herself her reaction in finding it. This time as she left, she made her way toward the professor's office while trying to decide whether to share what had occurred. Emily decided to simply say goodbye to Professor Rancor, but the professor noticed the distressed look on her face. It had not taken much inquiring to cause Emily, who was legitimately anxious, to let the cat out of the bag.

Immediately upon coming into work on Monday, Emily, Emerson, and I were called into Professor Rancor's office, where I had no choice but to tell her everything I knew. I started by explaining how it had only been in due diligence to solidify the evidence of what had occurred before turning the lab's world upside down that I had not shared the discovery with her immediately.

The professor listened to my story in complete amazement. She sat quiet the whole time I spoke, but I could see her scientific mind buzzing while she took in all the information pertinent to both the first accidental run and our subsequent second run.

I didn't know how, having first learned of the event Saturday night from Emily, Professor Rancor had managed to wait until Monday to learn the details.

Her first remark after I had completed telling her what we had learned, pointed out how, from a scientific perspective, both runs had been successful. She followed immediately with how incredibly astounded she was.

I trusted the professor, and though I would have preferred to keep the findings close to just Emily, Emerson, and me, Professor Rancor was the next person I would trust with the discovery. I knew the professor well enough to know she respected the implications of such a discovery and would do her best to handle it appropriately. Her complete understanding and agreement that we should not tell anyone else about it only supported this feeling. In fact, she had even agreed that, had she been in my shoes, she would not have told her professor yet either.

I left the meeting that morning feeling much more comfortable about her knowing than I had when I had initially found out she knew.

The rest of the day proved uneventful. I went home after work confident and happy, relieved we would be able to proceed with both the official project FHM720 and further testing of our new discovery.

Tuesday, the very next day, this confidence proved to have been formed from a false sense of security.

Emerson and I had just entered the lab. Again, we were immediately summoned to Professor Rancor's office for yet another emergency meeting. This was only the second time this had happened to me—to any of us as far as I knew, and yet this was the second day in a row it was happening to us now.

Emerson and I stepped in to find Emily already in there as well. She did not look happy to be there, and it only took a moment for me to realize why. Though Professor Rancor had yet to even speak, she did not need to for us to understand the importance of the news we were just about to hear. All we needed to do was see the Crown's royal insignia on the Crown's royal envelope and document she now held in her hands.

Heaven forbid the king have anything that looked common. Even his paper was so unique it was identifiable on sight—and smell, for that matter. The insignia was stamped in 18-carat gold, the value of which had the king declare that the letter's recipient must have the envelope returned.

Emerson had just closed the door behind him when the professor, with difficulty and in a failed attempt to veil her emotion, began to read the royal document. In literal fear of saying something she would surely regret, she stuck to reading the letter verbatim.

Minus the addressee and addressor formalities, the professor read, "Royally funded Anderson Raines Lab has been assigned the honor of serving its highest majesty, King George VII, in the pursuance of successful completion of Royal Project FHM724. The primary goal of said project is to enable controlled and timely communications being of the benefit of hindsight and extreme security, to His Majesty's eyes only."

The professor paused for a moment but did not look up from the letter. She appeared to be trying to regain control and composure before continuing.

Moments later she resumed. "Project FMH724 is to receive any and all necessary funding and attention essential for success. All resources previously assigned to FHM720 are immediately and effectively pulled and reassigned specifically, solely, and with highest confidentiality to FHM724.

"Under royal order, any and all knowledge of, and participation in the project is limited to the following: Professor Elisabeth Rancor, Joshua Franks, Emily Etheridge, Emerson Flanders, Geoffrey Talbrook, and Jeremy Bilkes. Should any additions to this list be required, only a direct line request from Professor Rancor to His Majesty, and upon His Majesty's approval can grant them. A secure direct line of communication with priority has been granted for said purpose.

"All approved participants are required to sign this document, recognizing their commitment to their duties and the project's nondisclosure requirements. Any disclosure of information surrounding this project to anyone outside of the above-approved list will be considered an act of treason against the Crown and will result in immediate execution of the traitor(s)."

Upon completion of reading it, the professor passed the document and a pen to me.

It was then, and with the weight of having to sign my life to further and precarious servitude to the Crown, when I saw a sticky note on the document. It read simply, "Meet me tonight, 8:00 p.m., at Chancellor's."

I looked up startled and received a hushed nod of acknowledgment from the professor. After signing directly below where I had seen the professor had already signed, I discreetly nudged Emily and handed over the document and pen. Emerson looked over her shoulder and saw the note and then Emily's "shush" look. Emerson had seen that look enough to know what it meant. Emily gave him that look every time I would fall into a deep thought to solve a problem. Emerson being Emerson, loud and full of nervous energy like spittle on a griddle, had effectively grown to respond accordingly to the signal.

After we had all signed the document, Emerson returned it to the professor. Though the professor had not read it, we could see where there were further instructions on the document, addressed specifically to her, to hand deliver the completely signed document to the king.

The professor said nothing else but dismissed us to our duties and to a long and stressful day dealing with our new assignments and royal pains.

Though I knew I had to contain it for my own survival, I was enraged. The selfish king had somehow already learned of our discovery and had pulled us from doing noble work on FHM720 to focus on increasing the power of the world's most powerful man.

We went from fighting tooth and nail for appropriate funding to provide an alternative and cheap power source for the people to being handed an open royal checkbook requiring us to provide an all-expense-required increased power source for the king.

To add to the misery, I thought of who we were tasked to work with on this assignment. Jeremy Bilkes was an excellent programmer, though I would have preferred to work with Emily's friend Samantha.

Samantha had started working FHM720 with us but was demoted after taking the rap for programming errors early on. The whole thing seemed shady and unbelievable. At the time, it had seemed a story in and of itself. I still believed Samantha was one of the best programmers we had, second only to Emily.

In some ways, I actually felt happy for Samantha, as she had luckily been spared from working on this project. FHM724 would not be a project most would want their name attached to—that is except for Geoffrey Talbrook. Geoffrey undoubtedly added to the misery. We all knew that, blinded by his ambitions, he would be dangerous to work with on a project with such polarizing visibility as the one we were about to embark on.

Emily, Emerson, Samantha and I had known Geoffrey for years. In our years at school together, we had gotten to see a side of Geoffrey the mentor's never saw. Geoffrey was like the moon. He had a dark side that always faced away from the earthly-grounded teachers. It was a side left visible only to those who sat next to him in class or, even worse, worked with him on projects.

My mind shifted and drifted from anger to curiosity. And 8:00 p.m. could not come soon enough. I was dying to know why the professor was secretly having us meet at Chancellor's. I also wondered if she had shared the invite with any of the other signers, Jeremy or Geoffrey.

— CHAPTER 20 —

C HANCELLOR'S WAS A RUN-OF-THE MILL HOLE-IN-THE-WALL PUB AND restaurant. It was as "not great" as it was "not bad." It was not fancy inside. Nor did it reek of the swill-infested throng so often found in most other pubs located in the western outskirts of George's Cross.

It was because of its nothingness that Professor Elisabeth Rancor had chosen it as the place to meet with Emily, Emerson, and me, whom she now dearly referred to as her "trio." We used to be her "quad' until Samantha's having fallen out of favor.

These days, most in George's Cross had forgotten Chancellor's existed. But to the scientists who had worked at the original lightning lab less than a kilometer west of it, it had been a regular haunt.

The three of us, Emily, Emerson, and I, shared a cab ride that night.

As we rode the lone stretch of Ghinger Road en route to Chancellor's, I recalled the time Professor Rancor had taken her group of young scientists there and treated us each with a root beer.

Though just a root beer, it truly was a rare treat for us.

The group back then had consisted of me, Emerson Flanders, Emily Etheridge, Samantha Edmunds, Geoffrey Talbrook, Jeremy Bilkes, Benedict Windham, and Eli Trussnor.

The latter two had buckled under the pressures of the PURPOSE program. Branded as societal disgraces and proclaimed as N'er-do-wells, they had been sent home by the local program committee to be dealt with by their families.

Secretly, the professor had always told us she hated the program and what it did to the innocent youths. She had also said she knew and hated how the families would be punished by more taxes to compensate for the loss of contribution by their children. I believe it was having witnessed what had happened to Benedict and Eli that had driven her to step in when Samantha's programming failures surfaced. We knew she suspected sabotage, and I bet it had taken every string the professor could pull to get Samantha only demoted to an administrative position.

Emily and I had figured Jeremy Bilkes had to have been the programmer to code in the bugs and, thus, set up Samantha. After all, Jeremy was a brilliant programmer. He was definitely good enough to have successfully hacked Samantha's code, but he didn't have a mean bone in his body to have done such a thing unless under duress. If duress had a face, it would look like Geoffrey Talbrook's. What Geoffrey lacked in scientific skills, he more than made up in ambition and survival instincts.

To cool things down, the professor reassigned Jeremy and Geoffrey to separate responsibilities, leaving the three of us—Joshua, Emily, and Emerson—directly involved with FHM720.

I suppose her belief in us pushed her to take the risk she was now taking by meeting with us secretly. She wanted to meet with us discreetly, and Chancellor's was the perfect place to do so.

We had just pulled into Chancellor's dirt lot and were exiting the cab when we spied her car pulling in.

After a quick round of nervous greetings, the professor asked, "Why did you come in a cab? Is your car OK?"

Emily replied, and in a hushed tone, "We were concerned about driving the GIV" (government-issue vehicle). "It gets tracked everywhere you drive it." Then she added and much more dramatically, "Only a few days ago, we were a bunch of nobodies, but somehow the king's caught wind of our scientific endeavors. I think our suspicions are more than warranted."

Nervously, I glanced around the lot. Our cab had parked behind us. The driver appeared distracted by his own conversation on the cab radio, and there were no other people in sight.

The professor mumbled something as we turned to enter the pub, and though she had her back to me, I swear she had indicated we were more right about our suspicions than we knew.

Once inside the pub, we saw what a bad friend time had been to the establishment. It was darker than I remembered, and aside from the two patrons at the bar whose builds wrapped around the stools they were sitting on as if they had grown attached to them like barnacles on the bottom of a ship, or moss on a boulder by a stream, the place was empty.

We sat ourselves in a booth hidden from view, as if in a place like this it would matter.

Using napkins found on the table, Emily and I began wiping the table off. It was not so much dirty as it was dusty.

The professor offered to buy a round of root beer and, upon seeing the three of us nod in agreement, headed up to the bar to order. Though we were all now over the drinking age of eighteen, I think the memory of the last time she had offered years before had warmed us up to another round of the same. I looked over at Emerson and saw he had lit up at recalling the happy memory. It was one in a short list for the three of us in our teens.

Before the drinks arrived, the professor could only manage small talk. The air about us was tense with uncertainty—both ours as we wondered why the professor had called us together there and probably hers as well, as to whether she was doing the right thing.

Emerson, as usual, got us to laugh as he recalled how, on his previous visit here, the floor had been so sticky he'd spent the evening traipsing around entertaining himself as his shoes belched the sound of Velcro separating.

The bartender slogged by and then plunked the drinks on the table. He said nothing, just turned and slogged his way back to the nothingness we had apparently disrupted.

It was then the professor started to convey why she asked us to join her there. As fast as the laughter had dissipated, and as if someone had flipped a switch somewhere to trigger it, our moods turned a somber color that blended in with the establishment, matching the atmosphere's grays and melancholic hues. If where we sat left us hidden, the color of our present mood left us camouflaged.

She began with an apology. "First, I want you three to know how incredibly sorry I am that things have come to this. Our current situation has only come about as the result of an accidental, albeit incredible

143

discovery. By itself, it is a wonderful thing. However, this discovery has somehow become known by the last person in the world we would have wanted to learn of it. What I am about to share with you must not go beyond your eyes and ears."

Simultaneously, Emily, Emerson, and I glanced at each other. I could tell by even Emerson's demeanor we all understood the gravity of the situation.

The professor continued, "My assumption is you might think I had revealed the breakthrough somehow, directly or indirectly, to the king."

She looked at each of us, as if for confirmation, and I would say, at least from me, she had gotten it.

"I want to make sure you guys know that I did not tell anyone about your"—now directing her eyes to me—"amazing discovery."

In my case, the professor was right with her assumption. I had assumed she had shared the find, though I figured it was done merely to fulfill her sanctioned responsibilities. I had not even thought it could have been done otherwise. I didn't know about Emily but doubted Emerson had even given it any thought.

She continued, "When I received the RPA" (the Royal Proclamation of Assignment) "you had to sign earlier, it was the first I had learned the king had known about it. I was quite literally blown away. I know none of you three would have told anyone else. I have been thinking about this ever since I got the RPA, and I believe the fact he found out, and so quickly, could only mean one thing—"

I then blurted in discovery what should have been obvious, "Your office is bugged." I shrunk in my chair as I realized how naive we were to royal reach. But as I had figured the professor had told the king of our finding, I had not suspected something so devious. I made a mental note to check our apartments for bugs as well.

She quickly looked around to make sure no one had heard and then continued, "It gets worse," she continued.

She then proceeded to pull a newspaper page from her purse. She also retrieved and unfolded a paper she had hidden in her blouse. Judging from the way it had been folded and stashed, it contained something she did not want anyone to know she had. Once unfolded, I recognized it was a copy of the FHM724 RPA.

As she flattened the copy on the table, I spied some highlighting on the document and noticed the professor's hands were now shaking. She then opened the newspaper to a page that revealed an article with some highlighting of its own, including images circled. The date on the newspaper showed the article had made yesterday's headlines.

The headline of the article read simply, "Fiery Crash Claims Three Lives." The professor's hands were still shaking as she pointed to the first highlighted picture. "I know her ... knew her. She is ... was Hillary Jane Ellison, the royal drafter for the king. I met her back when I was petitioning approval to rebuild the newly designed lightning lab. She never got involved until a final draft of a document was needed and only when it was either written on behalf of, or ready to be submitted to the king. The money needed to finance the lab needed the king's approval, and she had been assigned to draft my submission."

To confirm further connection, she now pointed to the back of the RPA and specifically to the initials highlighted at the bottom of the document. "These are her initials; she drafted this document as well.

"I know the paper claims this was an accident, but I do not believe it."

Emily, eyes and jaws wide open from what she was seeing and hearing, finally spoke. "Do you really believe she was murdered because of what she knew about our new project?"

"I know ... I know, this alone could just be a coincidence, but take a close look at the two men who also died in this supposed accident. Do they look familiar to any of you?"

Now focusing on the images of the men, I realized I did recognize the first of the two but could not place from where.

"It took me a while," she continued, "but I finally made the connection. A couple months ago, I had requested some facility maintenance to better accommodate monitoring the power levels stored in the battery cells surrounding the lab. This request was not unlike any of the other countless requests I have had to submit. As it is a government-owned lab, I have to request these things through our sponsoring government agency. The two men pictured here were two of the men sent by the agency in response to this specific request. I only recognize them because they were not the usual workers I had seen before but had only first appeared toward the end of the job about two weeks ago."

Now pointing to the man pictured on the right, she added, "I recognize him because I recall thinking how he looked a lot like Anderson Raines.

"I now believe they were only brought in to install cameras and bugs in my office and who knows where else in the lab, so they could monitor our activities and progress—to make sure we were making good on the government's investment. And if I am right, they were killed because of what they had since overheard, as I would bet, they were also tasked as the government's eyes and ears."

Looking back to the image of the man on the left, I remembered where I had recognized him. The memory came back as the professor had pointed out he had been at the lab.

Now pointing at him I said, "I remember where I saw this guy. It was at the lab last Saturday, the day of the discovery. I ran into him in the main hallway right outside the lab."

I did not recognize the name under the picture, but surmised if what we now suspected were true, the name I had seen on the coverall patch would not have been his.

Thinking of the coveralls jarred yet another memory. I added, "At the time, I had just thought it peculiar, but I also now remember when the man had turned to leave, I spied a suit and tie underneath his coveralls."

The professor summarized, "It is too coincidental that these three should end up dead in the same single fiery vehicle crash. This crash was no accident, and I can only guess that the king must have ordered them killed, no questions asked, to reduce the number of people who knew about his new power project. As if the king does not have enough power in this world, he is hungry for even more. If he can manage a means to convert hindsight into foresight, he will have found a way to at least temporarily satisfy that hunger."

For the next couple of minutes, the four of us sat silent. We stared at the documents in front of us as we absorbed the tangibility they provided to the professor's theory. Ultimately, they were all we needed to believe.

Emerson broke the silence, "We're dead."

"We are only safe as long as the king still needs us to complete and implement the project. Correction," I replied. "We are only safe as long as the king believes he still needs us."

Again, we sat through a long period of silence.

Emily finally spoke, "Why not convince the king that it was Geoffrey Talbrook, not Joshua, who made the discovery. Tell him we know nothing about it. Besides, Geoffrey is hungry for the attention!"

"I would not wish this on anyone, but believe me, if the king did not already have your names attached to it, I can think of a few 'Geoffries' out there I would prefer to put on it to make sure it would fail."

I chimed in, "The problem is, the king knows too much about this already. In fact, we had better be very careful moving forward, because I'm afraid, we are all now under his all-seeing royal microscope."

"I agree. Supporting my fears on this," the professor continued, "I have led and worked on royal programs for over twenty years. I have never, however, been involved in anything that ever drew the undivided attention of the king. This project is all his, and everything that comes of it is for him. He has a direct interest in everything about it, and that interest landed me my first encounter with him. I believe the whole encounter was intended to intimidate, to make sure I knew how much he knew. We are dealing directly with the most powerful man in the world. He has unlimited resources and a thirst for even more power, and worst of all, we now have his immediate attention."

Suddenly, the professor shuffled in her seat nervously, as if she was just going to get up and leave.

She finally added, "I remember one final thing the king added at the end of our one-sided conversation. I absolutely hate to say this. But for your safeties, I had better."

Now looking specifically at me, she continued, "The king made specific reference to the message you burned into Emily's journal. He had interpreted it to be one of affection and reminded me that he did not feel it appropriate that a relationship should interfere with his project. In his own words, I believe he put it, 'Their relationship is a fire that should not kindle lest it burn holes in the landscape of progress.' That was all he said, but it was enough."

Glancing back and forth between Emily and I, she added, "I am very sorry to have tell you both this. I think nothing but the best of the both of you and personally love learning that you have found each other. But I fear it would be dangerous to even give the appearance that you are in a relationship. I think the thing I hate most about this is how this"—she glanced around for turned ears—"stupid and senseless, self-serving, royal pain in the arse project is stepping on the petals of such a beautiful and blossoming relationship!"

Her voice had actually risen, and now we were all concerned. It was evident the king's last request had struck a personal nerve with the professor but even more evident that a royal wedge had just been driven between Emily and me.

As if the tear from Emily's eye was a counterweigh, as it fell down her cheek, she rose from her seat in the booth. Wiping the tear, she excused herself from the table, grabbed her coat, and made for the door.

I felt a sudden fury. Meeting Emily was the best thing that had ever happened to me. Now this selfish, greedy king who had already drained his countries to serve his every whim, felt it was important enough to step on my only chance for happiness.

The professor, after seeing Emily's departure, and probably my anger flare, knew we had to get out of there. She may not have actually thought there was anyone there who cared, but that did not afford us the luxury of making a scene.

She wisely asked Emerson to help her get me out to the car without exploding while she took care of the bill.

Emerson succeeded, but when the professor came out, she found Emily crying out in the parking lot, with me trying to console her. I just wanted to hold her, but she refused.

As if she intended her scream to reach the royal ears, she shouted up, "Nooooo! Heaven forbid we stoke the relationship flames that make us happy! Nooooo! We would not dare want to burn any fucking holes in his royal fucking landscape!"

She continued ranting, and though I only wanted to console her, now with very real fear that someone would hear, I finally pulled away as my attempts only drew more of her yelling, "Stop stoking! Stop stoking!"

Emerson stepped in, and in a way only Emerson could, he managed to distract her from the anger. Once Emily had calmed down enough, the professor called us a cab.

When the cab got there, Emily, still crying, climbed into the back. Emerson followed, leaving me to sit in the front.

I looked around and noticed how truly isolated we were. Not one car had driven by. Nor could another person be seen outside the establishment. Given our overall situation, if the wrong ears had heard Emily's rant, it could have dangerous consequences. I was just as furious as Emily, if not more, but the fury boiled dangerously inside me. Before I had gotten into the cab, the last thing the professor managed after repeating again how sorry she was, was how she feared for our safety. She begged us to be careful about anything we said or did.

On the way back, I wanted to sit in the back with Emily, to hold her. I knew we would have to distance ourselves to try to manage through this. But was there any opportunity to manage through this? It seemed a futile effort, as we were all on borrowed time anyway. Once the king felt he no longer needed us, we would wind up in our own fiery crash pictures buried in the pages of a newspaper.

It was a long and silent ride home. I wondered if the cab driver could hear the anger boiling inside of us.

— CHAPTER 21 —

Two days later, Thursday, October 14, 2021, 5:00 p.m.

M Y DAY WAS WINDING DOWN. UNDER ROYAL EYES, THE DAYS SEEMED both longer and more stressful. I'd also found that all the wind had been taken out of the sails, as none of us had any desire to help the king. I now wished I had never discovered tapping into the time dimension and was just glad to have made it through this day—or so I had thought.

"Hey, Traveler."

I heard the call but had not turned around, as I had not realized the voice was referring to me. I also did not turn because I had recognized the voice as Geoffrey's. But he repeated himself, only this time flicking me on the shoulder.

"So, Traveler, I got my papers on our new project, our great new secret adventure. Are you going to give me the low down? Or are you going to hoard this for your own, you squelcher?"

I expected nothing less from Geoffrey. The only surprise I got was his referring to me as Traveler, although the way he said it was coated with sarcasm. I had not thought about it so much in that perspective, but in a sense, I had traveled back in time.

"Good morning, Geoffrey. It's always good to see you too."

"Oh, please do away with the false niceties. You dislike me as much as I dislike you, and I hate you. You think you're so smart." Then in character,

"Ooooh, look at me. I am Joshua the Traveler! I tripped and fell into time! Ouch, I just poked myself in the eye with the past!

"Well, Joshua, let me in on your little accident. I'll turn that little accident into something glorious."

Geoffrey was almost right. I did dislike him. He was a blindly ambitious git who could not find his way out of a rabbit hole if he were stapled to the rabbit's arse. But hate was a strong word, and I had never even given enough thought about him to feel anything so strongly.

Now I knew where he stood, but it was no surprise.

If I snapped back, he would only continue, so I tried to keep it official. I had no choice but to try to work with him. Besides, we were in the lab, and as I had learned the hard way, the walls had eyes and ears. He had just gotten there, pulled from another lab and from another project, while I, thankfully, was just about to leave for the day.

Turned now and looking directly into his coal black eyes, I said, "Geoffrey, believe me, I look forward to sticking you on this one. But I'm still trying to validate what I believe prevented the lightning from frying me."

Though I know he did not believe me, I actually meant what I had said. Then a brilliant idea just popped into my head. I could just let Geoffrey lead the project. If Geoffrey led the project, it would certainly fail. This was the first thought I had had toward taking an offensive approach. But fear won out, and I'd purged the thought as fast as I'd thought it. Apparently, as much as I hated the king, I was still that much more fearful of him.

"Oh bullocks! Whatever, Traveler. I heard all you did was stand over by the core when lightning struck. I know how to stand by the core, and I know how to make lightning strike. You're no genius, just a right lucky git-bastard."

"You're right about one thing. I was very lucky to have survived. I must tell you, please don't try anything rash. I have some theories and will get everything I find documented and available to you as soon as possible. I have a speech I have to give tomorrow at school, and I'm going to the flat to prepare for it but will attend to the documentation straightaway after."

"Right, you hoarding traveler you. You just do that." With that he walked away, and with a saunter that suggested he had just won something.

As for me, I left the lab for the flat as I had told him I would.

At the time of my distraction the morning after my kingly kidnapping, I had only known the details of the events leading to Geoffrey's demise that I had been provided by the king. The king had only shared the bare minimum necessary to make his point.

I had since heard a firsthand account from Jeremy Bilkes.

— CHAPTER 22 —

Friday, October 15, 2021

J EREMY BILKES WALKED INTO THE LAB. IT WAS JUST AFTER 5:45 A.M., and he was not due in until 6:00, so was early as usual.

"Jeremy Bilkey, it looks to be just you and me! I wonder how much work the one and a half of us'll get done."

Geoffrey Talbrook. Jeremy cowered at the voice as, under his breath, he corrected his last name in response, "Bilkes."

He would much rather work with Emily or Samantha.

He had been supporting programming on FHM720 but had just received his papers on his new assignment to project FHM724. It looked like, for his part anyway, code was code, and his work would not change much.

He had been OK with that until hearing Geoffrey approach.

"I have plans for us today, Germy, big plans!"

Jeremy hoped if he ignored Geoffrey, he would go away. He logged into his computer to check the project docket, secretly hoping, though he knew he'd be working with Geoffrey, there'd at least be some distance between them. Jeremy should have known better than to hope. He knew hope was fool's gold, and any such fantasy was as hollow as the *o* in the word.

"I thought you weren't scheduled in until noon, Geoffrey, when Joshua joins us after his schooling?"

"Oh, you don't think we need to wait for that balloon head, do ya? Don't you see what we have in front of us here? No, I came in early; I've been here since five. Hell, I woke up the rooster so he could wake up the farmer!"

"What are you up to now, Geoffrey?"

"Nothing yet, but we'll reach our own grand heights this morning, you and I."

"Look, Geoffrey, I don't know enough about this program yet to be out there cavalier'n it. It's too risky."

"Ah come on now, Jeremy. Here you are, handed an opportunity to succeed, make your family proud. Besides, your part is no different than it was on your previous project. I've read the papers on both; I've done my homework."

"I have my instructions for FHM724, and I'm sure you have yours. I'm in operations, and you're the programmer—"

"You are a backup in operations, and I, a supporting programmer who will do what he, as a supporting programmer, is formally instructed to do."

Completely ignoring Jeremy, Geoffrey tossed his version of how their day's assignment should go. Jeremy only looked at it enough to notice it reminded him of the projects he'd been forced to do as a child in the PURPOSE program.

Geoffrey continued, "Look, it's really simple. You load the date, and I stand over there!" he said, pointing to the core. "You have an opportunity here to succeed big; you don't want to fail, do you? You know, as acting program manager in balloon head's absence, I report on our activities. Somehow the words *missed* and *opportunity* are not the two words I think you want written together. Why I can spell those two more efficiently as one word, *failure*."

"You are messing with things you don't understand, Geoffrey."

"You are messing with failure, Jeremy! Now get over there in the control center and do what you already know how to do. I'll be standing over by the core, soon on the other side of time, rewriting history."

Jeremy was rattled. Images of his family appeared. He could see the pain in their eyes while paying the cost for his failure. Without further thought but for his family, he walked mindlessly into his place in the control center.

Geoffrey had not shared with Jeremy his intention to write a deliberate message, sure to be seen by the king, only with his name as the successful initiator. He had also not shared with Jeremy the date he wanted him to dial into. So, Jeremy, who only knew from his previous project's work to load the current date into the computer, did just that.

As the control center had no windows, Jeremy was used to not seeing anything of what nature's fury did on the other side of its main walls.

He was also accustomed to hearing the muffled thunder from within the control center. Thanks to the soundproofing walls of the control center, it was muffled to a dull rolling rumble, as if the lightning were kilometers away.

He was, thankfully, spared the sights and sounds of what happened to his controlling, glory-seeking coworker. The scream alone would have haunted him for years, add to that the sight of Geoffrey being fried to a crisp standing outside the core just on the other side of the control center. Together, they were the parts list used to build nightmares.

— CHAPTER 23 —

Saturday, October 16, 2021
Joshua Franks

I WOKE UP THIS MORNING, EYEING THAT I HAD A GOOD HOUR BEFORE the alarm was to go off.

I tried to roll back over, as I really wanted that hour's sleep. But instead, an unanswered question had popped into my head. How had I survived my dive into the time continuum unscathed, but Geoffrey fried? I know Geoffrey wanted glory's light, and though I would not wish what happened to him on anyone, sometimes you get what you ask for.

I may not get that hour sleep I so badly need, but at least I had found a distraction to pass the time.

Since I had learned of Geoffrey's demise, I had spent a lot of time wondering why the lightning had killed him but spared me. I still believed my original assessment best explained why, and Geoffrey's example only supported it. What saved my sorry arse was the luck in the fact the system still had the coordinates of the previous day's lightning in it, directing my connection to it. I was saved by the difference in time between the lightning that occurred and the one the system directed me to.

In Geoffrey's case, he had Jeremy follow the normal procedure for triggering the environment in the core that would invite lightning to strike. Therefore, he must have had Jeremy load the real-time coordinates, leaving no time buffer for him between lightning strikes. In essence his "from" lightning and his "to" lightning were the same, so he'd been fried by both.

I rolled over and looked back at the clock. My self-distraction had succeeded, but the alarm had two minutes yet before it would sound. I turned the alarm off, as it was close enough to the time for me to get up but growled under my breath at being robbed even those two precious minutes sleep. Apparently, I had already forgotten the previous couple hours I missed while mentally reliving my past.

The date was Saturday, October 16, 2021. It was also my birthday, my twenty-first birthday, and I had a train to catch to visit my parents. Going to see my parents was always a trip I both longed for and dreaded. I guess after the day I had before, royal kidnapping and all, I was actually a little more happy than usual to be getting away, even if just for the weekend.

Within an hour, I had showered, dressed, and was ready to leave for the train station. I was wearing the same shirt I had worn the previous day, as it still smelled of Emily. On top of that, my mind had been too occupied to remember to pack a complete change of clothes; I would find myself wearing the shirt again tomorrow.

I headed out the door, bag in hand, for the nearly two-kilometer walk, with the first block taking me down Fusilier Road and then turning north up Hillsborough Avenue and onto the train station.

Along the way, I passed countless flats identical to Emerson's and mine, all homes of the thousands of other government employees working in the city—rectangular buildings of thousands of bricks put together to make them look like one giant brick with windows.

The train station was conveniently located within five kilometers of any government home in our burb. It was a centrally located hub to pick up George's Cross government employees or drop them off from where a train had picked them up in their respective villages. It was nothing glamorous to look at but was functional.

I thought of how nice I had heard the station looked in the city, the one used by the "thin upper crust," or TUCs (pronounced *tucks*), as we liked to call them. The only way into TUC-dom was through bloodline, either by birth or marriage.

They lived well off their statuses alone, having done nothing to earn their gains.

Best not to dwell on the layers of society. I was just about to embark on a trip from a station that was merely functional to a village that was barely habitable.

It had been a year since I had last made this trip.

There was always exactly a year's time between trips. It was no coincidence, because the only day you could take off for personal use was your birthday. It was also, for that reason I suspect, that I always recognized most of the people on the train. They must share the same birthday.

The government did not pay for the trip, but merely allowed you the day off. You weren't even officially told you about this rare allowance. Therefore, if no one was nice enough to unofficially share it with you, you would just go to work like every other Monday through Saturday.

I got to the station in time, boarded the train, and did everything I could to help get this trip rolling, which amounted to nothing more than wishful thinking.

The train, apparently, had not shared the same sense of urgency, as it was a good hour before it finally made its way out of the station.

I would spend the next two hours staring out the window, trying to ignore the ladies gabbing on my left and the man snoring in front of me. As with each time before, I watched as the ornate buildings of the glorious royal city of George's Cross bled into barely habitable communes and huts. These huts, tucked in tiny villages, were the homes of the people whose families built and paid for the cities, paid with their blood, sweat, and tears.

Once you got past the homes of the workers, the city was rich with all a royal city was allowed to support its government, not unlike the many other royal cities of its kind throughout the country of New England. I would expect George's Cross was even more well adorned than the others I had heard about, as within its limits was Wellington Palace, the primary residence of the royal family.

Almost instantly, upon reaching the outskirts of George's Cross, the landscape progressively degraded, as if each outer neighborhood was a stair down a steep stairwell. Witnessing this societal chasm was always such a sad reminder of the have-all or have-none world we lived in. As with each previous birthday, I had spent the past year trying to forget, but no matter how badly I felt about my life of servitude to the Crown, I was reminded how it was so much worse for the poor people in these villages. I was spoiled by comparison.

After numerous stops in the line of villages that, in the big picture, more resembled stepping-stones to the cities, I had finally reached the well-worn stepping-stone I knew as the village of Cloister. Before my required commitment to PURPOSE, I used to call it home, but I had been so young at the time, I only had memories of it as the home of my parents, Nolin and Bethel Franks.

Just the thought of their names, especially my father's, triggered memories. The first was of my mother, stressing how important it was that my middle name was Nolin. That I was named after my father's first name was a given, but the reminder would always be followed with how the name had been passed down for over two centuries. Lastly, she would state how our last name, Franks, "is all we have to take to the banks." I had never understood why she said that. And every time I'd pressed for an explanation, she'd never elaborated further beyond suggesting I just take her word for it.

My first name, Joshua, was more enigmatically derived from biblical lore. She never provided more specifics to its meaning or origin. But when I visited when I was younger, she would always tell me stories with the character Joshua cast as their hero.

I had never understood why my parents put so much importance in our family name, but beyond me, it was the only thing that they valued. I was resolved to believe it was because it was all they had that as truly theirs.

As I stepped off the train, it felt like I stepped back a century in time. What made it worse was knowing I stood in the "progressive" end of the village. I still had a kilometer walk through the village before I would reach my parents' patchwork cabin.

When I finally reached it, I could not believe how it had not appeared to change at all. I guess I have gotten used to how the city seemed to constantly change, and it made me expect to see something different, something new here as well.

By the time I reached the door, I had also reached an emotional low. Realizing I had a tear rolling down my face, I quickly wiped it away and took a moment to pull myself together before knocking. I did not want my parents to feel they had to worry about me; they had enough to worry about just surviving.

Finally, having regained my composure, I knocked on the old wooden door before me. My father, Nolin, answered, and right before my eyes, I witnessed a transformation of about twenty years dropping off his face. Wide eyes and a ridiculously large smile quickly replaced a lifetime's mask of suffering. He lit up at the sight of me at the door, the sight of which warmed me inside; I no longer felt the chill of the October wind whipping on my face as it made its way through the valley.

As if they had practiced the same response, my mother, Bethel, did the same as she stepped out from the musty shadows.

As I stepped in, I stepped directly into their hugging grasps. I tried carefully not to transfer any of the weight of responsibility I felt as the one bright light in their dim lives. It was a responsibility I dared not fail, and fulfilling it would always have me performing as best I possibly could, at whatever I could, to shine brightly for them.

The village of Cloister did not exist on any postal delivery maps. Though many times I had thought to sneak letters to my parents, sending them back with others I knew who returned to this village on their birthdays, I never did so. As far as I knew, my parents could not read.

The annual visit was the only opportunity my parents had to hear from or about me. I would spend the next two hours answering a barrage of questions from my father about what I had been doing the past year. I'd always been amazed at how my father remembered exactly where I had left off from the previous year's visit. It was as if we were merely picking up from where we had left off.

Meanwhile, my mother bounced around busying herself, while always bending an ear toward our conversation and throwing in her own share of questions.

I struggled to avoid telling them anything about FHM724, the king's project. Primarily, I was disgraced by what he had us doing, not to mention revealing anything about it was royally forbidden. I could not even tell my parents about being royally kidnapped. It would draw too many questions about why. And again, it would make my parents worry. So I skirted the whole event.

Instead, I told them of our progress on FHM720—how we had successfully been capturing the power of lightning and were working on the storage and distribution of the power. I reiterated how our hopes were that tapping into this naturally occurring power source may eventually provide affordable power to the villages. At least I still dreamed it would someday, but I kept to myself the fact the project had recently been cast aside.

Another thought leaped into my mind that I immediately suppressed. Never mind the fact that the capability to get traditional forms of electricity out to the villages had already long-existed. The royal cities had had fully implemented power grids for decades, but the king had no desire to spend the money it would have taken to extend that traditional and expensive infrastructure to the outer villages. It was of no benefit to him to do so. FHM720's saving grace was it was comparatively inexpensive, enough for the king to be convinced he would cobenefit from the effort and at a much cheaper cost. Therefore, getting electricity to the villages would merely be a token gesture, giving the king a rare and cheaper opportunity to look good in the eyes of his people.

My mother had listened all the while as she had gathered and thrown together the meager ingredients to make her meat-wish pie.

Both she and my father still wore peculiarly and awkwardly large smiles, and their eyes seemed to water from being held open so wide. They were always glad to see me, but I had never seen them look like this before. Smiling was something they had little reason to ever do, but my visit was the one thing that gave them reason to. While that day's expression conveyed their happiness, it also looked to be physically painful for them. They simply weren't used to using the muscles required to smile. From the looks of it, though, they apparently could not help themselves.

For a brief moment, I likened my parents' smile ability to Professor Jonathan Elders V. As fast as the thought came in, I drove it away. I felt guilty, almost to the point of apologizing for even making any such association between my parents and that poor old sod.

Within the hour, I had sat down to the same tiny old wooden table I had every year with them, for a serving of my mother's heart-filled dinner. It was a good thing she poured so much love into making it, because there was little else in it. Meat-wish pie consisted of water, nut mash, and whatever vegetables you were able to scrounge together, all encrusted in homemade breading.

I noticed my mother had added a pinch of salt to it this year. I had meant to bring them some, as salt was somewhat a luxury in the villages. How selfish of me to have forgotten. When I brought it to her attention how I had noticed the salt she added, she lit up even more, as if she had not already been wearing a painful enough smile.

My heart sank even further, though I could not let on, when she conveyed that she had saved the table salt remaining from last year so she could add it to our dinner this year.

After polishing off a relatively large portion of dinner, I set off to help my father patchwork repair a hole in their roof.

I had told my mother two white lies. For one, I had told her that the food was delicious, and, two, that I had eaten so much I was full. The prior was only a half lie, as, though it did not taste good, it did warm me inside.

The latter I told more because I wanted to make sure they had enough to eat. I knew none would go to waste; they would stretch the leftovers out over the next couple of days. Also, as this was the heartiest batch my mother would allow herself to make all year, it would also be the most nutritious meal for them.

By the time my father and I completed fixing the roof, it had already begun getting dark outside.

We were both chilled to the bone. I was eager to sit by the fire that my mother had built in the old stone fireplace.

Like everything else in the house, the fireplace was handmade. Also like everything else in the house, it was only a reflection of the tools and materials used to make it. Even my father's straightedge was naturally curved.

The fireplace was no different and was but a misshapen build of stones. The stones jutted awkwardly out at the left side of the fireplace. They stuck out just enough to form a place to sit on, with the stones close enough to the fire to be safely warmed. It had always been my favorite place to sit when we had fires. Tonight was no different. Taking my seat there, I believe I wore my own first genuine smile of the trip.

My father and I sat there in silence, warming by the fire.

Within the next twenty minutes or so, my mother finally settled down enough to join us. She had always been a busy bee, generally only sitting down to give her time to think about the next task she could be doing, even though there was little that ever needed done.

She motioned me to join her on the bench on which she and Father always sat.

My father had gotten up again, and I noticed his crazy wide-eyed smile had returned. My father looked as if he could hardly keep himself together as he tried to speak.

It was then that it all started, and I genuinely feared my parents had lost their minds.

— CHAPTER 24 —

STANDING UP BEFORE THE FIREPLACE, MY FATHER BEGAN SPEAKING. His voice was elevated, and he spoke like the words he was saying were tripping over each other, trying to escape his mouth more than just be spoken.

"Joshua Nolin Franks, it's a very special birthday for you." As he spoke, his animated movements, incessant smile, and bulging eyes made him look like a puppet. "You are twenty-one now, and it's finally time. Your ma and I've waited for this moment your whole life. We have something to give you."

I knew this was my annual birthday visit, but as usual, expected nothing but parental love and a warm meal. My parents had nothing, so I had no idea what else they could possibly have to give me. My first thoughts were of concern over what they would have sacrificed to get me anything.

My father made a comical leap toward his tool bin, a simple half barrel he kept his tools in to the far left of the fireplace and near the front door. As he turned, I saw he had retrieved and now wielded a homemade sledgehammer.

For a fleeting moment, I believed he intended to give me the hammer as a gift.

I stared completely speechless and puzzled as I watched my father turn back toward the fireplace, hammer over his shoulder, and motion my mother and I to scoot back—an action my mother had already started doing, while trying to take the bench with her, even with me still sitting on

167

the other end. I had no clue what was going on but instinctively followed suit, lest I find my arse on the floor, no bench beneath me.

I had not realized my mouth was hanging wide open, until my mother reached over to close it.

I turned to her, hoping she could provide a sane explanation for what Father was doing. She not only failed at explaining but bore her own mad smile and wide eyes, only her eyes were illuminated by the fire, which, while still trying to hold my jaw closed, only made matters worse.

Turning my eyes back to my father, I saw he had started what appeared to be practice swings of the heavy hammer, marking where I had just been sitting on the stones to the left of the fireplace.

Again, his macabre, crazed expression lit up by the fire would have had me fearing for my life had he been directing the hammer toward me. Instead, hammer back on his shoulder, he proceeded to clear a wooden bucket, broom, and stoker, as if to provide more swinging room.

Was he about to smash my favorite spot in the hut?

I sputtered, "Wha-what are you doing?" My glance went back and forth between my mother and father, and I found no answers, solace, nor sanity in either.

I repeated the question. And by the time I had made another glance back to my father, he had begun taking a full swing at that left extension of the fireplace.

I leaped into action to stop him, but my mother grabbed my arm and pulled me back down.

The only thing she managed to say legibly, she repeated, "It's OK … Your present … It's OK … Your present … OK … OK."

The pain in her comically stretched smile and insanely wide eyes screamed to me otherwise, but I sat back down having resolved it was the safest thing I could do, aside from run for my life out into the freezing night.

I sat, jaws wide open again in amazement, as my father proceeded to smash away at the side of the fireplace.

A hit spit out the first of many chips of stone, one of which whizzed by my left ear.

My father stopped only long enough for my mother to jump up and throw an old wool blanket over the extension. She immediately sat back down beside me, as if it had been all part of the plan. My father resumed slamming the hammer down. He had completely broken out in a sweat, and stone dust floated all about him.

Their faces were locked in maniacal expressions. My parents had completely lost it.

Again, the thought occurred to me to run for my life. I had no idea what was in store and feared I had already completely lost my parents. At some point, I had started crying.

As I reached the brink of my own sanity, the hammer made a connection with the stone resulting in a huge thud. Apparently, the section my father had been slamming away on had had enough and collapsed.

I was relieved the stone collapsed before my father would.

The only change in my father's demeanor was the added ingredient of exhaustion. He set the hammer down and plunked down as heavily as the hammer next to me into the seat my mother had just cleared as she leaped up to take over.

It all appeared to be part of their grand and mad plan, as she went to work clearing the debris my father had left behind. She removed the now shredded blanket and put broken pieces of stone into the bucket my father had set aside minutes earlier. She looked no less crazy cleaning the mess than my father had making it.

My father was taking long massive breaths, as if he were trying to regain control, fighting to come back. But it sounded as if he were losing.

I had regained enough of my own composure and courage to shout, "What the hell is going on?"

Ignoring my plea, my mother exclaimed, "I have them!"

I could see, amid the stirred stone dust, she was now holding a package in her hands. It must have been heavy, as it balanced and shifted precariously in one arm while she frantically dusted it off with the other.

She stumbled over to my father, who, though still heavily winded, had his arms out. eager to take hold of the package.

I was so shaken by the events, I had forgotten what my father held in his arms was intended to be my birthday present.

Though still struggling to breathe, he spoke. "Joshua," he began, taking pause long enough to sneak in a deep breath, "we've patiently waited your whole life for this moment when we could pass this on to you. We've dreamed of this day," another deep breath, "as what I hold in my hands is the most prized possession our family has ever and probably will ever own. What I'm passing on to you has been handed down a good dozen generations, to each generation's eldest son to be carried forward."

"Before I give you the package, Joshua, I must share some things about your family heritage, things we've never told you before. You've always known your last name as Franks. Publicly, it needs to remain that way. Now I ask your patience. You'll understand more of this in due time. It is most critical, before I give these to you," he said as he struggled to shake the odd package he held tightly in his grip, "that you understand and accept the gravity of owning them."

It had not escaped me that my father had just referred to the package as "these" and "them," plural.

He continued, "I need for you to promise to do what is right by what you're about to receive. You must promise to honor them and strive to do what is right by them, as we've done all these years, protecting them and waiting to pass them on to you. You'll see how, to our family, these gifts represent riches beyond the king's. They represent truth—truth in history, truth in lineage, truth in identity. And we've guarded and should continue to guard these truths with hopes that someday, if and when the world is ever ready to hear them, they can be told again. Son, you're finally at the age to learn your truths. The gifts this package contains hold those truths."

With that, my father handed me the package. My mother simply started crying. They both looked exhausted, but there was still a hint of madness in their eyes and pain in those damned, wicked smiles.

I stared at the package before me. My twenty-first birthday presents and the first material presents I had ever received. They were heavy and shifted within the packaging, which smelled very old and musty. The outside was wrapped in burlap and still covered by the dust and debris from the stone hearth it had been buried in my whole life.

I untied the ropes, securely holding the burlap bag closed around them. Opening the bag from the side, I carefully slid its contents out and into my hands.

The contents were sealed in plastic. I assumed the plastic was to keep them from being ruined by moisture. My question now was not so much *why* they were wrapped in plastic, but more *how*? How had my parents gotten plastic in the first place? I had seen plastic such as this in the city but never anywhere else, certainly never in the village of Cloister and especially never in possession of my parents. Lastly, as the package had been buried there my whole life, they had gotten ahold of this plastic over a lifetime ago, when I should have thought it even more difficult for them to get a hold of any.

These thoughts lasted only as long as it had taken for me to open the sealed plastic enough to discern the contents it protected—books. Wrapped within the plastic were four very old large leather-bound books and, apparently, a fifth, though it was wrapped in even more plastic.

I reached inside the bag and pulled out the top book. It looked very, very old, and on its cover of ornately stamped brown leather was embossed the name "Benjamin Franklin."

After reading it in my head a second and then a third time, I looked back up at my parents to find both of them crying. I was, thankfully, able to recognize their tears were happy ones.

I sensed another new emotional characteristic about my father I had never before witnessed—pride.

"Benjamin Franklin?"

"Yes, Benjamin Franklin. Joshua, you and I are living descendants of Benjamin Franklin. Our last name was changed to Franks some time before the Signers' Day of Reckoning. You see, it wasn't safe to be associated with the name Franklin after the great revolution was lost."

My mom added, "By the way, it also allows us to explain your father's first name and your middle. Nolin refers specifically to what was removed from our last name—and, therefore, is more appropriately translated as 'no … lin.'"

My father, Nolin … Franklin, continued, "What you hold in your hands is Benjamin Franklin's unpublished autobiography. He had started writing it while still in London back in 1771. It began as a letter to his son William. He brought it back with him to the colonies of America in 1775 when he had finally realized the colonies and the motherland could never reconcile. He never got to finish the autobiography but attempted to draft a second part, picking up where he'd left off and while he was imprisoned awaiting his fate on Signer's Day. In what we refer to as the prison journal, Benjamin recorded his account and actions during the revolution, as well as included some very interesting revelations and insights on the events that led up to the Signers' Day of Reckoning. It includes an addendum our ancestral lore believes to've been written by his son William, and including his own firsthand account of what actually happened that fateful day."

Having finally gotten his breath back, my father stood up again, as if what he was saying required it. "By the way, the second half was copied into one of the leather-bound books you hold. The handwriting matches the addendum, so it is also believed to have been written by his son William."

As if on cue my mother added, while pointing to the still wrapped book in the stack, "The original draft is sealed airtight in its own packaging to protect it, as it had been written in pencil."

I sat there listening in awe and, yet again, displayed a wide gaze, my jaw dropped. Not only was I holding Benjamin Franklin's autobiography, I had also just learned I was his living descendant.

If those were not mind-blowing discoveries enough, I had learned, too, that my father had a detailed knowledge of the history and had studied firsthand accounts of it. I had never even known he could read. Then, above all that, and after just having watched him tear up the side of the fireplace to retrieve the journals that had been buried in it for over the past twenty-one years, I realized he had to have been telling me all this from memory.

I pulled out the second book, which contained the transcription of the second part of the autobiography my father mentioned.

"Mr. Franklin stated he used a pencil, ultimately whittled to a stub, to complete the original. He considered it of utmost importance to complete."

"Joshua," he continued, "you should take a serious look at the other books as well—particularly Mr. Franklin's book *Experiments and Observations on Electricity*. With as much as you work with lightning, you should find it extremely interesting to read of a specific and groundbreaking discovery your great forefather made."

I pulled out the third book, which I assumed to be the book of experiments, but it had been written in a language I did not recognize.

As if sensing my confusion, my father explained, "That copy was written in French, a language that hasn't been spoken or written publicly for two centuries. King George III, building on the success of what you have always known as Third's War, beefed up his army and navy with 'volunteers' from his newly conquered country and sent them to France and Germany to expand his old country. To make sure the Crown-fearing newly converted Loyalists would fight honorably, he held their families as hostage collateral, threatening that any news of dissension would be the equivalent of putting nooses around their families' necks.

"The fourth journal, you'll see, is a version of the third, translated into English. It's also believed that William wrote the translation—an amazing discovery, as William was a staunch Loyalist. In fact, at the time of the Signer's Day of Reckoning, William was the royal governor of New Jersey, the province we know as Britannia Red. Even so, the handwriting in the second and the fourth journals match that of William's alleged account of the Signers' Day at the end of Benjamin's prison journal."

I sat in utter amazement. I was now the one who struggled to even form words in response.

Ignoring my failed effort to say anything, my newly discovered history scholar of a father continued. "History outside of these books only tells us of how William Franklin's loyalties leaned towards the Crown. But they never tell you of his visit to his father the day before Signer's Day. They would also never tell you how, after the visit, he tried to leave the city. He didn't want to witness the tortured deaths of the signers, but most importantly, he wanted the final image of his father to be of the fiery man he had witnessed in the prison. He attended only under the invitation and implied insistence of the king.

"Lastly, in William's account of the Signer's Day in the back of Benjamin's prison journal and thus transcribed, a completely different story is told than anything you'd likely hear today. Today we hear only lies—"

My father would have continued but was cut short as my mother began to speak. "Joshua, you remind your father and I so much of the Benjamin Franklin we read about in those journals so many years ago. We can't be prouder of you than we are.

"We've lived our lives as we have," she continued, "so that you could receive the education you've gotten through PURPOSE. That program, as bad as it is, gave you the best opportunity to become the brilliant young man we always knew you could be. You've so much of your great ancestor in you. Your father and I've always seen it in you, even at a very young age."

"What do you mean you've lived your lives this way?

"Son, what your mother means is where you have the intelligence, inventiveness—the brilliance of Benjamin Franklin—we too have a part of him. We have the fire and desire to stand up against all that is wrong with today's monarchial world. If we could think of any way we could to stand up and fight it, with even the slightest hope for success, we would do it. But we refrained from doing even little things, like changing our name back to Franklin on the government's census records, for the ridiculous fear that it may somehow be seen as making a statement. The best thing we could do was to allow you your opportunities. I don't regret a second of having done so but feel a void in not having fought for the freedom that, as you'll read in these journals, is so worth dying for.

"The best your mother and I could do was dutifully guard these truths until we could pass them on to you. But we can dream, and dream we have. We may be wrong. In fact, it is more likely to be lucky if you're able to some day pass them on to your own eldest, should fate allow. But secretly, your whole life, your mother and I have dreamed of so much more. Secretly, we've always believed that you would somehow find a way to rise above it all—somehow find the fortitude and the means to do what seems impossible to everyone else in this sad world. But, son, don't feel pressured. We're both realistic and simple people, and the dreams are just that—the dreams of simple people.

"Lastly, I want to stress how much this day has meant to your mother and me. In passing Benjamin Franklin's journals to you, we've achieved our own life's dream. At a minimum, our hope is that you'll read them, so you too will understand the gravity of their truths and respect the importance of at least carrying and passing their truths on through time."

Suddenly, even by just the flickering lights of the fire, I could see the exhaustion in the faces of my parents, Nolin and Bethel Franks. As I registered that thought, I instantly corrected myself—*my parents, Nolin and Bethel Franklin.*

I had never felt so proud of my parents. I had always seen them as I had everyone else in the world that was not royally connected, as victims. In many ways, they were just that. But as I learned that night, their lives were fueled by a higher purpose. They had dreams and had done everything within their abilities to achieve them—even if it meant burying their most prized possessions and living in the shadows of their histories.

The madness in their eyes and painful smiles gone, they looked as though they'd aged ten years there before me. Though I knew I would not be able to sleep that night, I told them how all the travel and excitement had worn me out.

After a round of hugs and genuinely thanking them for the best presents I could have ever imagined receiving, I retired to the cot behind the hanging tattered patchwork blanket that had always constituted the wall of my room.

As I had hoped, they went to bed, as well. Within minutes I could hear them sleeping. It was a deep sleep, but they were spent. It was the sound and peaceful sleep they so much deserved.

— CHAPTER 25 —

I WAITED A FEW MINUTES LONGER TO MAKE SURE MY PARENTS WERE IN a deep enough sleep that I would not wake them. Finally, by the light of a stub candle my mother had hand-dipped, I began reading about Benjamin Franklin.

My initial thought on him, based on what I had learned from my parents earlier, was he was a would-be revolutionary hero slighted by fate.

As I read on, however, I found him to be so much more.

I learned about his experiences as a printer turned writer. From submitting letters to the editor under the guise of a female named Silence Dogood to publishing pleas to support the British in the French and Indian War.

For the latter, he described how, in 1754, for a political cartoon and editorial, he had drawn a snake sliced into segments representing the colonies and then captioned the image with the phrase, "Join or die." It represented a cry for the colonies to join, alongside British soldiery, to fight in the French and Indian War for the protection of the colonies.

Though he included no image with the description, he indicated he had only mentioned it as it represented how his own personal views had once been in support of living under the Crown.

As events took a turn, by late 1775, that same image had morphed in meaning and image into a coiled snake. Mr. Franklin had first seen it on an American Marine's drum, sparking an anonymous editorial from him providing thoughts on why he felt the coiled rattler should be chosen as the symbol of the country he dreamed they could be—America.

Though it had never come to represent the country, he was proud it had found its way onto a yellow flag flown on the ship, the *Alfred*, by the colonies' first and only navy.

By that time, however, the snake's message had reversed. The flag had flown against the very British it had previously cried to support. Its message, directed to the Crown instead of for it, now declared, "Don't Tread on Me."

Mr. Franklin's description of this snake was supported by a sketched version in the journal, along with its revolutionary phrase. The image in the journal had an annotated caption, which appeared both in form and content to have been added later. Captioned beneath the image, Ben, or most respectfully, Mr. Franklin had ominously added, "The outcome of our efforts does nothing to negate the importance of our message, so our commitment holds firm and our voices remain strong, for the echo that remains will long outlive our final breaths."

A chill shook me as I read the image's footnote. I read it several times, trying to absorb his state of emotion, conviction, and resolution in writing it.

I was rapt by the image and emotionally connected as I reflected on the lives of our present generation, incessantly trod upon more than the most common sidewalks. We as a people had been trod upon our whole lives. The very thing for which Mr. Franklin and the Signers had given their lives was, to date, in vain.

The image of the coiled snake had etched and burned itself into the back of my mind. I could not shake it, as it had forged a bond, a connection—as if time had stopped, and where Benjamin Franklin ended, I began. The message was still alive. The message had survived his final breath, and I asked myself, *How firm is my commitment? How strong is the power of the message in me?*

I looked up and around at my parents' shack. Even the darkness could not hide the despair.

A strange and powerful feeling crashed over me. It was but a taste of what my newfound distant forefather had felt. It was only a taste, but it was enough for me to understand.

The crest of the crashing wave that had hit me carried its own message. A single word, and though I had no idea how Benjamin Franklin's speech sounded, I would swear in my mind it had been spoken in his voice—"Revolution."

Still staring at the image, my body shivered. The feeling was not one of fear but more of a release of energy. It was as if, somewhere in the recesses of my mind, body, and soul, lightning had struck.

I had broken out in a profuse sweat. I was exhausted but knew there was no way I would be able to sleep.

I switched gears and turned to reading about Benjamin Franklin's experiments and inventions and then nearly fell out of the cot as I read of his direct involvement in the planning and development of the University of Pennsylvania. My reaction was due to the realization that the college I attended, King's Gift, the University of Cornwallis, was ironically and originally more the gift of my newfound and amazing forefather.

I read on through the night, and as I dove deeper into the untold truths, I reached the part in *Experiments and Observations on Electricity* that my father had referred to regarding an experiment with lightning. Against anything I had ever learned about electricity, I read how it was Benjamin Franklin who had invented the lightning rod.

Then I read how, before that, on Monday, June 12, 1752, he had carried out a secret experiment with a kite, a key, and a storm. With only his young son William as a witness, Benjamin had set out and successfully proved that lightning carried electricity.

The scientist in me had suddenly taken over. I sat in a frozen daze and in awe of the fact that I was holding Benjamin Franklin's personal account, his notes, and his details on his scientific experiments.

I did not know how long I had sat there motionless, but when I finally snapped out of it, I found I had my index finger pressed on the open page. It pointed at something that must have subconsciously and summarily enthralled me. My eyes followed my finger to its tip and then on to the paper, to find the finger pointed to a single word that my ancestral and fellow scientist had written 260 years prior—*lightning*.

I felt compelled to keep reading but wanted to mark this page for its connection. From one of the tattered bedsheets I was using to try to keep warm, I tore an already loose corner and stuffed it between the pages as a bookmark.

Closing the science journal, I picked up the next in the stack to then read Benjamin Franklin the prisoner's account of the events that had occurred during his time in Hell's Gate. This journal I knew to be the transcription of the prison journal had been simply titled *Autobiography*.

On the first page I had turned to, he mentioned, as if they were just an annoyance, how the sounds of the gallows being constructed all around him were distracting his ability to focus on more important things.

I remembered hearing Professor Elders speak of his own ancestor and namesake, the King's Guard Jonathan Elders's account of the imprisonment of the Signers.

Benjamin Franklin's account confirmed it was Elders who had spoken the words, "'Philadelphia, Pennsylvania, fill'd with death, ya pens'll hang ya!" Those words found their place in time, destined, upon being heard, to become the famous catchphrase of what would become known in history as Third's War.

Mr. Franklin's account was different, however, in the telling of how the event surrounding the assertion had occurred. After reading it, I was more inclined to believe the words of a man with nothing to gain than that of a newly promoted King's Guard seizing his only opportunity to make a name for himself and having done so while standing safely on the outside of the jail cell bars.

Benjamin Franklin's version told of the fear, not the courage, in which the words were spoken.

Nothing, however, was as fascinating as Mr. Franklin's capturing of General George Washington's speech to his fellow comrades, tethered together by the ropes of their fates. His speech, Benjamin stressed, had strengthened the resolves of men who then believed themselves truly free.

As I had flipped toward the end of the journal, I found Mr. Franklin had written a collection of thoughts in reflection. He'd recorded his own and also those he had heard or overheard from his fellow prisoners.

These reflections had been made in retrospect of all that had occurred leading up to them now sitting in jail awaiting their date with a noose. They pointed out several key and specific observations, with the design to recognize that, if they, the Signers, had done things based on how they saw these opportunities through the filter of hindsight's eyes, they would have had a greater chance at success. The reflections formed a list of sorts, which contained what they would do if they could do it all over again.

Lastly, I read his son William Franklin's account of what had really occurred on the Signer's Day of Reckoning. I was nothing less than inspired by the courage of the Signers and the resolved strength shown in their fight for freedom and to their very end.

The telling of the event equally blew me away. It went against every account I had heard before. What was taught and celebrated today stressed how King George III had had his glorious day.

The gilded map of the gallows bookmarking the section in the journal was the only evidence supporting the fact that this "history" we'd all learned was actually an illusion. From what I had just read as a firsthand account of the event, the gilded map only represented the king's intent but not the reality of what had occurred.

By the time the morning sun made its way over the horizon, my head felt like it would explode from all the information and revelations—all the firsthand truths—I had learned. I was still on a high, wired and fully awake yet exhausted, when I heard my parents stirring.

Upon seeing them, I felt a pang of sadness. It seemed the combination of the previous evening's excitement, and probably the emptiness left from having fulfilled what they considered their most important life's goal and responsibility, had taken its toll on them.

I wanted to do something for them, anything to let them know how proud I was of them and of my newfound heritage.

The image of the coiled snake sprang back into the forefront of my mind. It had never left, but it was if it had just sat quietly coiled in the dark recesses, waiting patiently for the right moment to spring. By then, the image had left an indelible burn in my mind's eye.

I could not express how their gifts made me feel, so all I could muster was to tell them of all I had read and, most significantly, the importance of all I now understood.

Reflecting on the sacrifices they had made and the fact they had successfully achieved their goal, I ended by telling them how incredibly proud I was of them. Though I had loved them all my life, I had never loved them more than I did now.

They were my Signers, and I realized they had sacrificed everything for me and in the only way they knew they could.

At that moment, I realized I could do no less. In fact, in my position, I believed I could do much more.

I remember being struck by, and unable to shake, the sense of guilt and shame as I experienced yet another revelation. My most recent duties for the king involving, of all things, lightning, were helping all that Benjamin Franklin had died fighting against. My recent efforts were giving more power to the royal establishment he stood against for freedom. By doing so, I then reasoned, I was helping the king take even more from my parents, my friends, and my people—who had nothing more to give.

I struggled to hold the disappointment and shame in my current project from showing. I wanted to make my parents proud, and if they knew what I had been working on as of recent, though they would understand I had no choice, I feared it would devastate them.

As I ruminated on that, the word *choice* burrowed its way into my mind. Again, it came in a voice I imagined as Benjamin Franklin's. I resolved to reassess what choices I had. Then, as if on cue, the word *revolution* crept back. The wave it had ridden had cycled through its ebb to crash once more on the shores of my mind.

I understand the thought but did not know what I could do with it yet. I had a growing feeling this wave would continue to crash until I did. At this moment, however, I was just glad to see the gleam of happiness reappear in my parents' tired faces, upon hearing how honored I genuinely felt to have received the gift of my true heritage.

I made a promise I felt I was directing solely to my parents, but over time I have come to realize I had made it as much to myself. I promised I would do anything and everything I could do to bring honor to the name Franklin. It was a promise I could not have meant more by intention, though my conscience reminded me my present reality was going in the wrong direction toward fulfilling it.

I had to catch the 10:00 a.m. train back to George's Cross.

My parents and I shared a quick breakfast of hand-ground oatmeal and homemade tea. The tea leaves my mother used were considered weeds in the city.

After breakfast, my parents and I said our goodbyes, and I began my trek back to the train station.

I could not wait to get back home and change, as I was still wearing the same shirt I had worn for the past two days. I no longer smelled Emily; instead, I smelled a hint of smoke from last night's fire when the breeze hit me just right.

I laughed, recalling the comical sight of my father maniacally hammering away at the fireplace side. Looking at my shirt, I spotted and then swiped away at some of the resulting dust that had landed on it. With all that weighed so heavy on me now, the comical image still managed to put a smile on my face.

I found a chip of the fireplace stone that had managed to somehow latch itself to my side. It was shaped like the diamond in a card deck, though not so perfectly sized; rather, one half was more elongated than the other, so I progressively settled with the thought it was more the shape of a kite. With the image of a kite in my mind, I thought of the kite-flying experiment in a lightning storm that had taken place so long ago. I had almost flicked the chip away but decided to keep it as a memento of sorts or, perhaps, a reminder how the longer I did nothing, the longer it chipped away at my soul.

I stuck the chip in my shirt pocket, deciding it would later find its home in the pages of one of Mr. Franklin's journals.

The walk had been tiring enough the previous day, but in my sleepless and overwhelmed state, I found the walk back exhausting.

The bag I carried had the additional weight of the books I had inherited. They felt like they added the weight of the world with the newly added responsibility that came with them. Nothing, however, felt as heavy as the thoughts in my mind, including one that had reared its ugly head and insisted I had just seen my parents for the last time.

Having finally reached the station and boarded the train, my focus switched from where I was coming to where I was going. I pulled the journals in tight, though no one else even knew they existed, much less knew I had them.

I would not dare bring the journals out. They had been Benjamin Franklin's; now they were mine. I feared letting anyone else even know they existed. In my own journal, however, I doodled my own version of the coiled snake. I figured no one alive would recognize it or know its origin or meaning, so doodling it was harmless yet self-gratifying.

Reflecting on the journals' contents, all their revelations, I had so much I wanted to share with Emily and Emerson. What I wanted to tell and could safely tell, however, were two very different things.

Within ten minutes, and without any control on my behalf, I collapsed into sleep. A couple hours' nap later, the gentleman who had apparently sat next to me, courteously woke me up at the final stop in George's Cross.

I almost wished him happy birthday as I thanked him. I refrained, though I suspected I was correct in my assumption.

— CHAPTER 26 —

Sunday, October 17, 2021

I DO NOT RECALL THE WALK HOME. MY MIND WAS ELSEWHERE. BUT having finally reached the flat, I was torn between wanting nothing more than to pass out on my bed for the rest of the day and diving back into my journals.

I had not even had time to take my coat off when Emerson rushed me. He was wide-eyed and wired. I might have just mistaken it as one of the many familiar faces of Emerson, but this was different; something was wrong.

"Joshua! I did what I had to do! I got it all done!"

"Got what done, Emer?" I noticed he'd called me Joshua. I could count on one hand how many times he had ever called me that, and I would still have enough fingers left to play a piano.

"I got it all done, the modifications for FHM724!"

"When? You were supposed to be off today as well."

"We had visitors—royal visitors!"

As he said this, he made a gesture with his hand at his head. I imagined he intended it to represent a crown.

He continued, "They woke me up before five and wanted us both. They wanted us both to work. I don't think we get days off anymore,

Joshua! They tried to reach you too, but cell phones don't work deep in the villages."

"Work? We only get one day off a week usually anyway. They're taking that away too. Or should I say *he's* taking that away!"

"They were going to send someone to the villages for you. I told them the remaining prep work was mine. I assured the king's advisor I'd have it done in time for your return. I went in way early and just got home myself a few minutes ago."

Ever since the original project morphed into the king's pet project, we'd felt an intense and immediate ramp-up of pressure. Most had been directed at Dr. Rancor, but we too had received communications from and now visits by royal advisors making sure the king was kept current on our progress.

I thought that, more importantly, these advisors were just trying to figure out what we were doing that had his focused royal attention.

The king had surely stripped all bugs and cameras from the lab? Even basic details of FHM724 were need to know only.

After Dr. Rancor made the connection between the royal drafter, my friend "Howard Reskin," the Professor Raines look-alike, and their deaths in a suspicious fiery single-car crash, I would not think anyone in his or her right mind would want to know anything about what we were doing.

Finally, under direct instruction from the king, Dr. Rancor was required to provide encrypted updates directly to him. The only official task the advisors could have had would be to round us up and get us working on what should have been our day off, and they didn't even know what work they were demanding us to do.

No sooner had Emerson finished updating me than there was a knock at the door. "Knock" was being nice; it was really more of a singular hinge-splintering pound.

I looked out the window to the side of the door and saw two King's Guards standing stone-faced. Even without expressions, they reeked of impatience. They looked like they may be the same two who had picked me up before.

I had to answer the door. I didn't know how many more of their "knocks" the door could take. I figured they knew I had returned home, or they would not have been there.

While opening the door, they did not allow me the chance to offer them a false greeting. Immediately one of the guards, whom I will refer to as Frick, began to speak. Using the cold monotone voice I believe he learned in the required Talking Like a Statue 101 class at the Royal Guard Academy, Frick simply stated, "Come."

A man of many words, he even looked like a Frick.

I pictured the patch a newbie guard in training would have received for successfully draining all sense of humanity from his voice.

With no further wasted energy on Frick's part, I was taken by the arms and led to what looked like the same car as last time as well.

There was a chill in the wind, and I was suddenly thankful I had not had a chance to take off my coat. They would not have let me retrieve it otherwise.

At least my bag, journals and all, rested safely behind on the floor by the front door, where I knew I would find it when I returned.

The ride was a complete déjà vu. Though the direction and path were different, it all flew by in the same royal blue blur of the Royal Lane.

In roughly ten minutes, we had reached the destination or at least the entrance to how we could proceed to it. It was another Crowning Jewel Car Wash. Having experienced this before, I was much more attuned to what was happening and took in more of the surroundings along the way.

As before, the guard behind the wheel provided electronic identification and then the car proceeded into the front of what would have been an ordinary car wash for anyone else. Like last time, however, once hidden in the structure, we began our descent underground.

I laughed at the irony of the obvious expense and effort to keep this access secretive, yet again they had not even bothered to darken the windows to prevent me from witnessing it all. My snicker drew a piercing yet somehow expressionless glare from Frack in the passenger seat. Or was he Frick? Regardless, it was then I noticed he had a scar riding down the left side of his face. Like looking at a cloud, I found myself instantly trying to pin an identifiable shape to it. I landed on the musical note, treble clef. Or in this guy's case, maybe it is more a "trouble" clef. It was the first unique identifying mark I had ever seen on a royal goon.

The glare was successful at instilling fear in me. I may have been silenced, but I could not prevent my damned internal defense mechanism from kicking in. I wondered whether my not being blindfolded in the car was because the king did not feel I was a threat. Or was it because his inept guard clones lacked the depth of mind to think it through enough and realized I should not have witnessed the transition from the public world to the underground royal world?

I assumed it was the latter, and their ineptness was just a side effect of inbreeding.

I randomly thought of asking the goons whose turn it was to wipe the royal ass next so immediately bit my lip.

The snort that followed earned me two icy cold stares as we proceeded into the darkness of the gap between the aboveground and the underground. The driver's glare, of course, came via the rearview mirror.

As we descended, the royal blue lights of the tunnel began to illuminate the inside of the car. As my eyes adjusted, I could see Frick and Frack still glaring at me through the blue filter. The blue lights only enhanced the icy cold effect.

When the car stopped descending and began moving forward, I looked back to see our car's clone begin its ascension behind us.

I had a sudden bout of curiosity, wondering whether my return home would be in the same vehicle. Thinking quickly, I searched my pockets for anything I could leave behind. All I came up with was a little wad of pocket lint. I smiled as I feigned stretching and placed the lint on the rear window well surface, rubbing it into place as I returned my arms to a normal position.

Within the next minute I was dragged out of the car and led down yet another lavish and tapestried hallway. Having experienced all this before, I was not surprised by the chain of events that ultimately led me to my second one-on-one with the king.

I even looked forward to getting a whiff of the unique smell that I assume ever enveloped his high-n-mightiness.

As soon as I entered the final chamber, I instinctively knelt down. The smell was all I needed to know I was in his presence. For the second time in my life, among the sudden and unusually fresh air, I smelled royalty.

As with our first meeting, the king barked an order for the guards, which amounted to only one word, "Post." While speaking it, he directionally motioned where they should take their positions as royal gargoyles.

I kept my eyes down, knowing I could look up once the king directly addressed me. This was his game, and I had better play it and play it well.

"Joshua."

I obediently and immediately responded with attention.

"I trust your birthday weekend left you refreshed, and your visit with your parents was ... appropriate."

I knew he had not asked a question. Nor had he been making small talk. It was more that he had posed a hanging threat.

"I also understand your colleague, Flanders, has prepared new equipment for you to test. This equipment, my equipment, will aid in your ability to navigate your activities while in the fourth dimension. I expect you will need to test the ability to stretch further back in time but equally expect you to expediently proceed toward successful implementation of ... my project."

Yet again, I hung in anticipation of hearing the king refer to his project by the naming conventions I was accustomed to calling them, with the prefix FM. He let me down.

The only difference this time was the realization that I must have inherited my sharp, though safely inner dialogue from Benjamin Franklin. I recalled the wit that emanated from his writing, even though he knew it would be his last. He had written it while counting ticks down toward his final breath.

"I understand there are further pilot exercises to be done to grow toward my goal, but I have taken the royal liberty of drawing up the contents of the first real run of the project. I have also provided the location and architectural dimensions you will need to carry it out."

Not one to say anything he felt unnecessary, the king wasted no time or breath but cut straight to the quick. Besides, a greeting would have been awkward, as I had been kidnapped.

"You, and only you, will know what I am going to tell you. You, and only you, will load these coordinates. You and only you will ever know. I need not ask if you understand.

"You are to write a message through the lightning, as you had to your *ex*-girlfriend." Stressing the prefix, 'ex', he waved off the statement, as if by doing so he had just shooed her away again with one royal swipe.

"This message will be written on the inside wall of the now collapsed and demolished Anderson Raines Lightning Lab. I have spent my precious time and energy to pull together in an envelope how you can identify the wall. Pictures of me standing in front of said wall, as well as the time-date coordinates of the lightning, are included."

He then snapped his fingers once. A King's Guard appeared out of nowhere and forced the envelope securely into my hands. The guard was gone as fast as he had appeared.

The king continued, "You will also find the exact verbiage of the message you are to burn on the inside of that wall."

I stared at the envelope, but instead of wondering what his message would be, I had a sudden epiphany of what mine would be in the next pilot. I only needed to recall the image burned on my retinas of a coiled snake and the phrase, "Don't Tread on Me."

Then a strange thing occurred; I heard the singular ring of the hour bell of a clock chime somewhere in the room. It struck once to signify it was now 1:00 p.m., something not completely strange for a clock to do. It was not the clock's ringing that was strange but the immediate connection I made to the clock in Third's Tower—the clock that had so recently stopped for its first natural time in history, the clock stopped by lightning no less.

I had an instant revelation and determined that specific lightning provided the perfect location and time for my next pilot experiment. I resisted the smile that wanted so badly to stretch its way across my face and could not believe how brazen my thoughts had become.

The king continued, unaware my attention had strayed, as if it were not possible for anyone's attention to stray from him. "Lastly, I expect you to provide Rancor with your timeline of testing to completion, with the date I can expect you to be ready for carrying out this first task I have assigned. I respect the complexities of this science enough to know it's not realistic to expect you to be prepared to carry out the task today. But know this, if there is any way for you to do so, you had better."

He was done; therefore, in my second one-sided conversation with the king within a week, I was done as well.

A simple gesture of his hand cued the immediate appearance of two guards, thus confirming the meeting was over.

Upon seeing the guards, though they looked almost exactly like every other guard I had ever seen, I made the eerie realization that I had never seen the same two guards. These guards were just numbers to the king, his numbers, and he had a seemingly infinite supply of them. They too were mere pawns, as with his public, as with me, to carry out His Majesty's every command.

As if to confirm my suspicions, I saw no hint of the scar I had noticed earlier on one of them. I did register, however, that neither guard liked that I had even looked at them.

— CHAPTER 27 —

WITHIN MINUTES, I WAS THRUST INTO THE BACK OF YET ANOTHER royal vehicle cloned for the service of the Crown. I knew it was a different vehicle than the one I had arrived in, as my lint smudge was nowhere to be seen; or had they already cleaned it?

I knew the ride back would take much longer than the ride there had. There would be no Royal Lane this time.

I decided I would use the time to go through the contents of the envelope the king had given me.

Reflecting on the king's words and reviewing the details of his instructions, I was yet again amazed at the king's detailed knowledge of this project. Likewise, the instructions solidified my understanding of his intentions.

Remaining in monarchial power over centuries was no easy task. On the surface, for this king at least, instilling fear in the minds of his public kept them in their places. That much was ever present and, for the most part, had always proven effective.

Underneath the surface, however, the monarchy relied on information to keep up with the "who, what, when, where, why and how" of credible enemies and their threats to the crown. The never-ending flow of information through the vast, complex, and intricate web of providers had always been the best initial defense against these enemies, enough so that the list of credible enemies to the crown was a short one. The key word there was *credible*.

Though today's technological advances enabled far more information to flow much more swiftly, it also made it increasingly more difficult to efficiently swim through the plethora of the incredible to pluck the credible tidbits. Then, even if you did find solid information, did you find it quickly enough to act on it? It was for this reason the king so valued the hindsight's heads-up he could give himself via FHM724.

The king's game plan consisted of using the collapsed wall at the remains of the Anderson Raines Lab as a message board to communicate timely threats he had learned of in hindsight. In the instructions, the king provided detailed information about the location of this wall. Though less for me but probably just a natural flow of his thoughts on the event, he included how he had uncovered and viewed burn marks from the lightning on the backside of that wall. It stood to reason, if the lightning touched that wall, it would make an excellent surface to burn a message on—assuming he, meaning I, could successfully tap into that lightning.

There could not be an "if" in being successful. I had no choice but to be successful.

I shuddered in genuine fear at the thought of what it would mean when I succeeded. This king, who already has most the entire civilized world in his grasp, had found a way to take more. Hindsight may help him defend his crown, but I also saw how, if used on the offensive, it could help him expand his kingdom.

The only remaining viable threats to the British Kingdom rested in Russia and China—both of which had lost ground and power over the past century to the ever-expanding empire of British rule. Global Britain's power extended through them like a network of veins but had yet to entirely conquer them as it had all Europe, Africa, South America, Australia, and of course the country of New England.

It would not be difficult for the king to act on information he learned after the fact to turn it in his favor in completely taking over these remaining two countries.

The more I thought about how much I would be helping the king, the more it made me sick to my stomach. As if its potential alone was not bad enough, the knowledge that the potential existed because of scientific advancements I had helped make made it almost unbearable.

As if to protect me, the coiled snake sprang forward again from the shadows in the depths of my mind. This time, however, the snake spoke. It spoke the same two words I had heard before, each their own complete sentences, needing no more words to convey their intention—*choice* and then *revolution.*

Subconsciously, my hand reached for the chip from the fireplace, still safely nestled in the bottom of my shirt pocket. I do not believe my conscious mind remembered the chip was there. Apparently, while my conscious mind dealt with what was happening, my subconscious focused on what should happen.

Holding it triggered a reminder of what it now represented—how inaction would continue to chip away at my soul.

I thought again of the lightning that had struck the clock tower. I remembered the exact date and time it had struck. It had been the big news for months since it had occurred, especially since the clock had successfully been repaired in time for the Signers' Day of Reckoning. The legend of the lightning had been shown, told, and sold repeatedly. I had even seen T-shirts with the clock's image, big and bold, time frozen at 4:10 a.m. The articles and news segments had been reinvigorated as the first anniversary of the event and then Signers' Day had passed as time marched its way around the calendar again.

I recalled having seen a recycled interview with the resident clock maker. He looked exhausted, having just appeared from the tower after initially assessing its damage. The media had swarmed the poor man, but he had been gracious enough to provide a reply to their incessant buzz of questioning.

He'd indicated the clock's escapement had stopped functioning, causing the whole clock to stop. Ironically, the purpose of the escapement, he explained, was to isolate the clock's pendulum from the effects of wind and weather, and then with a tired smile, he added how it appeared the escapement needed its own escapement. As it was, he then knew the damage had been miraculously minimal, leaving him to believe the damage had been caused more by the proximity of the lightning and rattling of its thunder. After yet another tired smile, he stated he could not blame the clock, for he too had been rattled by the thunder. Finally, and probably the main reason he could afford to smile at all, he indicated the clock could be repaired in time for the Signer's Day of Reckoning.

The only reason I thought I even remembered the interview was because I associated it with the need for my own escapement, our own escapement, and the heavy understanding of just what that escape meant.

The images of the clock face the media had injected into the IVs feeding the TVs of the world had been seen by billions of eyes.

The shiver I had experienced the night before while reading Mr. Franklin's annotation to his snake sketch hit me again. Again, his words began to stream through my mind.

The outcome of our efforts does nothing to negate the importance of our message.

It hit me as I realized I was now firm in my intention to burn the image of the coiled snake onto the face of the clock that would be seen by billions—ensuring that, therefore, my message would as well.

Given another moment on the thoughts, I might have talked myself out of their bold intentions. I was afforded relief as I was distracted by the sudden stop of the vehicle. I looked out the window to find us stopped in front of my flat. I was thankful they had at least dropped me off at home this time. The excitement of the afternoon had depleted any energy I had restored on my two-hour nap on the train that morning.

Emerson trapped me in the entryway, bombarding me with questions. I had just enough energy left to pick up my bag, which still sat where I had dropped it earlier, and fill in Emerson on the highlights, making sure not to include anything for my eyes and ears only.

I wondered how I would ever be able to share my newfound lineage.

I kept my story generic and short and then turned to retire to my room. As I turned, I spotted a partially folded sheet of paper that had inadvertently made its way under a chair in the living room. Figuring it was just a casualty resulting from an afternoon with Emerson alone at home, I picked it up to throw it away.

A quick glance revealed, however, it was Emily's list from Professor Elders's rant. She had told me the story of the rant upon the return of my first kidnapping to see the king. That seemed so long ago now, and so much had happened since.

Simply because it was from Emily, I pocketed the sheet, now a neighbor to the stone chip, and resumed my path to the bedroom.

I wanted so badly to go to sleep but had some research and calculations to do first. My mind would not let me rest until I completed them. I needed to look up the time, date, and location coordinates I would be using the next day for our test.

On my computer, I searched up the longitudinal and latitudinal coordinates of Third's Tower. Then I searched publicly available archives for stats on the clock tower. I was able to find an architects blueprint rendition with measurements providing me with the vertical adjustment I needed to add to compensate for the tower's height and ultimately determine the height of the clock face that I would burn my message on.

Within an hour, I had all the information I needed and had written it on the back of Emily's list, the piece of paper I'd found under the chair earlier.

I safely stuck the list, and its neighbor the fireplace chip, under the front cover of Benjamin Franklin's journal, *Experiments and Observations on Electricity*.

With all I already had on my mind, finding the piece of paper, Emily's paper, put her on the forefront.

Even so, I was out cold the moment I lay down and slept straight through the night. I slept so deeply I could not remember my dreams. I wanted to believe they were happy, and imagined they were of Emily and me.

— CHAPTER 28 —

Monday, October 18, 2021

I WAS AMAZED TO FIND AT 6:00 A.M. WHEN THE ALARM WENT OFF, I awoke instantly. The exhaustion must have put me in so deep a sleep I was allowed a deep charge and quick recovery.

In my mentally refreshed state, I beat myself up for having used my laptop last night to do the research. How stupid, as my laptop could be being monitored as well.

It was too late to do anything about it.

I jumped into the shower and then got ready for work. Today would be the same, only different, as the days last week. It was what would be different that had me excited.

I came out of my room to find Emerson ready to walk out the door.

I grimaced as we jumped into the GIV. Having recently ridden twice in royal vehicles, just the sight of our medical blue government-issued vehicle nearly made me hurl in comparison. It was yet another reminder of the chasm between our worlds. The car's engine barked and sputtered as if in agreement and then hesitantly lunged forward as if it would have stayed put if offered the choice.

While Emerson drove, he filled me in on the changes and enhancements he had been able to complete yesterday. As usual, Emerson was fully prepared for the job. God love him, he was a nutjob at everything else in life but a genius when it comes to drawing up blueprints and hardware schemas and performing installs and upgrades. He was a whiz at turning whatever plans we threw at him into reality—that is, as long as he had the materials needed to complete them.

It was usually difficult to get your hands on any supplies, tools, and hardware necessary to complete a job. Moreover, many of our past efforts, and their corresponding timelines, had been halted and delayed by nothing more than the lack of basic supplies needed to complete them.

But since this had turned into a project for the king, all materials requested at the end of one day seemed to magically appear the next. It was as if it was the parts and materials that had to wait for us as we unnecessarily delayed the project by doing crazy things like sleeping and eating.

As we entered the hall leading toward the lab, I asked, "So you were able to install both the fiber grid to the middle layer of the core as well as the drives with the new logistics and swarm programs Emily coded?"

"I walked in yesterday, not only finding all the remaining materials I had requested, but a crew at my disposal to do the grunt work. That's the only reason I was able to get it done so quickly. It was more difficult to get the high score on the *Palace of Pigs and Pugs II.*"

"I cannot believe you played the *Palace of Pigs and Pugs I*, let alone its sequel. The graphics sucked, the pugs were ugly, and the theme song was so annoying it was an instant headache, just add water!"

"Hey, careful," he shot back as he lifted his sleeve to reveal the tattoo he had penned on his arm, "You'll hurt Penelope Pug's feelings."

"No way. And I trust the equipment and hardware you configure and install with my life! Maybe I'm the one who is crazy."

That was the first time we had laughed in a while. It felt good.

Though the swarm logistics program Emily had coded was strictly for the king's project, FHM724, I was still excited about it. FHM720 was no longer a royally-sanctioned project, but I refused to let go of it. Even though the swarm program benefited FHM724, it inherently benefited FHM720 as well. If successful, it would offer the most productive increases in our ability to efficiently capture the power from the lightning. Working with the fiber grid Emerson installed, it would allow the core to respond in nanoseconds to the electrical impulses off a lightning's branches.

For this reason, along with the message I intended to burn, I was actually looking forward to testing. The only other reason was an opportunity to see Emily again.

Sadly, the swarm project should also greatly improve our fourth dimensional connections between the two strikes of lightning I would be channeling through. Benefiting from the same enhancements enabling a stronger connection to the lightning in the core, it would also enable a stronger connection to the lightning in the past. What makes it sad is how much sooner and easier it would allow for helping the king.

Where the swarm program helps the connections at both ends, the logistics program helps the connection in between. Its enhancements are necessary to allow us to move forward to tapping into not only lightning in the past, but also lightning in the past that had occurred at a different location. All our previous testing had allowed us to successfully tap into lightning that occurred in the same relative location, the core of our lightning lab. Today's test would be the first to tackle adding physical distance to the equation, as well as a greater distance in time.

I wanted so badly to tell Emerson where and when the lightning of the past would occur, but as I was the only one to know what the actual coordinates and message would be, I felt I had better incorporate the secrecy into the tests as well. I also figured, as I was about to burn a revolutionary message onto a clock billions of eyes would be watching, Emerson would be better off not knowing.

I reasoned that no one in the present day would understand the message, as it was spoken in a revolutionary voice that had long been silenced. I figured there would be no harm done. Actually, I thought it might add some real intrigue to an event that had just naturally occurred, though it seemed the media would have you believe lightning had never struck before.

I had no intention to log or report on the test I would like to call "Don't Tread on Me."

Upon completion of my rebellious act, I would simply tell Emerson I had failed to make a good connection and needed to tweak the coordinates. He would be none the wiser, as only a flash of time would have passed for him. It would give me reason to perform a second test that I could then log and report on for progress.

— CHAPTER 29 —

ONCE IN THE LAB, WASTING NO TIME, EMERSON WORKED DOWN HIS list of safety and quality checks. With the recent additions he had made, the list had grown. He was more than sufficiently preoccupied with his own tasks to prevent him from being involved with mine.

For my part, I had just learned from Professor Rancor that I now had the added duties previously performed by Emily. Emily's programming functions had been completed and tested, ending with her loading it onto the new hardware Emerson had installed.

Emily's remaining tasks had been administrative, involving keying in time and space coordinates. Up to this point, those coordinates had been the time and date of the previous lightning we had helped trigger, and with the lab as its location. Even though today's effort was just a test and Emily had provided me with its coordinates and settings, as I was to be the only one in the future who knew the when, where, and what in this respect, the king had had Professor Rancor reassign the task of entering them to me.

This turn of events had me genuinely worried for Emily. I feared for her safety, as I felt the only thing that kept us safe hinged upon how useful we were to the king. Once within the circle of knowledge of FHM724, you did not want to become disposable.

I wanted to ask Professor Rancor about Emily but could tell by her demeanor she feared saying anything. The only thing she said further about it was that she was doing what she could to get Emily onto a new assignment. If her voice had not quivered so much when she added that, I might have believed she could.

The more I considered the message I would burn, the more I realized it was but a token gesture. Though billions of eyes would see it, my parents and I owned the only eyes able to take it in and understand it.

On top of that, my parents would never see it but would probably only hear about it later. In irony, my work on project FHM724 was preventing me from working on FHM720, the one project that could someday provide the electricity to their village that would enable them to see the message; no telly, no message.

But I needed to do something. I needed to find a way to act and not just allow our destinies to be controlled as if we existed only to be the king's old puppets, soon to be disposed and replaced by newer ones with easier strings to control. Token gesture or not, burning the message on the clock was taking a step, and I needed to start taking steps. Hell, I needed to start running.

Concerns were progressing, especially for Emily's safety, but also for Professor Rancor, Emerson, and me. The ball had started rolling, and snowballing would not be far behind.

I have heard some say knowledge is power, but in my opinion, knowledge seemed to have only put us on the wrong side of the power cord. Our power was being drained.

Once our level of knowledge slid past the thin line from being needed to knowing too much, our duties would also be reassigned and chunked out in smaller pieces. No one remaining would know enough to be a threat to the program or, more importantly, to the king.

An image ran through my mind of all our replacements. They all looked and acted like the Geoffreys of the world.

Though I had yet to even rattle the eyes of the world with my rattler, I realized, if I was going to truly honor the gifts from, and promises made to my parents, I was going to have to do much more than just burn a snake and an obscure message.

But for now, at least I was taking a step.

I keyed in the coordinate time and date range of the lightning I would be tapping into. The date was June 30, 2020, and I set the time down to the second the "King of Clocks" had stopped. As the clock was designed to be accurate within a second of time, it seemed the exact time it had stopped should get me close enough to the lightning for a successful connection.

The clock faces, however, do not have second hands. Thankfully, my research turned up the exact time, to the second, as reported during yet another interview with the resident clock maker. The clock maker professed he had determined the clock had stopped ticking at exactly 04:10:22. My curiosity naturally wanted to understand how he could tell, but for now I simply loaded the range of the lightning's time stamp as from 06/30/2020 04:10:20 a.m. to 06/30/2020 04:10:25a.m.

With a range loaded, once we triggered the lightning, the system would initiate the timer starting at the exact from time up until the precise time an instance in that range aligned with the time the lightning of the past occurred. This ability was one of the tricks we had picked up in our previous testing efforts. I think that was just last Thursday. It was amazing how far we'd come in so short a time.

Time coordinates loaded, I then set out to key in the logistical coordinates I had written on the back of Emily's list.

With my new perspective on the value of the list on the front, I no longer considered it as just a scrap of paper.

As I pulled it out of my pocket, I unfolded it to the side of her list. Before flipping it, I glanced at what she had written. This list, this rant, contained the professor's telling of opportunities he had learned in hindsight that may have changed the outcome of that war so long ago. Upon reading the first on the list, "Do not fight the formal British fight," my mind turned tangent to a corresponding message Benjamin Franklin had written in his journal supporting the same theory. Mr. Franklin had written what he had overheard General Washington discussing with John Adams—how he wished he had ignored the traditions of war.

I made a mental note to reread portions of the journals, as I believed Benjamin had documented what he and his co-revolutionaries had learned in hindsight as well. I guess at the time I just wanted to compare and or validate the professor's rant with Mr. Franklin's firsthand accounts.

Flipping the piece of paper, I continued my task of keying in the coordinates I had calculated. Time and space coordinates loaded, I was then prepared to initiate the day's first, albeit unofficial test.

Looking on how things in life had developed and how time had turned so quickly against everyone I cared about, my resolve to burn my rebellious but enigmatic message hardened. The feelings of the message's inadequacy in making a real difference fueled my mind to search for what I could do that could truly make a difference. How could I keep my promise? The question continued to burn in my mind. It was a promise I had initially made to my parents. But like the ripples from a stone tossed into calm water, the promise has since extended to all whom I cared about, as well as all in the present and the future trapped under the crush of royal heels.

Following newly revised instructions Emerson had provided me to successfully initiate the program with the changes Emily had coded, I keyed in my password to trigger hiding the coordinates I had loaded. I was sure that feature was a result of the king's insistence that any of the information surrounding coordinates of his future self-messaging remained securely hidden.

Having completed loading the parameters for this test, I checked on Emerson's status. He had been inspecting the updated fiber grid and had nearly completed his checklist.

I sat back down where I believed I was successfully concealed by the lab's control center walls and broke out Emily's list again. Staring at its contents and reflecting on what I could remember from Franklin's journals, I had a thought, or perhaps more of a wish, pop into my mind. I wished I could share with Benjamin Franklin not only what we had learned in hindsight, but also what he himself had recognized in hindsight. He and his fellow revolutionaries, during their year-ish time rotting in the jails of Hell's Gate, had had plenty of time to reflect and would more than likely have come up with some or all the professor's list, maybe more.

It was less about *what* they knew than *when* they knew it. Knowledge may be power if you know the right things at the right time. I would do anything to be able to somehow get a message to them before their revolutionary war, to share with them all we'd had the benefit of seeing in hindsight.

My planning was interrupted when I heard Emerson approaching. I noticed he was then whistling the theme song to the *Palace of Pigs and Pugs*. I hated that song.

If I dared voice my thoughts on that song, he would only whistle louder. I needed to distract him. "Hey, Emer?"

In between screeches, "Yeah, man?"

"Remember that dog food commercial, the one with the dog in a dress?"

I knew he did. I spent the three months listening to him hum the music bit in his version of a dog voice. I cannot believe I reminded him of it but knew he would instantly switch to humming it from whistling the pollution he was spewing now. At least it was a catchy bit, kind of like hold music you didn't mind holding to.

As if he had just changed his song selection with a remote, Emerson simply answered my question by humming the tune. I had just recalled it was bearable except for the part where—

As if on cue, Emerson bellowed, "Bow woo woo! Bow woo woo woo!"

Yeah, that part.

Having now finished the ditty, Emerson looped right back to the beginning. I figured I had about thirty seconds to lose myself in the test so leaped up, leaving Emerson to the controls.

"You know what to do from here. I will get into position and then give you the go-ahead to kick in the environment."

"Bow woo woo! OK. Bow woo woo woo!"

Well, at least I know he heard me.

Then in position behind the core, probably out of habit, I pulled the pen from my pocket. I have used the same Pilot G-2 07 black gel pen from my original and accidental run for every test we had completed to date. Aside from the fused tip, making it no longer capable of writing like a regular pen on paper, it was none the worse for wear. I considered it more of a stylus. Then, however, would be the first time I had used it for drawing. Looking at the small pen though, I realized, it would not result in an image large or bold enough to stand out on the huge clock face, so I put the pen back in my pocket and ran back down the ramp to find something bigger to use.

It took another good ten minutes before I found an old broom in a closet in the lab. Most of that time searching I had also spent trying to explain to Emerson why I could not use the pen. I ended up simply telling him I could not tell him, hoping the newly heightened secrecy of my tasks would suffice. After unscrewing the wooden handle from the broom, I then drove its handle end several times into the concrete floor to provide a broader tip to draw from. As I ran back into position, I peeped my head into the control center and hollered at Emerson to start a ten-second countdown to allow me to get into position before initiating the strike.

I had learned to love this part—that is, kicking in the environment. You can feel the change in the air, the stir of energy as the lightning inducers pumped negative ions into the core, while, beneath it, coils buried below generated positive ions. The area inside the core acted as a lightning magnet.

Each of the previous week's tests had taken a couple minutes for the environment to set, but with the new grid liner in place, it had taken less than a minute. I had already begun to experience the then familiar sensation of transitioning from what started as the clashing of positive and negative ions in the third dimension, to slicing into the time continuum via the fourth dimensional characteristics of lightning.

In the fourth dimension, lightning occurs when the ever-fluxing walls of the time continuum rub against themselves. Lightning is merely the resulting friction of two moments in time scraping each other like the shoulders of people walking through a crowd.

I knew from experience what Emerson was seeing, hearing, and feeling. He had his commercial grade shades over his eyes and his ears plugged and covered, as he sat nestled behind the safety of the control center walls.

How strange was it that I could be so much closer and seemingly less protected and yet I saw no flash, heard no boom, and walked unscathed from an area less than five feet from where lightning had just struck?

Even stranger was how I would spend the better part of the next few hours in the dimension, but to Emerson, on the other side, the whole test would take place within the half a second it took for the single flash of lightning to flash and its thunder to crash.

I imagined what I believed Emerson would accomplish during my time spent dimension hopping. The only image I could conjure amounted to Emerson successfully bellowing another, "Bow woo woo woo."

I was surrounded by the then familiar glow and dreamlike haze. My eyes had quickly adjusted, and I realized as quickly how surprised I was to actually see what I intended. I had not realized how much I had expected the added lengths in time and space to have not worked. I was not sure what I expected to happen, but much to my surprise and before my eyes, I saw the city of George's Cross spread out before me.

Its expanse loomed large and in vivid color, spread before me like an intensely detailed map. More importantly, however, was the perspective of the view. I was looking at George's Cross as if through the eyes of Third's Tower's clock face.

The view would have been nothing short of beautiful in natural light, but in the rich hues and pronounced clarity provided by my viewpoint through lightning, it was beyond breathtaking.

Where I had known I would be tapping into a strike that had occurred farther in the past, as well as farther from the lab, I just recognized this was also the first lightning I would witness from the past that had struck outdoors instead of within the confines of the lightning lab's core. Reflecting on that revelation, I recalled how this lightning had also occurred in an intense thunderstorm that occurred at night when it was still dark. The sun would not rise for another hour or so on the third-dimensional side. I was tapping into wild lightning.

The view before me, however, was wonderfully illuminated—again, the result of the fact time had, in essence, frozen in the outside dimension; and it had done so while the lightning I peered through showered the cityscape with light. The air was filled with tiny glowing crystals. I came to realize they were raindrops, suspended and frozen in time, reflecting the light from the lightning. It all made for a spectacularly beautiful sight.

I recalled how the core of lightning carries five times the proportional power of the sun, and as if it were in fact just an arm of the sun reaching down to strike the earth, it shined as I imagine any part of the sun's body would.

The freeze of time in the third dimension, though not in mine in the fourth, afforded me the luxury of taking my own sweet time. I did not need to hurry and could take all the time I needed. No matter how long I took, upon crossing back into the third dimension, I would find less than a second had passed.

So, for now I just absorbed the view, knowing that, as I had been facing east from my vantage point, the giant eastward-facing clock face of Third's Tower loomed behind me.

Taking in one last glance at the pristine view before me, I followed along on my bridge through time, which consisted of the ramp circling along the top of the core inside the lab. I found myself using the broom handle as a walking cane, as if I were walking a trail through the mountains.

As I walked around, approaching the clock from the right, its immense face entered the periphery of my view. I was dwarfed by it. The tower lived up to its name and towered proper and majestic before me.

A quick glance to my right and down gave me a clear view of Hell's Gate. My eyes were drawn to it, like how they say the eye is attracted to the brightest spot of an image.

Ironically, with virtually everything illuminated by frozen lightning, Hell's Gate was the only spot shadowed by a storm cloud. Therefore, it was the contrast provided by its darkness briefly attracting my focus. The coincidental symbolism of a dark cloud hanging over freedom's tombstone would stay with me. This perspective reminded me why I was there in the first place. I turned back left, towards the clock face, and to my task in time.

As I got closer, the clock face quickly consumed the scope of my view. Up this close, I found it perfectly imperfect, with the stains of nature and time. As the clock face I was looking at had frozen, I imagined it trying so hard to move its hands again, to get back to its never-ending attempts to wipe away the effects of the time it kept and in an effort to always put on its best face.

I stopped, standing directly in front of an intimidating looking Roman numeral III.

I was taller than the number, though it lay on its side, and I wondered if it were standing whether that would still hold true. Though for no other reason than to satisfy my curiosity, I studied its length and surmised it would only be just over a meter and a half standing. I almost had it beat by a third of a meter, but that realization took nothing away from the thought that, though it was physically smaller, it represented time, and time towered above all.

My eyes caught the web of the mosaic patterning as I peered into the mouth of the clock face. The mouth was formed by the minute and hour hands, frozen in their respective positions with the minute hand pointing to the two and the hour hand to the four. This image of a mouth on the face of a clock had me think how we are all ultimately being swallowed by time. Since this was the face of the King of Clocks, I also saw it as another representation of how the king was swallowing our lives, feeding on us to give himself more strength, more time.

As breathtaking the view of the city was, I cannot deny, this close-up view of the seven-and-a-half-meter clock face before me stole the show. All negative analogies aside, I acquired an immediate appreciation for not just the face, but also the clock as a whole. Before this experience, I had never given it a second's thought.

My newly found appreciation, however, had neither exceeded nor diminished my resolve. I got to work.

Not knowing where on the face I would be able to reach to actually burn my intended message, my focus turned to determining just that. With the Roman numeral II towering above my head, and the IV below, I figure I would draw my coiled snake in the space between the II and III and then add the "Don't Tread on Me" between the III and the IV. Let the mouth on the King of Clocks chew on that for a while.

There would be no eraser to use, so I proportioned the image in my mind and then set out to draw it.

If I had not had my own watch on, I would not have known over four and a half hours had passed before I finished. Something else I had learned, since the watch was simple mechanics, it kept time as if it were in the third dimension still. I would need to reset it when I returned.

As I looked upon my handiwork before me, the length of time passed made sense.

The coiled snake stood almost a meter and a half. It looked taller and thinner than the picture Mr. Franklin had drawn in the journal, but I was working within the space I had available and wanted to make sure it would be visible. I was sure the fact I had drawn it with a broomstick and stretched over the railing of the ramp around the lab's core had some influence on its shape as well. I was just glad it actually looked like a snake.

The lettering of the message capped out at a third of a meter in height. I had to shade it all in to make sure the billion eyes that would be looking would be able to make out what the image was and what the message said. It was easier to solidify the shading of the letters than it had been the snake. Not only was the location for the message easier to reach, but I was also able to stand in a more natural position, not reaching up.

Given all this and that I was burning it through lightning and time with a broomstick no less, I was impressed by the facts the message was legible and the broomstick was not on fire.

Instead, like my pen had suffered a fused ballpoint tip, the broomstick's tip seemed to have rubbed itself to a glossy black shine but had not even smoked and was otherwise none the worse for wear. Wetting my fingertip, I carefully and quickly tapped it on the tip. I expected it to burn my finger, but the tip wasn't even hot.

Task completed, my thoughts turned, as if in harmony with my body, toward a return to the third dimension. I imagined what thoughts, words, and actions had occurred from the time of the lightning's strike and message burned to the time I would meet back up with Emerson in the lab. What would he be able to tell me?

Then I remembered he would not know what I had done just now, as the results of my handiwork would have been seen over a year prior. For all our safety, I could not tell him or anyone else for that matter. Knowing what they knew now, would Emily or Emerson have figured it out? Would anyone have figured it out? Would the king?

I began to panic. But to fend off the fear, I reasoned that I had burned the message in a time long before the king even knew about the ability to do so. There was a good chance he would not make any connection back to it by the time he did learn of the ability over a year later.

Unlike the first time, my accidental stretch through time and when none of the safety measures to protect us in the lab from the lightning we danced so closely to in our work were on, all subsequent instances had every safety measure activated. In fact, with what we had learned, more were added.

This resulted in a much smoother transition between dimensions. Where I had been thrown the first time, it now just felt more like when you drive fast over the crest of a hill causing your stomach to rise and then suddenly fall. At least, that was the best way I could describe the feeling as I made the final descent from the core's ramp and then past the threshold of the lightning's grip, making my stomach jump.

The first thing I had noticed that was different transitioning this time, as it had been my first time traveling to a location outside the lab, was how I could not see the lab beyond the ramp until I crossed the dimensional threshold. Up to that point, it looked as though I was going to walk out above the city I had been looking over, as if stepping from the edge of a crow's nest, from my perch on the ramp.

If I had taken any time to think on it while I was walking, it probably would have freaked me out. It might have left me wondering whether I would have actually come back into the lab, or if I would have been stuck in either the space between the dimensions or the time in the past. If the latter were the case, what would happen when I took the final step from the ramp? Would I fall to the ground below?

Thankfully, instead, my mind was on the impact my message would have had and not the impact my body would have made on the ground in the past. I stepped forward without giving it a thought and, thus, made my transition without the anxiety I would have experienced had I been paying attention.

Holding my now queasy stomach, I made my way into the control center to find Emerson mid-hum on the jingle I had left him howling. He jumped when I called out his name, breaking wind as he did. It was bad form in such a small confined space as the control center, but I laughed anyway.

"I thought you were going to be gone longer!"

He did this every time, but usually Emily was here to explain it to him. God, how I missed her.

Now for the lie. I reminded myself how it was for Emerson's own benefit he knew nothing about what I had just done.

"Emerson, according to my watch, I was in the fourth dimension for about five minutes, but it's only ever going to last the time it takes for lightning to strike on your end. I came back quickly, as I was unable to succeed at burning a message. I am going to tweak the coordinates, as I believe I know why they were off. Then we'll do a second run."

Thankfully, Emerson took my story at face value and asked no questions.

I looked at my watch and reset it to a minute past the time I remembered to have left. There was so much still to learn about this dimensional jumping. If it had this impact on time, what was it doing to me?

Curiosity was killing me. I needed to know the reaction to my message.

My curiosity had to wait. I needed to run at least one other test so I would have results I could share when the king would no doubt inquire.

Emerson made his second round of safety and equipment checks, while I reviewed official notes Emily had put together, providing the necessary coordinates for lightning that had struck a power line post a couple weeks ago in a neighborhood not too far from my flat. The lightning gad caused a power outage, so a simple check with the power company provided the time stamp, and the local newspaper provided the location.

I was pleasantly surprised to find Emily had even translated the location into its coordinates.

I could not wait to get through this second test, as we would spend the rest of our working day investigating its results and then planning for the next.

Where Emerson had only been at work less than an hour, I had already gotten in six with my time in the fourth dimension. It figured; only I would find a way to shove more work hours in my day.

— CHAPTER 30 —

T HE SECOND TEST RAN SMOOTHLY, WHICH MIGHT SOUND GOOD, ONLY
it just meant we were getting that much closer to the king's ultimate
rise and, probably, our demise. At least our workday had finally wound
down.

I didn't know where Emerson had found a paper bag, but as I removed
it from his head and as curiosity was killing me, I asked, "Emer, can you
tell me anything that has happened that you feel may have been a result
of me burning a message in the past?"

"Not that I know of. But wait, I almost got bit in the ankle by the
neighbor's dog the other day. Did you tell the dog to do that? What's its
name again, Roofus Aexavius Sasparilla?"

"Puffy," I replied and then thought, *This is not going to be easy.*

Instead of trying to get any information of substance from Emerson,
I came up with a better idea.

"Hey Emer, do you want to get a muffin at Brown Gold?"

Brown Gold was Emerson's favorite coffee shop downtown, but more
importantly, it was also located near the library.

He didn't answer but just jumped up to leave.

As we got into our GIV, I remembered that it could be tracked. Given
our current royal assignment, I figured our vehicle stood a far greater
chance of being tracked than it would have just a couple weeks ago.

I could not shake the experiences I'd had with my visits with the king.
Each time the king had made a point to show me how much he knew,
knowledge seemingly attained with no extra effort on his part. I was

reminded that he had the world at his disposal and, thus, reminded of the disposal everyone else lived in because of it.

It was because of my fear of being tracked that I had asked Emerson if he wanted to go to the coffee shop and kick back for a few. Being at the coffee shop would get me close enough to the library where, as I would tell Emerson when we got there, I had a little history to brush up on.

As far as the car was concerned, therefore any tracking eyes, we had just stopped at Brown Gold for a cup of joe.

I also knew going to Brown Gold would have us drive past Third's Tower, thus giving me a chance to see the clock face for myself. I didn't know why, as the lightning striking the clock had occurred over a year before, but I half-expected seeing the clock tower might jar a comment from Emerson about what had happened.

I was not overly surprised, however, when all he talked about were the ravens that resided on the tower. Whatever memories or thoughts Emerson may have had on having seen the lightning and the message had long since been buried by the two things his life revolved around—science and high game scores.

This unkindness of ravens had long been considered a lucky omen for the Crown. The ravens' existence, protection, and care at the tower had existed for a lot longer than I had been around.

I could not have cared less about them, but they had always captured Emerson's attention and imagination. Aside from electronic games, not much else could hold Emerson's attention successfully for very long.

As Emerson drove south on Wingate Lane, just before turning left onto Chestnut Street and then past the tower, I looked down at the road and saw the Royal Lane lines. The lane lights were not lit; therefore, we were driving legally in the lane, but I could see them nonetheless.

Images of my being royally kidnapped reappeared. My imagination added the blue filter I had peered through on those drives when the lane was illuminated. It was only upon turning left onto Chestnut Street that my thoughts snapped back to present.

A block down Chestnut, and we were finally passing the clock tower.

Glancing up as we drove by, though I had a clear view of the eastward facing clock face, I saw nothing of my message—and no sign that it had ever existed. As over a year had passed, I guess I should not have expected to.

It was then that I realized I could not recall any memories of having seen the clock face with the message there or even having heard any news of it. I guessed it was possible that I may not have the memories, but I wondered if Emerson had any.

I had to get to the library. I needed to find out what anyone else had seen, assuming they had seen anything at all. If my actions truly had influenced this dimension, I needed to read about how the world responded.

A thought of failure had flashed across my mind. I doubted whether I had been successful at burning a message at all. Or maybe I had but in some other dimension.

If I hadn't, what was it I'd done?

I gave Emerson a few pounds, as I knew otherwise he would have tried to trade game cards for a muffin again. I left him with the currency and a plan to check out the results of the second test afterward, and then we would head home.

At the library, I stepped up to a public PC to scan the internet for news on lightning striking the clock tower. At this point, I had no idea whether lightning had even struck the clock tower. Had I somehow altered that history too?

As I keyed in the words for a simple search, my fears quickly subsided. I had typed in the word *lightning* and had just finished typing the *o* in clock, when the dynamic search instantly returned over 230,000 hits, and the numbers kept climbing.

The first headline on which I had clicked screamed off the screen, "For It Is Written: Don't Tread on Me!" a reference it made to stress the connection between the clock stopping at 4:10 a.m. and Matthew 4:10. The article pointed out how the message was intended for its audience of the non-God-fearing nature.

After reading the article tied to the headlines, as well as several others, it appeared my message had added fuel to the media's fire in its efforts to tout the occurrence of lightning striking the Great Clock of the Palace at George's Cross as a message of biblical proportions, from the almighty Himself.

I read on, and in awe, finding it reported how the image of the clock face and the message it carried had been seen around the world. It turned out I had not been exaggerating when I had thought over a billion eyes might see the message.

Other headlines that caught my eyes ranged from "We Found the Message Striking" and "The Eleventh Commandment" to those that supported the belief the message was a bunch of overly hyped graffiti, such as "Don't Write On Me" and "Shedding Some Light on Graffiti."

One article answered my questions surrounding what had happened to the message. A resident clock maker, a man by the name of Samuel Thatcher, stated he had immediately and impressively received all of the royal resources necessary to get the opal glass of the clock face repaired. He had further added how it had been no easy task, but the whole operation had been completed within hours of kicking off the Signers' Day ceremony two days later.

He described the makeup of the markings itself as being similar to the black smoke residue on the glass of a well-used candle.

As to how the message had gotten there in the first place, he tried passing it off as just having been graffiti that had somehow gone unnoticed until the lightning striking the clock had everyone looking at its face.

Lastly, an investigation had been opened to find the offenders, and he believed there had to have been many to pull of such a feat.

I learned in another article later in the week from the same paper, *The Howe Chronicle*, that the decision to remove evidence of the message from the clock face before allowing for a complete investigation was being questioned. Some members of Parliament argued having it removed before Signers' Day should not have taken priority over completion of a proper inquiry. They believed doing so had successfully removed any solid evidence that could be used to investigate the message's creators.

Knowing I was the "creator," I realized I owed a huge thanks to a clock maker, his team and resources, and even the crown for destroying evidence that, in a wild stretch, I feared could be tied directly back to me.

Though the clock's face appeared back to normal, the prior images captured by the media had already burned themselves onto retinas all around the world.

A very recent article in Mother England's primary media for all His Majesty's Europe, *The London Times*, contained an artistically and digitally altered version of the clock face, message and all. The picture had cropped the full clock face shot seen in every paper, magazine, or website I had seen. It had been cropped to zoom and focus on just the clock hands and the message. What I liked most, however, was how the image had been artistically enhanced. The artist tinted the image with an antique sepia filter and digitally illuminated it from behind, giving it a glow as if it were an old lamp shade.

The article, like most others I had read, repeated highlights of how it had been the first time the clock had stopped in its existence, which was of course aside from times when it had been intentionally stopped for maintenance. It also provided the same details in respect to the event surrounding the clock stopping.

I had nearly jumped out of my skin upon reading the one unique statement the article offered. It stated that the king had demanded the investigation into the incident be reopened and that any available materials from the message removal efforts be retrieved and sent for analysis.

I scrolled up to look more closely at the date of the article, finding it was Wednesday, October 13, 2021, less than a week prior, and timing wise, not long after the king had learned of the accidental discovery of the fourth dimensional aspects of lightning.

I had broken out in an instant sweat. Had the king made a connection?

My attention leaped back to finishing the article.

Worst-case scenario, the king was somehow successful at having the year-old remnants analyzed and discovered how the message had been burned onto the clock face.

I was relieved to find, however, that the article later reported the materials used had long been disposed of. The priority had not just been fixing the clock before the holiday but making it presentable as well.

Even still, I believed the king—with all his resources and his ability, which he had already proven to me, to have everything about anything he wanted provided to him—had probably pieced enough of it together to suspect a connection. He was the one person I feared smart enough to connect the dots and somehow recognize the message had been intended for him.

For the first time since I had decided to carry out my first rebellious mission, I realized the potential repercussions of my actions. Like stepping back through ripples extending from the epicenter of a stone tossed into calm waters, had the king traced the ripples back to the stone?

Again, I realized that I had no memories altered. Things in my mind had occurred as they had before me going back into time and changing history. I had no memories influenced by the occurrence and felt at a great disadvantage of not knowing my own current level of standing in the eyes of who I now recognized I considered as my enemy, the king.

Of all people to have as an enemy, I had somehow managed to get the most powerful person in the world.

I cleared the cache memory of the PC I had been using and then rushed back to Emerson at Brown Gold.

Through the window of the coffee shop, I had spied him playing his DS3 in his typically animated fashion. Emerson was like a brother to me, and though I had often felt sorry for the life he'd had to endure, I felt sudden warmth wash over me as I sensed he had found his way to escape to somewhere happy.

As for the message I had burned on the clock, I decided to keep it to myself and figured it would not be likely anyone would know the wiser. I would leave the storytelling to the media.

PART IV

Accidents Happen

— CHAPTER 31 —

Friday, October 22, 2021

PACING IN A PRIVATE STUDY, THE KING RUMINATED ON HIS END GAME and how to deal with the loose ends—yet only after getting all he needed from them. He would often go there as, from the security of this study, he could think through and resolve issues he knew he could not share.

No one, not even his trusted advisors, knew details surrounding his latest pet project. He knew he needed to keep it that way, lest it make his plans vulnerable.

So, pacing from within the security of his study, his initial thoughts turned to his greatest dependency and biggest threat, Joshua Franks. He knew he could not get rid of him yet. The key word being *yet.*

He imagined himself pacing a path toward his solutions, with each thought a stepping-stone. *I believe my breaking of his relationship with the Etheridge girl has helped, but I also know I cannot break the hold she has on his heartstrings. I need to use that to my advantage. That girl is the ace up my sleeve, the token I can play to apply further pressure on Joshua to perform.*

I cannot prove it, but I know that boy had a hand in the clock message, so maybe it's time I played my ace.

I need to remind the rogue scientist of his place.

As he paced, he planned an innocuous yet effective threat. Though he had decided he could not directly "tread" on Franks yet, he could definitely "tread" all around him.

A simple investigation had provided him with an opportunity. With just the snap of his fingers, he learned that Emily Etheridge drove to Peneford Heights monthly, and like clockwork, she left Sunday morning. It had not taken long to see the pattern. Emily left at 8:00 a.m. every fourth Sunday of the month to make the two-hour-long drive from her flat in George's Cross to the Peneford Heights Communications Station. She had network maintenance responsibilities at the station, testing the servers and connections, performing updates, and the like.

Peneford Heights sat a couple of hours north toggling the border of the provinces Burgoyne to the south and Sandwich to the north.

Upon learning of her monthly visits, he thought, *I don't want to throw my ace, just show it. I can have some guards follow her. All I need now is simply to scare her. That alone will keep Joshua Franks on the straight and narrow.*

When the time comes, and with a wave of my hand and royal smile on my face, I will have them both eliminated, as well as that dolt of a technician, Flanders.

The king knew Emily's car, like those of all PURPOSE recipients', was just a royal rental.

Keeping costs to a minimum, all such cars were identical. There were no additional costs associated with managing the manufacturing of multiple designs, colors, amenities, and the like.

Emily's rental, as with all others, was a dull blue four-door sedan, the blue typically referred to as medical blue. Most vehicles on the road fit this description.

The king also knew all such government-owned program vehicles came loaded with technology—not for the comfort or entertainment of its user but so the government could monitor its investments, both the car and its PURPOSE-ful driver. The ability to track any vehicle by its tracking identification number, its TIN, was the one such technological feature the king had in mind.

Another quick search, this time on the plates of Emily's car, gave him the TIN he needed.

And so, the king assigned two of his guards with the tasks of tracking the TIN he provided, intercepting the car as Emily made her way to Peneford Heights, to put a Royal Lane scare into her and send a message that should be as obvious to Joshua as the burning of the message onto the clock face had become to the king.

— CHAPTER 32 —

Saturday, October 23, 2021

I HAD JUST GOTTEN TO THE LAB WHEN I RAN INTO JEREMY BILKES. With the look on his face, I knew he wanted to talk.

It had not been until after Geoffrey Talbrook's death by ambition that Jeremy Bilkes finally got the courage to confess to Samantha Edmunds what had really happened that had led to her demotion. And even then, it was not until a chance encounter where I now know he had run into her that he had given her any indication he had something to confess.

They had agreed to meet yesterday at, of all places, Brown Gold before work.

Jeremy had briefly confessed as much to me and shared his telling to Samantha.

Upon learning the details behind the truth, I realized I had had the illustrious honor of being royally kidnapped and delivered to the king twice so he could tell me all the things he knew, yet he made no mention of Geoffrey's hand in sabotaging the programming and implicating Samantha. I found it hard to believe the king had not known. He had not shared these details with me as it would not have benefited him to do so, but he knew.

His knowing, and Professor Rancor's pleas, may have been the only things that truly spared Samantha the disgrace of being sent home branded as a N'er-do-well.

As it was, Jeremy had been riddled with guilt, and upon spilling his story to Samantha in the coffee shop, he said she sat stunned.

Jeremy said Samantha realized that, if she were in the same threatened situation, she would have probably done the same. Though it was not without a degree of shame, I wasn't sure I would have done any differently.

Geoffrey Talbrook had always been a threat to all—a black cloud in the already and always dark gray skies hanging over the heads of his PURPOSE-ful peers and their families.

I was not overly surprised by Jeremy's confession and especially Geoffrey's influence in the scheme. But it was what Jeremy shared afterward that left me stunned. We had been talking in the lab when he motioned me toward the control center.

"I have some program changes I want to show you," he said as he directed me in.

"Sure. I wasn't aware of any other changes on the docket. What's up?"

Having both entered the control center, he closed the door behind me and, when he had turned back around, was handing me a letter. Jeremy's hand was shaking.

Pointing at the letter, all he had said and in a whisper was, "From Samantha," as he motioned nervously for me to read it.

I unfolded the letter and anxiously read through.

I had known Samantha's demotion had landed her a much lower position as an assistant processing files in the Placement Services department in PURPOSE's administrative office.

In the letter she mentioned how it had been in her task of creating job profiles and processing results of candidate matching that she had reviewed a high-level request, a royal request by mark, titled Pieces of Eight. It had been submitted to fill eight positions, and the responsibilities were all the same—to manage code partitioned from the project FHM720.

There was no way Samantha knew anything about project FHM724; it was a need-to-know project only, and she had no need to know. She even had no idea how lucky she was for that.

What Samantha did know, however, was the programming details behind project FHM720. FHM720 was the program she had been working on alongside Emily before her unwarranted disgrace and demotion.

She explained in the letter how the program code for FHM720 had eight segments, previously equally divided between her and Emily.

I already knew that, in the balance of things, Samantha's demotion was offset by a promotion, if you could call it that, for Emily, as she had inherited Samantha's code and responsibilities. It had not meant an increase in pay for Emily but an increase in value; therefore, any failure would only translate into an increase in penalty.

So, where this offset left Emily holding the bag of all programming responsibility, it also left her as the one person with full knowledge of the program's code.

Samantha knew this, so for her to see a request, her first and only royal one no less, to parse the code ownership into eight separate chunks, she knew it could not be good for her lost friend. As she explained in the letter, Samantha saw the writing on the wall and believed the plans requested would make Emily obsolete.

Upon reading this, I looked up at Jeremy, who had not moved or said a thing while I had been reading. He even still had his hand held out as it had been when I had taken the letter.

Samantha had not even known about the new project, in which Emily's responsibilities had not even really changed from the prior, and she was worried. She had no idea how right she was to be worried.

Jeremy and I both know how much higher the stakes were now. And to be royally deemed obsolete—I saw why Jeremy had been shaking when he handed the letter to me.

In my mind, my initial question was why Samantha had not directly communicated to Emily. Emily had recently told me how, since they were younger, she and Samantha would secretly send messages to each other via a special and simple sublevel messaging program they had coded. They called it the undercurrent. The code was nested deeply on the servers and used very little resources and bandwidth; it had always gone unnoticed. She even felt secure enough about it to share the access with me.

I answered my own question, as I figured Samantha had probably tried, but Emily would have to answer the initiating call. And with their fallout, she may not have answered.

Finally, with the letter now shaking in my hand, I spoke. "Jeremy, I have to get this message to Em. She needs to know."

Emily was attending required classes today, so I would not see her, but I decided I would call her tonight to initiate messaging on the undercurrent. I need to get Samantha's message to her and feared a large boulder had been pushed down life's hill and was gaining volume and momentum as it hurled toward her.

I thought to myself, *How fast our meager lives have turned on us, and all because of an accidental discovery and an evil man. My love denied, Emily is in a perilous position now. And as bad as that is, she merely represents the first domino in this line that includes everyone I hold dear.*

— CHAPTER 33 —

Sunday, October 24, 2021

I HAD TRIED TO CALL EMILY A COUPLE OF TIMES LAST NIGHT, BUT SHE'D never answered. I didn't want to raise alarms to prying ears so decided I'd just try again this morning.

I had intended to call her at eight o'clock, but here it was before seven, and she was calling me.

She rarely called anymore. It was too hard emotionally and not safe to talk, at least about anything we would want to talk about. We had even tried the undercurrent messaging a couple nights, but to her, it seemed wrong. She would get angry, so the calling and messaging had stopped.

When I answered her call now, she spoke only two words, "Hello, Joshua."

The call would be short and bittersweet, as its true intention was to direct me back to undercurrent.

The fact she had even called me back triggered my anxiety. My leg started twitching the way it did whenever I got nervous. I remembered how, whenever Emily saw my leg start twitching, she would say my nervous reaction was like a dog being pet behind the ear.

"Hello, Joshua."

Had she repeated herself, or had I let her voice echo in my mind?

Catching the hidden but expected intent, I replied, "Hello, Emily."

She continued, "I am about to head up to PH and may swing by tonight upon my return with some of Emerson's favorite pastries."

She would not even mention the name, but I knew, she meant the bear claws from Peneford Heights Bakery.

Shit, I forgot she'd be making that drive today!

I pulled it together as quick as I could and replied, "Uh, he's still asleep. But I'm sure he'll appreciate it." After another pause, as the concern that flooded over me almost made me feel as if I were drowning, I added, "Drive carefully."

Her voice wavered as she responded, "Of course, always. Goodbye."

With that, the call ended.

Things are moving way too fast, and I don't have a hand on the steering wheel. I need to do something, but what?

I immediately jumped on my laptop and plugged in the external card Emily had given me to access the messaging program. As I signed in, the card altered the identity of my laptop, diverted its location, and sent all communications down a hopefully still secure and obscure path.

In a physical sense, however, this virtual underground communication pathway reminded me of the hidden network of roads and locations I now knew existed beneath the kingdom, and at the king's disposal. It seemed anymore, everything reminded me of yet another reason to feel unsafe and vulnerable.

I only hoped eyes with royal interests would not recognize us since our altered IDs were off their watchdog list and search grid.

Once in the messaging program, I saw where Emily had already forwarded me the rundown on Samantha's revelation and apologies, but more importantly, the warning that had prompted Samantha to reopen communication with her. So, Samantha had somehow found a way to get through to Emily.

The message Emily typed uncharacteristically contained misspelled words. I saw that as another sign that she was shaken and legitimately scared.

I replied, "Em, don't go to Peneford. I now feel like we need to do something to try to get some semblance of control of our lives before it's too late."

I could read the anxiety in her reply. "What do you think we can do, Joshua? There is nowhere to hide in the king's world."

She was pushing herself away from me by calling me Joshua.

"We can escape to the villages, Emer included. It wouldn't be easy, but at least we'd have each other."

I realized how desperate I was now sounding. I'd never felt I had much of any control of my destiny, but even the small amount I had held onto had now seemed to fall like sand through my fingers.

Her reply showed me she had already resolved that any effort to alter the course would be futile. "Joshua, you know what that king will do. He will first go after everyone we care about. Even if we did escape, it would only be a matter of time. And at what cost? I don't know how much time there is before he has implemented his Pieces of Eight, but I don't think he's one to waste time when he is to benefit. I don't know how long my wick is but just that it is a short one."

There was a pause in the messaging. I didn't know what to say in response, but I could tell by the active text ellipses she had more to say.

I sat in silence for what seemed several minutes and then finally received her follow-up. "Josh, you know my parents live just north of Peneford Heights. I'm not sure whether waiting until my next birthday to see them is going to be an option, so I'm going to try to see them, even if for only minutes, before I head back tonight."

Emily had already convinced herself resistance was futile and that it might be the last time she would get to see her family.

Realizing there was nothing I could say to convince her otherwise, as well as believing her fears were not unfounded, I relented and asked her if she would at least message when she reached her parents. Thankfully, her parents lived close enough to the communication station that they were within reach of an internet connection, though they had no means o utilizing it, and Emily promised she would take her fully charged laptop with her.

I asked her to keep the laptop on during her drive. She promised she would but questioned why. I danced around answering, moving back to having her promise she would message when she got there. I did not want to tell her why, as the reason would have only stressed her more than she already was.

Using the Find My Device app on my laptop, I had added her laptop as a device of mine so it could be located. I did not want to tell her I wanted her to leave her laptop on so I could digitally locate her, which I would be frantically trying to do if she did not text me within a few hours. The drive to Peneford Heights was just over two hours.

I typed our secret message, "Indigo lights, on violet evenings, yellow orange undertones," to which she replied, "Indigo lights, on violet evenings, yellow orange undertones trail on ominously."

I countered simply, 'Touché,' to her addition in reply but shivered as I absorbed the choice of words she had selected to answer back in code— *trail on ominously.*

As a result, my final reply was simply a reminder for her to message once she got there safely.

⸺ CHAPTER 34 ⸺

E MILY WAS NEARLY TWO HOURS INTO HER DRIVE, HEADING NORTH ON, at this point, a relatively empty Darby Highway around the Pocono Mountains when the Royal Lane lights kicked on. Another ten kilometers, and she would have reached the end of the Royal Lane on the Darby Highway. There, it finally crossed the border leaving the George's Cross Expanse and seemingly stepped back in time to the lesser-developed outreaches, where the Peneford Height's Communication Station, she had told Joshua and Emerson, was literally the only location similar to something they'd see in the city.

She had not even been driving in the Royal Lane when its royal blue lights kicked on, but she knew the black Jaguar quickly appearing larger in her rearview mirror was there for her.

You could call it paranoia, if only she had not been correct.

There was no comfort in being right. Emily panicked.

This panic was the wild card held in this stacked card game of control the king had been trying to play against Joshua.

As the Jaguar was now quickly upon her and no longer even in the Royal Lane, but in hers, Emily lost it in panic. The knowledge of her obsolescence as a catalyst combined with the high-speed pursuit by the guards created a fear that pushed her over the edge.

She lost control of the car, missed a turn and sent the car careening over the literal edge, mirroring her loss of self-control. The car flipped several times as it sped and tumbled down the hill and into a massive boulder at the bottom of the ravine. The impact immediately caused the car to explode. As if in an act of mercy, the impact from the boulder made sure Emily had not suffered.

⌘

Upon hearing the outcome of his plan, the king was not pleased.

He instructed the guards to report to him immediately upon return.

There, less than three hours after the accident and now kneeling before him, they pleaded their case. They unemotionally explained that it had been an accident, over which they had no control.

The king waved a hand. Another two guards appeared behind them immediately, though remaining stealthily in the shadows.

Stating how he understood, though with a note of sarcasm, that, "Accidents happen," the king pretended to forgive. The second wave of his hand, however, was not as good at pretending. It had not pretended to forgive, as it gestured for the final act and inevitable conclusion of the guards' assignment, their final assignment.

The two guards, themselves disposable, were shot in the head and killed instantly.

From the shadows, another pair of guards stepped out to finish their current assignments. They were to remove the bodies and the mess. Any sign that the two dead guards had ever been there, much less ever existed, were to be wiped away and for no other reason than cleanliness. The king had already moved on.

To himself, as the king had walked unemotionally away, he muttered, "Oops, accidents happen."

238

PART V

When I Lost Her Again

— CHAPTER 35 —

I HAD JUST GOTTEN OFF THE COMPUTER WITH EMILY WHEN EMERSON had gotten up.

I had him help me "clean up" the place. I had whispered to him the intent was to search for bugs. Validating the paranoia, we'd found two. I'd found one attached to a lamp in the living room, and Emerson had found one in the dining area under the corner of our table. I'd told him not to say anything if he found one but to merely get my attention. We weren't able to find any more. Then we took a quick step outside after I had announced I needed his help to replace the light bulb in the front door lamp. I told Emerson we needed to somehow diffuse the bugs without making listening ears aware we had found them.

He came up with the brilliant idea of very quietly moving them to his underwear drawer.

The voice of paranoia still screamed in my head to keep my voice at a whisper. It knew, as I did, that the information I now planned to share with Emerson could get us killed.

A nervous wreck, after having swept the flat, I jumped back to my laptop and repeatedly clicked the refresh icon in the device location application.

Emerson understood what was going on. And I was reminded that, although Emily was my love, she was one of his best friends—one, as in one of two, the second being me. Together, we followed Emily's progress at every click of the location app's refresh button.

In between clicks, I flipped through my journals, divulging to an amazingly captivated Emerson, the recent revelations about my heritage. Even though we believed we had taken care of the bugs, I continued to speak in a whisper. At first Emerson laughed at my still whispering, until that is, the gravity of what I was sharing hit him.

While we witnessed Emily's progress north and to the outskirts of George's Cross, I shared with Emerson the story of what had really happened leading up to the Signers' Day of Reckoning. Then I told Emerson about the true heroes as written in a firsthand account by my newly discovered ancestor, Benjamin Franklin. "Speaking of his name, I proudly prefer my newly discovered correct surname, Franklin," I added.

After quickly agreeing to Emerson's instant preference to now be referred to as "Flanderslin," I continued. And when I reached the real story behind the King's Guard Jonathan Elders's fifteen minutes of fame, we saw that Emily was well on her way up the Darby Highway.

By the time I told him of General George Washington's speech that forged the freedom fighters' resolution into hardened and fearless steel, Emily, an hour and a half into her trip, had reached Felder's Point, a town at the junction where Darby Highway crossed another east-west counterpart known simply as Earl's Way.

Emerson stared at the laptop, repeating under his breath the old saying I had told him George Washington had referred to in his speech. "Men make history ... Men make history ... Men make history."

Lastly, and in between several more refreshes on the locator program, I told him how I saw us as being in no less of a position to warrant revolution. The fire had been smoldering inside, but it only seemed to get hotter and hotter as I continued.

For his part, Emerson sat seemingly stunned into attention. He seemed to absorb every word, only whispering to express concern for Emily. "Where is she at now, Josh?"

I clicked refresh. She had just reached the northern edge of the George's Cross Expanse. On the one hand, I was happy she had made it that far without incident. But that thought only led to the fact she would need to drive back. And what then? Was every day going to be spent worrying about becoming the next discard played by the king?

It was Emily today, but Emerson and I were not far behind in having been tapped out of our usefulness. We would be replaced by a handful of other pawns.

The king would use his time-messaging process to alert him of dissension, or opportunities, so he could strengthen his already most powerful position in what truly would become his world.

I paused long enough in my rant to click refresh once more.

At first, I thought the screen simply had not refreshed. It seemed to show that Emily had not moved since the previous click, which did not make sense, as the area she was in did not exactly have a place for her to stop.

I clicked refresh again, but again her location put her on the Darby Highway at the northern edge of the George's Cross Expanse. Something was wrong. I looked at Emerson and could see he sensed it too. I clicked refresh again and then again, anguished, as it was all I could do. It would not be of any help to Emily if she was in trouble, and it was certainly not helping Emerson and me now.

I looked at the coordinates provided by the location. I grabbed a pen and paper, intending to write the coordinates and the time down. I didn't know what I was going to do. I just felt I needed to do something, and those coordinates were all I had to work with. I had inadvertently tried to write with my lightning pen. Its fused tip would no longer relinquish the ink I needed, stubbornly holding its position and causing me to tear the paper as I nervously tried to scribble the coordinates.

Emerson made the connection, silently grabbing the pen from my hand and replacing it with another he had found.

I jotted down the time, 10:18 a.m., and then the coordinates on the torn sheet of paper; 41°14'55" N 76°17'52" W. In desperation, I clicked refresh again ad then again. We hoped to find that she had continued on or at least expected to see that she had still not moved. What we saw in response to the refresh had not been an option on our list. The results returned indicated that the laptop was now offline.

I must have clicked another twenty times before finally stopping. There could have been any number of reasons why the Find My Device app continued to show Emily's laptop as off-line; maybe the network was down, maybe her laptop battery died, maybe a storm was interfering. My repeated clicking was no more fruitful than a doctor trying frantically to revive a patient already lost; though the flat line would not go away, the "doctor" in me refused to call it.

I stared at the coordinates I had written—41°14'55" N 76°17'52" W.

Turning to Emerson and snapping him out of a state of shock, I asked, "Emer, you know how you hack into your games to reveal game codes and unlock powers?"

He stared back, simply nodding—showing my question had reached him enough to subconsciously respond.

"Have you ever hacked into any other programs, say, for example, at work? I want to see if you can hack into the Royal Lane digital files for these coordinates to see if the Royal Lane kicked on near them."

It was a stretch of an idea, and I wasn't even sure at first how I had made the connection. The pieces were there, though—my own recent experiences with the Royal Lanes, the king's endless resources and knowledge of everything, Emily's programming experience with the program that archived the footage, and so on.

It was Emerson's single word response, however, that made the stretch of an idea seem possible. "Sam."

— CHAPTER 36 —

"**Y**OU'RE A GENIUS, EMER."

The past had put some bad blood between Samantha and Emily, Emerson, and me. But I had to hope Samantha's recent revelations concerning what had led to her downfall, not to mention her already expressed concerns for Emily, would have her willing to help us, if only for Emily.

I pulled her number up on my cell and was reminded that I had changed her name from Samantha Edmunds to "S-a-bitch-a Edmunds."

I thought of Emily and then closed my eyes and pressed call.

It took three long rings.

While it rang, I remembered I would have to speak in the code that would tell her to go to the messaging program. I would call her by her full name, Samantha, and only hope she would recall that, in better days, I had always called her Sam.

I didn't know if it was out of restrained anger or whether her shared fears about Emily's well-being and royal ears had preempted her, but when she answered, she simply said, "Joshua?"

"Samantha." I paused, however, because I had not thought this plan through enough to know what I was going to say next.

As if she were reading my mind, she spoke first, and with an inconspicuous lie. "Are you looking for Emily's journal? She mentioned you might call if you couldn't find it for her. I'm afraid I haven't come across it either."

Playing along, I replied, "Well it was worth a try. I hope I find you well."

"Yes, thank you. I'll keep looking for it."

We said our goodbyes. The conversation as a whole would mean nothing to other listening ears, but I hung up believing Samantha was on the same page as me.

I immediately plugged the program card Emily had given me back into the laptop and then signed into the secret connection. Again, eyes with royal interest should not recognize me, if they noticed the connection at all.

Back in the messenger program, I recalled that the last time I had been in it was my last communication with Emily. I prayed it would not be so in a literal sense.

I messaged Sam, who I was relieved to find had, in fact, understood the underlying message in the call and immediately pinged back.

Wasting no time, I jumped into my intended plan and typed, "Sam, I need to ask a huge favor, for Emily. I know this will put you at risk and would not ask if I truly did not believe we are all at risk anyway."

Sam quickly responded that she understood.

I continued, and after explaining to her that Emerson and I had been following Emily via the device location app, I typed, "Sam, I have both the time and coordinates where we had last tracked Em. I need to know if the king had anything to do with why she has disappeared off the map." Unless Emily had shared something with her, Samantha still did not know about FHM724. I did not have time to explain so added, "I can't go into details, but there's a project you probably aren't aware of that has us working directly for the king. The project's utmost secrecy and Em's obsolescent status in it have us genuinely worried about her safety."

"How can I help?"

To confirm what I believed to be true, I asked, "You worked with Em on the program to track and archive Royal Lane usage, right?"

"Yes, program FHM682."

"Does that program record times and locations of activity?"

"Yes, as their digital recordings are used as evidence in trials to officially prove when someone broke the law and drove in an activated Royal Lane."

"I know this is asking you to take a big risk, but can you tap into the program to see if the royal lane was activated at the time and location where we last tracked Em?"

There was a pause in communication, I presumed because Samantha had to think it through, both the capability and the willingness to take the risk.

After a couple minutes and numerous refreshes on the still open locater app, I received her reply, "I'll see what I can do and will ping you as soon as I know."

I quickly provided her with the coordinates and time stamp and then began the eternal wait for her response or, even better, any indication Emily was ... alive.

— CHAPTER 37 —

PICKING UP WHERE I HAD LEFT OFF IN MY WHISPERED DOWNLOAD TO Emerson, I looked at the list on the other side of the paper, Emily's paper, where I had written the coordinates I had provided to Samantha.

Suddenly, it was as if I had been struck by a lightning. I think my download to Emerson provided a cohesive spark but believe the credit for the lightning could only be attributed to the culmination of all that had recently occurred—both in the revelations of truth in history and all that had led me, and everyone I cared for, into a seemingly inescapable corner, each trapped there by the Crown. Though the head under the crown may have changed over time, what it represented had not.

The Crown, and all it had represented in detriment to all it had ruled throughout relative history, had provided the negative ions forever raining down on our world. However, and in irony, the project for the king, FHM724, or at least the discovery that had led to it, provided the enabler for the existence of positive ions.

Positive ions had last reared their revolutionary heads centuries ago but had failed to seal the necessary connection with the negative to generate the lightning that would have allowed them to succeed in striking. Because of their failure to connect, we as a society still drowned in the deluge of injustice that the revolutionaries had fought so hard to end. As if being reminded every day by our own struggles was not enough, we were reminded of the Signers' failure each year on July 2, "celebrating" the Signers' Day of Reckoning.

The simple spark provided by whispering all I had learned to Emerson allowed me to recognize the reemergence of the positive ions. It was our time, our turn, and our responsibility to try to strike. It was our turn to throw the positive ions at all the negative raining down upon us—the clash of which could result in a lightning that could strike down the very crown that enabled them.

Having just been struck by the lightning of revelation, I must have frozen in place. I snapped out of my frozen state at the hands of Emerson, who had been shaking me by my shoulders. The look in his eyes alone conveyed belief he had lost me.

"Josh … Josh!"

"I'm OK, Emer. I'm OK," I finally responded, though with the revelation I was just about to share with him, even I was not sure what I had said was true. Not to mention, the optimist in me kept me in denial about my true thoughts as to Emily's well-being.

I reached for the chip of stone, the remnant from my parent's fireplace; I had retrieved it from its safe haven in the journal that morning and placed it in my shirt pocket, close to my heart. Rubbing it with my thumb, I repeated in a whisper the general's words, an adage in which he had resolutely believed, "Men make history. Men make history."

Still whispering, I added, "Emerson, what do you think's going to happen to us—me, you, Em, Sam, Professor Rancor, and everyone we care for?"

A sad look took over him. "We are so screwed."

"If you thought you could do something, anything to fight back, would you do it?"

He replied without hesitation. "For everyone I cared about, yes."

"Even if it meant risking all that we know to be our world today?"

"What do you mean?"

"I mean, what if we could do something that would strike at the root of why we're so screwed, for that matter, could do something that would strike at the root of why our world has been screwed for centuries, would you do it? Even if it meant risking a change to the histories of our own existence?"

At that moment, I recalled yet another statement I had read in Benjamin Franklin's journal. It too had been a quote from General Washington's speech to his comrades of fate. Without realizing I was now speaking aloud, I made the declaration as if it had been my own, "It is against extraordinary odds that one needs to take extraordinary actions."

I was not sure whether Emerson understood where I was going with this. Again, I had failed him by forgetting how truly intelligent he is. I realized my mistake as soon as he answered, although he too had just been speaking to himself aloud.

He whispered in response, "Men make history."

— CHAPTER 38 —

THE OPTIMIST IN ME HOPED THE NEXT CALL OR MESSAGE I WOULD get would not be from Samantha, but from Emily. I wanted so badly for the optimist to be right, but the more time went by waiting for any call, the more I genuinely feared time would prove him wrong.

All we could do was wait. I decided to follow my thoughts down the planning path they had since led me. If anything, it provided us with the blessing of distraction, and though the ordinary man in me felt the path led only to a land of fantasy, the extraordinary hinted otherwise. This path seemed the only tunnel with the possibility of light at its end.

Quite honestly, however, I was not sure I could stop myself from continuing anyway. With all that had pushed us down this path, it had become a snowball rolling down a mountain of snow, picking up mass and steam as it continued to roll.

So, with time singing its foreboding tune louder by the tick and Emerson still by my side and at full attention, I would share the fantasy of a plan I had been formulating.

I would start by retrieving the journals from their place stashed in my room. I especially would need the one Benjamin Franklin had written while in jail awaiting his fate. It contained his and the other Signers' reflections—specifically those, in hindsight, he felt could have made a difference in enabling perhaps a different ending to his story, to history.

As I got up from my chair, Emerson immediately responded, "Wha'? Where're you going?"

"I'll be right back. I have to get something I want to show you"—I paused long enough to formulate what I would say next, fearing we were being listened to—"but, more importantly, that we will need to continue our efforts."

With that, I ran to my room and retrieved the journals. Wasting no time, I put the jail journal on top of the stack and opened it toward the back, before the pages where Benjamin's Loyalist son William had entered his account of the Signers' Day of Reckoning. By the time I got back to Emerson, I was already rereading Benjamin's reflections.

I plopped back down in the chair, looked up at Emerson and caught the expression of awe on his face at what he was seeing—tangible proof of what I had previously whispered to exist. I was appropriately alerted, by his expression, that he might say something aloud in response and potentially give away their existence to ears we could not afford to share them with. I quickly motioned him Emily's shush signal, whispering to answer the question I knew he would ask, "Yes, these are the journals."

I grabbed the list, Emily's list, and a pen, remembering to make sure this time that it was the one Emerson had given me earlier and not my lightning stylus. Emily's list contained what Professor Poopypants had ranted about as historical hindsight—a collection of realizations that, had the Signers had them in time, would likely have led to us telling and living a completely different story. I intended to add to that list what the Signers themselves had learned in hindsight.

As I looked at the paper, I realized I was reading its back, where I had written the coordinates for Samantha. I flipped it over, not realizing the pang that would hit me when I recognized Emily's handwriting. I reminded myself to focus on the distraction at hand and began reading the list. It was not in an outline form or even numbered but was scribbled, more like the letters were just thrown on the sheet. Having always seen Emily's writing in her journal, however, I had long become accustomed to her note-taking style. Where I could read it, I knew I would need to rewrite it and in an organized format. I needed some paper of my own. Lost in my train of thought, I had turned to get up and run back to my room for some paper when my eyes caught Emerson. The poor guy had been sitting there frozen, staring at me with hungry eyes, eyes that were starving to know what the hell was going on, but disciplined enough to know not to interrupt. I had yet to share the plan.

"Emer," I quietly stated, "I need to grab a sheet of paper, but I promise I will share the plan as soon as I get back."

With that, I was off again. Having returned to my room, I grabbed at my book bag on the floor next to my bed. I remembered the notebook I had come for was in its back pocket, but as soon as I grabbed the bag, I also remembered what its front pocket held. In its small front pocket was where I had stuffed the envelope the king had given me with the instructions, coordinates, and message I was to send him at his spot behind the wall of Anderson Raines's fallen lightning lab. The rebel in me, growing stronger by the minute, insisted I grab the envelope instead of the notebook. I figured the list I was about to write was far more worthy of royal stationary than the drivel of a power-hungry tyrant.

The birthday card Emily had made for me was standing open on my nightstand. I grabbed it and stuffed it gently into my shirt pocket.

As I turned to return to Emerson at the table, I was startled by the sound of loud music. I recognized the song instantly as it was the intro music to one of Emerson's favorite video games, *In the Rocks of the Ingerglock*. I swear I'd had to listen to that annoying music over a million times. Was he actually going to start playing that game now?

The song, and variations of it, played throughout the game. The intro, however, was the only version that contained lyrics. I had heard it enough times, as it blared every time Emerson started the game up, that I was already aware of what was coming. In about three seconds, a choir of angels would sing, "Saved by the warriors of Ingerglock, safe haven found in their world of igneous rock." The angels' lines would be followed immediately by monks chanting in the background, "Hard rock ... bedrock." They would repeat the line three times, with Emerson always right there with them. And when playing the game, he would repeat the monks' lines when it fit in appropriately with the music variations playing throughout gameplay.

As I made my way down the hall, the angels' song kicked in. I was about to yell at Emerson in disbelief, until I noticed he was not sitting propped in front of the screen prepping to play the game but had actually returned to the table. Then it clicked. He was merely providing noise so we could stop the awkward whispering and speak more freely. With the game stuck on its intro, its annoying music would loop, providing us with nonstop interference for any ears trying to listen in to our conversation. I had never appreciated that annoying song—or Emerson's inner genius—so much.

Back with Emerson at the table, I witnessed his expression's metamorphosis before me. It began the moment his eyes caught sight of the royal envelope. I remembered I had not shared, under royal threat of course, the fact the king had personally handed me instructions he had written using his royal stationary, fully emblazoned with the royal insignia.

Emerson began sniffing the air like a dog. I would have thought he had lost it, and then it hit me as well—the smell, the royal smell that I had smelled before and in the company of the kidnapping king. That smell was now emanating from the envelope and had made its way to our noses, mine for the third time but Emerson's for the very first.

"That smells amazing."

My immediate thoughts concurred, but I caught myself and slammed the door on the foot of agreement. "No, Emer," I murmured, "it's the smell of evil and all that's wrong. These are instructions the king gave me, containing what he wanted me to tell him via lightning in the past in his quest for more power."

Having tried to explain the letter to Emerson, I realized, when I got to the writing in the past through lightning part, how we had not yet given that ability a name. The only way we had been referring to it, since it had become a project, was by its project name, FHM724. I was not intending to do it "For His Majesty" any longer so needed to quickly rectify that situation. Anything but what we had been calling it would be better, so I settled on the first thought that came to mind—*writening*.

Wow, writening, *I thought.* It was so punnily lame, but I liked it anyway. Then, providing another bad pun and yet a valid reason to support the new name, I respelled a variation of it in my mind as, *rightening*. I knew neither *writening* nor *rightening* were words, but I connected to them phonetically. And to me they had appropriate meanings.

The music, cranked and locked in a loop, had returned to its only lyrics, starting in falsetto with, "Saved by the warriors of Ingerglock, safe haven found in their world of igneous rock." I looked at Emerson just in time to catch him only mouthing the, "Hard rock ... bedrock," in unison with the monks.

With the new project name reverberating through my head and the video game intro in my ears, I smiled and opened the envelope, pulling the paper out and flipping it immediately, as I had no interest in the side the king had written on.

Before I started rewriting the list, I knew I owed Emerson further explanation. I needed to share my plan. I grabbed from the pile of journals Mr. Franklin's *Experiments and Observations on Electricity*. I carefully flipped through its old pages, scanning for the corner of the bedsheet I remember I had stashed as a bookmark on the page for which I was now looking. Having found it, I set the journal down opened on the page found. The corner of fabric made me think of my parents. I decided they would be proud of what I was now planning—of my taking action.

Not wanting to waste any more time, I cut to the chase. "Emer, what I'm showing you now is from Benjamin Franklin's science journal. In a nutshell, he was an amazing scientist among other great things, and the pages you're looking at now contain his notes on his experiment with lightning."

"Whoa!"

"Yeah, whoa. You see, Emer, we have the date, time, and coordinates of when lightning struck and when Benjamin Franklin happened to be out in the storm flying a kite."

The angels returned, "Saved by the warriors of Ingerglock, safe haven found in their world of igneous rock."

Let it go, just let it go, I thought to myself, though I still paused long enough for Emerson's favorite part to play through.

Moving the journal carefully aside, I pointed to Emily's list, "We also have a list of things we have learned in hindsight. If the Signers had known this list's contents back then, we quite possibly could be living in a completely different world today. My plan is we're going to tap into that storm, more specifically that lightning, and burn a message on Benjamin Franklin's kite, filling him in on all that has been learned in hindsight. We're going to try to rewrite history. And I can only hope that we succeed and that we find ourselves living free in its happier ending."

I imagined I had tidbits of this plan floating in my mind since the first time I had read the journals. I now pictured these tidbits trying to connect like skydivers as they dropped together, trying to form a circle while free-falling toward terra firma, victims of their own gravities but armed with the choice to, only moments later, pull their cords. My "skydiver" thoughts, the tidbits, had finally formed their circle as a cohesive ring. And for the first time, I had spoken their collective results aloud.

Had I actually found we had a cord we could pull too?

Again, my thoughts jumped back to the promise I had made to my signers—my parents—that I would do everything I could to bring honor to the name Franklin.

I looked at Emerson, who by now had fire in his eyes. I imagined the flames were lit by a combination of the thread of hope I had presented and, perhaps, a reflection of the flames burning in my own eyes. This newfound fire, however, had not prevented him from mouthing along with the monks again.

Again, I let it ride and then resumed, "Emer, I'm on the border between believing we're insane to think we can do something as risky as this and thinking that, not only can we do it, but we have to."

My thoughts turned tangent again, this time to the inscription Mr. Franklin had written under the image he had drawn of the coiled snake. I grabbed that journal and flipped until I found the image. I handed the journal to Emerson, pointing to the statement my ancestral hero had written himself so long ago, "The outcome of our efforts does nothing to negate the power of our message, for our commitment remains firm, and the echo of its message will long outlive our final breaths."

I looked to Emerson, I had to ask him the same questions I had asked myself when I had first read it. "How firm is our commitment? How strong is the power of our message?"

It seemed by his response that the adage he recalled from my own telling of historic truths discovered had embedded itself in his mind. Without hesitation, he again replied his newly adopted mantra, "Men make history."

Pressing to continue, I went on to point out that, beyond the list Emerson was already familiar with, Mr. Franklin had made his own list of sorts.

I returned the journal from Emerson to the stack and picked up the one I had originally been reading when I had first returned to the table carrying them. The journal was still opened to the page I had flipped to.

I handed it over to Emerson, "Read this, Emer."

He eagerly yet gingerly accepted the old journal I had just passed him. The angels sang their piece.

While he read on, Emerson and the monks followed with theirs, though this time by the third, Emerson's voice boomed, "Hard rock … bedrock!"

I began the undertaking, rewriting a concise and complete summary consisting of both Benjamin's and Emily's lists.

As I wrote it, I tried to take into account how Benjamin Franklin would respond. If Emerson and I were to succeed at what we seemed committed now to try, Mr. Franklin would find this list burned onto his kite after lightning had just struck it as he had set out to discover its electrical properties.

As I considered the event, I recalled that it had occurred many years before any thoughts of separating from the Crown existed.

From memory, I believed it was in June 1752 that he had flown the kite, but it would not be for another twenty-three years, in 1775, before he would make his way back to America from England with the intent of separation from British rule.

The list I would be writing him would not make any sense to him at the time he received it. I realized the impact this would have on him being able to take the kite seriously but reasoned the sheer fact he had just received a message burnt by lightning onto his kite might be enough for him to feel some amount of prophetic connection worthy of at least holding onto it. I decided I would supplement the list with a preface explaining the importance of not just holding onto but hiding the list until the time was right.

I had hoped the planning, and maybe even the game's music still looping, would keep my mind off my immediate concerns for Emily. Not even plotting a history-changing act against the Crown via writening— more appropriately, rightening—has proven successful at that. I checked the computer again for any updates from Samantha or, even better, a word or sign from Emily; still nothing.

Emerson was right there over my shoulder, sharing the same sigh of disappointment at still not having heard from either.

I had to believe Samantha was doing everything she could and would succeed with tapping into the Royal Lane digital files. I also believed that, as soon as she did succeed, she would contact me. I had to leave her to her work, as I knew interrupting wouldn't help.

My belief, however, that something had happened to Emily and that she would not be calling me as we had planned grew stronger as time ticked on. I pushed out the negative thoughts and forced myself back to the graces of a historic distraction.

I chose to dive back into drafting my message. I diverted my attention to the length of time between Mr. Franklin's and ours. I also had to take into account the time between his receiving the message and making any sense of it.

In the process, I stumbled across another connected consideration. It was amazing how everything seemed so connected, but I recalled one of the many facts I had read about my time distant relative, this one in reference to an almanac he wrote, and more specifically his ideas on leap years.

I turned to Emerson, who by now had finished his reading and was just sitting there staring at me as I drifted in and out of thought. It was like he was waiting patiently for his next assigned task, and thankfully he was ready, because I had one for him. "Emer, I need you to check into something."

He answered eagerly, "What?" But nothing would apparently prevent him from still mouthing with the monks.

"I need you to sign into Astoria" (our system at the lab) "to check its calendar program, and make sure it'll take into account leap years when we dial in a date that goes back in the past through them. You brought your laptop home, right?"

"Yeah." Then after a long pause, had said, "I can do that. I know the calendaring system takes care of automatically recognizing leap years as the calendar moves forward, so it stands to reason its path in reverse would. Also, we're in the same time zone, so I don't think that should influence anything, but we may have to account for the daylight savings. I'll check their histories and compensate for them as well."

With purposeful task in hand, his demeanor changed instantly. Again, I kept forgetting how this current situation with Emily and everything related to it directly affected him too. I could see how my assigning him a task he could do to help brought a sense of usefulness and purpose to him. He had even responded with a complete and appropriately logical statement and followed up by identifying additional variables to consider. I was impressed to say the least and watched on as he leaped up to get his laptop.

It was then when I noticed he had pulled his "king kissing my ass" boxers over the pants he was wearing. He must have put them on when he stashed the bugs in his underwear drawer. I couldn't believe I hadn't noticed sooner. God, I loved that guy.

I jumped back into my own efforts, and the more I thought about things that could influence our attempt to change history, the more of a pipe dream it seemed. What other option, what other weapon did I have? I was increasingly convinced the king's program would only make life worse for everyone else. I also firmly believed anyone who knew too much about the program would find his or her days were numbered. Lastly, I recognized that even my parents, though they had nothing directly to do with the project, would inevitably be impacted.

Checking the time, I realized that several hours had passed since Samantha had communicated that she would try to find out whether the Royal Lane had been activated. I checked the computer for any word from Samantha, catching myself subconsciously mouth with the monks this time. But still no word from Samantha. And still no call from my Emily.

I grabbed the royal envelope to focus my efforts on the only productive thing I could think to do—draft the explanatory prelude to the list. Before flipping the envelope to its blank side, I took my pen, and in another small act of defiance, I frantically X'd out the royal insignia.

I couldn't deny a smile appeared on my face. For a very brief moment, the smile felt wrong; it felt evil. But that feeling was gone as fast as it had appeared. The true evil in this madness lay symbolically under the X I had drawn.

— CHAPTER 39 —

LESTER GRYNTHAL WAS A CAREER, ALBEIT LOW-LEVEL SPY FOR THE Crown. He worked in a division with no name, which provided grunt work services for espionage. It didn't get a name for the sake of recognition (or lack thereof). That way, if anyone in his line of work were to be caught, there would be no connection to recognize.

It may be grunt work, but it was typically high-risk grunt work. Lester was well aware he was on his own in his job and carried all the risk. He also knew he had never been given the option to choose his career. He had seen what happened to people who tried to control their destinies so had long succumbed to accepting his life's assignment. Lester was a good worker bee, a quiet worker bee. You would not hear a buzz of complaint out of him.

Lester had received this specific assignment earlier this week.

Getting a camera securely in place was easy enough, as he had been given the inhabitants' work schedules, and how to break into locked government-owned establishments had been covered early on in Spying 101.

He did not know, however, why he'd received orders to watch these two men. He merely knew he had orders that had come from above him to install the camera and watch their activities within the flat for any peculiar activity, anything out of the ordinary. If he witnessed anything, his instructions were to notify his superior, Lydia Portence, and provide her with the footage in question.

Aside from one missing item of instruction, this assignment had come across no differently than any other. The missing instruction that made the job unique to Lester was that he had not been given direction or approval to listen; therefore, he had only been given a camera and could only watch and record but not listen. He'd thought it peculiar when he'd received his instructions and found it more peculiar when, while installing his camera, he had found a couple hidden microphones in the flat.

Lester, however, knew his place as a buzz-less worker bee. He was not high enough in the chain of any command to question anything. So, for several hours now, he had sat and watched, though not listened to, two young men in the video-bugged flat. They had spent the first hour or so of this morning cleaning. Since then, they had sat huddled around a laptop around their dining area table.

Because of the position of the camera, he could not see what they were doing on the laptop. He could, however, see the gravity of what they were doing by the expressions on their faces. He could see this as clear as if it was a distinguishing mark on a face, like a mole or tattoo.

He figured, if he were to be instructed to continue with this watch, he would sneak back into the flat and reposition the camera, or add another, now that he knew where they chose to sit.

He watched as one of the two men got up and disappeared into a side room, only to reappear moments later carrying a stack of old-looking books. He watched them lean closer when speaking, as if in whisper. Then, one of them started a video game but never played it. He then watched him pull a pair of boxers over his pants, as if he were playing superhero.

Lester deemed none of these activities important enough to constitute royal alert. While he found the boxers over the pants unusual, he did not find that act constituted royal alert either—that was until he got a closer look at an envelope one of the men had carried back with him from his second trip into the side room. He could not zoom in closely enough to read either the envelope or the document that was removed from it, but he did not need to zoom in to catch the royal insignia on the envelope.

When the royal insignia caught his eye, the actions of the two men captured more of his attention. As he watched on, he tried to figure out anything he could as to who these men really were, such that their activities warranted the separated visual and auditory spying he knew was occurring.

Why do they have a distinctly royal communication in their possession?

Spying the royal insignia on the envelope in their possession, in and of itself, was not suspicious enough for him to warrant alerting his boss. It was enough to trigger his focus and attention, but if that were the only red flag that surfaced, he would probably not even mention it in his report out at the end of the assignment. At least that was what he had reasoned with himself up to the point where he witnessed the second and related red flag when the man who had retrieved the royal envelope scribbled a hard-pressed *X* across its insignia. As if that were not enough, the malicious smile he witnessed on the man after crossing out the insignia provided red flag number three.

Lester Grynthal cropped a copy of the footage containing all three elements, together constituting enough evidence for concern to report it. Much to his surprise, he would be giving Miss Portence far more than just the end of task summary he had been expecting.

He saved the file off, attached it to an email to Miss Portence, and continued watching for further evidence of ingredients for royal dissidence.

— CHAPTER 40 —

E MERSON HAD COMPLETED HIS INVESTIGATION INTO THE VARIOUS hiccups in time, like daylight savings and leap years. He then sat as he had before his assignment. It would look as if he had not even moved were he not now holding his laptop while waiting to present his results. He waited patiently for me to complete what would be my fifth rewrite and attempt at a prelude to the list. He watched on while I scribbled on what used to be a clean side of royal stationary envelope.

I had been trying to identify not only what to say but also how to say it. After all, I would be trying to convince and inspire into action a genius of the eighteenth century to accept, well before he would eventually be ready to, courses of action to be taken against a Crown he then believed in. I had to make him believe in something that, from his perspective and time, would make absolutely no sense. Never mind the fact I had to do this convincing via burning a message through lightning onto his kite.

Each of the five attempts progressed closer to the intended and concise message I believed I could write on a kite flying in a lightning storm that occurred over two hundred and sixty years earlier. Thankfully each was shorter than the prior, as I was running out of room on the envelope. The last few words I had written had to be written over an embossed crest, the royal coat of arms. I had been avoiding it for no other reason than knowing the pen would not write well on it. Having run out of room, I scraped away at the last couple of words on it, and then finished by drawing a moustache on the lion's face in the crest.

My setting the pen down was the only trigger Emerson needed to start communicating his findings.

I had been so lost in my thoughts I had shut out the game music still looping loudly throughout the flat. It was as if setting the pen down also shut off my mind's ability to filter out the music. I snapped out of the silence to the chant of the monks. "Hard rock ... bedrock."

I simultaneously winced at the sound and watched on as Emerson showed me a spreadsheet containing notes, calculations, and the resulting analyses he had made. Even while sharing his findings, Emerson managed to lip-synch to the tune as the chorus repeated, twisting his face as he emulated the angels' high notes. "Found in their world of igneous rock."

Emerson had just enough time to explain how he believed he had been successful but not enough for me to attain his level of understanding when it finally happened; my laptop dinged, alerting me I was being messaged. It was not the normal message alert I had been familiar with over my years of messaging friends and coworkers but the one I had only heard a handful of times at best. It was hopefully Emily but probably Samantha, pinging me on the private, secure, and incredibly illegal messaging program.

As if on cue, Emerson had frozen in the tracks of his explanation. We both turned our eyes and attentions back to my laptop, which had come alive from its sleep mode because of the incoming message.

I maximized the program's window to find Samantha's communication. If hope were a stairwell, I had just fallen a flight or two—still no Emily.

It revealed simply, "Josh, you need to see this."

I had a feeling deep down inside all along about what she would find, though I had mummified the belief in an immeasurable shroud of hope. The shroud disintegrated as if Samantha's message was a lit match easily burning its fragile fabric away.

I looked at Emerson, who sat stoic but for a tremor of emotion that appeared to be rippling through him.

Taking a deep breath, I typed in response, "Sadly, I am not surprised you would have something you would need to show me." It was as true as me also not being surprised by the feeling of an abysmal pit swallowing up my insides.

"I was able to trace two activated Royal Lane cameras that'd been activated in the coordinates and time you provided. The file contains footage the from both, and ..."

I think Samantha just could not finish the sentence, for after a long pause, she followed with, "Josh, Im am so sorryhn." The errors at the end of her message only conveyed the emotional state she was in, and all alone.

Along with the message, she had attached a video file.

I had to see it. If it was what I believed it to be, I had determined earlier it would be the deciding factor to proceed full force down a dark path with no return. The path might be dark, but I firmly believed it held the only opportunity for light at its end.

Opening the file, I watched it load, while on a frozen screen flashed a stretch of highway with mountains in the near distance but with no cars visible. My eyes burned as they stared at the royally illuminated lane. I should have known I would be seeing it, as its activation was why the camera had turned on in the first place, yet I was still taken by surprise. I watched the bar at the bottom of the program window move slowly to the right, indicating the file was loading, though not nearly fast enough.

Finally, the video clip kicked in. For the first ten seconds, nothing changed, and then a flock of birds made their chaotic flight across the video horizon and over the side of the highway, where they flew down and disappeared. The ground past the edge of the highway must have dropped down into a valley. Their movement let me know the file had been playing, and I shivered at the sudden belief their path foreshadowed that of Emily's fate. A vision popped into my head of Emily's car being forced to follow the path of the birds.

The first part of the video contained footage from the first camera where Samantha identified Emily's car.

Emily's car had just entered the camera's view, clearly driving outside the royal lane and two lanes to the left. She was driving in the furthest lane from the royal lane. I was angered at the thought of the fear she must have felt when the lane kicked on. Her car had just reached the horizon's reach for this camera when the black Jaguar sped its way into the scene, blazing up the royally lit lane.

I did not need the Royal Lane lights to recognize the car. I had been in my share of them recently.

The video skipped up to the next camera, activated from its position a kilometer farther up the highway. The mountains were closer, and from this angle, eerily, the valley looked deeper, more ragged, and hungrier.

Emerson and I watched as we saw Emily's car enter the scene. This time, however, it was visually evident she was swerving in a panic.

The black Jaguar came into view immediately after, only now in Emily's lane and riding her tail. The Royal Lane remained visibly lit but empty.

All we could do was watch the event that had already occurred.

The Jaguar barreled down on Emily. I motioned a silent shout as if to cry out for her, but it was as if some part of me knew shouting would do nothing.

Suddenly her car swerved sharp. I could not tell if the Jaguar had hit her car or if, in a panic, she had merely lost control of it. Her car spun as its tires hit the dirt shoulder along the side of the road. It looked as if she had attempted to regain control, but a sharp reactive turn of the wheel only worsened things, sending her car into a series of flips.

The internal mechanisms that prevented me from shouting earlier did nothing to stop me from jumping and screaming out for Emily as I could only watch on as her car careened over the edge of the highway, crashing down into the jagged jaws of its hungry valley.

Lester, deep in his job of observation, jumped in reaction to seeing the men he was spying do the same. He had not seen what made them jump but had not needed to. It was visually evident the men had just seen something on the laptop that had triggered such a violent and emotional response.

Lester tried to shake off his own emotionally connected response, as if it were a chill.

It continued to become increasingly evident to him, there was much more to this job than he had been let on to.

He saved off yet another file of the video, immediately attaching it to yet another email to his boss.

Miss Portence had replied to the first email, stressing for him to continue, though she also continued to provide no additional information as to why these two men were so important.

Still, this bee would not buzz.

I do not know if this actually happened or if it was a mere continuation of the premonition I had earlier, but I would swear I saw a flock of white birds fly up from the depths of the valley that had just swallowed Emily. I imagined them carrying her off to heaven and how lucky heaven would be to have her.

On the video, the Jaguar had come to a screeching halt, and two thugs jumped out and ran over toward the edge.

The camera shook, and I could see the thugs recoil, as what I can only imagine in my worst nightmares was the result of an explosion.

Emerson screamed, though I could not even register what he had said. He jumped up and ran into his room.

I looked back at the screen, and through the tears that flowed freely, I noticed the video had ended. I had just witnessed the death of the woman who, in any other scenario, I would have spent the rest of my life loving.

I had just enough sense to remember Samantha alone on the other end of the delivery and having witnessed her best friend's death. I could not type much, but managed, "I am so sorry for your loss as well."

I had chosen my path. This path would lead to the end of my life and the lives of all those I loved—a fate I believed to be true regardless which path I were to choose at this point. This path was tied to the promise I had made to my parents and a vow of love I'd just made for Emily. This path was the only path I had available with a shred of hope of making a difference. Lastly, this path was my first chosen as a free man.

Anger kicked in, and I threw the laptop, smashing it against the wall. The wall shook enough for a picture to fall. It was a picture of the three of us, Emerson, Emily and me. Seeing it broken, I ran over to pick it up and salvage what was left of the memories it carried.

When I bent down to pick it up, I found a little black object next to the broken old brown wooden frame. Grabbing the picture carefully with one hand, instinctive curiosity had me retrieve the black object with the other. I stared at the picture, wiping tears off it with my sleeve. It was then I noticed what I held in my other hand was a tiny camera device.

The instant realization I had, that someone may have just witnessed what had transpired and with eyes of royal intent sent an awakening shudder throughout my body. The time for action was now; I would not even be allowed time to grieve.

That was probably for the better, as grief would only melt away the strength I needed to continue down the path I had chosen. Something in me was smart enough to suppress the grief. It too must have known I could use the anger and emotion as fuel. But if I gave myself a moment longer, I might have resisted what this part of me had enabled.

While consumed by this anger and emotion, I ran to get matches from the kitchenette pantry.

Picking up the sheet I had drafted the message on, I tore away the final draft. I stuffed it in my shirt pocket along with the list, and then took the matches, lighting one and setting the remains of the sheet on fire. I held onto the paper as long as I could, making sure the insignia could be seen on the camera I had picked back up in my other hand.

When I could hold it no longer, I dropped the camera on the floor and then dropped the burning paper on top of it.

After crushing the camera with my heel and stamping out the remains of the flames, I snagged the journals and then checked my pocket to make sure I had both the list and message I intended to communicate, as well as my pen come stylus. I also found I still had the kite-shaped chip from my parent's fireplace.

I had no time for doubts so shoved away the fear that tried to creep its way into my head. The fear laughed at me, at the thought I believed I stood a chance of succeeding at anything but getting myself killed.

I had everything I needed in hand, so I rushed into Emerson's room. As much as I just wanted to console Emerson, I knew he had no time for grieving either; I stood zero chance for success without him.

When I first saw him, I could only describe the look of my best friend as broken. I imagine I looked no different, though I also could not forget how this government had already taken his parents, and now Emily. I was the only person Emerson had left in this world.

As I froze grasping this realization, Emerson jumped into action. He put on his jacket and picked up his laptop in one hand and car keys in the other.

He grabbed my arm to snap me out of it, stabbing me accidently with the keys he held in his hand. His eyes were red and streaming, his shoulders sunken, but though his voice wavered, what he repeated had not, "Men make history ... men make history."

PART VI

History Repeats, History Completes

— CHAPTER 41 —

I DID NOT NEED TO SAY ANYTHING TO EMERSON. HE KNEW WHAT WE had to do, and that we had to do it immediately. I was relieved, as I was not sure how well I would be able to communicate it to him or inspire him otherwise.

I grabbed my coat, and within a minute, we were on our way out to the car and off to the lightning lab.

Lester Grynthal had been surprised twice by what he'd witnessed. At least he thought what he had seen was worthy of surprise—that was, until he witnessed a man throwing a laptop and, thus, inadvertently revealing his source for eyes to the events. He had not realized for certain if his camera had been found, until the close-up view of the carpet he had seen since had turned into a pair of eyes looking directly back at him. It was evident the man who had thrown the laptop was then aware of the camera he had exposed from its inconspicuous location on top of the picture frame.

It was what the man did next, however, that taught Lester the true meaning of surprise. The man had not only started burning the sheet of royal stationary but was clearly trying to make sure the eyes he had now found upon him could see the insignia as it burned.

Moments later, the camera found its way back to the floor. This time, however, instead of carpet, Lester's close-up consisted of flames and then nothing. His screen had gone static, and he could only imagine his camera had just been destroyed.

He sat frozen, taking in all he had just witnessed.

Several minutes had passed before he snapped out of his contemplative state. He was struggling to believe he had just witnessed a direct and intentionally visible threat against the Crown. He was also struggling with his own personal feelings about it. As if in the recesses of his being, a part of him, like buried but still burning wood embers that had just been stirred bringing the flame back to life, had felt an alien spark of liberating hope.

For the first time in his life, Lester Grynthal felt the urge to buzz.

He shook the thought off as ridiculous, shoving it away by returning to the job at hand. He quickly clipped a video file of the events and emailed them to his boss. The verbiage he typed with the email simply contained an alert code he had never used before but one that alerted his boss of the threat identified. It contained no evidence of the buzz he had already silenced and directed to go back to wherever it had come from and out of his head.

Now the only thought in his mind was of the flurry of activity his email would instantly initiate. He wondered how high the alert would go.

Emerson and I reached the lab within minutes of leaving the flat. The drive there was, as Emerson liked to declare, "only a hop, skip, and a jive down Hillsborough Ave."

Time was not on our side—at least yet, I told myself. We had to hurry, knowing full well our car was being tracked, which gave us even less time.

The few minutes the drive had taken, however, were the longest I could remember. The whole drive I spent imagining who would know what by when and what they would try to do about it. Whose eyes were on the other side of that camera?

I knew my royal burning and then subsequent burning and stomping of the camera had been fueled by the emotion of all that had occurred.

I did everything I could do to fight back the tears from losing Emily. As if I were somewhere above myself looking down, I witnessed my immense sadness suddenly twist into a hardened and focused anger. I realized I must not let it get the best of me. I must not let it turn into the unbridled rage I felt hid behind anger's door but had to control it and use it to my advantage.

I could not beat myself up too badly, as, at worst, I had merely sped up the inevitable. The king could not afford to let those who knew too much keep breathing. With us still breathing, we could still think and act on the knowledge and accesses we had. The king would do anything to stop us, so I intended to do anything I could to bring his fears to fruition.

His whole intention was to use writing as a means to put and keep himself a step ahead of all his enemies and to take even more from his world. I could see him having messages sent back to him every time he learned of any missed opportunity to seize more power, more control.

He would not stop until the entire world was his.

He would also use it to squash any sign of rebellion, getting the jump on any attempt by knowing exactly who, what, when, where, why, and how before it ever got a chance to occur in the new history he would draw. With the ability to tell himself in the past what he learned in the future, he would not be putting out rebellious fires that had the potential of spreading fast so much as pinching out lit matches of discord between his royal index finger and royal thumb.

Since it was Sunday, I expected to see the parking lot of Anderson Raines Lightning Lab empty except for the usual maintenance vans. However, as we turned to pull into the lab's main parking lot, we could already see two black cars parked up by the entrance, and judging from the plumes of exhaust, both were still running. These were not maintenance vehicles, but like the maintenance vehicles, I recognized them. I should, as I had ridden in them several times as of late and had just watched helplessly as one took the love of my life.

This type of vehicle tended to come standard with a pair of goons.

I was near panic when, as if Emerson had suspected it in me, he said, "No worries. They may be guarding the front doors, but I know another way in."

Emerson drove past the main entrance and appeared to be driving past the lab entirely until he turned left down a road I had never known existed.

We continued down the road for half a kilometer and then looped back left again onto a rocky road heading back toward the lab but at a lower elevation and approaching what must be the back.

I had never seen the lab from this perspective before and often forget that Emerson's job got him involved in much more than just inside the lab where I found myself imprisoned. How many more places had he seen that I never knew existed?

Again, apparently sensing my curiosity, Emerson provided an explanation as he completed the drive up to an entrance that looked as if it had been misplaced. "This entrance takes you to the bottom of the core in the lab. There is a ladder built into the inside portion of the core that will take us up into the lab."

The core! We were going inside the core. A ladder? I had never noticed a ladder.

I had always assumed Emerson was the more sheltered one but found myself feeling like I need to get outside my bubble more.

Just the thought of the word *bubble* triggered a memory—so close yet so far I could not make the connection. Then it hit me. The dandy Emerson and I had run into in the school hall. It seemed so long ago but really wasn't. I actually snickered as I recalled the connection, sharing it with Emerson, "I find your driving skills both fitt-a-ging and capa-bubble!"

My use of humor as a defense mechanism was kicking in again.

Emerson snorted as he broke into laughter.

He pulled the car up off the road, driving right up to the side of the door. As we got out of the car, I sensed a low but strong vibration beneath my feet. Again, I was the only one surprised by it.

Emerson, adding to my newfound understanding of his broad experience at the lab, pointed out, "We are standing directly over one of the power cells, and just to the right here"—he pointed to what looked to me like just a grassy knoll—"but another ten meters below are conduits for the positive ionizers."

As he finished the sentence, he approached a security keypad and began keying in what I thought was his access code. The image of someone seeing and reporting the digitally recorded actions of us badging in crossed my mind, but before I could even state my concern about goons having potentially already locked us out, Emerson stated, "I used a generic maintenance code I spied used by one of the government temps they had me work with when I added the fiber layer to the core."

As if in confirmation to his statement, the door responded with the unlocking click of an approval.

I was amazed we were going to be able to get into the lab here but more so at how Emerson had suddenly started acting intelligent and mature. I had always known him to be a genius of sorts, but the severity of our current situation seemed to have broken down his eccentric childlike layers. The realization left me both impressed and saddened.

His normal demeanor may have always been a little peculiar, but I had always seen it as a mechanism to allow himself some degree of happiness in his life. As if the fact it had been a project for the king that had taken Emerson's parents from him were not enough, yet another project for the king was stealing his remaining happiness, his life.

As we stepped into the dark entryway, I could not tell whether the chill I felt was from the draft that hit us upon entering, or the darkness of our realities that hit me as I reflected on its influence.

Emerson felt his way, with confident familiarity, to yet another door.

I could not see very well for the darkness, but by the sounds of the metal latch he raised and the shoulder he put into it to open it, I imagined the door to be quite heavy. Even with the bang of his shoulder, it had barely opened enough for us to squeeze through.

Instantly we were bathed in the light of the day. We stepped into the first part of this side journey that I recognized, the core in the lightning lab, though I had never before seen it from the inside. I stared at the slate-black metallic walls, following them up to the gap I recognized having viewed through its honeycomb grid from the other side in the past. I could almost see myself standing there the day I burned the message on the clock face.

Emerson had not paused a second. As I returned my focus to ground level, I could see he had crossed the coal-black ground of the core and had made his way to a ladder I had not previously known existed. He stood before it, waiting for me to join him.

I turned back to close the door we had gone through, only to find Emerson had already done that as well.

As I walked toward Emerson, I could see why I had never noticed the ladder. It was made out of the slate-black wall itself, comprised of indentations into the wall, deep enough to grip with your hands and slide the fronts of your feet into. Lastly, looking at the placement of it in the core, I saw it would have been just to the side beneath me from my viewpoint through the honeycomb grid. I could now see how it actually extended up a solid column to the top of the core, past the exposed grid and vents.

Remembering the urgency of the task, I put my curiosities aside, and joined as Emerson began ascending the ladder.

I was directly behind him—and the outline of the king Emerson had drawn with marker on the backside of his boxers. Even in this darkest hour, I snorted a laugh.

When he reached a vent, I witnessed the effort he had to make to get his leg up and over the rim. He paused, pseudo-straddling the rim and with a look on his face that showed he was fishing blindly, presumably with his foot hanging on the other side of the rim, for a wrung on the corresponding side's ladder.

Within a few seconds, he swung his other leg over and then descended, disappearing from my sight. Less than a minute later, it was my turn. I was saddled on the rim and doing the same foothold, fishing, only to have him unexpectedly grab my foot, and stick it in the rung for which it had been kicking below.

I must not be too observant; I should have known this outer core ladder was here. I had been on this side of the core many times before. I must have been too lost in my work to take notice.

Once we were both over, we began the familiar descent down the ramp alongside the outside of the core.

— CHAPTER 42 —

ONCE IN THE LAB, EMERSON AND I MADE A BEELINE FOR THE CONTROL center, and Emerson began setting up his laptop. He needed to be hard-lined in; we had Wi-Fi, but it would get disconnected when the lightning struck.

I gathered the papers I had written the coordinates on and set them down next to the laptop and then checked to make sure I had all the other papers I needed to complete the mission. I found them folded and secured in my shirt pocket alongside Emily's card; my stylus; and, after another second of digging, the kite stone.

"Emer, as soon as you get up and running, can you do the parameter check?"

"Will do rhymes with mildew."

I saw Emerson was keying in his password. A fleeting thought jumped through my mind as I tried to imagine which game or character name he used for a password. The thought didn't last long enough to trigger the smile it normally would have. I reminded him, due to the new security, he'd need to use my password. Given what we were about to attempt, security was pretty much out the window anyway.

After I got him signed in, my eyes jumped back to the lab door. At that point we had no way of knowing whether anyone would be trying to stop us or not, but I had witnessed firsthand how much the king knew about anything he desired. I would not put it past him to already know about and have jumped into action over all that had recently occurred.

After all, those were not ice cream trucks Emerson and I had seen out in front of the lab. Luckily, we had yet to see who had come in them.

I quickly headed to the closet where I had previously found and used the old broom to draw a snake on a clock face. While there, I grabbed the broom and looked for anything else I could use to jam the doors in case we had any company. I had thought about blocking the doorway with the tables in the lab but remembered they are all attached to the ground. Instead, I made the best use I could of the old broom come paintbrush, a mop, and some rags I quickly tied together to run through the lab door handles. Looking through the thick plexiglass of the doors, I realized this bought us seconds at best. Not wanting to risk needing those seconds, I turned and rushed back to Emerson.

By the time I had returned to the control center, I saw Emerson had finished his setup and was making shadow animals on the wall from the light of the laptop. I was so relieved to still see some remnant of the Emerson I had grown up with and learned to love like a brother.

Interrupting what I believed to be his attempt at an elephant, I said simply, "Emer?"

I hadn't meant to startle him, but he jumped. Maybe it was just the effect of returning to his stark new reality.

"Are you OK?"

"Yeah … yeah. This is it though, isn't it? If you're successful, we'll be living in a different world, our souls as different people, free people. Do you think we'll know each other?"

I did not know the answer to that question but replied from my heart not my head, "Emer, I cannot imagine a world where we would not." An instant reflection on my response told me I believed it to be true.

I spotted a pencil and paper on the table and remembered how Benjamin Franklin, while in his jail cell, had kept a journal he figured no one would ever read. Thankfully Mr. Franklin's son gave him the opportunity to prove his fears wrong. In the moment, I decided I might try to capture some thoughts of my own, so I folded the sheet and stuck it with the pencil in my back pocket.

Still following down his train of thought and in his forever optimistic perspective, Emerson added, "If you don't succeed, Josh, we'll get to see Em sooner, and as free men of sorts. So I guess we can't lose."

I was about to agree. I was about to tell Emerson how genuinely proud I was to have had the honor of living in this world of wrong with someone so off-kilter and yet so right. I was about to tell my best friend goodbye. My attempt was interrupted by a loud bang.

I stuck my head out the control center door and peered across the open area separating it from the lab doors I had jammed.

It was King's Guards, two of them. The loud bang was their learning the doors were jammed, and though there was a little distance between us, I swear I could see the confusion on their Frick and Frack faces. The only difference I could detect between the two was how one of them had a hand over his nose, presumably after having just planted it onto the plexiglass of the jammed doors before him.

I turned back to Emerson. "Emer, are we ready? There're royal goons at the outer doors!" I quickly loaded the coordinates while Emerson keyed in the trigger sequence.

"Go, Josh. You have about twelve seconds to get into place!"

As I ran out of the control center, I heard a much louder bang and saw the goons had nearly broken through.

Ten. Picking up the countdown in my head, I ran left around the walls of the control center and then through the last door that would protect me from the lightning, unless I reached the fourth-dimensional range around the core.

I imagined the goons would be following. The solid and heavy door had not yet closed, so I could still hear the outer lab.

Eight.

I had not been prepared for what I heard next.

"Joshua Franks, if you do not stop, you will be executed for treason, but not before witnessing the effects of your actions on your family!" It was the voice of the king, and hearing it nearly froze me in my tracks.

Five. My subconscious mind kept me on track, and my feet managed to keep me running.

Four. I slid to a stop to my spot by the core.

I turned to take one last look. *Three.*

Then, through the remaining gap of the door, I witnessed my final vision from the third dimension. It was the king. He had been running toward the inner lab. I could see his royal arm extended toward me. I lost vision as the heavy door was nearly closed, but the last word I heard before it shut completely was the fading sound of the king shouting, "Nooooooo!"

In the back of my mind the countdown had concluded, and only a blink later, the lab was gone.

It was replaced by the darkness of a storm cloud, and yet the lightning below it provided a patchwork of illumination.

I completed my way up the ramp and around both it and the cloud and then peered down over the railing's edge. It was raining hard; at least, that is, it would be in the third dimension.

The glow of the frozen flash of lightning illuminated the ground below.

Aside from the crystalline raindrops as I had witnessed before when burning the message on the clock, something new caught my eye as its darkness contrasted with the enlightened view before me. It was a raven hanging midair, though in the third dimension in full flight.

I allowed no time to ponder whether it being there was an ominous sign or just a twisted coincidence.

I continued and had finally reached the top of the core. I was less than a quarter of the way around it when I first saw Benjamin Franklin. It had to be him underneath the tri-horn hat down below. Who else would be out in the storm on this date, at this time? He even had a boy next to him, his son William I assumed. The man was also holding a string. I followed it up, making my way farther around the core's rim until I could see the string's end. And there it was—the kite. It was a couple meters down, so I turned around to make my way back down the ramp to reach it and all the while wondered how the hell I had not noticed it on the way up.

I completed a full rotation down the ramp to find the kite just above my head level. A quick assessment, and I realized I was not near the ladder Emerson and I had climbed down and would need to balance myself on the railing and the honeycomb side of the core to reach the kite and bring it down to where I could write on it safely standing on the ramp, but reach it I could.

I also saw why I had not noticed the kite before. Without having known it was there, it had been easy to miss, as it was camouflaged within the spray of color and light compliments of the lightning-lit sky.

— CHAPTER 43 —

As I reached for my rightening stylus and the draft of the message I intended to write, I glanced down in awe of what I was witnessing. I was looking over 260 years back in time and into the eyes of my time-distant and heroic relative, Benjamin Franklin. He stood frozen and appeared to be looking directly at me, though I knew he was focused on his kite. I wondered whether he could see me, even though, if this were a movie, I would only appear on one single frame, more a mere subliminal image than a fully realized vision.

I looked over at the boy, William, and could see he had his head down with his hands over his ears, probably preparing him for the thunder that would boom as the voice of the lightning. He had willingly joined his father to witness the experiment but could no longer hide the trepidations of a child in a storm.

Eyes back to Benjamin, I waved as if he might see me and, in response, wave back.

I knew in this dimension I need not hurry but still feel a sense of urgency to complete what I had set out to do.

I turned back to the honeycomb core and, at my present level, tested the ability for me to get a strong foothold in it. Thankfully, my shoe slid right into one of the core's pentagonal spaces, its heel allowing it to stop and nestle itself into place.

My other foot would need to rest its heel on the first of the two poles making up the horizontal frame of the ramp railing directly behind me.

This would have the top pole rest just below my knee, providing yet more support and balance.

I put the stylus up to my mouth, biting down on it with my teeth, and stuffed the paper back into my shirt pocket. I realized I would not need it, having memorized what I intended to write as if it were as burned in my mind as I intended to have it burned onto the kite.

I spied a vertical pole just to my right that I could use to stabilize myself. Grabbing the top pole, I lifted my right foot up and into its position on the lower pole. Still holding onto the top, with my other hand gripping, as best possible, an edge of the honeycomb on the core's outer wall, I lifted myself up.

Now using the strength of my foothold on the railing while leaning with a firmed grip on the core wall, I positioned my left foot, testing several of the five-sided holes that would provide the best support and balance. Finally settling my foot into the one that felt most comfortable, I extended my left leg, spreading the support and balance between both my legs now and butting my right knee up painfully against the top railing.

Settling into the most comfortable position I could get to extend my reach; I turned my attention to the kite. The kite would have been so much easier to reach if I had the broom. As if the king had directly ordered me to use the broom in the lab doors, I relished the thought of yet another thing for which to blame him.

The stability would not get any better. I reached in for the courage to reach out and grab the kite. My arms were fully extended, as were my right hand's fingers, but I found at best I could just barely touch it. Touching it was not a good thing, as my doing so actually pushed it a centimeter further away.

I stood there balancing between the poles and the wall, my right knee aching from leaning on the pole. To have risked everything but not be able to even reach the kite would be an epic failure. In frustration, I bit down harder on the pen, come stylus, in my teeth, causing my jaw to pop.

The stylus!

I reached up to my mouth, grabbing the stylus from it, and worked it in my right hand as best possible for grip and extension.

I pulled myself back up to extend and looked out at the kite for the best place to snag it with the pen without inadvertently pushing it further away. Spying the kite's framework, I reached underneath it and then up until I could feel the pen hook its tip on the frame and then safely pulled the kite toward me. Carefully putting the pen into my shirt pocket, I reached out and pulled the kite the rest of the way to me, pulling it right up against my side as I leaned back to the core wall to step down.

I saw the wire sticking out of the kite and was reminded that, while writing this message through lightning was an experiment for me, so too was this kite flying in an electrical storm an experiment for Benjamin Franklin.

I had to kneel as I stepped back and down because my descent was pulling on an already taut string.

On the fly, I realized I would not need to write on the kite from my perch on the railing but could pull the kite down with me to the ramp. Once safely back onto the ramp, I took the kite, carefully hanging it just over the railing and then moving it hand to hand until I was able to pull it under the bottom pole of the railing and lay it flat on the ramp floor to begin my rightening.

I stared at the kite before me. Benjamin Franklin's hands had built this kite, and I imagined my holding it would be the closest I would ever come to shaking hands with him.

Before continuing with my task, unsure whether I had bent it or if it were already twisted down, I reached over and straightened the wire from the kite. Also, though I didn't know if it mattered, I used my hand to gently squeegee the rain from the kite's surface.

When I retrieved the stylus from my pocket, Emily's card came out with it. My hands were soaked, as was the ground, so I handily stuck the card gently under the frame of the bottom and drier side of the kite, and I set to work.

I had the world to say but the space of a kite to say it on. I knew I would need to forego standard formatting but felt the words were too important to sacrifice. Taking my time and pressing the stylus gently enough to make sure I would not damage the kite but hard enough so my message would be legible, I spent the equivalent of a good two hours third-dimensional time penning what I could only equate to hope.

Upon completion, I sat up to give it one final review. I would not get a second chance to do this. My thoughts jumped back to Emerson. I hoped the goons had not reached him yet, and he had been spared any pain.

As fast as thoughts can jump, they jumped back.
I read the kite out loud to myself:

Mr. Franklin,

Everything about this message is extraordinary—the kite medium on which you are reading it and all epiphanies contained. It asks for nothing less extraordinary from you.

My list, my pieces of eight, make no sense now but will when the winds of change whistle for freedom. And they will. Hide this kite, this task list, until freedom calls for you.

When the time is right and the circumstances extraordinary, prepare to do the extraordinary things it begs, for the first breath of a free nation depends upon it.

With respect, sincerity, and hope,
Joshua Franks

1) When you take Fort Ticonderoga, do not forget to take its cannon.
2) Have General Washington surprise the Hessians during the rites of spring.
3) Portray an American as the French romanticize him.
4) Let Benedict Arnold be a hero, but he will turn when you give him a turn to point.
5) Do not fight as formal tradition holds but as necessity demands.
6) Eat the elephant one bite at a time, or it will eat you. Slavery must end, but divide it from your revolutionary efforts, or it will divide your revolution.
7) Think outside the box, for inside is a snake that will tread on you. You do not need to win to not lose.
8) Your son William will remain lost to your cause, but in the end, know he loves you.

Mr. Franklin,

Everything about this message is extraordinary: the kite medium on which you are reading it, and all epiphanies contained. It asks for nothing less extraordinary from you. My list, my pieces of eight, makes no sense now, but will when the winds of change whistle for freedom... and they will. Hide this kite, this task list, until freedom calls for you. When the time is right, and circumstances extraordinary, prepare to do the extraordinary things it begs, for the first breath of a free nation depends upon it. With respect, sincerity and hope, Joshua Franks

1) When you take Fort Ticonderoga, do not forget to take its cannon 2) Have General Washington surprise the Hessians during the Rites of Spring 3) Portray an American as the French romanticize him 4) Let Benedict Arnold be a hero, but he will turn when you give him a turn to Point 5) Do not fight as formal tradition holds, but as necessity demands 6) Eat the elephant one bite at a time, or it will eat you...slavery must end, but divide your revolutionary efforts, or it will divide your revolution 7) Think outside the box, for inside is a trap that will tread on you. You do not need to win to not lose 8) Your son William will remain lost to your cause, but in the end, know he loves you

After reading it, I did not bother to ask myself whether it was good enough. I had no eraser, backspace button, or Wite-Out. It had to be.

I remembered and retrieved the kite stone from my shirt pocket and then pressed it down beside where I had signed the kite. It lightly burned a kite-shaped impression beside my signature.

I slowly and carefully hand-by-handed the kite back up to where I had found it, back above the railing. I had no way of knowing whether the core structures in my dimension could possibly get in the way with the kite's safe return to its owner but couldn't take any chances. With the kite securely in hand, a slightly smoking kite I might add, I climbed back up the core's footholds and onto the lower pole of the railing to where I felt I could appropriately release the kite, safely away from my obstructions. Not knowing whether it would be beneficial or not, I gave the wire one last straightening and then tended to the hemp string to make sure it was taut and would not get snagged or knotted. I then shoved the kite far enough away that I would not be able to retrieve it again, even with my stylus-enabled extension.

I asked myself, as my eyes drifted back down the kite string to its owner, whether the message I had written would prove to have a hand in rewriting history. Then a prophetic answer presented itself as my eyes landed on the brass key Mr. Franklin had tied to it. In the instant of the lightning strike I stood dimensionally frozen in, a spray of sparks illuminated the key. In my mind, I could see Benjamin Franklin as my key and believed my message would provide a spark illuminating a path to freedom. I thought it fitting my message would be delivered via lightning.

I turned to begin my descent down the ramp and into whatever life existed beyond and resolved, however influential my efforts had been, the hands of a free man had carried them out.

I remembered the caption Mr. Franklin had written beneath his representation of the "Don't Tread on Me" snake. It read something to the effect of, "The outcome of our efforts does nothing to negate the importance of our message."

I remembered the paper and pencil I had stuffed in my back pocket and the desire to try to somehow tell my story. It had been an impulsive decision, and in my exhaustion over what had all just taken place, the time to put some thoughts down would give me a moment to catch my breath.

Like Mr. Franklin sitting in the jail cell for over a year, as long as I stayed in dimensional range, I had all the time I needed. I plopped down from where I was standing to put my thoughts to paper. While I may have time, I seemed to lack any idea of where to begin. I laughed, as Benjamin Franklin had nearly filled a journal, but I had only brought one piece of paper. The best my mind could muster regarded all the history surrounding and connecting Mr. Franklin's world and mine.

The importance of my journaling effort paled in comparison to the actions I had just taken. I was determined nonetheless to complete the task, though I imagined if anyone would ever get to read it, with my luck, it would probably be the king.

My mind zeroed in on histories, so I ran with it, and my pencil followed:

> The king wants me dead. I should feel hopeless and scared out of my mind right now. And I suppose I do. Still in this flash of a moment, I find I ponder histories.
>
> Funny thing about histories, we all have them—personal histories; family histories; and even local, cultural, and global histories. We all have them and, to varying degrees, we all share them. The broader a history's scope, the greater the chance it is shared.
>
> I can think of no history with a broader shared reach than the king's. As of recent, the king has consumed not only my history but also my future. He has pushed me to the point where I must try to make some global history of my own.
>
> My options are to either die by the king's hands, the very hands that already have a stranglehold on most of the world, or die by my own in my fight for freedom from them. In an attempt to make my decision as a free man, I choose the latter.
>
> Others in history have faced these choices as well.
>
> A moment in history over 240 years ago shared the same opportunity for transformation. It was a time when some very brave revolutionaries, my newfound heroes, faced the same decision.

I've always known how their story ended but have only recently learned some truths surrounding it, by reading a firsthand account written by Benjamin Franklin's son William. In it, William, having just witnessed his father's hanging, provided revelations on how his father and the fellow rebels were resolved to their fates. Their lives were a price they were more than willing to pay in their fight for freedom.

As it was, these so-called "rebels" paid that price, as they were publicly hanged, drawn and quartered in a single event now known as the Signers' Day of Reckoning.

Coincidentally, the spectacle occurred in nearly the same location where I am. Back then, however, the city was not known as the royal city of George's Cross in the Province of Burgoyne, but as Philadelphia. And a map of its time would place it within the colony of Pennsylvania.

I am amazed and equally saddened at how a path taken in a fork in the road at that time could lead to such a history as ours.

I am also amazed at how I managed to get my life so tightly knotted within the results of such a history, and all in just the past couple weeks. Two weeks ago, I was a no one, just another cog in the machine doing my royally mandated part to keep the machine running. In the short time since, I've turned from a no one into a someone with the most powerful person in the world wanting him dead.

Two weeks ago, I would have thought my story had begun at my birth. However, I now understand it is merely and hopefully the long overdue end story of a fight for freedom and the end of a revolution that began over two centuries ago.

I apologize for my rambling. But like a clock at the end of its wind, I am exhausted and out of time.

I know I have been vague. I know my story sounds as if I have told it all without having yet told you anything. In my current state, I have merely provided a fifty thousand-meter view, though in doing so, I have laid the groundwork on which my story might run.

My story is one of histories. More significantly, however, it represents the classic battle between the history that makes you and the history you make.

I had nearly filled the page within the time it took to exhale. I looked up at what I had written—not to read it, but more to inhale and breathe it in. In the pause, I recalled what General Washington had repeated in the inspirational speech Mr. Franklin had captured in the jail cell. Those three words would probably add more value to my so-called journal than all the others combined, so I ended with them.

"Men make history."

I may not need to hurry back to whatever the third dimension held for me, but I was spent and had accepted that whatever will be will be. I stuffed my journal and pencil back into my back pocket and pulled myself up to make my way toward my whatever.

As I descended the ramp, I pictured my parents, as if they had any way of knowing what I had done and hoped I had made them proud.

With that, and having reached the base of the core, I reimagined what I believe to have been William Franklin's telling of the Signers' Day of Reckoning.

I pictured myself, head in noose, standing in the gallows alongside heroic men preparing to leap for their freedom. In my mind, it was as if I could actually hear General Washington's words as he shouted down to the king before stealing his thunder, "Hear ye. Hear ye!" Then with the unexpected attention of the crowds, he uttered the swan song of revolutionary freedom. "Give me liberty, or in a final decision, and as a free man, I choose death!"

As I pictured the Signers leaping, I too took my own leap back into the third dimension and into whatever the world in it held for me.

—PART VII—

On a Path to the Country of the United States Benjamin Franklin Flies a Kite

— CHAPTER 44 —

Monday, June 12, 1752

O N A STORMY MONDAY IN JUNE AND IMPATIENT FOR THE COMPLETED construction of a church steeple, Benjamin Franklin decided he would take advantage of the storm at hand.

Upon completion of the steeple, he would attach a grounded metal rod to its top, with hopes to prove the electrical properties of lightning. The steeple may not have been ready, but the storm was, and Benjamin had already determined another means with which to prove his theory.

Attaching a wire so it poked out of a kite and then attaching a brass key close to where he would be holding the kite's hemp string, he decided he could attain the height of the steeple and, with the wire, the same result the metal rod would provide.

He intended to fly the kite in the thunderstorm, predicting the wire would attract the lightning, whose charge would travel down the wet string until it reached the key where the resulting release of electricity would generate both a powerful spark and proof by illuminating the existence of the electricity the lightning carried.

With his son William as his only witness, he hoisted the kite up and into the stormy skies.

The storm did not disappoint him.

Within minutes of getting the kite into position in the sky, a bolt of lightning struck the kite's wire, sending a powerful jolt of electricity down the wet string until it terminated at the brass key.

Benjamin Franklin's experiment was a success.

The slight shock he had felt reminded him of the danger he had put not only himself but also his son in—and for the sake of an experiment. He quickly turned to his son, unable to hide his elation but instantly aware of the fear in his son's eyes, "Quick, William, our adventure was a success. But you must return in doors for your safety! I will retrieve the kite and then join you."

He did not need to complete his instructions. Little William was already well on his way to the door upon hearing the word *quick*.

After seeing his son reach the door safely, Benjamin began winding the string around his arm as he walked toward where the now smoking kite had landed.

Thunderous lightning illuminated the sky again. This lightning revealed a frightened raven flying dangerously close past Benjamin as it made its way to anywhere but there. Startled, Benjamin jumped aside, nearly falling in the process.

Where he had not been surprised by the experiment's results and was merely startled by the raven, what he saw next completely threw him. He would later imagine the only thing that could have shocked him more would have been the lightning, save for the key.

He had picked up the smoking kite to find, though it had probably seen the last of its flying days, it had not been damaged too badly. However, upon gently shaking the kite, thus clearing the smoke-like fog that enshrouded it, he saw what he instantly recognized as words written upon it. At that same moment, he smelled the smoke he had mistaken as fog. Without having read a single word on the kite, he nearly leaped out of his skin, losing his tri-horn, dropping the kite, and falling backward, saved only by his own hands and rump.

He sat there in the rain for several minutes staring at the kite that had since stopped smoking but sat before him, soaked from the rain.

Though still completely blown away by the discovery of words printed on his kite, he snapped out of his stupor enough to climb to his knees and then to a stand and finally went on to retrieve his hat and walk back over to inspect the kite.

Initially afraid to touch the kite again, he was thankful it had landed words up. He walked around the kite to align himself with the message it carried.

Lightning, and its resulting counterpart, thunder, continued to try to make their presences known, but Benjamin read on unhindered, intermittently aided by the light from the lightning to read.

In all, he read the message completely three times before he dared pick it up.

What does it mean? Extraordinary? Epiphanies? Take Fort Ticonderoga's cannon, and even, surprise the Hessians! What would necessitate carrying out the items listed? It makes no sense. Or maybe, as the message on the kite states, it "makes no sense now."

Who is this "respectful, sincere, and hopeful" Joshua Franks?

Benjamin Franklin did not know the answers to these questions any more than he understood how the message had gotten there in the first place. He also knew no reason to believe he would ever need to carry out such a list of tasks—and to free a nation of royal colonies no less.

As strange as the whole event seemed, it was equally as strange how he felt compelled to trust the message. At least, that is, he trusted it enough to do as the kite also stated he should—hide it.

His focus landed on the last item in the list stating how his own son William would "remain lost to the cause." At first, he laughed at the idea of a cause existing. It took only moments, however, for the laughter to gravitate to thought. Within minutes, while still out in the storm, soaked and between the continued strikes of lightning, he decided the burden of the prophecy carrying any truth rested in the hands of fate. Until such time, Ben would keep the message a secret, even from William, his son and only witness to the lightning experiment. It seemed reasonable, for now at least, until he could try to make any sense out of what had just occurred.

In search of any potential clues, he turned to look back up into the skies where the kite had flown and found nothing but stormy skies.

Gathering up the kite, he headed for the house, opting for the rear door closest to his office and desk. He would stash the kite behind it for now, until he figured anything else out otherwise.

Having pondered the mysterious message all night, through the next morning, and alone, Benjamin Franklin set out to build a replacement kite

301

he would state he had used in the experiment. He would use the frame of the original kite, replacing only the material of the kite itself.

Benjamin had also determined how he would preserve and hide the kite material containing the message.

Still in shock from having received the message, he could hardly have believed he could be shocked so much again. Flipping the kite to begin its removal from the frame, he found something he had not previously noticed. It was a card of sorts, held in place between the kite material and its frame.

If the message on the kite were not enough to rock his world, the card helped take him the distance.

After a good hour of reading, rereading, and pondering the seemingly impossible, Benjamin placed the messaged material between two tanned hides, rolling it up tightly enough to make it fit within a wooden chest. It barely fit. He then took the chest and buried it behind an old oak tree he and the family frequently picnicked under. It was the family's favorite tree, and he would often tell stories under it. Often the stories portrayed the tree as if it were the infamous Hyde Park hanging tree at the end of Abbey Road in London.

The tree rested atop a steep hill, so no one tended to go behind it. Ben knew, however, that burying it there would provide a safe place to store the chest, at least until the day, should it ever really occur, when he should actually need to heed the message it carried.

He resolved that time, again as the message had stated, would shed light on the causes and opportunities to which it referred.

— CHAPTER 45 —

January 29, 1774

BENJAMIN FRANKLIN HAD LONG FORGOTTEN ABOUT THE CHEST AND message he had buried over a score ago.

He had not found a reason to remember them. It had not been time.

The winds of change had started blowing in recent years and strong enough into his "colony representing" sails to have docked him back in London for the past five years. He had been commissioned and sent there to represent several of the American colonies as their agent.

One cold day in January, over twenty-two years after his escapade in a storm, he wondered whether it was colder outside or inside, where he was being hit by an altogether different type of front.

Benjamin Franklin, for his involvement in passing on incendiary letters in what was to become known as the Hutchinson Letters Affair, had become Britain's scapegoat for some of the rebellious acts the empire had recently endured back in America.

Though he had been in Britain at the time, it seemed the British believed him partially responsible for the "Tea Party" that had been held in Boston Harbor the previous month.

So, for his part in sending the letters, along with the rebellious baggage he inherited, Benjamin stood before the privy council led by Solicitor General Alexander Wedderburn.

Benjamin stood in the "cockpit" of the amphitheater in Whitehall and in front of the entire King's Council. He also stood silent and stone-faced as the council orally tore into him. The crowd laughed and jeered as he stoically withstood the verbal assault.

The verbal storming culminated with Lord Sandwich thundering, to equally thunderous laughter, how the "deft ingrate American should stick to flying kites in lightning!"

As if remembering was a gun and words could pull its trigger, the words of Lord Sandwich triggered a shot. They fired a memory at Ben, the memory of a smoking kite; a buried chest; and, most importantly, an extraordinary message he had received on a kite in a lightning storm so long ago.

Benjamin Franklin recoiled in response.

The incident proved the fall of a final domino from a trail of many over recent years. Before its fall, Ben had firmly believed the American colonies could reconcile with Mother England, thus prevent the war at the end of the path on which the colonies had been traveling.

Lord Sandwich, along with the audience in the amphitheater, mistakenly believed Benjamin's reaction to have been because of the insult.

Only Benjamin knew he had not reacted to the insult but to the memory it jarred free. Therefore, it was only Benjamin who understood why his reply to Lord Sandwich consisted of a broad smile; a hat-tipping bow; and a genuine, "Thank you!"

The audience froze, silent.

As Benjamin was escorted from the amphitheater, he whispered to the council leader, Wedderburn, how he would "make your king a little man for this."

It was quiet enough in the amphitheater for the whisper to echo.

A year passed with the new fire building inside him before Benjamin realized what he had to do. He would return to America to retrieve the chest he had buried so long ago. The winds of change whistled for freedom, and the circumstances were indeed extraordinary.

On a brisk morning in March 1775, while with his friend Joseph Priestly, Benjamin read an American newspaper for information on the local impact of Britain's closing Boston's Port as punishment for its Tea Party against tea tax. He shed a tear as he read the resulting hardships the colonies endured.

It was time to go home, to the colonies, and it was time to fight for that home.

Benjamin Franklin realized he would need all the help he could get to accomplish the extraordinary things required to free himself and fellow Americans from the taxing grip of Mother England. He would take it from any friend, from any opportunity, from any place, and he would even take it from a kite with a message burned on it by lightning nearly a quarter century earlier.

— CHAPTER 46 —

Monday, July 2, 1782

I T WAS A HOT SUMMER DAY IN PHILADELPHIA. IN FACT, THE SUMMER OF 1782 had been one of the hottest people could remember.

Thankfully Jonathan Elders, the lowly ship prison guard, had been granted a day's leave. It was his first day of leave in over a month. He had been pulling duty on the HMS *Romney*, primarily standing deck guard over the prisoners stuffed down in the ship's hull.

He was especially thankful his leave had been granted today, as today was the weekly scheduled day to remove the bodies of the prisoners that had died festering in the summer heat down in the hull of the ship. The stench was more intense when in the tight confines of the hull. He did not feel sorry for the incessantly moaning and wailing prisoners but more for his back having to heave their dead rebellious arses out of the hull. In milder weather, he could usually force a live prisoner to do it. But in this intense heat, if the prisoner was not dead, he was a bayonet's length from it.

Disposing of the dead was not to be his problem today, though. He was going ashore today, and he knew exactly where he was going to go. He planned a trip to a tavern he frequented on Chestnut, the Fraunces Tavern, and he was cooled just by the thought of the pint he imagined he would have freshly poured before him.

The only thing he had not been looking forward to in this leave was that he'd been instructed to remain with the other lucky sods also on leave. It was not safe to be a lone redcoat in the colonies. As this war had dragged on, the winds that carried it had swayed westerly as of late.

Captain George Montagu's directive, to stay together, meant Jonathan would be saddled with a fellow jailer, Miles Westbrook, and the young and mouthy quarter gunner, Horatio Fennel.

Miles and he had seen many a prisoner pass through the phases of capture, defiance, desperation and then death, while rotting in the hulls of the ships they had guarded together.

But Fennel had only joined the crew on the HMS *Romney* a few months prior. He'd taken advantage of a connection with Captain Montagu to get his assignment.

All Jonathan Elders really knew of him was that he liked to run off his mouth, especially at and about the Americans.

Elders wanted no trouble today; he just wanted a cold pint.

After the three reached the tavern, it did not take long for him to get his wish. Within minutes he had a cold draft in his hand. He held it up against his sweating forehead and then pounded a snort, leaving himself a frothy moustache that he took care of with his sleeve.

As if keeping a natural balance to things, however, it took equally as long for Fennel to stir things up. Elders turned to find Fennel standing over a table with a man who had been writing something the quarter gunner had apparently found a reason to object.

Fennel was already shooting off his mouth at the man. "You pen words of freedom, do you?"

"Mind your own, lad," replied the man with quill in hand.

Elders was not even certain Fennel could read and had no idea what the other man had been writing. But as he turned to the commotion, spilling draft as he did so, he witnessed the man pointing the quill pen at Fennel as if it were a weapon.

Instinct had him intervene. Within moments, Elders stood between Fennel and the writer, but it was too late. Fennel was not to be bested by a pen-wielding fool and had begun to draw his sword. Apparently, tempers feel compelled to flare higher as if to keep up with the elevated temperatures.

The man with the pen held in defensive stance declared to Elders, "Yew had be better'n to let loose your young wild dogs in here."

"He's not me dog, young or other, and it is you'd best stand down for you'll soon find yourself trading ink for bullets and blades."

"The quill need only be guided. It can write powerful words, though I doubt either of you can read. But be assured to this, you will get the point."

The man with the pen was no ordinary man, no ordinary writer, and by no means an ordinary fighter for the cause. He had the skills to turn nearly anything into a lethal weapon, and a pen was just as good as anything to fill the need at hand. His patience and tolerance had worn as thin as the paper he had been writing on; the same thickness described how far two redcoats were from having their fates sealed in ink.

"I have grown weary of your presence on this side of the big water. Why don't you and your young dog here make your way back to your boat? You can use his hot air to fill your sails and make it home in time for tea. I would offer you some from Boston Harbor, but that blend was only intended for the free."

He had not so much as cracked a half smile as he spoke in wise turn, and his eyes darted about, assessing the strength of his opposition. He had devised a plan of offense, should the tiff escalate to offensive heights, and he worried not whether it would.

Westbrook had been watching on as the tensions rose. He had prepared himself to witness Elders's witty retort, as he believed Elders, a wit with words himself, was mentally preparing to deliver. He had only too late just noticed how quickly the environment had turned on them.

Elders, however, was speechless. This was not what he had wanted but was exactly opposite. He truly only wanted a cold draft or two and relief from the stench of prisoners' rot.

It was more instinct than desire that triggered his actions. His instincts had him reach for his pistol. His instincts, as usual and as the buildup of scars on his back should have reminded, were wrong.

The pistol was only half from its holstered position, as was Fennel's sword only half into whatever action the young fool thought it might carry out, when it happened.

The man with the pen used his free hand to flip his ink well up, over the shoulder of the older soldier, Elders, and into the face of the young dog.

At the same time, in a focused, swift and sweeping motion, he stabbed the older soldier in the main artery in his neck. The point of the nib provided ample puncture, and the quill's hollow shaft ample blood let.

Elders had not known what had hit him, and Fennel, stunned by the ink that now coated his face, lunged forward, only managing to bury his sword into Elders's side. It did not matter; the wound left by the quill was more than enough to kill Elders.

The pen was not done writing its death sentences. It took but a second for its handler to recoil in fluid motion and help it find its second artery. This one already had been targeted with ink as it belonged to a young dog that did not know when to bark or when to tuck his tail and run.

The young dog would not find the tail it had been chasing but would find its end.

Miles Westbrook stood frozen, having just witnessed something he could never have seen coming. He had watched as, within seconds, Elders and Fennel lay dead or dying on the floor. In his present and frozen position, eyes locked tightly onto the pen-wielding assailant, he lacked in visual periphery and failed to notice the knife swinging around from behind him.

── CHAPTER 47 ──

Saturday, October 16, 2021

MY NAME IS JOSHUA FRANKLIN.
My whole life I have heard the stories and accomplishments of the genius with whom I share last name and bloodline.

I have equally been amazed how I could find evidence of the genius's legacy and inventions in so many places—from my wallet on a good day to almost any nationally historical museum that held his journals and courses that taught of his revolutionary influences and from the tops of skyscrapers to my father's bifocals, no less.

All my life I have been told how proud I should be to carry the name Franklin, and I have always genuinely been proud of it. I have even read my namesake's autobiography numerous times to use as a guide for my own approach to life. I would obviously contemporize my own methods to help them apply to the world I live in, but the ideologies still apply nonetheless.

Today is my twenty-first birthday. I have long outgrown the birthday parties I had as a kid, but my parents, Joshua and Evelyn Franklin, insist this specific birthday is special.

We would be meeting up later with the love of my life, Elle, and my goofball best friend, Edward, or Edwardo the Great, as he most recently prefers to be called. But for now, my parents requested I join them in the living room by the fireplace.

Once there, I felt the instant warmth from the fire, and my mom asked me to have a seat on the couch.

No sooner had I sat then my dad leaped up from his chair as if someone had left a hot coal on it.

They both had been acting strange this morning. They had both always seemed so happy, but today they were smiling so hard it looked like it hurt.

I was about to ask my mother what the hell was going on, when my father began speaking, or at least trying to through his elongated smile. "Joshua, you know we're very proud of you. And while you've long known and understood the importance associated with your last name, Franklin, today I share with you why you're a *Joshua* Franklin in a very long line of *Joshua* Franklins. It's a family secret that's been handed down for generations, and today, on your twenty-first birthday, I'm handing it down to you."

With that, my father turned back to the fireplace, moving over to its left side by the protrusion I had always sat on as a kid to keep warm by the fire on a Christmas Eve while the family told stories and opened gifts from each other. Just looking at that side of the fireplace sparked memories of Christmases past.

I shot a glance back to my mother for understanding, but she simply motioned me to direct my attention back to my father.

As I did so, I could see my father had begun to pull on a brick on the underside of the mantle.

He still wore a crazed smile, and the combination of its strain on his wide-eyed face, the vein popping in his neck, and the force from the effort he had been applying to pull on the brick made him look as if he had gone mad.

Thinking I should try to help, I instinctively jumped up, only to be gently pulled back down by my loony-eyed mother.

I sat baffled, with anxiety building up, wondering if my parents had lost their minds.

Suddenly, there was a cracking sound from where my father had been tugging away at the brick. He circled around to get a better grip on the brick that now appeared to have shifted slightly outward.

Why was he dismantling the fireplace?

By now, he was panting.

My mother began to ask him a question, "Franks?"

Franks was the nickname she had always called him, and like everything with these two, I am sure there's a story. My guess was it had some connection to the Phantom Franks stories she would tell me when I was younger. Phantom Franks was a mysterious character, who no one in the stories would ever meet, much less see, but who would always seem to find a way to save the day. He was an enigmatic hero.

My father interrupted simply but in between breaths, "I got this, dearie. I am almost there." As if in confirmation, the brick gave off another but smaller crack.

Finally, it gave way. Then I could see, as if it were on a pivot, the brick had turned perpendicular to its normal position, giving an altogether different sounding thud as it reached its final position.

My father turned. Sweat dripped off his forehead; a bead appeared ready to jump from the edge of his bifocals; and his hair, normally combed back, was askew bangs now hanging down his face. But his outlandish smile remained intact.

My mother nodded back to him, and he then turned back to the fireplace, leaning now and grabbing the corner of the fireplace extension. Squatting into position to increase leverage, he proceeded to pull on the corner, as if to pull it way from its hold on the side of the main fireplace.

Then, and with the combination of a grunt from my father and a scrape from the fireplace corner, I could see that pulling it away was exactly what he was trying to do. With a swooshing sound, as if it were a vacuum inside that sucked air in with the breaking of its seal, I could hear he had finally succeeded.

It was then I first realized that, perhaps, this was what the corner had been made to do. He had pulled it open enough now that I could see the dark space behind it and even a metallic shine of something hidden within it.

Two more heaves, and my father had opened the secret door entirely.

From my seat on the couch, I could see it was a hidden compartment by design and now sat completely open, revealing the owner of the shiny reflection I had seen moments before. Inside the compartment sat a wooden chest barely small enough to fit in it. The wooden chest had brass framework, and a brass keyhole on the front secured it shut.

All of the brass looked as if it had just been shined, but judging from how difficult the hidden safe appeared to be to open, I assumed it had been cleaned before being placed in the safe and that the safe had been sealed airtight.

Still out of breath, my father kneeled even further down to reach into the compartment, retrieving the chest.

Chest in hands, he stepped back until he had reached the end of the couch where my mother and I sat and then proceeded to shift into a position on the end.

To give him some room, I moved over, closer to my mother, who I noticed as I turned, now sat dangling a big old brass key in her fingers. It rocked back and forth while her smile rocked on.

I had no idea where she'd retrieved the key from and had not noticed her with it prior.

"Joshua Benjamin Franklin," she said.

I thought to myself for the millionth time, *Yeah, my middle name is Benjamin.*

My father tagged in and picked it up from there. "Your mother and I've waited your whole life for this moment. There's something about the mystery, another part of our history no less, that's intrigue has long held our family's imaginations captive. Oddly, among all the things we have to cherish with our heritage, this enigma has always been one we have treasured the most. It's time we pass this treasure to you."

With that, my father handed the chest over to me, and my mother nearly took my eye out with the key.

"Open it, son. Open it!" she barely managed, as the freaky smile prevented her from completely sounding out the *p* in *open*. I imagined her saying it as if she were attempting ventriloquism.

Chest in lap and key in hand, I stared at the two objects, mesmerized by them. They looked so incredibly old and yet capable of and appropriate for the mystery they were tasked to conceal.

My parents stared on with wild anticipation.

I inserted the key and gave it a twist. The chest lock fought back, though only to argue, not fight, giving way with only a metallic tumbler clank in protest.

Anticipation getting the best of me, I gently opened the lid to respect its apparent age. It creaked, as if screaming for WD-40, but opened nonetheless to reveal the objects it contained.

The first object was a frame—not an ordinary picture frame but one designed to protect its contents from the elements. I knew the frame was nowhere near as old as the chest, but by first glance at the frame's contents, I could see they were.

The frame contained two articles, a shard of material with a salutation of sorts apparently burned onto it and a very old letter.

The words on the shard of material simply read, "With respect, sincerity and hope, Joshua Franks."

Next to the name was a diamond shape burned into the fabric.

Reading the shard again slowly, thus allowing the revelation it carried to sink in, I repeated the words aloud, "Joshua … Franks?"

"Yes, son, Joshua Franks," my father confirmed.

Turning to him, I asked, "But who is he? I mean, is this why we're all named Joshua? Was there really a Phantom Franks?"

My mother added, "The answer to both is yes."

"But what does it mean? Who is Joshua Franks?"

"Read the letter, son, and you'll know almost all your mother and I've ever known of its origin. By the way, the shape burned next to the name has long been determined to represent the shape of a kite, though nothing is known of its purpose or design."

To get a better look at the letter, I pulled the frame completely out of the chest, placing the chest on the floor before me.

Holding just the frame now and angling it to remove the glare of the fire off the glass-like surface, I read the letter it contained.

Future Franklins,

I leave this message for you to give credit due in reference to the many extraordinary things that have occurred serving purpose toward successfully achieving the freedoms I hope you still enjoy.

I do so in secrecy, as I feel compelled to share this, though if publicly, I fear it would not be understood.

Many questions would be asked that I myself could not begin to answer.

However, it is in the spirit of honesty, I must confess this, if only to those who hold my name.

I have included with this letter a swatch, so you will know from what I reference when I say Joshua Franks deserves credit. It was the close of a message delivered me, presumably by Mr. Franks, and it precluded a list of extraordinary tasks. That is all I will share, as you would not believe the details surrounding the topic anyway.

No one would believe the prophetic message I received with it, the method or medium in which I received it, when I received it, or anything else about it.

That said, I have decided the only item of importance worth sharing is the salutation itself. It is the only proof I have seen myself of Mr. Franks existence.

I kept this swatch because I firmly believe this Joshua Franks, who left me the message with respect, sincerity, and hope, most certainly deserves immense credit for all he has done to help free the colonies, these United States, from the tyranny that once gripped them. I firmly believe we would not have succeeded without his assistance.

If legacy and honor should be awarded to the likes of General Washington, John Adams, and the many more who have fought valiantly for our freedoms, me included, then it could not be done in justice without honoring and smiling upon Joshua Franks equally in their ranks.

If I could tell you more about him, I would; however, I know nothing more.

With that, I ask that his name carry on as proudly as I hope would the names Washington, Adams, or even Franklin and that his enigmatic and heroic story remains with you.

Live free,
Benjamin Franklin

Once they could tell I had finished reading the letter, both my mother and father tried to speak. Then my father bowed out to let my mother. I believe he had intended to say the same thing anyway.

My mother continued, "As we pass this family heirloom on to you, Joshua, the only thing we ask is that you honor Benjamin Franklin's request to honor and help carry on the name, Joshua Franks. And we ask that you do so as Benjamin and the bloodline of Joshua Franklins on up to your father have before you—both openly by name and in secrecy by story, until the day it's your turn to pass this story on."

My father, still wide-eyed, added, "There's another item in the chest, Joshua. If you thought the first was an incredible mystery, you're in for a shock."

Looking back into the chest, on the inside bottom, I could see there was yet another frame.

As I pulled the second frame out, I saw it contained a card with a picture drawn on it. The colors looked weathered, like the paper had been wet but dried intact. I could still tell the image represented a sunset of sorts, where sunset to dusk meets twilight.

In the bottom right corner, I could make out a signature, presumably of the artist, that read simply, "Emily."

Looking up at the top of the image, I could see that the image had been drawn on a sheet, a page from a calendar journal. The date was today's, Saturday, October 16, 2021.

To its immediate left, I read an inscription, wishing simply, "Happy 21st Birthday, Josh Franks!"

It took a second for both to register, but this item from the chest had to be new, as it was dated today and wished *me* a happy birthday.

I turned to my parents and asked, "Is this my birthday card. And if so, why the frame and who is Emily?"

As if he had been waiting all along for me to ask, my father jumped in, "Joshua, that's not *your* birthday card. Read the name again."

Puzzled, I did as he had instructed and noticed, this time that the message was in fact addressed to Josh Franks, not Joshua Franklin.

My head started to spin.

He continued, "Joshua, what you're holding has been passed on through generations, along with the salutation on the shard. The questions you already have, along with more to come, have already been asked by all down the string of generations, right back to the man that originally passed it on, Benjamin Franklin.

"The answers to all the questions, however, have never, and probably will never, be revealed."

Then my mom chimed in. "Joshua, we believe today marks the most special gifting in the history of our family's greatest secret and closes the time loop on an over 260-year mystery.

"The calendar item is dated with today's date, on your twenty-first birthday, and coincidently addressed with a twenty-first birthday wish to the very Joshua Franks Benjamin Franklin felt so very important to honor and remember.

"Even more strange is the fact that Benjamin Franklin excluded mention in the letter but must have decided after having written it to pass on this birthday card. And finally, take another look at the framed shard. Do you recognize the handwriting?"

I looked again at the shard of material in the first frame. I focused this time on the handwriting rather than the words written.

"Th-that's my handwriting. But I didn't—"

"You didn't write it." My father finished. "Yet another mystery of seemingly impossible coincidence, but yet, there it is in your hands."

My mother then added, "Son, all this feels as if it's made up of puzzle pieces that should fit together somehow. But for the life of us, we cannot make them fit.

"This puzzle, however, is a secret legacy we now pass on to you. And, Joshua, I believe you're somehow quite literally connected to it. I've long determined you're tied by your soul to it and to Joshua Franks.

"Finally, and though I suspect you too may never be able to figure out how or understand why, I firmly believe, at some cosmic level, your receiving this gift will provide answers and closure to your soul. Your soul is free. And freedom, son, is something worth cherishing."

"And, Joshua," my father further added, "we must never forget or take for granted that we are free and that our freedom was attained by the efforts and sacrifices of the men and women who fought to win or continue to defend it. Always respect freedom and recognize its fragility, because it is far too precious of a gift to lose.

"It's easy for our family to remember our lineage, our heritage, because of our bloodline connection to Benjamin Franklin. I feel blessed to be able to say I am a part of it, but my pride is not in his name as much as it is in what he stood for. We live free today because he and his fellow revolutionaries risked their lives fighting for our freedom.

"We may not know much about Joshua Franks, but thanks to Benjamin Franklin passing on this gift, we know we can include him within those revolutionary ranks."

CPSIA information can be obtained
at www.ICGtesting.com
Printed in the USA
LVHW111213130321
681457LV00036B/942